The Weaver's Heir

Book Two: Musician

TS McCarthy

Thank you...

To my siblings – my exuberant pack of brothers and sisters who fill the world with energy, curiosity and passion, and so much creativity. A capable and enthusiastic bunch of great humans. Thanks for supporting me on this journey, and being my cheer-leaders.

To my sister Gita, generous, courageous, and true. She would never let anybody else call me a weirdo. She is The Possibilist, making the world a better place every day. There are no words for how much I appreciate you and everything you do for our family.

Thank you to my friends and colleagues, who have lived the Weaver journey for the last few years, and are always so encouraging as I balance my corporate life with my writing life.

To all the people who read the first book and sent me such lovely feedback, asking for more, thank you.

This book is for Patrick, who makes the writing possible.

Contents

Chapter One

D'rona

Asher sat up slowly, rubbing her sore head. The crossing of the Void had been fast and furious, and she had crash-landed awkwardly into the ground. The feel of grass beneath her hands and the hot sun on her face was disorienting. Clearly she had not arrived in Hesta's library but somewhere outside.

Carefully she collected the globe and the bangle that were lying next to her and placed them back on her neck and wrist. She breathed deeply to steady her racing heart and then took a good look around.

She was sitting in a field and the Manor was nowhere in sight.

An ear-splitting roar tore the air around her. Something large whooshed above her head, sending vibrations all around her body. In terror Ash flung herself to the ground, covering her face.

The thing landed with a light thump not far from where she lay. Asher was shaking with fear, trying to disappear into the long grass, fervently hoping it had not noticed her.

Heavy footsteps moved closer. The earth trembled beneath each step. Warm breath caressed her head.

It had definitely noticed her.

Gathering all her courage, Asher raised her head and stared straight into a huge pair of lizard eyes. She screamed as she scrambled backwards, desperately trying to get on her feet and run. But her body was sore and bruised and it protested against every move. Realising she could not outrun the beast Asher rummaged in her pockets, seeking the harmonica. If she couldn't run she would have to Craft.

The first note had barely been blown when a firm puff blew Asher backwards onto the grass and knocked the harmonica out of her hand. Before she could scramble to pick it up, a great clawed hook flicked the little instrument up into the air, and it disappeared somewhere above her.

"Hey! Give that back," she demanded, lifting her gaze to look directly at the beast. Further and further back she tilted her neck until she could see the creature's head.

Towering over her, gleaming in the hot sun, was a creature of myth and legend.

The large dragon body was covered in gleaming scales, each one bigger than her hand, the colours melding and shimmering so that it was impossible to decide if they were blue or gold. A tail three times longer than her height stretched out along the ground, and enormous wings were neatly folded along its flanks.

It bent down to bring its huge head level with hers. Hot breath seared her skin.

"Hello small human Crafter. You are a very long way from Andera."

The words were not threatening, and neither was the tone. Deciding she was not in immediate danger of being eaten or burnt to a crisp, Asher carefully stood up and backed away so she could see the dragon's face easier.

"How do you know I came from Andera?"

"All Crafters come from Andera," rumbled the dragon, "that is a fact."

"Not this one," said Asher sadly, "this one is even further from home." She turned around, looking at the endless grasslands and the wide blue sky.

"How do you know I am a Crafter?"

The dragon snorted, a hot burst of air that sent Asher stumbling backwards.

"The only humans that can open portals through the Void are Crafter Wens. That is a fact."

He sounded so confident that Asher almost grinned. She thought of Darven and his squads going to Earth to take Evie.

"Also not true," she could not resist telling the know-it-all Dragon.

"True!" insisted the Dragon with another great puff of hot air. Asher quickly stepped further back, keen to stay on her feet. "Crafters are from Andera. Fact. The only humans who can manipulate the portals are Crafter Wens. Fact."

Arguing with a dragon three times her size seemed rather foolhardy, but some mad devilry must have taken hold, for Asher just could not keep her mouth shut. Maybe she had switched personalities with Levi during the last crossing.

"Hmmm, that's odd. Because I am neither from Andera, nor am I a Wen. And twenty-four hours ago I had no idea this planet even existed. So I guess we are both learning things today."

The dragon huffed and the air shuddered. Asher swayed but happily did not end up on the grass.

"How old are you?' she asked.

Huge golden eyes blinked sideways.

"7000 moons," was the enigmatic reply. "How old are you?"

"Fifteen years old. Well, sixteen in another two days." She shook her head in disbelief. In two days it would be her birthday, and she had no idea where she would be, or who she would celebrate with. A wave of sadness washed over her.

"You are sad. Is it sad to be your age?" The deep voice rumbled and the huge eyes blinked from the outside in.

Asher nodded slowly. "Not to be my age, but to be alone. My friends are gone."

The dragon blinked again, seemingly unsure as to why this was a sad thing.

"You speak D'ronic very well," it said.

"I'm not speaking D'ronic," said Asher. "We are both speaking English. My Earth language," she clarified when those big eyes blinked again.

"Not possible," said the Dragon confidently, "Dragons only speak D'ronic. Fact."

This time Asher did grin. Sometime during this strange conversation she had lost all fear of her arrogant blue and gold companion. Regardless of his size and rumbling there was something in his manner that suggested he was young.

"Phew it's warm out here!" she said, reaching into her pack and pulling out her water bottle. The cloudless sky seemed incredibly bright and she could feel a headache building. A quick scramble back in the pack produced her sunglasses, but no hat. She had packed for a cold autumn camping trip, not for this heat. She really needed to find some shade.

Shielding her eyes with her hand Asher spun around, scouring the horizon. There did not appear to be a tree in any direction.

"Is there some-where I can rest out of the sun?" she asked. "I need to work out how to get back to Andera but this heat is making my head pound."

The Dragon pointed with a long claw.

"Just over there - where those rocks are is my home. The caves are cool."

Asher peered and squinted in the direction he indicated but could not see anything other than grass and sky. Dragon vision was better than human vision, and *that* was a fact. She would just have to take his word for it and head in that direction.

Pulling the pack onto her back Ash began the slow, hot walk to the caves. She was desperate to rest somewhere cool and dark. Every step in the long grass felt sluggish and her head was thumping. She thought longingly of Kate's painkillers.

Beside her the Dragon hopped in a strange step and flight motion. One step, two steps, hop into the air and spin. With each odd step his long tail whipped the air around Ash.

After a few minutes the Dragon huffed with annoyance. "You are very slow and this is a very boring way to move! I will meet you there."

With a great whoosh of his wings the Dragon pushed up into the sky, each giant flap moving him upwards and forwards. Within a few breaths he was disappearing into the great blue ahead her.

Envying the ease with which the Dragon covered the distance, Asher trudged on step after step feeling more and more heat affected. Dizziness and nausea dogged her every movement and her eyes were beginning to blur.

The minutes seemed to be getting longer and the air was getting hotter. When she looked up she could see a second sun, and Asher worried that she was starting to hallucinate. Recklessly she skulled the last of her water, desperate to ease the heat that seemed to be everywhere within and without her body.

How much further?

Sweat stung her eyes and effected her vision as Asher strained to see into the distance. This time she could see a rock formation rising up ahead. Close, so close, but yet still so far to go. She willed her exhausted body to keep moving. One more step, one more step. She was not going to make it. The last thing she saw was a huge shadow blocking the sun before she collapsed unconscious to the ground.

***

Coolness. Darkness. Softness. Snuggling deeper into her quilt Ash tried to go back to sleep. But some-one was whispering in her room, creeping around.

"Go 'way Evie," she muttered.

The whispering ceased but the movements did not. Pulled from the edge of a dreamless slumber Asher tried to focus. What was Evie doing?

With a burst of awareness Asher woke fully and remembered. Evie, Evie. Princess of Andera. No longer her sister. Grief sat heavy on her chest and her breath constricted. Carefully she sat up to try and ease the crushing sensation.

She was in a dark, cool cave wrapped in soft furry skins. A few metres away daylight glowed at the entrance. Her body and head no longer ached with dehydration and heat but she felt weary all over. She was tempted to lie back down and seek sleep once again. But something had woken her, some-one whispering and rustling.

Carefully Asher peered around the dark cave. There was not much to see, just a bowl full of water beside her. There were no furnishings apart from her makeshift bed. Which meant the rustling had to be coming from... aha... Over by her pack Ash could just make out two small figures crouching, trying not to be seen, the contents of her pack strewn around them.

"Hello?" she said carefully, "Can I help you?"

Her words ricocheted around the cave louder than she intended. Startled, her visitors jumped up and ran for the entrance.

"Wait!" called Asher to their retreating backs.

Once they were gone Ash plopped back into the blankets and decided to rest a moment longer. Until she heard the screeching sound of her flute being played, badly.

In a heartbeat she untangled herself from the furs and leapt up.

She stepped through the cave entrance and stopped abruptly, her mouth dropping open in wonder. She was on a wide stone ledge, at least one hundred metres off the ground. Around her and above her many cave openings led out onto their own ledges. Her cave appeared to have the smallest opening, most of the others were large enough for a dragon to fit through, some even larger.

On one of the ledges to her right the blue and gold dragon lay snoozing in the afternoon sun. Asher plonked to the ground, leaning back against the cool stone walls, her wide eyes trying to take everything in.

The cave system was part of a large mountain. Far below the ground was covered in the same green grasslands that she had trudged across, and beyond the rocky mountain there was an undulating forest of trees and a large lake area. Every so often a huge shadow would darken the sky above her, and a thunderous rumble would split the air. She did not have to look up to know what flew above her.

There were no steps up or down, no connections between the caves. She was marooned.

"How on earth did I get up here?" she wondered aloud.

The blue and gold dragon opened one eye. "You were carried up."

"Thank you," said Ash with sincerity. If he had not brought her to the coolness of the caves she would surely have died on the grasslands.

"I did not know how weak humans are," he grumbled as though she had admonished instead of thanked him. "It is not my fault."

Asher frowned in confusion. "I'm not blaming you for anything."

"How was I to know that you were not meant to walk in the two suns? Hmmmm?"

Asher shook her head. "I told you, I'm very thankful. I mean it. You saved my life."

The dragon shook his head mournfully. "It was not me who collected you from the ground. And it was not me who gave you the life-liquid. That was *him*."

"Who?"

An almighty roar split the air sending her tumbling back into the mouth of the cave. Huge gusts of wind from enormous wings battered Ash and she curled up into a ball to protect herself.

"Him."

The tornado eased and cautiously Asher raised her head.

The new arrival was magnificent. His purple scales were vibrant and iridescent, refracting thousands of shards of light. He perched proudly on the ledge opposite her, twice the size of the blue and gold dragon. In her own world Ash was considered tall for a teenage girl, but next to this beast she was tiny. She had thought the first dragon was huge. Her concept of huge had just been adjusted.

The giant dragon turned his golden gaze on Ash then opened his mouth and roared.

With a cry of pain Asher stumbled into the cave and buried her head beneath the furs. Her eardrums were ringing so loudly it felt like they would burst.

After many long minutes her hearing settled to a light ringing and Asher tentatively raised her head. It was all quiet outside.

Gathering her courage she crept to the mouth of the cave and peeked out, keeping her fingers firmly in her ears.

Both dragons were still there. The purple dragon raised a claw as long as her forearm and beckoned her outside. It was not a request. As she headed onto the ledge, she desperately hoped the purple dragon meant her no harm.

The golden claw reached for her and Asher closed her eyes, her heart thumping and her legs shaking. *Please, please, please* she silently prayed.

A cord was plopped over her head and for a second Ash staggered under its enormous weight. Then the crushing sensation disappeared and she could breathe easily again. She opened her eyes.

A strange curved white shell hanging from a leather strap lay comfortably against her chest. It weighed barely more than a few grams, but when she tried to lift it off it was heavier than anything she had ever felt before. Straining with exertion Asher tried again and again to remove the pendant.

"You cannot remove it little Crafter. It is a dragon tooth." The purple dragon had a warm, deep voice, far more mature than that of the smaller blue and gold.

"A dragon tooth! Wait, I can hear you clearly. And my ears don't hurt."

"Welcome to D'rona small human. The dragon tooth adjusts the sounds waves of our language so you can hear and understand us clearly, without destroying your fragile hearing." He sounded amused. "Now, to what do we owe the pleasure of your visit?"

"Well actually," Asher tried not to squirm under that direct gaze, "my visit is rather unintentional. I'm lost."

"Is that so?" rumbled the dragon. "Where have you travelled from, and where were you travelling to?"

"I went from Earth to Andera, then back to Earth briefly and I was trying to get back to Andera when I ended up here."

The dragon's ginormous head leant in closer until Asher could smell the fresh pine on its breath. His golden eyes gleamed unblinking. They were so large Asher could not look at both at the same time. She focused on the right eye.

"That is a great deal of journeying across the Void for one so young. What is your name little Wen?"

"Asher. Just Asher, no Wen."

"I see. Hr'tom tells me you speak D'ronic even without the tooth. This is very, very rare among humans."

Asher shook her head. "No, actually I've been speaking English the whole time. You sound to me like you are also speaking English."

The purple dragon blinked slowly, the great lids moving from left and right to meet in the middle.

"Hmmmmm, interesting," he rumbled quietly, though Asher suspected if she were not wearing the tooth it would have sounded like a thunder crack.

"You travel the Void with no ill effect, but you are not a Wen. You speak and understand our language, but you are only a human. There is only one explanation. You must wear an Object of Great Power."

He spoke with such certainty Asher could almost hear the unspoken word *fact*.

Although she did not feel she was in imminent danger Asher hesitated to show him the globe. They knew she was a Crafter and had treated her with care, but she had no way of knowing if the dragons were friend or foe of the Weaver. In fact she had no idea about the protocol surrounding the globe. Was she allowed to tell people, or dragons, of its presence? Against her skin the golden globe buzzed happily, offering no wisdom or course of action.

Asher settled for nodding her head.

"Yes I am," she said simply. From high above the screechy sound of her flute echoed around the caves.

"Please may I have my flute back?" she asked, "and then I will be on my way to Andera."

The purple dragon snorted, small tendrils of smoke wafting out of his nostrils. Hastily Ash pressed back against the rock wall, wondering if a stream of fire was to follow. But it did not.

"Small Asher human, you cannot open a portal when the two suns are in the sky. You would disintegrate with the pressure. You must stay the night. Tomorrow you can leave."

Stay the night! Her stomach churned. She needed to get back to Andera and find out what had happened to Hesta.

The flute squealed again. Another snort of smoke from the big dragon.

"Pe'tul! Lr'vin! Cease that dreadful racket and come here at once. Bring the Crafter's instrument."

Silence followed this command. Asher craned her head, wondering where in the rambling cave system her little thieves were hiding. Then a tiny breeze curled around her head, whispering over her ears, and announcing their arrival as two identical green dragons wafted into view. There was no need to protect her face or block her ears. The arrival of Pe'tul and Lr'vin was a muffled sneeze in comparison to the dramatic thunder of the purple dragon's appearance.

Ash said not a word as the flute thieves landed on the ledge beside her, one of them clutching the object in its claws.

"Pe'tul and Lr'vin are sorry," mumbled the dragon as it held out the flute.

The second green dragon peered at her from its hiding place behind the first.

Compared to the purple dragon and Hr'tom these dragons were miniature, no bigger than Ash herself. No gold teased at

their scales in the same luminous manner as their larger coun-
terparts. Rather they were the green colour of the endless grasslands, apart from their claws and eyes which were a deep brown.
The other dragons would dominate the skies, but this little pair
looked like they had been born of the earth. Even their wings
were small in comparison to their bodies, designed for drifting
or current surfing rather than soaring at altitude.

Asher retrieved the flute with a small "thank you" then carefully inspected the golden instrument for damage. The dragons
inched away from her and settled on the edge of the ledge.

"Dragons do not steal!" thundered the purple dragon,
his displeasure reverberating in the very air around them.
"Dor'tiem has made this very clear to you."

"We are very sorry Dor'tolen, please not tell Dor'tiem. Pe'tul
and Lr'vin were not stealing, just looking, we promise," said the
designated spokesperson contritely. Its silent twin kept its head
hidden beneath its wings.

"Floooot," continued the dragon, pronouncing the strange
word carefully "is not fun, makes a terrible noise." The dragon
glared at Asher accusingly, as though she had deliberately given
them a defective toy.

"Taking without asking is still stealing," enforced Dor'tolen.
"Dragons do not steal. And that includes field dragons. You
must atone."

The green dragons shuffled uncomfortably, their short tails
twitching unhappily along the ground. They clasped their claws
together and turned their faces away from Dor'tolen.

"Small human Asher, what do you choose?"

At the sound of her name Ash looked up from her inspection
of the flute. She had been imagining a melody of winds in the
grasses, and the hot sun beating down on the earth. Of giant
wings beating against the wind. She was arranging notes in her
head and she had paid no attention to the dragons' interaction.

All four dragons were looking at her. Beneath their unblinking gazes Asher fought the urge to squirm.

"Sorry, what do you want me to do?"

"You must choose a punishment for the field dragons."

Asher shook her head. "No thank you. I'm just happy with the return of the flute. No need for punishments."

Dor'tolen raised his head and roared. Even with the tooth Ash felt the force of his displeasure reverberate through her body and eardrums. She slapped her hands over her ears. The green dragons cowered in fear.

"Choose something!" the blue and gold dragon hissed at Asher from behind his wing. "If you do not *he* will, and it will be more unpleasant than anything you can think of."

"What do I choose?" said Ash desperately. She had absolutely no idea how justice was administered on D'rona.

Hr'tom grinned gleefully. "Sentence them to listening to you make the squealy noise from the flooot. That will serve them right."

Asher made the offer to the purple dragon who rumbled his approval. Pe'tul and Lr'vin groaned and curled up into a tangled ball of wings and tails on the ledge. They had found no pleasure in the strange sounds of the flute and their misery exuded from every green scale.

"After the Gathering while the sky dragons hunt, small human Asher will play the flooot and you must sit in her cave and listen until the moon is high. Then your atonement will be complete."

Dor'tolen stretched his humungous gleaming wings wide and shook them out as he stood up on his hind legs. Ash braced against the rockface for the wind he generated as he leapt into the sky.

The two green dragons waited only until Dor'tolen was gone, then leapt off the ledge without a glance in her direction, gliding around the caves and out of sight.

"What happens now?" asked Ash.

The blue and gold dragon shifted his shoulders in a casual movement that reminded her of Levi's shrugs.

"It is the hottest time of the two suns, even for dragons, so now we rest. Then we meet at the evening Gathering and then we hunt."

He rolled over, smoothly adjusting his wings and long tail. Clearly he was finished with her.

Asher stood staring at Hr'tom's back for a moment, then she grinned. "I think you should return my harmonica before it occurs to me that *you* have stolen it, rather than simply kept it too long. You might find yourself enjoying the flooot with Pe'tul and Lr'vin."

With a huff Hr'tom sat up, the smug expression wiped from his face. He rummaged around under his wing and from a small pouch of skin he pulled out the harmonica. It looked miniscule hanging from his claw.

"Here," he flicked it at her across the divide.

Asher leapt forward and grabbed it from the air.

"I did not actually mean to keep it," he said, the closest he was going to offer to an apology, "it is just so tiny I forgot I had it." He turned his head and closed his eyes.

Even in the shade of the giant rock formations the heat was becoming increasingly oppressive. It seemed a good idea to rest in the coolness of her cave while she waited for whatever the evening gathering would bring. Besides, she thought ruefully glancing at the gaping spaces between the ledges, it was not as if she could go anywhere.

Once inside she drank deeply from the cool, fresh water in the bowl, relishing the feeling of the liquid rejuvenating her body from within.

Before she curled up to sleep Asher tidied her pack and tightened the fastenings. As an added precaution she tucked it up beside her, an unusual but comforting bedmate. Dor'tolen may think she travelled the Void with ill effect, but he was wrong. She was tired down to her bones. Within minutes she was fast asleep.

Chapter Two

The Gathering of Dragons

The two suns were low in the early evening sky when Asher awoke.

She lay in comfort for a few minutes, mentally assessing her pain and exhaustion levels. To her surprise she felt rather fantastic. She sat up and stretched her arms above her head. The great weariness that had accompanied her for days had eased. Her thumping head and battered eardrums felt clear and light.

For the first time in a long time Asher felt healthy and strong. A huge grin split her face and she kicked off the furs. How wonderful it was to be rested and rejuvenated. With her body restored her spirits felt brighter and her mind clearer.

A loud grumble from her stomach reminded her that sleep was not the only requirement for a strong body.

Ash pulled the last of Cook's supplies from her pack, leaving the packaged muesli bars and chocolates from home for later. She munched happily on the cake and slightly stale sandwiches and fruit, then drank nearly all the delicious water from the dragon bowl. The last few mouthfuls she used to wash her face and clean her teeth. Her skin tingled.

Feeling invigorated Asher also felt inspired to brush her hair, wincing as she pulled the brush through the tangled curls. A quick sniff persuaded her to change her top and apply deodorant. This was the cleanest she had felt in days.

Minute by minute the cave darkened as the suns set outside. There was no apparent lighting inside the space, so soon she would be alone in the dark. It was a rather unpleasant thought. She pulled a torch from her pack and sat it beside the bed in readiness. A large whoosh announced the arrival of a dragon onto her ledge.

"Small human Asher, it is time to attend the Gathering," boomed Hr'tom, in his best imitation of Dor'tolen.

"Just Asher will do," she said as she joined him outside the cave. "I don't think we require the small human bit every time."

Hr'tom blinked. "You are small and you are human. Fact."

Asher grinned. "Yes I suppose so, mid-sized blue dragon Hr'tom."

He did not respond to her jest. Instead he twisted frantically, looking at his gleaming scales from every direction.

"Am I blue? More blue than gold?" he asked anxiously.

It was obvious that this mattered greatly, so Asher took her time peering at his scales.

"Honestly I don't know," she admitted, "some seem quite blue but then you move and they are clearly gold. I can't tell if they are changing colour or if it is a trick of the fading light."

A puff of smoke enveloped Ash as Hr'tom sighed with relief.

"What's so important about the gold?" coughed Ash.

"There is already a blue dragon on the Council, but the gold seat is vacant and I hope to claim it when I reach 10,000 moons. My sheen will settle then."

"That sounds important."

"It is the most important thing to me. Now come, I must take you to the Gathering."

"Just a second." On impulse Ash dashed into the cave and grabbed the small black case that housed her flute. She had no desire for that to be taken again.

"So how do we do this?" she asked Hr'tom when she was once again on the ledge. He pulled a swing from behind him. Swing being a generous description for the piece of wood hanging from rope-like vines.

"Oh no!" exclaimed Ash, backing away, "absolutely no way."

***

On the evening when the two suns set, the dragons of D'rona gather together at the Rocks of Dor'atar. From far and beyond they come, whole clans or lone representatives of families unable to travel - the large, the small and every size in between.

For a hundred thousand cycles it has been so. The dragons gather at Dor'atar in unity, but only twice before has a human been in attendance. The first time to witness the end of the Clan Wars and the creation of the Council. The second time to farewell the last Dragon King.

Asher was unaware of the honour being extended to her, and to be truthful she would not have cared, she was too focused on not throwing up.

She held tightly to the ropes that supported the wide plank of wood on which she sat, swaying precariously from Hr'tom's grip. She swallowed hard. It was difficult not to panic as they veered through rock formations and dipped and soared to avoid obstacles.

Around them more and more dragons joined their flight, eventually gliding into an enormous amphitheatre. On every ledge and crevice there perched the dragons, rumbling and roaring greetings to each other, great wings creating gusts that buffeted her as she and Hr'tom flew into the Gathering Place.

Most dragons paid her no attention and those that noticed her showed only mild curiosity in the tiny, feeble human dangling in their midst. Only one small yellow dragon pressing close to its parent squealed in surprise.

"Look papa! What a strange thing Hr'tom brings. Is it food?"

The large yellow dragon rolled one black eye in her direction.

"Ah that is only a human. Not for eating. Mostly harmless," he said dismissively. "I wonder what brings it here," he added, but the lack of interest in his tone suggested he did not actually wonder at all.

"A human!" mumbled the little one with excitement, flapping his wings as Asher was carried past.

Shyly Ash gave the juvenile a small wave, then quickly grabbed hold again of the plaited vines that held her swing in place.

With relief and a roiling stomach Ash jumped off the swing onto the ledge Hr'tom chose. From her vantage point she could see most of the amphitheatre and the array of colourful dragons. Her own spot was small and unobtrusive. Sheltered by Hr'tom's much larger body she could observe without really being seen herself.

Directly ahead of her was a huge stone platform designed for twelve dragons to sit together.

One by one enormous dragons thundered out of the sky, taking their place on the podium. First to arrive was the purple dragon, followed immediately by a red dragon of the same size. A green field dragon arrived next.

Two much smaller dragons arrived together. A creamy white and a royal blue. As they landed a huge roar erupted from the crowd. The white dragon gave a wave to the assembly.

"Tonight is her first Gathering as a member of the Council," rumbled Hr'tom beside her. "She is very popular. Her appointment was unanimous." He sounded envious.

The five dragons were soon joined by another three – yellow, soft grey and blueberry coloured.

"Eight in total?" asked Ash. Hr'tom shushed her without replying.

Suddenly huge flames erupted across the twilight sky, followed by a roar so intense that Asher had to cover her ears despite the tooth. The assembled dragons roared in response. Wingbeats later a midnight black dragon glided smoothly onto the platform.

It was neither the biggest nor the smallest, but it was clearly the leader. It landed in the central spot and lifted its snout, sending plumes of fire over the amphitheatre. Around the ledges wooden torches burst into flame, illuminating the darkening space.

This time Asher responded quickly, covering her face and ears just in time to muffle the roars and beating wings that followed.

Against her chest the Weaver's globe hummed with excitement. It had been many generations since it had attended a Gathering and farewelled the king.

The black dragon raised its arms and the crowd fell silent.

"Welcome," it said, the quiet voice completely at odds with the dramatic rock-star entrance. Asher felt that soft, powerful voice pulse through her very being.

"The two suns are setting and the dragons of D'rona gather in peace. Tonight we right any wrongs, celebrate new life, and then we hunt together, asserting our dominance over the land and sky."

On cue the crown thundered their approval and pleasure. Again the black dragon raised its arms requesting silence.

"Firstly a warm welcome to Dor'ienna as she takes her place on the Council."

More cheers.

"A reminder to those of you nearing 10,000 moons. There are three vacant places on the Council. To earn a nomination and be considered for selection you must prove your courage, honour, and loyalty. Only the finest candidates will be considered. Remember – if you wish to supplant an existing Council member you must challenge them to a fight to the death."

More roaring.

Asher considered the Royal Blue Dragon sitting on the Council. She was not much bigger than Hr'tom. Perhaps if his scales did deepen to true blue rather than gold he could fight her for his spot.

As though he had read her thoughts Hr'tom rumbled fiercely, "I will never fight her."

Asher had no opportunity to ask why not, before the Black spoke again.

"Bring forth any complaints. The Council will hear and decide."

The dragons shuffled in anticipation, glancing from one to the other. Eventually a small grey dragon stepped forward nervously to share its grievance.

For the next hour various problems and arguments were laid before the nine dragons of the Council. No matter how petty or grave, each complaint was given its time. Each was carefully considered and arbitrated.

If the applicants or defendants were unhappy with their ruling they made no public display. Finally the last matter had been presented and resolved. The dragons of the Council stood and shook out their wings, stretching their bodies. In the firelight the gleaming, many coloured scales looked like a rainbow of stars fallen to earth.

"Now for the celebrations," announced the Black in its mesmerising soft voice. "Five hundred moons have passed since the two suns last rose and set above D'rona. Tonight we celebrate our hatchlings and the continuation of our species. Present your offspring to the Gathering."

The yellow dragon that had been so dismissive of Asher raised his wings. All eyes turned to him.

"I present my son Lo'sen," he boomed with pride.

The little yellow dragon immediately hid behind his papa as the crowd cheered. With a puff of displeasure the papa dragon pushed little Lo'sen forward. The youngster glanced up at the yellow dragon on the podium and waved. The yellow Councillor beamed with pleasure, shaking her wings in reply.

Then the members of the Council raised their heads and in unison sent streams of fire into the dark night sky. Asher exhaled and wiped the sweat from her face with her sleeve. The air was pulsing with heat. Six more infants were presented to Council, each one receiving a large cheer and a canopy of fire.

After the seventh little dragon had stepped back behind its parent the crowd fell silent, waiting expectantly for the next baby. As the minutes dragged by they began to murmur in concern.

The Black perused the crowd. "That is all?" it asked incredulously, "only seven? Nineteen eggs were registered this cycle. Only seven have hatched?"

The murmurs were growing, the crowd was uneasy.

"Bring forth the unhatched eggs," commanded the Black sadly.

Four brown and green field dragons flew to the podium, each clutching the corner of a large skin. Lying on the skin were twelve gleaming silver eggs, each one three times the size of Asher's head. The skin was laid carefully at the feet of the Black.

Reverently the Black touched each egg in turn, like a blessing. Then it roared and aimed a shard of fire onto a pile of wood beside the podium. It burst into flame. Carefully the Black lifted the first egg, presented it to the assembly then tossed it onto the funeral pyre.

Not a blessing after all. A farewell.

One by one each egg was given to the fire in silence, until only two remained. Asher was feeling hot and bothered with the roaring heat. The globe burned and buzzed against her skin, filling her ears with agitated music.

What do you want? She sent the thought, pulling out the globe to hold it in her palm. For the first time since she had been given the globe Asher heard it clearly.

It lives.

Asher shook her head in confusion. *What lives?*

Images filled her head. A small life-form curled up asleep within its silver egg; its heartbeat so faint and feeble that its own parents had not detected it.

The eleventh egg was presented to the silent crowd and consigned to the flames. The Black picked up the twelfth and final egg.

It lives, it lives.

Asher stood up and stepped forward.

"What are you doing?" hissed Hr'tom.

Asher barely heard him. The music of the soul inside the egg was filling her ears.

"STOP!" she screamed.

Time slowed; every giant dragon eye turned in her direction. Outraged rumbling and puffing filled the air.

"Human! Be quiet!" roared one furious dragon.

"How dare you interrupt the sacred pass-beyond!" boomed another.

Asher would not be quiet and she would not sit down. She felt very unlike herself. Asher the invisible wanted desperately to be seen. Insistent music tangled with the energy that was pulsing within her.

The universe wanted this baby to be born and the Threads had sent her to ensure that happened.

She ripped open the case and clicked her flute together. She did not hear Hr'tom's groan as she lifted it to her lips. The dragons roared their objections.

"Silence!" thundered the Black, and the dragons obeyed. "Let the Crafter play."

The music was fast and light, notes of awakening and excitement, of hope and beginnings. Ash sent each vibrant, staccato note into the egg, to the sleeping baby inside.

She closed her eyes, picturing the notes tickling at the baby, enticing it, encouraging it. *Wake and discover your world.* The tiny dragon stirred and the egg jumped slightly within the Black's claws.

Asher poured more energy into the tune to strengthen that fragile heart. Her own heart strained in response, beating faster and faster. The notes began pinching and gently biting the baby: *wake now, live now.*

With a great yawn the hatchling stretched and cracked the egg. The crowd erupted as little claws pushed their way through the shell, followed by a small scaly head.

The Black lifted the baby above its head, the tiny scales gleaming the colour of flame. The Council roared fire above the cheering assembly as the last of Asher's song swirled around the dazed newborn.

Then, for the second time that day, Asher crumpled to the floor.

Chapter Three

The Birth of the Fire Dragon

The Black Dragon sat alone on a large rock gazing at the star filled sky.

Behind him rose the vast mountain cave system, before him seemingly unending grasslands rustled in the light breeze. His keen vision spied the occasional rabbit or fox creeping through the grasses, but he did not hunt.

For the first time in his life the Black Dragon was uncertain and he did not enjoy the sensation.

The newly hatched baby had been reunited with its ecstatic parents, a rather unassuming set of white and greys that had been dazed and awed by their sunset coloured hatching.

They had not understood the significance of the flame-coloured baby but the Black most certainly had. As had Dor'tolen who had sought him out as soon as the Gathering left for the hunt.

"Dor'tiem," the purple dragon had rumbled quietly, "the hatching. That was no ordinary birth, and no ordinary colour."

"Indeed," sighed the Black, scratching his belly with his long claws. "How is the small human Crafter?"

"She sleeps," replied Dor'tolen, "she exerted herself beyond sense tonight. We have given her the life-liquid. She will wake restored."

Dor'tiem stared into the still burning funeral pyre. "What she did tonight required great courage."

He remembered the passion with which she had played, the energy pulsing in the music. Then the way she had fallen to the ground.

"She is strong. There is power within her. But she does not yet fully control it. She reaches too deep within. She must learn to control the Crafting or it will consume her."

The two dragons fell silent, both thinking of the tiny newborn, his gleaming scales shimmering with Crafter energy and dragon fire.

"It is foretold –" began Dor'tolen. The Black raised a claw.

"I know what is foretold," said Dor'tiem. "I just never expected it would come to pass in my lifetime."

"If the Weaver has need we will be called to war," pressed Dor'tolen.

Dor'tiem said nothing. He thought of the fragile human girl who had saved the most precious of dragons tonight. He thought of a promise made to a Weaver generations before his own birth.

"Even by human standards she is only a child," he said. "I need to think."

So he had flown out here to the rock to ponder in silence.

A flurry of light wings announced the arrival of Pe'tul the field dragon.

"She is awake Dor'tiem," he said respectfully.

"Thank you Pe'tul. I shall join her shortly. Please make sure she is well fed."

The little dragon fluttered off back in the direction of Dor'atar leaving Dor'tiem to his wonderings and his worries.

***

Asher sat up gingerly, her sore head still lightly pounding but overall feeling not too bad. She was snuggled once again in a bed of soft furs, but she was no longer in the plain cave where she had spent the afternoon.

Her current accommodation was much more luxurious as caves go. It seemed she had been upgraded.

The walls were painted a soft cream, allowing the light from flickering sconces to bounce around the room. Large pelts covered the stone floor. A huge screen divided the room in half, behind which light reflected off water.

Curious to know what lay beyond the screen Ash unwrapped herself from the furs and went to find out.

To her amazement and delight she discovered a steaming rock pool of fresh spring water. Her pack and a pile of towels were placed conveniently at the side. Asher gratefully climbed into the warm water, soaking her hair and body.

Unlike a bath, the natural springs did not cool with time, so Asher did not rush. She floated happily, enjoying the warmth seeping into her muscles.

It was the smell of something delicious that finally lured her out of the pool.

The towels made of tightly woven grasses dried her body and her hair. Then with great pleasure Asher pulled on her last clean outfit.

She stepped out of the cave and onto the large ledge which had been set up with a makeshift table and a tree stump for her seat. A bowl filled with steaming stew was waiting for her, as were the two field dragons.

The dark night was filled with stars. Occasionally the far-off sound of dragons on the hunt was carried back on the breeze. After the intensity of the Gathering the calmness was soothing and rejuvenating.

"Sit and eat small human Crafter," said one of them imperiously, the one she suspected was Pe'tul.

Ash swallowed a grin. It was one thing when the giant dragons referred to her as a small human, quite another when it was said by a dragon no larger than herself.

"Thank you." She sat and lifted the bowl to her lips, sipping carefully.

"This is delicious!" she exclaimed. The dragons puffed with pleasure, small tendrils of smoke dancing from their nostrils.

Savouring each mouthful, Asher gulped her way through the entire bowl of rabbit and vegetable stew.

"Thank you so much," she sighed. She was definitely 'filled to the gills' as her Nana Blake used to say. "That was really tasty."

A change in the breeze drew her attention to the sky.

Through the expanses of the caves the Black soared, landing with a quiet thump on her ledge. He settled on his haunches and inclined his head to the field dragons. They bared their teeth to Ash in what seemed to be a smile and flapped away.

She stood to greet the Dragon Leader.

"I am Dor'tiem, head of the Council of D'rona," said the Black.

"I am Asher Blake," she responded in the same formal tone.

"You are an Earth human," stated Dor'tiem.

Asher nodded. "Fact."

"You are a Crafter."

"Fact."

"You wear the Weaver's Globe of Power."

Unconsciously Asher raised her hand to her chest. "Fact."

"But you are not the Weaver." This time there was a lilt of a question, a shade of uncertainty.

"No," she replied, "I am not her."

Dor'tiem nodded his giant head. "You are the Musician," he declared.

"Yes."

"You were sent here to save the fire dragon."

Asher nodded slowly. "I think so."

"Do you understand the importance of the fire dragon?"

Asher shook her head. The Black blinked his slow sideways blink and said nothing for a long time.

"Dragons are clan creatures," he said eventually in his soft, deep voice. "Each clan is clearly marked by its colours. For thousands of moons the clans waged war on each other, fighting for control of the High Throne of Dor'atar. It was a dark time for D'rona as dragon slayed dragon and clans were brought to the edge of extinction."

Asher realised she was holding her breath.

"A pact was agreed upon. A Council representing each of the twelve clans would be established. The last Dragon King stepped aside, living out his days in peace while the newly elected Council assumed the responsibilities of government and stewardship. So it has been for 100,000 moons."

He pinned her with his unblinking stare.

"We are a long-lived race, but our hatching rates are low. Even after all these years some clans have not fully recovered from the loss of the wars. We number only a few hundred and each cycle we mourn more deaths than celebrate births. Every new life is precious. What you did for us this Gathering is a priceless gift, in more ways than one."

Ash paid great attention to the flute in her hands so she did not have to meet his gaze. She did not want praise or thanks.

"There has not been a fire dragon since the clan wars. That seat has been empty on the Council from the day it was established. The return of the fire dragon is auspicious and the manner of its birth was written into prophecy."

That word again. The last time prophecy had been bandied around had not yielded a positive result. Asher raised her face.

"What is the prophecy?" she asked nervously.

The Black blinked. "It does not translate to anything of sense to you, but I will summarise. When the fire dragon is born of the Musician's song, the dragons of D'rona will experience prosperity and fertility once more."

Asher smiled with relief. "That's a good thing then!"

Dor'tiem stood up and stretched his matte black wings.

"We are grateful for your actions. Know that when the time comes little Musician, the dragons will repay our debt."

Asher screwed up her nose in puzzlement. "What does that mean?"

But Dor'tiem had said all he was willing to say. With a push of his powerful legs he leapt into the sky.

Now that the heat of his large body was gone the chill of the cloudless night settled upon Ash. She shivered. It was time to make use of those furs once more and get some sleep. First thing tomorrow she was heading to Andera.

Chapter Four

The Laneisian

When the sun peeked above the mountains of Dor'atar, its warm rays cutting through the frigid morning air, Asher was already awake.

She had slept well enough at first, but restless dreams of fire dragons and clan wars had forced her from slumber.

The air in the cave was still cold, and her face stung. The warmth of the heated springs beckoned. With a happy sigh Asher sunk beneath the water and enjoyed a quiet soak. By the time the sun's light had fully reached into the cave Asher was washed, dressed, and packed, ready for her journey.

She carried her pack onto the ledge and watched the sun rise. The solitude and calmness buoyed her for the journey ahead. She tried not to think of the Void crossing, and instead focused on being back on Andera.

She had only been with the dragons for a brief moment, but some-how she felt different here. Far less awkward and anxious than she had ever felt in her real life. Stronger, braver. There had been none of the anger that she had spent years denying and the last few days trying to control.

Maybe there was a way to hold onto that when she returned to life on Earth. The solemnity and earnestness of the dragons had resonated with her. She connected with their straightforwardness far more than she ever had with the emotional complexities of human beings. And that was a fact.

It felt wrong to disappear without farewell, but she could not go in search of Hr'tom or Dor'tiem as she could not leave the ledge unaided. She was unsure if they could read English if she left a note. When another ten minutes passed without a dragon appearing, she decided it was time to go.

This time when Asher prepared to open the portal she was not in such a state of panic. Both her mother and Hesta had said that preparation was the key to a safe crossing. This seemed like a good time to learn how to use the bracelet properly.

Carefully Ash ran her fingers over the enamel flowers, learning the feel of each carving. The bracelet warmed to her touch. She rubbed the bracelet and imagined the energy in it releasing.

As the portal opened before her, Asher played a tune on the harmonica to surround herself with her own Crafting. She brought to mind the image of Hesta's library and focused on the portal opening there.

The globe hummed in agitation, distracting Asher.

"Shush!" she commanded.

Ash returned her attention to the portal, twisting the bracelet around her wrist to widen the portal. The familiar bleakness of the Void filled her with dread. No light guided her to the other side. Asher closed her eyes and tried to picture the exact spot in the library where she wanted the portal to open. There, beside the table.

The globe burned against her chest.

"Ouch!" she yelped, opening her eyes and losing the image of the library. "Stop doing that!"

But no matter. A pinprick of light was visible. The portal had opened on the other side.

"Here we go," she muttered, taking a few steadying breaths.

It was one thing to leap madly into the Void when escaping certain capture and possible death, quite another to deliberately step into the nothingness with full conscious choice. Before hesitation could weaken her resolve, Asher inhaled deeply and stepped through the portal.

Numbness seeped into bone and muscle, but she did not lose focus or her sense of purpose. She could not feel, but she still had control over her thoughts, which was reassuring. Each step brought the light closer.

With a huge gasp of relief Asher stepped through the portal and into a gleaming street lined with crystals and gold. By the Threads, not again! This was definitely not the Manor and she suspected not even Andera.

Behind her the portal evaporated.

Ash ran her fingers over the enamel bracelet once more. It had barely begun to warm up when the globe burned her skin with such intensity that Ash yelped and let go of the bracelet so she could pull the globe out of her top.

'*Stay,*' came the thought. Asher really, really did not want to stay. She rubbed the bracelet. The globe burned so ferociously she could feel it through her clothes.

"Okay you win," she muttered, "so what now?"

The globe, having achieved its objective, fell unhelpfully silent. Asher took a long look around.

She was tucked in a deep doorway overlooking a crowded street. Figures walked at varying paces along streets quite literally paved with gold. Buildings made of crystal towered high into the white sky. It was beautiful and stark and completely devoid of colour.

She was the only person not wearing a large white fur coat that almost grazed the ground. Each coat had an oversized hood which completely covered the heads and faces of the passers-by.

Asher shivered. The air was more than cold, it was like heat just simply did not exist. Her thin long-sleeved t-shirt provided no protection against this intense bitterness.

She needed help. Hesitantly Asher stepped out of the doorway and onto the golden street. She waved at the first cloaked figure who walked her way.

"Excuse me," she said tentatively. But the person stepped straight past her without any acknowledgement and continued on their way. Embarrassed and uneasy Ash tried again with a second passer-by. Again they walked straight past her. As did the next person and the next.

Cold radiated off the glistening buildings and her fingers throbbed due to the extreme temperature. Her chest and throat ached from the panic she was barely keeping at bay.

What was happening?

She wished Levi and Kate were with her. Levi would find a way to charm some-one into helping, while Kate would have some practical solution to keep them warm. Charm was out of the question when she seemed totally invisible, so Asher tried to think like her practical friend. The first thing Kate would do was delve into the packs to see what they could use.

Ash rolled her eyes and whacked her face. What an idiot. With numb fingers she pulled her mother's brown woollen coat from the bottom of the pack. Then she found her soft woollen gloves. They were not thick and thermal but they were definitely better than frostbite. She rubbed her hands together ferociously.

Her entire body sighed with relief as feeling started returning to her hands.

No longer in imminent danger of freezing, Asher was able to focus on the comings and goings of the cloaked figures. Most of the figures were hurrying away from the dense city buildings, disappearing to her right. But a few were moving rapidly in the other direction.

Ash hesitated on the stoop for a few minutes longer until she realised that her outfit would not protect her indefinitely. She hauled her pack onto her shoulders and stepped out onto the street. She glanced at the figures disappearing to her right, and then fell in behind the last of the figures heading left. Without exchanging a single word they walked quickly through the streets, occasionally acknowledging another passer-by with a nod. No words of greeting were exchanged and the hoods were never lowered.

A few silent minutes later they arrived on the edge of the city. Where the golden streets stopped an enormous field of crystals began. There was no gentle transition. Quite simply the tall buildings ended and the crystal fields began.

Her companions wordlessly joined others that were harvesting crystals from the ground. Carefully they inspected each of the clusters without disturbing them, until they found one that met their criteria. Then it was plucked from the ground and vanished beneath their voluminous cloaks.

Ash stepped off the golden path and into the crystal fields. Chaos exploded in her head. Thousands of voices clamoured and whispered and jostled for attention.

Immediately Ash covered her ears with her hands which did not help at all. The cacophony was inside her head. In shock and pain she stumbled back onto the golden path and the blur of thoughts stopped.

Relief flooded through her. She sank to the ground and rubbed her pounding temples until the headache eased. When she was able to focus once more, Asher turned her attention back to the cloaked figures. Not a single word was being spoken.

An idea began to bubble.

Very carefully Asher reached into the field, being certain to keep her body on the path. Her fingers closed gently around a large pinkish white cluster. This time the barrage of thoughts was far less but still too many. Ash chose again. A single, yellow white crystal that was the size of her thumb.

'Step carefully Morag, that's the second one you have crushed.'

'I'm just so anxious Fenley. We left the harvest far too late today. How much time until the dark storm?'

'We have enough time if we move with haste. Let's gather what we need quickly and leave'.

Much, much better. It seemed she was now only hearing the thoughts of the two figures closest to her. She watched curiously as they chose their crystals, telepathically muttering to each other the whole time. The thought that was repeated consistently was the fear of the dark storm.

Ash raised her gaze to the clear sky. So far everything looked just as it had when she arrived. A sunless, cloudless, white sky. The air still and cold.

'Done.' Satisfaction and relief. *'That will be enough to get us through the darkness.'*

'Are you sure Fenley? Not one or two more?'

'We have enough,' responded Fenley firmly, *'we don't want to over harvest. Look, already today there are less living crystals than last month.'*

Asher looked closely at the ground near her. There. Dark crystals without any glow. Slowly she reached out her hand.

'Don't touch it!' yelled a voice in her head.

Asher snatched her hand back. She turned her head from side to side trying to identify the thought speaker. Morag and Fenley were hurrying back into the city. Clearly not them. The rest of the cloaked figures had finished and vacated the fields. Soon she would be the only one here.

'Hurry, we must get inside before the dark storms.'

It was then that Asher noticed the small figure standing a few feet behind her on the path.

'Follow me.'

Ash hesitated, then frowned as she peered over the fields, sure her eyes were playing tricks. In the far distance beyond the crystals the white horizon now appeared to be a roiling grey mass.

'Hurry!' the thought was frantic.

Ash hurried.

Back through the golden streets they rushed, Asher only just keeping up with her small guide. Abruptly the hooded figure stopped and pushed open a partially concealed door.

Beyond the city the crystal fields were being consumed by a terrible thick wind that howled and roared. The sound filled Asher with immense dread. It was only a matter of minutes before the still silence of the city was invaded. Asher leapt through the doorway. With a firm thud the door closed behind her. All was quiet once more.

Gratefully Ash shrugged off her pack. She leant it against the door and turned to view the room. It was one large, windowless space bursting with crystals of every colour. From the high ceilings they hung, gently spinning as the small, cloaked figure moved among them.

The room itself was lit by clusters of white crystals and was warmed by clusters of glowing red crystals. The walls were made of amber coloured crystal, giving the room a gentle otherworldly glow. Which was apt considering she was most definitely on another world.

Apart from the crystals there was very little else in the room. Asher waited quietly while her host glided in and out of a room at the far end, the hood still firmly in place.

As she stood there Asher realised why she felt so unsettled. It was not the strangeness of the situation or the foreignness of the crystals and the room. It was the silence.

She had never realised how much noise existed in her life. Not only talking and music but also the continuous background hum of life. Even when completely alone she was never in silence. Cars, planes, phones, electrical appliances, birds, dogs barking, air conditioning...

Life on earth was rarely quiet and never completely devoid of sounds. The intense silence made her ears throb. Ash shuffled her feet just to hear the scrape of her shoes against the crystal floor.

There had never been a moment in her life when music had not been part of her being, part of her thoughts. With relief she tuned into that never-ceasing sound.

'You don't belong here,' the thought was rough, the tone accusing. *'If you had touched the dead crystal you would have been consumed. Become part of the dark storms.'*

'I'm sorry. Thank you. Why did you help me?'

Her formless, faceless host paused. *'I have heard of the human who comes to speak with the Old Ones. You look as she is described. Are you her?'*

Ash shook her head. *'No, I am not the Weaver. I am the Musician. Who are you?*

'We are the Laneisian.'

'When did she last come, the Weaver?'

'Many storms ago. The storms are getting worse, more crystals are dying. A piece of the storm almost broke free last harvest.'

Asher's heart pounded in response to the terror in the Laneisian's voice.

'What do you mean, broke free?'

'Broke free from the Laneisian, from the fields, from the planet. Seeking destruction. Hungry for whatever power it could devour.

I hoped you were her. She would know what to do. Do you know what to do?'

The thought was a plea and its desperate tone cut straight to Asher's heart.

'*No, I'm sorry,*' she thought. '*I don't even understand what is happening.*'

The hooded figure turned away. Asher felt helpless and useless. What was she supposed to do? Why was she even here?

Help me! She commanded the globe. *Please...* she added softly. But the globe did not answer. Even its usual hum was silent.

'*What happens if the crystals die?*' she asked tentatively.

'*The crystals die and are consumed into the dark storm. That is their nature. New ones have always grown. But now they do not. Only the fields of crystals keep the storm contained here. As they die, the storm gets stronger. Soon...*' its voice broke.

Asher did not dare ask what might come after 'soon'.

'*The dark storms come more frequently and the crystals do not grow. If they all die, we die. If the Laneisian die, the storm will be released. This has never happened before. It is not meant to happen. Something is wrong. Something has changed.*'

'*The balance is lost,*' they thought simultaneously.

Asher jumped as a jolt leapt through her. The balance is lost. The Threads are tangled. Darven's dark work with the Stolen Crafters was already having an impact. What would happen now Hesta was no longer weaving the Threads?

The thought when it came was soft and pleading.

'*Please. You must know what to do to save the crystals, to save us all. Only creatures of power travel between the worlds.*'

Asher felt frozen. What was the right thing to do? Stop the storms? Pour her own Crafting into the crystals? Could she even do what needed to be done? Should she? She didn't know when to interfere and when to simply let the Threads lie as they were woven.

"I don't know what to do," she whispered aloud, needing to hear a voice even if it was her own. Tears pricked and she swallowed hard. "I'm just a girl who plays the music around her. I am not the Weaver."

The Laneisian remained silent, unable to hear the spoken words.

The amber crystals pulsed. Perhaps they understood she brought no answers, no hope. Outside the muffled sounds of a raging storm made Ash wince.

'Can you hear that?' she asked the Laneisian.

'I can feel it. My body aches with its fury. The city is strong. It will stand.' But the thought was more hope than certainty.

'How long will it last?'

'Until it ends.'

Asher sank to the floor and leaned against her pack, her forehead resting on her folded arms. Her host disappeared into the far room. Beyond the safety of the crystal room the storm howled.

Time lost all meaning. Asher had no concept of how long she sat there alone surrounded by the flickering of the crystals. A change in the flicker drew her attention. One of the hanging crystals had begun to dance wildly, its luminous white core fighting for life.

Ash stood up, her heart thumping. The Laneisian rushed in from the other room.

'It is dying,' wailed the thought, *'too soon, too soon!'*

Asher froze, filled with uncertainty. The Laneisian stood utterly still beside the dying crystal. The fear and grief churning through the small figure's thoughts was unbearable. Asher remembered the overwhelm of those feelings in the months following her mother's breakdown.

On D'rona she had known exactly what was required. The Threads were fixed, she had simply been the instrument of fate.

But here the Threads were tangled and she was out of her depth. She had yet to master her own Craft, let alone weave the balance of the universes. Indecision raged within her as the storm raged without.

A second crystal began to flicker with the same desperation. The Laneisian's thoughts were filled with agony and despair.

Asher tore open the front compartment of her pack and retrieved the flute that was tucked there. Quickly she clicked it together and raised it to her lips. She blew and the notes played. Music danced around the room, bouncing off the crystals. The dying crystals flickered and Asher poured more into each note.

With the fire dragon she had been birthing a life-force that was destined to live, and even that positive act had exhausted her. Now she was fighting against death, twice over. Crafting the energy back into the crystals was excruciatingly hard.

The energy churned and struggled, wrestling with the great blackness that wanted only to consume.

Every note drained Asher a little more, every tussle with the dark made her own light a little weaker. Never in her life had music felt like this. She pushed and played until her breath was too ragged to blow and her fingers ached from pressing the keys against the darkness; until her shoulders and wrists ached with the pressure and she could not play another note.

Exhausted she slumped to the floor, her chest aching and her head spinning. She could not even look up to see what her Crafting had wrought.

'*You did it! You saved the crystals,*' the thoughts were jubilant. '*You can save the fields!*'

'*No, I cannot…*' whispered Asher, but she was drained and her thoughts were weak.

'*As soon as the storm passes I will send for the Old Ones and tell them the news. You will come and save our fields!*'

The Laneisian rushed into the back room once more.

Asher raised her eyes to the two happily glowing crystals. They blinked with life. But for how long? Had she truly banished the darkness or only delayed it?

The notion of trying to save the enormous field of crystals filled her with fear. Saving these two had almost drained her life force. Any more... she shuddered. She knew that once the Old Ones arrived they would not let her leave. They needed their miracle.

Every muscle aching, Asher pushed herself up. She reached for her drink bottle and gulped down the dragon's clear, rejuvenating water. Energy seeped back into her veins. Nowhere near enough to heal the crystal fields, but hopefully enough to get her across the Void.

The pack was once more on her back and the portal beginning to open when the Laneisian returned.

'No, no, no! Please... don't leave,' it begged.

Tears clouded Asher's vision as she turned away. *'I'm sorry, I cannot do what you ask of me.'*

'Please Musician... we need you.'

Tears rolled unchecked down her face. She was not strong enough. Her mother's breakdown. Evie's kidnapping and defection to Darven. Hesta's defeat. She had not been strong enough to stop any of it.

The person she had felt blossoming within her on D'rona did not exist. The strong, confident Crafter who wore the Weaver's Globe and birthed the fire dragon was an illusion. The dark storm seemed to have settled on her soul.

She would not make any more promises she could not fulfil.

'I'm so sorry. I cannot save you. Any of you.'

And she stepped into the Void.

Chapter Five

Return to the Manor

In the great house of the Weaver, Trinity and Cook polished already spotless silver in the kitchen. Wordlessly they rubbed the soft cloths back and forth over the intricately patterned platters and jugs. Outside the sun shone in the early morning sky, promising a beautiful day. Inside the atmosphere was as gloomy as their thoughts.

The room was chilly. The great stove lay dark and cold.

It had been two days since Hesta had left for Ostrin and never returned. Two days since Marten had pulled her from the Queen's dining room, the Weaver hovering at the final portal between life and death.

What had become of her or the children, nobody knew.

Anetta sat with Trinity and Cook in the kitchen, clutching a bundle of unread papers and staring sightlessly through the window to the great grounds beyond. The three women exchanged no words, taking comfort in the presence of old friends who shared the same fears.

Anetta fretted about her husband, gone where she could not follow. Trinity feared for her son, bonded by blood oath to serve, and perhaps die, at the Weaver's side. And Mariah the Cook guiltily guarded the secret of the children's journey to the Mountains and Asher's true identity. In her darkest moments she felt certain that both Weaver and granddaughter were lost.

A muffled crash startled them from their mournful thoughts. The sound of falling books followed.

"The library!" exclaimed Anetta, nimbly leaping out of her chair and rushing through the back hallway, Trinity close at her heels. Cook followed behind, moving as fast as her tortured knees and back would allow.

A crumpled figure lay face down on the floor, beside the fallen table and a cacophony of books.

"Hesta?" said Anetta hopefully.

Tangled red hair spilled around her head. A familiar brown woollen coat covered her body.

"Ginarwen," breathed Cook.

Trinity crouched down and collected the semi-conscious figure in her arms. Gently she pushed the curls back to see the face beneath.

"It is the girl, the trainee," she said wonderingly, her bemused face turning to Cook. "Where has she come from? How did she get here?"

In her arms Asher began to stir, struggling to sit up.

"Shhh, careful now, careful." Trinity crooned. "She needs some water," she said to Anetta.

The housekeeper sped off to the kitchen.

"Where...?" breathed Asher, struggling to open her exhausted eyes.

"You are at safe at E-Langren, the Weaver's home. Cook is here and Anetta, and me, Trinity."

Asher stopped fighting to stay awake. She had finally returned and she was safe.

When Anetta returned with the glass of water Asher was already fast asleep on Trinity's lap. The three women looked at each other with confusion and hope.

"Do you think...?" began Anetta, "Could the others be not far behind?"

"We'll discover it all when the child awakes. We need to make her more comfortable and release poor Trinity from that awkward position," bustled Cook. Asher was back. Relief threatened to overwhelm her and the best way Cook dealt with any high emotion was action.

"Righto, without Marten we will have to move her ourselves."

"Upstairs?" said Trinity in horror.

"Absolutely not. We shall settle her here on the sofa. She will be quite comfortable. You two grab her shoulders, I have her legs. Ready? One, Two, Three..."

The women pulled off the pack and then heaved and half dragged the much taller Asher to the sofa, where only a few days ago she had sat with Levi and learned the story of Darven and the Crafters.

Anetta hurried out of the room in search of pillows and blankets.

While she was gone Trinity and Cook held the limp girl and gently removed the heavy coat. As they lay her down something glinted at the edge of Trinity's vison, causing her to blink.

Trinity gasped. The golden globe shone brightly on Asher's t-shirt.

"Mariah! Mariah, look. The girl wears Hesta's globe. *The Weaver's globe.*"

Cook shuffled closer and the women peered at the gleaming, humming pendant, neither of them daring to touch it.

"How?" breathed Trinity. "What does this mean?"

Cook bit her lip hard. What was to be shared and what was to remain unsaid? She did not know anymore. The world as they knew it was shifting and the child wearing the globe marked a significant change. There was so much unwoven, so much in turmoil, and she felt certain that young Asher would need all the support she could get. She made her decision.

"I will tell you what I know Trinity, but you must swear absolute secrecy. On the very Threads themselves." Cook's voice was low and serious.

Eyes wide, Trinity made the pledge.

"Ginarwen did not perish in the Void all those years ago. She settled on Earth and built a family. This is her daughter, Asher. It appears Hesta has claimed her as her Heir."

With a great whoosh Trinity plonked onto the armchair, her cheeks bright with colour. "Well then," she said after a long pause. "And what of Carowen?"

"She knows none of this. And we will not be the ones to tell her. That is Hesta's choice."

An uneasy silence settled between them. Both thought, but neither mentioned, the feared possibility that Hesta was gone forever.

Ash stirred but did not wake. Beneath her lids her eyes were moving rapidly and every now and then her body twitched. She was lost in dreaming. Silent teardrops leaked from the corners of her eyes.

Trinity's face was full of compassion. "The poor child seems troubled even in her dreams. I wonder where she has been and what she has seen."

Cook said nothing in reply. She had lived in the Weaver's house for many years and experienced Hesta's return from countless difficult journeys. Sometimes the aftermath of the Weaver's decisions weighed heavily long after they were made.

Anetta trotted back in, laden with pillows and blankets. Before she could see the globe, Cook carefully hooked the chain with a pen and tucked it back under Asher's collar. She made sure not to touch the pendant itself.

"How is she?" asked Anetta as Cook gently manoeuvred a pillow beneath Asher's head.

"Restless and exhausted." Cook replied softly. "We will take turns to sit with her."

The three women looked at the sleeping girl. Her face seemed so young. Cook and Trinity exchanged a troubled glance. Would they be able to provide the support she needed to become the Heir Andera required? And where in all the stars was Hesta?

***

In the place Beyond, where here and there are nowhere, and yesterday and tomorrow do not exist, the Weaver and her Protector slept the deep slumber.

No dreams disturbed their consciousness, for such things do not exist in the Beyond.

They had no need of blankets or water, for such things are not required in the Beyond.

The Ralshok watched over them as they slept. No-one could enter the Beyond without him, yet he still maintained his silent vigil. The Weaver had been poisoned by her kinswoman on her own planet. The Threads were in disarray. He would take no chances.

In the place Beyond, where time has no meaning and the blurred line between life and death is ever changing, the Weaver and the Protector slept the deep slumber.

And the Ralshok watched and waited.

***

Cook offered to sit with Asher for the first shift. She pulled the heavy curtains shut so the sleeping Crafter would not be disturbed by the mid-morning sun. Then quietly she shuffled around, collecting the fallen books and piling them against the bookshelves. Once that was done she carried in the silverware and set up a polishing station on the table which had been restored to its previous upright position.

The flaw in her plan became immediately apparent when she sat to polish the candlesticks and realised her ageing eyes could not see clearly without the lights on or the curtains open.

She chuckled softly at her own foolishness and decided to sit in the soft armchair with her legs supported on the ottoman. For the first time in a very long time Cook had nothing to do and no way of doing it. For the first time in two days the grip of fear around her heart had eased slightly. She gave herself permission to relax for a few minutes.

The wheeze and puff of Cook's snoring greeted Trinity when she entered the room two hours later carrying a tray with tea and cakes.

"Oh dear, oh dear," fussed Trinity, rushing over to deposit the tray on the table. She gave Cook a firm shake.

"What happened?" mumbled Cook, wincing as she adjusted her stiff body.

"You fell asleep! In a chair. Oh your back will not thank you when you stand up!"

Never was a truer word spoken. With Trinity pulling and Cook groaning, she was finally back on her feet. But getting up was only the beginning. Now she had to undo the kinks that were so gleefully twisting in her back. With each hobbling step Cook screwed up her face in pain. Trinity screwed up her own in sympathy.

"It was just so comfortable at the start," moaned Cook.

"Perhaps you should go for a gentle walk around the garden," suggested Trinity anxiously.

With teeth clenched Cook nodded and slowly hobbled out of the room. Trinity went to sit down, then leapt back up in one swift movement, glaring at the offending armchair as though Cook's back pain was all its fault.

"Oh I don't think so," she said in a very stern voice.

Instead she choose the chair at the table and poured herself a steaming cup of tea. With a sigh of satisfaction Trinity breathed in its soothing smell and sipped.

The girl Asher who wore the globe of the Weaver still slept. The dreams seemed to have settled as she no longer twisted or cried out in her sleep. Trinity thought of her cousin Ginarwen, long considered dead but actually not. She wondered what Hestawen's plan was for this girl and when the Weaver would return. She thought of Carowen, the cousin she loved above all others and how this might affect her.

Then she shook her head to clear the ache all this thinking was creating and decided to have a piece of cake instead. Once the cake was eaten and her fingers wiped clean, Trinity reached into her deep pockets and pulled out her knitting. She could knit just as well in a darkened room as a light one. The familiar looping and interlocking movements were ingrained into her hands' memory, and the repetitive motion required no effort.

Some time later Fleur silently entered the room. Trinity smiled at her daughter and returned her attention to the needles and wool.

She paid no notice to Fleur when she went and sat on the floor beside Asher. Nor did she see the girl gently lay a warm hand on the Musician's forehead. Trinity had never felt the energy of Crafting within her own hands, never felt the weaving of the Threads. She did not feel the energy now as it passed between her daughter and the Heir. Beneath Asher's top the globe hummed.

Mother and daughter were still sitting there when Cook arrived soon after, her steps less pained and her back almost straight once more.

"I'm feeling much better," she said to Trinity. "Nothing like sunshine and movement to invigorate the body and the soul. How is Asher?"

At that moment the girl stretched and opened her eyes. She gazed unblinking at the ceiling for a few seconds, then her focus settled and she turned her head to see three solemn faces staring at her intently in the dark. Fleur's was so close Asher actually yelped in shock.

"Sorry," murmured the younger girl, standing up and moving back to the table beside her mother.

Cook stepped forward. She turned on the table lamp beside the sofa and peered at Asher's face keenly. She must have been satisfied with what she saw, for a pleased smile lit up her own face.

"You have your colour back child and your eyes are clear. That's a very good sign. How are you feeling?"

Asher sat up slowly, trying not to overly strain her bangs and bruises. She fervently hoped that was last of her Void crossings for a while. The crossings were strenuous and the landings were painful. Her body could not take too many more right now. As for her mind... *How was she feeling?* Sad. Lonely. Confused and uncertain. Overwhelmed. Frightened. And very tired, with a weariness that seemed to have settled deep in her soul.

Asher looked from face to face. Each of them was looking at her with kindness, with happiness, and with hope. They did not need her worries for they had enough of their own.

She smiled for the big-hearted old woman who hovered beside her.

"Hungry."

Cook's smile split into a wide grin of pleasure. "Well that, Miss Asher, I can definitely do something about!"

"Tea?" offered Trinity.

"Yes please," said Asher, taking the proffered teacup and drinking the luke-warm liquid gratefully.

"Ooooh, we'll have a wonderful Sunday dinner," declared Cook joyously, limping only slightly as she moved towards the door.

"I'll have it all pulled together in no time. Meanwhile I'll bring in some biscuits and fruit cake. That will set you right. Then there will be some sandwiches for lunch, not too many, we don't want to ruin our dinner."

"Wait, did you say Sunday?" asked Asher. The days had blurred together during her time with the dragons and the Laneisian.

"Yes indeed, Sunday all day," chortled Cook.

Ash stared at the teacup in her hands, her face still and un-readable.

"Why do you ask?" said Fleur softly.

Unexpected tears burned behind Ash's eyes and her voice caught as she answered. "That means today is my birthday. My sixteenth birthday."

"A special day indeed!" said Cook. "I will add cake to our celebrations!"

She was dictating a list to herself as she left the library and headed back to the kitchen.

"A special day indeed," echoed Trinity, her tone far more solemn than Cook's. "You know what it signifies of course. For you, the Heir. I suppose that's why you returned today."

Asher's eyes widened and her hand flew to the globe beneath her clothes.

"It is very important that you are here for this birthday. It is almost like the Threads were already woven," Trinity said in wonder.

Fleur gave her mother a brief hug. "Yes mama, it is exactly like that."

"Why? What happens?" asked Asher.

Trinity was clearly confused by the question. Her eyes flicked between Ash and Fleur, filled with indecision.

"If you do not already know then I am not sure I'm allowed to speak of it. This is Weaver business. Am I Fleur? Should I?"

"Of course you can and should mama. The Weaver is gone for the time being. Asher needs us to help her, to give her all the information she needs. Nobody else knows what you know. You grew up around the Weavers. You know the ways. Perhaps us being here is also woven in the Threads."

Trinity nodded, reassured. "Yes you are right Fleur, as always".

She smiled with deep affection for her sensible daughter, then turned serious eyes on Ash.

"Sixteen is an auspicious birthday for the Weaver's Heir. Today is the day you first hold the Threads."

Chapter Six

Carowen

Asher trudged slowly up the seemingly endless stairs of the Manor, her body weary and her mind numb.

When she arrived at the first floor landing her heart panged. Down the hallway to her left lay Kate and Levi's empty rooms. She felt their absence more keenly here than she had when she had been with the dragons or the Laneisian. They had been here at the manor together.

Ash took a deep shuddering breath and squelched the rising loneliness. Resolutely she turned down the hallway on her right.

Up the next flight to the top floor she continued, the weight of her pack increasing with every step.

The objects were humming when she arrived in the Crafter gallery. Their collective energy crackled within the light-filled space. Asher stood still and closed her eyes.

Generations of Crafting flowed around her and within her. She raised her arms out to her sides, picturing the energy as stardust surrounding her.

For a long time she stood like that, warmed by the sun rays and nourished by the Crafter energy. Then her back twinged, drawing her consciousness once more to the aches and pains of her human self. The uncomfortable reality of the cumbersome pack could no longer be ignored.

She opened her eyes and continued through the gallery to her bedroom.

As she shrugged off the pack onto the floor of the beautiful room she noticed she was smiling. The Crafter energy had buoyed her spirits and she felt lighter, calmer, and more optimistic. More like the Musician she had been on D'rona.

Today you hold the Threads. Trinity had been unable to tell her how that happened, or when or where. She had shrugged helplessly when questioned and said that was known only to the Weaver and her Heirs. She simply knew that today was the day.

Anticipation and trepidation buzzed within Asher. Today she would be one step closer to uncovering the mysteries of the Weaver, potentially finding Hesta and restoring balance to Andera.

The unwanted thought intruded. *You left the Laneisian to be consumed by the dark storm. You are useless, hopeless, friendless...*

The ugly words punched hard in her gut and chest. Asher collapsed onto the sofa, taking deep breaths to ease the pressure in both body and mind. The familiar doubts and fears were rearing their heads with glee. For so long she had allowed them to keep her small.

"No," she said aloud to the empty room, to the bully in her head. Her voice was shaking.

"No more. The Threads have chosen me. Hesta has chosen me. She believes I can, so I can."

Saying the words gave her courage.

'You go girl,' she imagined Levi cheering. *'As my gran always said - the words you say to yourself create the person you are. Choose with care.'*

The truth of that soaked into Asher, refreshing her spirit just as the Dragon water had refreshed her body.

The words you say to yourself create the person you are.

Yes but... began her fears and doubts.

"Oh shut-up," commanded Asher firmly. "No more today. Today is my birthday."

A sense of quiet settled within her mind and Ash grinned. The doubts and fears would return, she was sure of that. After all, they had been companions all her life. But for now she was choosing other thoughts, and that felt good. There was no time to wallow in a pity party, she had things to do.

And while one of those things was holding the essence of the universes, there were rather more practical needs to be dealt with. Such as the fact that the clothes in her pack and the clothes on her back were travel soiled and more than a little smelly.

Her mother's wardrobe produced a green and white checked dress and a box of new undergarments. She shook her head with a smile.

In the bathroom she was surprised to discover the dragon tooth still hanging around her neck. Tentatively she pulled at the leather strap and laughed when it lifted easily over her head. She laid it carefully on the shelf above the sink.

From her jeans' pocket she then pulled out the Laneisian crystal, relief gurgling in her tummy when she saw its vibrant yellow glow. The Laneisians were not destroyed. While the crystal lived there was hope they would still be saved.

Asher placed the crystal beside the dragon tooth, followed by the enamel bracelet and the golden globe. Finally she placed Brawn's small blue whistle alongside her other treasures. An odd little collection of experiences far beyond the ordinary. She gazed wonderingly at the mementos of the Musician's life. Her life.

The road ahead was unknown, and truth be told it filled her with fear. But this assortment of magical things reminded her of how far she had already come.

'Wow, you are thinking all the deep thoughts today,' imaginary Levi teased gently. Asher rolled her eyes then laughed at herself.

Once she was showered and dressed in her mother's dress and green boots, she headed back through the gallery with the intention to find the laundry and wash her dirty clothes.

She truly had not planned to turn down the hallway that led to Hesta's rooms, so it was quite a surprise to find herself outside the door to the Weaver's study. She stood at the closed door for a long minute, then with a sigh turned to leave.

The tiniest sound caught her attention, a whisper of rustling coming from the closed room.

"Hesta," she breathed.

Abandoning her washing to a pile on the floor, Asher eagerly pushed open the heavy wooden door and stepped inside. The woman carefully opening drawers and poking through their contents was not Hesta, but some-one quite welcome anyway.

"Carowen!" exclaimed Ash, her face beaming.

The Glass Crafter looked up in shock, her hands full of papers. With care she placed them back in the drawer and slid it shut.

"Asher! What a wonderful surprise. I haven't seen you in a few days, though in truth I have been rather busy. I thought you had left."

The pleasure in her warm voice wrapped around Asher. She knew she was grinning like a fairground clown but she was just so happy to see the Crafter.

"No, I'm still here. I accompanied my friends home and have just returned."

Carowen stepped around the desk and reached out to clasp Asher's hands in greeting. Asher moved to close the gap between them, her own hands outstretched. As she stepped forward she moved out of the darkened entry and into the lamplight of the desk.

Caro stopped abruptly, her hands dropping.

"You look so familiar to me," she murmured, speculation clear in her eyes.

"There's something..." she eyed Asher up and down, noting the dress, the boots, the red curls for once neatly brushed and tied back. "Like some-one I used to know."

Asher took a deep breath. Surely this was the moment to tell her everything. To spill the whole tangled tale and implore Carowen for her guidance and support. The words bubbled in her throat, racing each other in their haste to spill off her tongue. She so desperately wanted some-one to tell her what to do.

But a sensible, practical voice intruded on her excitement. This time her imaginary companion was Kate.

'Why is the room dark? The fire unlit, the curtains closed? Why is she pawing through Hesta's things like a thief in the dark?'

The eager words of confession skidded to a halt, tangling with each other and creating a coughing fit. Asher turned away to cough into her arm, and took the opportunity to layer her 'don't notice me' charm.

"Are you alright Asher? Here have a glass of water. It may taste a little strange having sat here for two days, but it will do the job."

Asher turned around as Carowen reached for a jug and glass. The Glass Crafter poured the water, the sound rushing in Asher's ears.

Queen Magda held out the glass to Hesta...

No, it was Carowen handing the glass to *her*. Asher shook her head to clear the memory.

"You do not want it?" asked Caro, misinterpreting the head shake.

"No, I do. I mean, yes please." Ash took the drink with a nod of thanks and raised the glass to her lips.

The Weaver collapsed to the ground...

With a determined frown, Ash swigged a mouthful of water, swallowing the cool water in one gulp.

"That seems to have fixed your coughing. Now what did you come in here for?" asked Carowen kindly.

Ash blinked and wriggled her nose, dispelling the memory of the Weaver's poisoning. "I heard a noise. I was hoping you were Hesta."

"Oh dear." Carowen's beautiful face was sombre. "I suppose you haven't heard then. Hesta is gone."

"Gone? Gone where?"

"We don't know."

A thought occurred to Asher, an idea so brilliant she could have slapped herself for not thinking of it earlier.

"Carowen, can't you find her in the Threads?" she waved her hands enthusiastically in a rather vague depiction of weaving. "You know, blood related Wens and all that."

Carowen shook her head. "I think you mean Blood Bonded, not blood related."

"Yes that," said Asher excitedly.

"It's a good idea young Pianist, but I am not Blood Bonded to the Weaver. I don't believe there is a Crafter alive who is. Now should we head downstairs?"

Carowen held out her arm, wriggling her fingers to herd Ash towards the door.

Asher moved slowly, her mind racing. "Excuse me Carowen, what happens if Hesta never returns? Who will be the next Weaver?"

Carowen screwed up her nose. "I believe that will be me. If I can find the globe of inheritance."

"A globe?" said Asher innocently as the damn thing chuckled against her chest. "What's that about?"

"Nothing important," replied Caro, "just an outdated tradition that we may have to do away with."

The globe burned. Asher hurried through the door so Caro would not see her grimace of pain.

"Why are you so cross with me? Stop it," she hissed to the seething pendant.

Back in the corridor Ash scooped up the bundle of washing. The globe no longer burned but it was definitely sulking.

"Asher," said Carowen as she pulled the study door shut. "How did you open Hesta's door?"

Ash frowned in confusion at the odd question. "I just pushed it."

"So it was closed shut and you turned the handle and pushed it open?" persisted Caro.

"Um, I really don't remember."

"It's rather important dear, so try to remember." Her usually honeyed voice was cool.

The hair on the back of Asher's neck prickled. "I, ah, think it was ajar. Yes, it was slightly ajar."

Carowen stared at her intently, trying to determine if she was telling the truth. Asher wondered why it was so important.

"It must have been ajar because I heard a noise. Yes, that's it," she said with relief, pleased to have an explanation for Caro. "I would not have been able to hear the noise if the door was fully closed."

"Yes, that seems plausible," conceded Carowen. For the first time she noticed the bundle of clothes.

"Are you looking for the laundry? Come, I will show you the way. Jenah from the village comes in each day to help around the house and do the washing."

Asher smiled in thanks and relief. The warmth in Caro's voice was restored. Asher no longer teetered on the edge of being cast out of Caro's good graces, and for some reason that was important to her.

They walked in silence to where the hall met the gallery. The wondrous objects gleamed in the cases and on the stands. Carowen stopped and looked around thoughtfully.

"It occurs to me Asher, that I do not know which room you occupy."

A heated flush crept up Asher's chest, inflamed her neck, and deposited two splotchy blobs of colour on her cheeks. How would it look that she was in Hesta's daughter's room?

"Um, the room on the far side of the gallery."

Her awkward grip on the clothes gave way and they fell in a muddled heap to the floor. Carowen watched her silently as she collected each item, Ash using the excuse of the clothes to not lift her head and meet that curious gaze.

"I see," said Carowen finally, her voice small and sad. "Onward to the laundry."

Cramming the clothes into a tangled bundle, Asher hurried behind her. She could not shake the uneasy feeling that even though she had said nothing, she had somehow given everything away.

At the laundry Carowen bid her good day and left Asher to her washing.

Once back in her own rooms, Carowen the Glass Crafter sat and cried. She sobbed for the cousin she had loved and lost. She sobbed for the many years she had served at the Weaver's side, waiting for her turn. And she sobbed for the great love that she feared would never be hers.

Once, many years ago, a young man had told her how much he loved and admired her, and she had loved him too. But Ginarwen was newly dead and Hesta had need of her. So she had turned him away, breaking both their hearts.

The years had marched by. He had built a family and a home with some-one else. She had remained loyal to the Weaver, within the lonely walls of E-Langren. Waiting for Hesta to pass on the Threads, the Weaver never once mentioning that she had no intention to do so. That she was waiting for another.

When her mind and body were drained of sorrow, Carowen wiped away the last of her tears. She washed and creamed her face, and brushed her glorious chestnut hair until it gleamed. Then she packed a bag of clothes and treasured Glass Craft.

She hesitated over the photograph that had graced her desk for these many years. She knew it well, having held it close in her loneliest moments.

Two young women beamed for the camera, sharing matching grins and matching dresses. The brunette in a blue check, the redhead in a green check, their arms entwined around each other's backs. Best friends, confidantes, cousins. She stared at Ginar's glowing face and thought of the quiet pianist, her daughter, who wore that dress today.

"Why didn't you tell me?" she whispered to the frozen image of her cousin. "All these lost years."

With a sudden burst of anger Caro thrust the photo deep inside a drawer. For thirty years she had lived here at E-Langren, believing herself loved, believing she belonged. She had carried the memory and the loss of Ginarwen with her for nineteen of those years. She would carry her no longer. As quickly as it flared the anger was gone, leaving only the pain. Her neck and chest ached with it.

"I have been a fool," she said softly. "Too much of my life I have given in service to the Weaver. Not a moment more."

Chapter Seven

The Weaving Room

J enah from the village had insisted Asher leave the clothes with her, and there was still a little while until lunch, so Asher had time on her hands. She considered going in search of Caro and telling her everything, but she was in need of time to recover and rebuild her energy after D'rona and the Laneisian, and there would be time later to talk with the Glass Crafter. So she headed to the only place where she could feel truly herself and settle her mind.

As she opened the door and slipped inside, the music room seemed to waken up to welcome her. The sun was still high on this side of the house, and the large windows poured light into the quiet room.

Ash took her place at the piano, reverently lifting the glossy lid and running her fingers along the keys. She was sure that countless unknown people had played here before her, but in this moment she chose to believe the piano was purely for her.

With the habit of many years, she ran her fingers up and down the scales, warming her fingers and her mind. Everything within her seemed to relax. Soon she was lost in Mozart, oblivious to anyone and anything around her.

Beyond the music room Carowen descended the beautiful oak staircase for the last time, her head heavy and her heart numb. She wondered whether anyone would notice she was gone, or if they would miss her.

Around the house the people who cared for her went about their day, unaware of the threads being woven around them.

Asher continued to play, lost in the music that nourished her soul, as Carowen ran her hand down the smoothly polished banister.

Mariah bustled about in her kitchen, humming happily, as Carowen crossed the wide hallway.

Trinity rested her fragile nerves in her room, as Carowen hesitated at the front door, longing for some-one to stop her. To tell her how much she mattered and they needed her to stay.

Fleur el Jesper stood frozen in the shadows of the library doors. She recognised Carowen's pain but was not sure it was her place to interfere. She did not know what had caused it, or how to ease it. So she stood quietly and agonised over what to do.

The Threads paused. In this moment multiple possibilities existed, multiple outcomes. But choices would be made and the possibilities would diminish to only a few, and finally to only one certain outcome.

Fleur told herself she was too young and unimportant to interfere in the affairs of the Wen. She made her choice, and walked silently back into the library.

Carowen looked back one long, last time. Nobody came. Her pride and pain told her that nobody cared. She made her choice, pulled open the heavy wooden door and stepped outside.

Asher the Musician played on, oblivious as something important was lost from the Threads and something else was woven in its place. As Carowen el Brawn walked away from E-Langren and everyone who loved her, without goodbye and with a soul nursing the fertile seeds of bitterness.

In the solitude of the music room, Asher felt the music seep within every element of her being. Energising and healing her depleted body and soul.

She played songs she loved, just for the enjoyment of playing them and hearing them. Just to feel her fingers move with lightness and ease. Around her minute particles of dust danced with the light and shadows. For Ash, lost in the music, time ceased to exist and yet she felt completely immersed in every heartbeat. The music swirled around her, and even with her eyes closed she could see the colours of each note. Vibrant strands of blues and greens, intertwined with warm yellow and jaunty orange.

Eventually her fingers ceased to play and the last of the notes wafted away. She stood up and stretched her back. Her fingers tingled from a solid hour of playing. Her mind felt clearer. It was time to confide in Carowen, to tell her everything that had happened and ask for her help and guidance.

She walked across the music room to the door that led into the service hallway. But there was no longer one door leading into the hall, there were two.

Ash stopped, wrinkling her mouth and nose in confusion. Surely there had only ever been one doorway.

Tentatively she pushed open the door on the left. It swung into the wide white hall. To the left she could faintly hear Cook singing merrily in the kitchen. To her right the hallway continued on to Cook and Anetta's living quarters.

Ash stepped into the hall and peered along the wall. Definitely no second door on this side of the wall. She stepped back into the music room and contemplated the mystery door. Should she? She reached forward and lightly touched the door. With a distinct click it unlatched and opened an inch, offering a clear invitation for Asher to step inside.

Heart pounding, she pushed open the door and stepped over the threshold into an enormous room. What it lacked in windows, for there was not a single one, it more than made up for indoors. It was impossible to count them all, layered as they were alongside, behind, in front of and above each other.

In the very centre of the vast door-filled space was a large wooden table, above which an old-fashioned loom hovered.

The loom clacked, its arms rising and falling, as threads of every colour were pulled from nowhere and woven into a glorious tapestry that spilled off the edge of the table and disappeared. The sound and movement of the loom was hypnotic, drawing Asher closer and closer. Her fingers itched to touch the glorious threads, to immerse herself in the countless lives and stories she could feel pulsing from them.

The loom lurched for a fraction of a millisecond, almost too brief to detect, then clicked back into place.

A rustling noise from somewhere to her left made Asher her jump. Her mind immediately jumped to rats. Nervously she peered at the floor.

"That was too long," muttered a worried voice from behind her, "those Threads tangled".

Ash leapt away from the voice with a small scream, twisting to find the source. There was no-one else in the room.

"There's no need for that!" said the voice rather crossly. "I didn't scream when I saw you."

"That's just the thing," said Asher slowly, still scouring the space around her. "I can't see you."

Piece by shimmering piece a being materialised in front of Asher. A long brown furry tail appeared first, followed by a wide round bottom and strong rodent legs. Ash screamed again.

"Now what's wrong?" said the human size rat crossly, its long pointy face appearing.

"Sorry. I just wasn't expecting a large rat," said Ash sheepishly, "I'm not particularly fond of the Earth variety."

"Well if I am a rat to you, then a rat must be exactly what you were expecting."

Ash considered this. She supposed it were true. She had been frightened of encountering a rat in this lightless, windowless space, and that had been her first thought when she had heard rustling beside her.

"So you are not normally a rat?" she asked.

"I am normally just me. You see me as you expect to see me," said the rat.

Its whiskers twitched. A shiver of horror trickled down Asher's spine.

"Can I choose again?" she asked tentatively.

The rat shimmered and morphed into a plump forty-year-old woman with soft brown hair cut into a bob and a pair of red glasses perched on her nose. Mrs McIntyre, her much loved fourth grade teacher, stretched out her arms and looked her new body up and down curiously.

"Comfortable enough," she said, "We'll keep this one for now. So you are Asher. Welcome, I am the Guide."

"Nice to meet you," replied Ash politely. "Where are we?"

"I take it you have not been educated about the Weaving room?"

Asher shook her head.

"And me? Surely you know about the Guide?"

Reluctantly Asher shook her head again.

"Clearly the current Weaver has neglected her duty," said Mrs McIntyre sternly. "It is expected that the Heir is trained and ready when she steps into the Weaving room at sixteen. This is unacceptable."

Ash was taken aback. The real Mrs McIntyre had never been so fierce when she was ten.

"It's not exactly Hesta's fault," she explained. "My mother raised me on Earth without knowledge of the Weaver or the Threads. I've only been on Andera for a few days."

"But you *are* Asher el Ginarwen."

Asher nodded.

"And today *is* your sixteenth birthday?" the Guide asked intently.

Ash swallowed hard and nodded again.

"Hmmm." Mrs McIntyre was clearly displeased, but after a moment of silent deliberation she decided that they would have to make do.

"As you can see, here in the Weaving Room is where the Threads of Existence manifest for the Weaver. Though she can physically attend to the Threads here, she of course can feel them wherever she is. The door to the room opens for her whenever she requires it. Is that clear?"

Asher nodded, though it really was not that clear. She did not want to ask a stupid question and draw Mrs McIntyre's ire, so instead she pointed at the many doors.

"And what are these for?"

The Guide looked around. "What? What are you pointing at?"

Ash tilted her head. "All the white doors," she said.

"You can see those?" Mrs McIntyre's eyebrows shot up in surprise.

Ash nodded. How could she not see them? There were hundreds of them, disappearing into the distance of the enormous space.

Mrs McIntyre stared at her. "Well." She stopped, at a loss for words.

"Is something the matter?" asked Ash eventually, when it seemed the Guide would say nothing further.

"It's just extremely unusual that some-one other than the Weaver can see the doors. They are part of her weave. I've never before had an Heir that can see them without the Weaver revealing them to her."

"Where do they all lead to?"

Mrs McIntyre sighed deeply. "Alright then. If you can see them, then I cannot see the harm in giving you a quick overview. Separating the galaxies and universes is the great Void of nothingness. You are aware of this of course. The Void exists to protect the planets from each other, to ensure stability among the galaxies and ensure continuity of the 100 billion lifeforms in the five universes. If beings could just travel between the worlds, imagine the chaos and destruction they could wreak."

The Guide pinned her with another piercing look of displeasure.

"Travel between the Void is deliberately difficult, almost impossible. Only creatures of power can attempt it at all. And they must be careful, not only to cross safely but also to protect the integrity of the portals, so others cannot follow. You have been barging through the Void for the last few days, creating a terrible racket. Ripping open the fabric of space itself with little regard for the scarring you leave behind."

Asher dropped her head. She was getting the distinct impression she was rather a disappointment to the Guide. It stung even more coming from the likeness of the much-loved Mrs McIntyre. She wished the Guide had chosen her current PhysEd teacher instead. Ash was used to disappointing *him*.

The weaving on the loom hitched and then continued. The Guide rushed over to closely examine the Threads.

"We need the Weaver to maintain the Threads," she said accusingly to Asher, as though the Musician herself was to blame for Hesta's absence.

Ash said nothing, choosing to nod in agreement only.

"As I was saying, travel across the Void is greatly discouraged, however the Weaver is required to travel through the universes and she cannot be ripping open portals to do so every time. So we have created some shortcuts for her."

Ms McIntyre gestured at the many doors.

"I thought the Weaver could only travel on nights of power. Mum said something about blue moons."

Mrs McIntyre huffed. "Ginarwen knows far less than she thinks she knows."

"So each of these doors leads to another World?" asked Asher slowly, stepping closer to peer at the nearest door. "How do you know which one leads where? They all look identical."

She thought of Earth's great oceans, or the sun battered grasslands of D'rona. "How do you know where the door opens on the other side? You wouldn't want to get that wrong."

"The Weaver knows where the doors open. She is the only one who can see these doors and use them. They do not exist for anyone else. If the Weaver needs a new door created, or one sealed, then we administer that for her."

"So because I can see them, can *I* use them?" asked Asher.

The Guide frowned at her. "You really should not," she said firmly, "not without the Weaver to teach you."

"But you are called the Guide. Can't you take me?"

Mrs McIntyre huffed and busied herself with polishing her glasses with the edge of her white shirt. Ash waited patiently. Finally the Guide raised her head and glared at Ash.

"Alright. I will take you. But no interfering or meddling. The Threads are already fragile, we certainly don't need an untrained Heir muddling around."

Mrs McIntyre looked closely at one door after another, muttering to herself as she assessed the suitability of the land beyond. After discarding more than a few she settled on one that looked exactly the same to Asher as all the others.

"Come along then," she said to Ash.

The Guide grabbed the silver door knob and twisted it to the right. Smoothly it swung open and Ash stepped through the doorway, onto a wide golden beach.

Beneath her feet soft yellow sand squelched. Above her head white clouds filled a pink and purple sky. Fifty metres in front of her, frothy light pink waves from a vast rose-coloured sea, crashed upon the shore. They were standing in a small cove, completely devoid of any other people.

The roaring of the surf crashing over rocks and rushing onto the sand filled Asher's ears, as the wind whipped her hair wildly. The immenseness of it filled her with awe and humility.

"It's beautiful," she said softly.

"This is Undula," said the voice of the Guide. She was formless outside the Weaving Room.

Beyond the frothing shallows a trio of fins were visible.

"Dolphins," breathed Asher.

The fins swam closer, diving above and below the waves, until one enormous leap brought them onto the sand. Asher swallowed hard. Before her stood three creatures with human legs and head and the torso of a dolphin, complete with smooth belly and a fin.

"You are not the Weaver," gurgled one, the words bubbling like the air in a fish tank.

"No, I am the Musician. Her Heir."

Disappointment flashed across their faces.

"We need the Weaver. She needs to know that the yellow birds have not followed the migration path this season. All the others have been, taking their clouds with them."

"What do I do?" Asher hissed to the invisible Guide. There was no answer. "What happens if the yellow birds do not migrate?" she asked cautiously.

Without warning a large yellow cloud appeared in the sky. The three creatures on the beach reared back in horror.

"That!" gurgled the lead creature. "To the sea, now!" he commanded.

The other two ran to the water's edge then jumped high into the sky, transforming fully into dolphins as they dove into the churning pink sea. As the third creature jumped to transform, a giant bolt of yellow lightning shot from the cloud and struck it down. Already transformed into dolphin form it landed with a heavy thud in the shallows and lay still.

Ash tried to run forward to help, but found herself held back by an invisible grip.

"Let me go!" she yelled, thrashing against the tight hold.

"And if I let you go, what will you do?" said the Guide.

"Save it, help it."

"How?"

"I don't know."

"And if you are hit by the lightning, what then?"

Asher sagged and the grip loosened. She watched helplessly as the dolphin's lifeless body was washed out to deeper water, where its friends nudged it repeatedly. Great wails of grief filled her senses.

The invisible hand guided her back through the doorway and into the coolness of the Weaving Room. Ash put her hand on the closed white door, tracing the small symbol of a leaping dolphin above a crashing wave.

Behind her the Loom clicked and clacked, weaving its trillions of threads. Asher turned to watch the tapestry form, wondering which of those threads wove the life and death of the Undulan dolphin.

Mrs McIntyre shimmered into view beside her.

"Do I find a way to restore the yellow birds to the migration path? Is this a tangle? Or is this meant to happen as part of the Undulan weave?" Asher asked.

Mrs McIntyre peered solemnly at her over the glasses. "These are questions for the Weaver."

Asher whirled around to face the Guide, her face red. "We don't have the Weaver, remember?" she blurted in frustration.

Mrs McIntyre glared back at her. "No we do not. So why don't you find a way to learn what you need to know? Or restore the balance on Andera and find the Weaver."

The loom hitched. Another tangle, and she had no idea what it meant. The only person who could train her had disappeared. She took a deep breath.

"Can you show me how to hold the Threads? I believe I am meant to do that today."

Ms McIntyre nodded, gesturing for Ash to follow her to the Weaving table.

"Here," she said. "Put your hands below the tapestry, there. What do you feel?"

Asher placed her hands just below where the thick tapestry dropped in a waterfall and disappeared.

Heavy, was her first thought. Though she appeared to hold nothing in her hands it was hard to balance the weight of the unseen woven threads. Once she had steadied them she realised she could feel millions upon millions of decisions, feelings, thoughts, outcomes. The weight grew heavier and heavier. Her head was spinning with every one of those moments. They filled her senses beyond capacity, her vision blurring as she struggled to maintain consciousness.

With a huge gasp she yanked her hands away and collapsed on the floor, breathing heavily.

"It can be overwhelming at first," said the Guide not unkindly. "It is a heavy burden, but I am told it lightens with experience."

Asher lay there with her eyes closed. Her entire being tingled with awareness. She had held the lives and deaths of billions upon billions of sentient beings in her hands, and she was humbled. She realised how very small she was, and how enormous the privilege and responsibility of being the Weaver really was. Every one of those lives was precious; every one of them mattered; every one of them was part of the rich, vibrant weave of the universes. No life existed in isolation.

The Weaver did not choose each path. She needed to maintain the overall tapestry to ensure the individual Threads could be woven as they chose. The magic bound them all together, making it all possible.

She needed to find the Weaver, and she needed help from some-one who had stood in this room. Who understood the Threads.

Ash pushed herself up off the floor as a brilliant idea occurred to her. "Where are the doors to Earth?"

The Guide gestured to a collection of white doors on the far right. Asher hurried over and ran her fingers over various marks. One of the doors was marked with the ancient formation of Stonehenge in Britain, another with the unmistakable shape of Uluru in Australia. Yet another looked like Niagara Falls in the United States. There was even one that looked like a city under water... Atlantis? Then she found it. A painter's palette criss-crossed with brushes. That had to symbolise Ginarwen.

"I'll be back soon," she called to Mrs McIntyre.

"You are not able to open the doors," said Mrs McIntyre archly. "The handles only turn for the Weaver, or myself of course."

Asher knew otherwise, she was sure of it. Heart pounding with excitement she put her hand on the silver knob and turned. It moved easily for her. The Guide gasped in shock.

"Asher el Ginarwen... Don't you dare!"

Asher pushed open the door and stepped through.

Chapter Eight

The Weaver's Daughter

Asher stepped into the coolness of her family's living room, grinning from ear to ear. Home, home, home. It was that easy! She turned to make sure the door back to the Weaving Room was still there. Yes, beside the fireplace.

If only the Weaver had shared the secret of the doors she could have been moving between the planets and the universes with ease. They all could! Actually, anybody could. Which of course was the reason she had not shared the secret.

Her giddiness somewhat sobered, Ash called out. "Mum! Dad! Are you home?"

"Asher?" Gin's shocked voice floated down the stairs, followed by the thump of her feet, then the rest of her appeared in a great rush. She paused at the bottom of the stairs. She was dressed for gardening in old jeans and a long sleeve top, with her white hair tied up in a bandana.

"By the stars it *is* you! How did you get here? I didn't hold the portal for you."

Her mother rushed forward and grabbed her for a tight squeeze while peppering questions the whole time. "Are you back to stay now? What happened with Hesta? Any update on Evie?"

"Mum, I have so much to tell you. About D'rona and the Laneisian and the Weaving Room," Ash was practically babbling with excitement.

"The Weaving Room! Oh my, of course, it's today! Happy birthday sweetheart!" Gin gave her another tight squeeze and stepped back so they could look at each other properly.

"You look older."

Ash rolled her eyes. "Mum."

Gin shook her head. "No, I'm not being ridiculous. You do look older. Or perhaps more mature is what I mean. Or maybe, like some-one with a huge amount of responsibility."

Ash nodded, not trusting herself to speak. If she said anything she feared a great gush of tears would pour out. She swallowed and took a deep breath in and out.

"I need your help mum. Hesta is lost and I don't know how to read the Threads."

They settled on the sofa and Ash shared her experiences over the last week, filling Gin in on the missing Crafters, the attack on Hesta and then her visits to the other planets.

"And the Threads keep hitching, little tangles," she added, "And I have no idea what I am meant to do about that."

Gin sighed. "I would love to tell you that you don't have to do anything about any of it, and that you should just stay here with us. But strange things are happening in the Threads, even I can feel them."

She stood up and paced around the room, rubbing her nose and chin as she talked. "Hesta is alive, I know that for certain. I would have felt the weave if she had died. But I cannot locate her without seeing the actual Threads themselves."

Asher jumped up. "Then come and see them!"

Gin stopped pacing and reached out to cradle Asher's face between her hands.

"I'm not sure I can cross the Void without Hesta holding the portal. I was injured in the last crossing and it's unclear if my sanity will remain intact. What's left of it that is." She wriggled her eyebrows and gave a light-hearted laugh as though she had said something funny, but her eyes were dark with worry.

Ash grinned. "Luckily we don't have to cross the Void at all. I have a short-cut." Grandly she gestured to the door.

Gin frowned slightly. "What are you pointing at Asher? The fireplace?"

"No mum! The door! It leads directly to the Weaving Room. Pretty nifty, right?" she was practically hopping from foot to foot with excitement.

Gin shook her head in confusion. "I have no idea what you are talking about Ash. There is no door."

Ash's mouth dropped open. Her mother could not see the door! The Guide was right. But could she walk through it, even if she couldn't see it? They had to try.

"Mum, please trust me. Here, take my hand and just walk behind me."

Raising her brows Gin reached out her hand. Together they walked to the white door. Asher turned the knob and pushed the door open.

"Please, please work," she muttered.

A few steps later mother and daughter walked into the Weaving Room and the ire of Mrs McIntyre.

"Asher el Ginarwen! This is outrageous, you had no right to use the – ahhhhhh!" the Guide's outrage gurgled into horror. "You brought some-one into the Weaving Room. This. Is. Not. Allowed." Her breath was laboured, her voice hoarse.

Asher dropped her mother's hand and moved toward Ms McIntyre, terrified the Guide was going to hyperventilate. But the Guide shrugged her away.

"Who have you brought into this most secret of places?" she demanded. "Show yourself."

Gin stepped out of the doorway and the Guide sucked in a shocked breath. "Ginarwen el Hestawen," she said. "So you have returned. What is it you want?"

Gin stood calmly, uncowed by the distinct lack of welcome, or the annoyed tone of the Guide. "Hello Guide. I have come to read the Threads, to find Hestawen."

Mrs McIntyre wanted to be outraged. She wanted to argue and insist that Ginarwen leave and never return. But it was imperative that the Weaver was found and restored to Andera and Ginarwen was the best hope they had. She huffed and stomped around, saying nothing, but making her displeasure known.

Gin watched her in silence, a small smile playing around her lips. "I do not need your permission Guide," she said gently, "This is my birthright."

"You relinquished it!" stormed Mrs McIntyre.

"Do you know why?" asked Gin.

The Guide said nothing, but from her stiff stance Asher suspected she did not. She herself burned with curiosity. What was her mother referring to? Ginar chose not to enlighten either of them. Ash mentally added this to the list of explanations her mother owed her.

"Then if you have no further objections, let me see what I can see. As per my agreement, I will not interfere with what is happening now, or what is to come. I am only looking for what has been, specifically to do with Hesta."

Ginar strode across the room to the Loom and watched the Threads weave. Her brow furrowed as the colourful threads caught or paused, and at one point she raised her hands above the weaving as though she was going to adjust the weave, but true to her word she did not interfere. Instead she carefully placed her hands below the tapestry, where Asher's had rested earlier. Unlike Ash, she did not buckle with the weight. With practised hands she lifted and adjusted the invisible tapestry, her eyes closed and her breathing even and deep.

Ash watched in fascination as her mother settled deeper and deeper into the Weave, her body shimmering with the energy of every magical life-form across the universes.

For a long time Asher and Mrs McIntyre watched the Weaver's daughter in silence. Around them lively glowing embers danced while Ginarwen el Hestawen held the Threads for the first time in nearly twenty years.

Eventually Ginar opened her eyes and stepped away from the Loom, letting the Tapestry fall from her hands. With a deep breath she rolled her shoulders and stretched her back, easing the kinks that had settled there from the weight. She turned to Ash and Mrs McIntyre, rubbing and flexing her fingers and hands.

"She lives," she said, but she was frowning, her eyes flickering with uncertainty.

"Where is she?" asked Asher, excitement gurgling in her gut.

"That's the thing," said Ginar slowly, "I don't actually know. She is not on any of the sentient planets in our universes."

The excitement whooshed out of Ash, leaving her deflated and disappointed.

"She was there in the Threads and then she wasn't," continued Gin. "She was a vibrant energy, then she diminished, I assume due to the poison, and then she simply vanished from the Threads completely. Not dead. Just vanished. And yet her energy remains, captured in a single unchanging Thread that is without colour, that does not interlock with the others. I've never seen anything like it."

"Oh!" gasped the Guide, then her hand flew to cover her mouth as though to silence the exclamation.

"What is it?" asked Gin sharply.

"Nothing," coughed the Guide from behind her hand.

Ginarwen seemed to draw herself up, her normally soft features hardening, her eyes darkening. Before Asher's eyes her mother transformed into the likeness of Hesta.

"Guide." The word was firm, her voice deep and bottomless.

Mrs McIntyre squirmed and refused to look Gin in the eye.

"Guide," repeated Gin. "Tell us what you know."

The command was unmistakeable.

Mrs McIntyre fidgeted with her glasses, then the buttons on her shirt. All the while Ginarwen waited. It seemed like she would wait until the end of time.

"Oh fine then!" the Guide burst out, "It's only a *thought*, I cannot know for sure." She hesitated.

Gin raised her eyebrows.

"Well, it sounds like she could be in the Beyond," conceded the Guide.

"What is the Beyond?" asked Gin. Asher was watching the exchange in fascination. She could not quite believe her artist mother could be this imperious, this commanding. Even dressed in gardening clothes.

"I'm not allowed to tell you," fussed the Guide.

"Says who?" asked Gin.

"The Weaver," she said unhappily.

"I am the Weaver," said Gin. But the words fell flat. Gin seemed to diminish back to her normal self. The Guide felt the change and her own confidence returned.

"No Ginarwen, you are not," she said tartly.

Gin wrinkled her nose. They were at an impasse.

Asher's ears filled with the sound of roaring; her body was buzzing. She stepped forward. The words spilled from her mouth.

"I am the Weaver and I release you from your oath of silence."

The words echoed around the room, filling their heads, thrumming in their blood, beating in time with their hearts. *Weaver, Weaver...*

Ginar and the Guide stared at her in wonder. Then the Guide held out her hands, and for the first time Ash felt her touch.

Her head filled with images: of stars and black holes; of supernovas and the birth of planets; of the movements of the galaxies and the great expanses of Void that separated them from each other. Her mind's eye reeled with the speed and volume of the images she was being shown. And then suddenly there was quiet. Everything else froze and Asher was in a place so still and silent that she could hear her heart beating like a drum. In a space quite simply, beyond.

And there lay Hesta and Penn, captured in an endless sleep.

The Guide released her hands and abruptly Ash was back in the Weaving Room. She staggered and Gin rushed forward to support her.

"What did you see?" asked her mother.

Ash steadied herself. "They are there, in the place Beyond." She turned to Mrs McIntyre. "How do we get there?"

The Guide shook her head. "I do not know how to get there. I do not even know what you saw. I could only open the knowing to you. The rest is up to you."

Asher wanted to scream in frustration. With difficulty she resisted the urge.

"It is time for you to leave Ginarwen," said Mrs McIntyre firmly, her poise well recovered. "I have allowed too much already today. Musician, you may escort your mother home. If you plan to return do not linger too long or the doorway might close completely. They do not wait indefinitely."

"Goodbye to you too Guide. It was good to see you again," said Gin with a cheeky smile.

The Guide huffed as she disappeared deep into the room.

"Is it just me, or did that last huff sound more affectionate, less offended?" asked Gin.

Asher laughed. Then she sobered.

"Maybe you could stay a little longer mum. Come into the Manor." She tried to sound casual and not betray the longing in her voice. "Cook would love to see you. We're having a birthday dinner."

Gin hesitated then nodded, her eyes suspiciously bright. "Okay, for a moment."

Asher's face lit up. She spun around looking for the oak door that led to the music room.

"Over here," she called to her mother as she opened the door. In the other room everything was just as she had left it, though the sun had risen over the house. Gin walked over to stand beside her.

"Wow," she breathed, "It's been a very long time since I saw this room. Not much appears to have changed."

Ash stepped through the doorway and into the brightness of the music room. The space felt airy and light after the intenseness of the Weaving Room. She took a deep, replenishing breath and stepped aside for Gin to follow her. But Gin did not move. She seemed to be struggling in the doorway, unable to cross over into Andera. She was mouthing something to Asher, but there was no sound.

In a panic Asher stepped back into the Weaving Room.

"What's wrong?" she asked.

"The doorway will not let me pass," said Gin.

"Take my hand, I think you can walk through with me."

But Gin shook her head, not wanting to try. "I should not enter," said Gin finally. "It is not my time."

She turned to Ash and took her face between her hands. "This is *your* time Asher. You are the one who must restore the

Weaver to the Threads. I will help you as much as I can. I will show you and train you, but it will be up to you."

Asher wanted to argue but she knew Gin was right. Knowing her mother would be there to guide and support her filled her with hope that she could do what needed to be done.

"Come," said her mother, "I can't stay here with the Guide, I doubt she will relish my company. It's best I go home. You can collect me tomorrow and we will begin training in the Weaving Room. In the meantime, have a look through Hesta's personal library in her study. See what you can find on the Beyond."

A moment later they stepped through the doorway into their old comfortable living room.

"Well that was perfect timing!" chirped a familiar voice. "I was prepared to settle in for the duration, but clearly the fates are working in my favour. Everything is coming up Levi!"

Chapter Nine

Hesta's gift

L evi and Kate stood in the Blake living room, grinning madly.

"Happy Birthday Ash," said Kate. With a shout of delight Asher flew across the room and engulfed her friends in a huge bear hug.

"What are you doing here?" she demanded once the hug was released. "How did you get here?"

"How did *we* get here?" said Levi, "Through the front door like normal people. Which was unlocked I might add. How did *you* get here? You two just appeared over there."

He waved in the direction of the white door to the Weaving Room, which he clearly could not see. Ash frowned, the door seemed slightly faded. Perhaps the Guide would hold true to her threat and disappear the door before she could return through it. Whether she could actually do that, Ash did not know, but she did not want to find out. She was not keen for another harrowing trip across the Void, when the alternative was so much better.

"Are you home for good?" "What's happened on Andera?" "Have you found out what happened to Hesta?"

Kate and Levi showered her with questions.

"No; Mum will fill you in; and no," she answered. "I really have to go." Ash looked anxiously at the door. It definitely looked less solid, slightly transparent.

"Across the Void?" asked Kate, her voice wobbling.

"Actually no," smirked Asher, "I have discovered the Weaver's shortcut. Much faster and definitely easier on the body and mind."

"Then I'm coming too," said Levi firmly.

"Me too," said Kate, though her voice lacked the same conviction as Levi's. She was not entirely convinced that Asher's new mode of transport was not as debilitating as the Void.

"Absolutely not," said Ash unconvincingly. Her heart had leapt when they had said they were coming with her, and secretly she longed for them to return to Andera. She could use their support and friendship as she faced the challenges of Darven and the lost Weaver.

"Just have us home by the end of the school holidays," grinned Levi, walking towards the fireplace. It was then that Ash noticed the small backpack he was wearing. Far more compact than his camping pack, but still clearly brimming with supplies. She glanced at Kate. She too was carrying a small pack.

"Are you sure?" she asked, torn between wanting her friends with her and wanting to keep them safe.

They nodded.

"Well I guess I can bring you home anytime now I know about the doorways..." her voice trailed off. Who was she kidding? She was desperate for them to come.

The door flickered. She turned to her mother and gave her a small smile. "I guess this is goodbye again mum. For now, anyway."

Gin smiled warmly. "I'll see you soon. Be safe."

Ash nodded. Then another thought occurred to her, and she pulled up her sleeve, revealing the enamel and silver bangle.

Carefully she slipped it off her wrist and placed it into her mother's hand.

"I don't think I need this anymore."

Gin wrinkled her nose. "No, I don't suppose you do." Her voice was filled with pride.

The door flickered again. Ash turned back to her friends.

"Alright you two, we have to go now. You know the drill. Hold on."

Levi and Kate grabbed hold of an elbow each as Ash turned the silver knob. Blindly they stepped with her across the invisible threshold.

Levi let out a low whistle as they stepped into the Weaving Room. To his eyes the large space was completely empty apart from a single oak door and the Loom clacking above the Weaving table.

A figure appeared from the far shadows. Levi squinted.

"Is that our primary school teacher Mrs McIntyre?" he asked.

"Asher el Ginarwen!" The Guide's voice bordered on the hysterical. "Never in a thousand years of being the Weaver's Guide have I experienced –"

"No time to chat!" declared Ash, practically dragging Kate and Levi to the Music Room door. With a firm shove she pushed them through, before leaping into the room and pulling the door shut. With a click she closed the Guide and her outrage inside.

"Well here we are!" said Ash, grinning so widely her face hurt. She flung her arms out and spun around giddily. Kate and Levi joined in, spinning with her for a few minutes, until they were so dizzy they were banging into each other. Laughing madly they collapsed onto the floor.

"*That* was a far more civilised way to travel across the universe," declared Kate. "What was that place?"

Ash shook her head. "You two already know far too much about everything. I seriously cannot tell you anything more. And you have to swear not to tell anyone about the doors or any of it."

"Lucky you mention that, because I was just thinking – hey, I can't wait to tell everyone at school about my new first class way of travelling across the 'verse," replied Levi, rolling his eyes.

Ash rolled her own eyes back at him. "You know what I mean Levi. Nobody here knows about the Weaving Room or the doors. You're not meant to know either."

"On my honour I swear," said Levi solemnly, hand over heart, his eyes sparkling.

Kate nodded and slapped her hand over her own heart. "Oh yes, me too. Now tell us everything that has happened over the last few days."

"Let's get some lunch and settle in the library," suggested Ash. "This is going to take some time."

Cook greeted them with delight when the three of them wandered into the kitchen. She loaded plates with sandwiches and fruit, refusing them cake despite Levi's pleading. The cake was for the birthday celebrations that evening.

She did not ask where they had been for the last few days, nor how they had returned. After forty years in the Weaver's House, Cook did not waste energy questioning the vagaries of the inhabitants of E-Langren. She was simply pleased to see all the children returned, safe and sound. It gave her hope that Hesta would soon follow. She gave Kate and Levi a warm hug and said their rooms would be ready in an hour.

Munching happily they settled in the warm library. Kate and Levi listened with increasing wonder as Ash filled them in on her travels to D'rona and to the Laneisian. Levi had many questions about the dragons, most of which Asher could not answer.

"So now we need to find the space where Hesta and Penn are being held. The place Beyond the universes," she concluded her tale.

"Another search and rescue," mused Levi.

"Exactly, and hopefully far more successful than our last one. By the way – how come you two were at my house? And what's with the backpacks?"

Levi and Kate exchanged a glance.

"Well," said Kate, "Some-one made a bit of a scene that first morning after we arrived back and realised you had left. That person, who shall remain nameless, but is not me, refused to leave unless Jennifer opened the portal and took us back to you."

Ash raised an eyebrow at Levi who widened his eyes as though he had no idea who Kate was talking about.

"Anyway, Jennifer refused and gave us one of her head pats. Next thing I was in my own bed at home. I had a vague recollection of mum picking me up, but I was shattered."

Levi nodded. "Yep, same here."

"But here's the best part," continued Kate. "Turns out that your mum cannot erase our memories, she thinks it is because we've travelled across the Void. It's probably a side-effect because non-magical beings aren't meant to move between the universes."

"We're immune to her memory meddling!" blurted Levi with glee. "So we just kept coming back to your place every day, bothering and harassing her until she would take us back to Andera. It was our regular 'let's bother Jen' visit when you arrived."

"And we get to celebrate your birthday with you," smiled Kate. "So what do you want to do?"

"Actually, we have a few hours before dinner, I'd love to see what we can find in Hesta's study that might help use locate her," replied Asher, leaping to her feet.

She was brimming with energy, buoyed by the return of her friends and the ease with which she could return home anytime she wanted. She was optimistic about finding Hesta.

They returned their empty plates to the kitchen, saying hello to the young village girl Evone who had come to help Hesta and Anetta around the house. She smiled shyly at them, her eyes wide as she looked at Kate and Levi in their jeans and hoodies.

The three of them headed upstairs. While Kate and Levi deposited their bags in their rooms, Ash took a moment to knock on Carowen's door, but there was no response. The depth of the silence beyond the door lay heavy on Asher's senses. A trickle of unease crawled down the back of her neck, but she shook off the feeling. Most likely the Glass Crafter was simply in her workshop.

On the top floor Levi was first to reach Hesta's study. He tried to turn the knob. "It's locked," he said.

"Here, let me try," said Kate, twisting the handle. "Yep, locked."

"As I said," replied Levi.

"That's odd," frowned Asher, "I don't think Carowen locked it when we closed it before. See, there's no keyhole."

She reached out and turned the handle, the door swinging open with ease. Waggling her brows at them, Ash stepped past her friends and into the study.

The room felt empty without the powerful presence of the Weaver. The richness of the room was dulled, and its layered textures seemed less comforting and warm. With the magic missing it felt faded and somewhat shabby. The overall feeling was melancholy.

Ash pulled open the heavy tapestry curtains, allowing the soft afternoon sun to brighten the forlorn room. Immediately the atmosphere lightened, but the deep chill in the neglected room still made them shiver.

"I'll get the fire going," volunteered Kate.

"And I'll bring up some hot chocolates," offered Levi, rubbing his cold hands together as he headed out of the room.

Asher wandered to the desk, running her fingers along the polished mahogany. A very light film of dust stuck to her fingertips. The glass she had drunk from only a few hours ago sat forgotten on the edge of the desk.

The energy of the room was still. It was waiting for the Weaver. Ash knew they had a good reason to be in here, but still it felt like she was intruding.

"I'm trying to find her," she murmured.

She padded over to the large bookshelf that ran the full span of the back wall. Her eyes jumped from book to book. There were volumes there that were possibly hundreds of years old, bound in well-worn leather with hand stamped lettering. Many of them seemed incredibly fragile and Ash was loathe to pull them from their shelves.

She ran her gaze along each row, looking for any mention of the planets, the galaxies, the Threads, or even possibly the Beyond. Unsurprisingly there was a large number of book titles that referenced all of these things, with the exception of the Beyond. One section of the bookcase was filled with books which each bore the name of a different Wen. Some of the volumes were very slim, others incredibly thick. Without reading any of the books, Asher instinctively understood these were the Weavers who had gone before her. She ran her fingers over the deep, gold lettering of the slim book that said *Ginarwen*. She wondered if all her mother's secrets were revealed inside.

She dropped her hand and stepped back to look at the magnitude of books. "It's going to be a slow process."

"Maybe there's an index, or a reference system," suggested Kate, walking up beside her.

"That is an awesome idea," said Ash heading back to the desk. "After all, each Weaver has to hand over to the next, so it makes sense they would have a master list. You check the drawers on the left-hand side," she said, as she opened the top drawer on the right.

The drawer slid open smoothly, the old wood having been cared for meticulously over the centuries.

"Mine doesn't open," said Kate, heaving against the tightly stuck drawer.

Ash leaned over and effortlessly pulled the drawer open.

"Oh for goodness sake! This room clearly likes you better than it likes me."

Ash laughed.

The top drawers were filled with pens and ink, beautiful gilt-edged stationery and a variety of keepsakes. There was also a wooden and rubber seal with a large W and a pot of hard wax.

The bottom drawers were filing cabinets that were filled with copious amounts of correspondence, all carefully filed by sender.

"I've found something for you," called Kate.

She handed a small package to Ash as the two of them walked to the sofa. They sank into the soft lounge relishing the warmth of the blossoming fire. Levi came back into the room balancing three mugs filled with steaming cocoa. He handed a mug to each of them and plonked onto the soft rug, his back to the flames.

"What do you have there?" he asked between slurps.

Asher turned the package over in her hands. It was a small brown box tied with a cream ribbon. An envelope with her name on it was tucked beneath the ribbon.

She pulled open the envelope and pulled out an embossed cream card, covered in neat black handwriting. Kate and Levi craned their heads to read its contents.

"Total gibberish," declared Levi.

"Very funny," said Ash, running her eyes over Hesta's note.

Kate peered at the card. "I have to agree with Levi, it's a mess of random letters."

"Well it's quite clear to me," said Ash.

Her friends just shrugged. The locked door, the stuck drawers, and now the unreadable message. Clearly the room and its contents were protected from unwelcome eyes.

"So what does it say?" asked Levi.

Ash cleared her throat.

"Dearest Asher, today you celebrate your sixteenth birthday and hold the Wonders of Existence in your hands for the first time. The stars rejoice as you take your rightful place in the Threads. Musicians are unique among Crafters, for they do not create items of power to carry with them. To ensure you always have your instruments to hand, I gift you this bracelet. It is the only one of its kind in the universes. Guard it with care. When you are ready, you simply select your instrument and say *Play*. Blessings on your birthday. Hesta."

Asher put the card aside and untied the ribbon that decorated the box. Inside was a black leather case no bigger than her palm. A shiny gold buckle clipped it shut. Heart pounding, she unclipped the latch.

The case was lined with soft black velvet. Lying neatly inside was a silver bracelet adorned with four tiny instrument charms. There was a violin and bow, a flute the size of a toothpick, a Christmas cracker sized guitar, and a keyboard that looked like it belonged on a novelty keychain.

"Aw, super cute," said Kate.

"I think we can safely assume these are magical objects," said Levi. "I'll be incredibly disappointed in Hesta if they are not. Pull it out Ash, let's see what they do."

Asher lifted the bracelet out of its velvet case and touched each charm. The silver was warm and smooth to touch. Each little instrument was attached to the bracelet by small hooks. Carefully she jiggled the small guitar out of its setting. She twisted it between her fingers, marvelling at the perfect replica in miniature.

"Play," she said softly.

The guitar began to vibrate, but it did not produce any sound. Instead it grew larger and larger until Ash was holding a full sized guitar in her hands. Tentatively she strummed the strings. The sound was sweet and clear, as though the guitar had just been re-strung and tuned.

Asher laughed. "This is amazing. Now how does it shrink? Stop playing. Shrink."

On cue the guitar shrank down to mini size and Ash gently hooked it back into its spot on the bracelet. She clipped the bracelet around her wrist and gave it a good shake. The instruments jiggled but did not fall off. On a hunch she held out her wrist to Kate.

"Kate see if you can take the bracelet off my wrist, or remove any of the instruments."

Kate rolled her eyes. "I think we all know the answer to that."

But she still attempted to unclip the bracelet. "It's stuck tight, and it is actually hurting my fingers to try. It's like a cold burn."

Ash tucked the now empty box into the pocket of the green check dress along with the birthday note. She was buzzing with excitement. The miniature instrument bracelet was quite possibly the best gift she had ever received. If she had been on her own she would have spent the rest of the afternoon playing with it.

Reluctantly she stood up, eyeing the large bookcases around the room. "Alright, we'll each take a section. If the book looks promising then pile it on the desk."

Levi and Kate clambered up beside her. With gusto they each chose a section of the large bookcase.

For the next few hours they chatted and laughed, reading out odd book titles or passages that were particularly interesting or appealing. Some books refused to open for any of them, including Asher. Others were in languages they could not decipher.

As the sun set over the lake they paused to evaluate their progress. Of the small number of books they had actually been able to review, only six had made it to the desk.

"Well that's rather discouraging," said Levi.

"Or really encouraging," countered Kate, "because the answer might be in one of those six books."

The faint sound of a bell clanged somewhere outside.

"Caro's dinner warning," said Ash. "I guess that means we should wash and change." She knew she sounded flat. Despite Kate's optimism Ash still felt concerned.

"Come on, let's celebrate your birthday properly. We can continue on tomorrow, and I think we are really close. I think tomorrow we will find what we are looking for." Kate smiled confidently.

Ash smiled gratefully at her friend. "Sounds like a plan."

They tidied the study, closed the curtains, and damped down the fire. Kate and Levi collected their empty mugs and the water glass and headed out of the room. Alone in Hesta's study Ash looked around the room. The atmosphere in the room was thick and tense.

"I know I did not have permission to poke around her study, and I apologise for the intrusion. Truly I mean no harm. I'm just trying to bring her home."

She followed her friends from the room and carefully pulled the door shut.

A moment later, as the top floor of E-Langren settled into silence, a small, unremarkable book wriggled from its place on the bookshelf and dropped onto the floor.

Chapter Ten

Fleur

T he household met for dinner at 7pm sharp. Asher insisted they eat at the large kitchen table rather than in the formal dinner room. She felt more comfortable with a relaxed birthday celebration.

She looked around the table at Anetta, Fleur and Trinity, Levi, Kate and Cook. Warm, friendly, smiling faces. Ash smiled back at them, grateful for their company but sorely missing her parents and Evie. This was the first birthday she had celebrated without them. The ache of their absence pulsed deep within her chest, curled around her heart, and tied her tongue for a while.

"Where is that Carowen?" huffed Cook after fifteen minutes had passed. "I have a lovely roast chicken and vegetables ready to serve."

Everyone looked at each other, shrugging and shaking their heads. Except for Fleur, who blushed a deep shade of crimson.

"Excuse me," she said softly, "I think I know where she is, or rather where she is not. She is not at the Manor. I saw her leave this morning with a travelling case."

"What?" asked Cook, her face creased with confusion. "Why?"

"I don't know, but it was clear she was going away," said Fleur. "She was carrying a case and wearing a cloak. She did not see me, so we didn't exchange words."

"You mean she has left permanently? For good?"

Fleur shook her head helplessly. "I really don't know. I'm sorry."

"But why would she leave? Where has she gone? She did not say a word to me. When is she coming back?" Cook's confusion bubbled out in a torrent of words. Carowen having left without a word, while Hesta was still missing, was upsetting for the old woman.

"Perhaps she has gone to see her mother," said Anetta soothingly.

"That does sound most likely," agreed Trinity.

"Do you think so?" Cook's voice was hopeful.

Everyone nodded, though nobody really knew. The anxiety eased from Cook's face as she allowed herself to be convinced.

Reassured that her chick had not flown the nest for good, Cook served her delicious dinner. She was clearly so pleased to create this birthday dinner that Asher put aside her misgivings about Carowen, and her restless homesickness, and resolved to completely enjoy the celebration.

And despite everything - Hesta's poisoning and disappearance, Evie's defection, Carowen leaving, and her parents being across the universe - strangely enough Asher really did enjoy it.

After they had eaten their fill of the meal and the marvellous chocolate birthday cake, Levi piped up.

"Now it's time for Ash to play. To the music room!" He leapt up and headed down the hall, confident the others would follow. Which they did.

Ash settled herself at the piano as the small party clustered around. "Any requests?" she asked.

Levi immediately suggested a favourite song, which he and Kate sang along to with gusto while Ash played. When they finished the others clapped enthusiastically and Kate and Levi bowed profusely.

Ash then chose a Handel piece, relishing the drama of the composition. Again the small audience applauded with appreciation.

"The music you play is unknown to me, but very beautiful," said Fleur.

"Thank you," smiled Asher.

"Are you able to play something I choose? Something that is just in my head?"

She looked into those serious eyes and she nodded. "Just hum the music and really think about it clearly. Be as clear as you can about the melody. I will do my best."

So Fleur sat beside her and quietly hummed her tune. Ash closed her eyes and let the notes materialise inside her head, pressing the chords.

"I think we should make hot drinks while they get this sorted," declared Cook. "Levi, come and help me."

By the time everyone had resettled with their drinks in hand, Ash was brimming with the music.

"Ready?" she asked the group. They nodded.

Slowly Asher began the piece, visualising the music that Fleur had passed to her. The music wove a tale of love and belonging, casting a web around them all. Asher could feel the energy tumbling from the notes, infusing the music with a depth of emotion that captured the audience's hearts.

And then Fleur began to sing.

Her pure voice rose above the notes, effortlessly filling the room and the spaces between them. Trinity gasped as the song whirled around her, and her eyes filled with tears. Fleur sang in a language never heard on Earth, the ancient language of the Ap'an people.

Beneath her dress the globe pulsed against Ash's skin. Around her Fleur's voice fed the Crafter energy, magnifying it.

The power was beyond anything Asher had ever created on her own.

The last notes of the song soared through the room, sending tingles down the spine of every person present. Asher's fingers stilled. Fleur fell silent.

"Wow," murmured Levi after a long moment. "I have no idea what you were saying but that was seriously incredible."

"That was beautiful," said Trinity, wiping the tears from her face as she stood. She gave her daughter a fierce hug. "Thank you."

"What was the song about?" asked Kate.

Trinity smiled. "It is an Ap'an ballad, sung for centuries by warriors, telling their loved ones that they will return safely from conflict. It is a song of love and belonging. Of hope. Fleur is reminding me that Penn is a warrior. He will return safely."

The party broke up soon after that. Mugs were returned to the kitchen and everyone said goodnight with their hearts full. The tight band of sorrow and homesickness around Asher's heart had dissipated.

She was keen to get to her room and play with the miniature instrument bracelet, but there was something she needed to do first.

She found Fleur in the drawing room off the dining room. The heavy curtains had not yet been drawn shut, so the wide dark gardens were clearly visible beyond the room. Garden lamps along the path provided pools of light in the darkness. A large table lamp cast light and shadow into the corner of the room, where Fleur sat curled in a large leather armchair.

"Hi Fleur, do you mind if I join you for a bit?" asked Asher.

The younger girl shook her head. Ash chose the chair next to Fleur and the two of them sat in silence looking at the darkened grounds.

"You are Hesta's Heir," stated Fleur, breaking the silence.

"Yes. And who are you?" asked Asher bluntly.

"Nobody," was the quiet response.

Ash looked hard at Fleur, who deliberately avoided her gaze. "Everyone in that room tonight felt the emotion of your song. They felt it within their bones. But I was the only Crafter there, and I felt the energy you created with every note."

Ash paused, allowing space for Fleur to speak. But she said nothing.

"The thing is Fleur, you weren't using the energy, you weren't actually Crafting with it. I can't quite explain it, it was like you created the energy for me to use."

"I don't know what you are talking about," said Fleur in a faltering voice, trying for one last bluff.

"Lying does not become you," replied Ash gently.

Fleur dropped her gaze to her restless hands, her face flushed with shame at her dissembling. "No-one has ever noticed before. It's never really mattered as our local Crafters are so low-level they are not aware of it when it happens. I knew it was a risk singing with you, a powerful Crafter, but my mother has been so desperate about Penn. I wanted to give her that relief."

Now it was Asher's turn to say nothing. She waited patiently while the girl struggled to put her thoughts into words.

"I am not a Crafter," Fleur said finally.

"Then what are you?"

"That's the thing," whispered Fleur, her eyes swimming with tears. "I simply do not know. I've never heard of anyone like me."

"Explain it to me."

"A Crafter uses the energy around them to create items of power."

Asher nodded.

"But I've never been able to use energy like that," continued Fleur. "It happens so rarely that I don't really know how I'm doing it. As the Crafter works I can feel the energy they are drawing on, and it is almost as though I can intensify it. I can't use it for any purpose of my own, but I can provide it for them to use. Does that make sense?"

Ash wrinkled her nose, sorting through what she had just heard. "So it happens when you sing?"

"No, it happens if I link my energy to the Crafter. Like with the painter in our village. If I mix the paints for her the Crafting is magnified. She creates her best works, but she is unaware that I have contributed."

"So if you were in Carowen's workshop while she was Glass Crafting, what would that feel like for you?" asked Asher.

"I would be able to feel her energy, and then I can add to it, if I wish."

Asher did not know what to think. She did not know enough about Crafting to know if this was unusual or problematic. But she did know it was potentially dangerous in the wrong hands. A girl who could magnify any Craft. It was mind boggling. It was best they continue to keep it secret for the time being. Tomorrow she would seek guidance from her mother.

She swallowed a yawn. "I think it is time for bed. We can sort through this some more in the morning."

They walked through the house in silence, parting ways at the top of the staircase with a quiet exchange of "good night".

A great weariness settled on Ash as she climbed the final set of stairs. Her mind was as exhausted as her body. It had been a day filled with revelations and explorations. It was hard to believe that she had only returned to E-Langren that morning.

She was desperate to rest both body and mind. After a cursory clean of her face and teeth she crawled into the soft bed and within minutes was fast asleep.

Downstairs the two village girls finished tidying the kitchen and living areas. They said goodnight to Cook who was settling in with a second glass of sweet wine, and quietly let themselves out.

The housemaids walked along the quiet lanes back to their homes. They had been working for the Weaver for only a few months, and they were proud to do so. It was considered prestigious to work at E-Langren. The conditions were excellent, the pay was very good, and in the home of the Weaver they met people of power and status. Many of whom were kind and generous to the staff.

But this week things had changed. As they walked together in the moonlight they talked of the outrageous rumours that had been swirling around the village.

That the Weaver and a group of Crafters had attacked the Queen and her Advisor. That the Weaver had been captured and was being held as a prisoner. That the Queen was outlawing Crafting.

They had been worried coming to the manor today, but as the residents of E-Langren did not seem concerned the girls felt somewhat reassured. They had even held a party tonight, with glorious music and the most beautiful singing the girls had ever heard. Perhaps it was all just gossip and trouble-making, by jealous minded people. Surely Hestawen would return soon and put such rumours to rest.

The night air was fresh and cool as they walked. The wind moved gently through the fields of grass and a night owl hooted softly from the branches as they passed beneath.

All was peaceful, and as it always was. So it was a complete surprise when four heavily armed men stepped out of the trees and onto the path, their eyes full of menace. Terror fuelling their steps, the two girls picked up their long skirts and ran.

Chapter Eleven

The Fall of E-Langren

The morning after her sixteenth birthday, Asher Blake el Ginarwen woke in the Weaver's house with a sense of possibility.

Her sleep had been peppered with confusing and twisted dreams, which had disrupted her rest. Regardless, when she pulled herself out of bed, she felt excited about what the day might hold.

Asher moved through her morning routine on autopilot, her mind occupied with what she might discover about the Beyond. She showered and washed her hair, drying it and brushing it into a semblance of order. In her room she hesitated over what to wear. A glance at the collection of items on her desk reminded her that she needed a high enough neckline for the globe and dragon's tooth, long sleeves to cover the instrument bracelet, and deep pockets for the little whistle from Brawn.

On a whim she disregarded her newly laundered clothes, and instead decided on an outfit from her mother's cupboard.

Among the fancy dresses and coats she found a plain, deep blue, woollen dress that dropped from her collarbone to her knees. Two pockets with zips were sewn into the heavy skirt.

Ash pulled on the dress, pairing it with navy tights and matching ankle boots. Carefully she concealed all her curios. Once dressed she made the bed and pushed open the curtains. A light rain was showering the landscape. She opened the window and took a deep breath of the cool, damp air.

Downstairs Anetta the housekeeper made her morning rounds of the Manor. She took great pride in the seamless running of the house, from daily deliveries to the hired village staff. With Marten gone, the additional help was more important than ever.

Polishing cloth in hand she wiped away fingerprints and specks of dust from tabletops and banisters.

In the kitchen Mariah the Cook nursed a slight headache as she kneaded dough to bake into bread later in the day. And in the vegetable garden Trinity and Fleur pulled weeds and turned the soft soil in the gentle rain, their faces sheltered by wide-brimmed hats.

The rhythm of E-Langren beat as it always had, awaiting the return of the Weaver.

Asher walked through the gleaming Crafter Gallery to Hesta's study. She turned the handle and let herself in. The room was cold and dark, but she did not bother with lighting a fire or turning on a lamp. Opening a curtain allowed enough light to illuminate the books on the desk. She gathered them in her arms, intending to take them downstairs to the warmth and welcome of the library. As she turned away, her toe caught on a fallen book.

Balancing her load, carefully Ash leant over and collected the book off the ground. It was a small, slim volume, no longer than her hand. She turned it over to read the title but the brown leather was unmarked. Her fingers tingled from their contact with the book, as it responded to the Crafting within her.

Asher added the book to her pile and padded lightly out of the room, taking care to close the door firmly. A second later she opened the door and stuck her head inside.

"Thank you," she whispered into the stillness. Then she closed the door once more, leaving the room with its secrets.

By the time Ash arrived downstairs she was ready for breakfast. She placed the books onto the table in the library, then made her way to the kitchen.

Levi and Kate were enjoying a hearty spread of eggs and toast with cooked mushrooms and tomatoes fresh from the garden.

Levi was wearing his normal jeans and hoodie to ward off the cool morning air, but Kate was a surprise. She had chosen to wear a dress almost identical to Ash, in a buttery yellow. Her tights were the colour of soft cream as were her kid boots. The girls laughed when they saw each other.

"You two make a pretty picture," said Cook with a smile.

Asher sat with her friends and shovelled forkfuls of eggs and toast into her mouth, giving herself the hiccups in her haste to finish eating and return to the library. As the hiccups increased in intensity her unsympathetic friends erupted into a fit of the giggles.

"Have a cup of tea," offered Cook.

"Thank, *hic*, you," hiccuped Ash, glaring at Levi and Kate. "I'm going to the library now. Any, *hic*, one care to join me?" she asked, not waiting for a response as she strode out of the room, mug in hand.

Kate and Levi grinned at each other, thanked Cook for the yummy breakfast and went to join Asher. She seated herself in the large armchair and pulled the small brown book from the top of the book pile.

"What do you have there?" asked Levi.

"I have no idea," replied Asher, her hiccups eased but her voice full of frustration. She flicked through the pages. "I thought it was going to be important but it's completely blank. See?"

She held out the book Levi. He plonked onto the sofa and carefully turned each page, twisting the book this way and that, holding it up to the light and even gently blowing on the paper. Finally he conceded defeat.

"Yep, it's blank."

"What a bother," said Ash, "perhaps it's just a notebook. I had high hopes." She placed the book on the table.

"You never know. It could just be part of its magical defences. The words might reveal themselves later," said Kate.

"You make a good point," replied Ash. She added it to the mental list of things to discuss with Gin.

"Let's see what the other books have to say. I'm thinking we cross back to Earth after lunch to talk with mum. That gives us a few hours to do some research and make notes."

Anetta poked her head around the door. "Good morning children. Have any of you seen Jenah or Evone? The village girls?"

They shook their heads. Anetta tutted in annoyance. "They were to bring the meat from the butcher. I will have to go collect it myself."

Her face disappeared from the doorway. Another moment later Cook appeared.

"Just letting you know that I am heading to the village with Anetta and Fleur. We'll be back well in time to prepare lunch. We'll eat at half twelve. Today it's pumpkin soup and freshly made bread." And she was gone.

The trio settled into the reading. They found pens and paper in the desk drawers and drew up a system to record and double check items of interest as they were uncovered. It did not take long for Levi to come up with a faster and more efficient way to record information.

He pulled his phone from his back pocket and started taking photos of the pages that most interested them.

"There is no signal, but the photo app works just fine," he said with a grin.

Levi and Asher focused on the small pile from Hesta's study while Kate perused the large collection in the library for any additional reading. The hours passed quickly. The sun moved high above the manor as the morning blurred into the afternoon.

"Should we review what we have so far?" suggested Ash, standing up and stretching her stiff back.

Levi stood up beside her, raising his hands high above his head to lengthen his spine. A large tummy grumble accompanied the stretch.

"It's lunch o'clock," he declared. "Bring on the pumpkin soup. I think better on a full stomach."

The girls grinned at him and agreed that a lunch break was definitely in order. As they left the library Ash glanced at the large ticking clock on the mantel above the fireplace. 1:05pm.

"That's odd," she said to the others, "I'm surprised Cook has not called for us by now. She's such a stickler for timely meals."

When they walked into the kitchen it quickly became apparent that not only was lunch not ready, Cook had not been there since the morning. And neither had the village girls. Breakfast dishes were piled beside the sink. The teapot on the stove was stone cold.

A loud bang at the front door echoed through the house, but they paid it no mind. Leaving Anetta to deal with the door, the three of them set to work tidying the kitchen and pulling vegetables from the crisper to make the soup.

A sudden horrified scream ripped through the house.

"What on earth?" exclaimed Ash. A second scream followed.

"Front hall," she said.

Levi ran out of the kitchen, Asher and Kate close behind. Through the house they raced, screeching to a shocked standstill beside Trinity at the open front doors. A severed pig's head lay bleeding at the terrified woman's feet.

On the great gravel drive three carts were standing. Large cages were bolted to the back of two of them. Inside one of the cages three figures were huddled together. Standing beside the carts were four foul looking men wearing familiar looking uniforms.

"That is the Queen's livery," whispered Kate.

The carts and captives were unsettling enough, but the true horror was the two young village girls who had been tied to the back of one of the carts. They were beaten and bloodied and barely standing.

Asher felt fury tingle up her face. Her nails cut into her clenched fists but she barely registered the pain. Roaring filled her ears. She had never felt anger like this before. She felt like she could pass out with the intensity. She took a few deep breaths to stave off the light-headedness until the fainting sensation passed and she could bring her temper under control.

Levi did not take a moment. He barged onto the wide porch. "Let them go!" he yelled, his whole body vibrating with rage.

The thugs laughed. A tall, bearded man stepped forward.

"What are you going to do lad? Hmmm?" he mocked.

Then casually he whipped Jenah's already tormented back with a heavy braided rope. Blood seeped through her dress. The young girl cried out in pain then fainted.

Levi screamed in fury. Ash grabbed him before he could run at them.

"Let me," she said coldly.

Asher walked down the wide stone steps. Silence descended on the courtyard. Around her the air crackled. The rain ceased and the sun peeked between the clouds, illuminating her like a spotlight. Her red hair glowed like a flame. She kept her focus on the two beaten girls before her.

"Let them go," she said quietly.

Her voice echoed across the expanse between them. She took a step forward. Three of the men stepped back.

"I said, let them go. Now."

The Leader, the one who had whipped Jenah, stood his ground. His face twisted in a snarl.

"We have come for the Weaver. Queen's orders. Hand her over without incident and you can have your little maids."

"She is not here. Return the girls and I will let you leave."

"Ho ho. So you must be the Crafter who plays the piano. These lovely girls told us about your singalong last night." He glanced at Jenah and Evone and snickered. "Unfortunately they didn't seem to know much else. So they had to be punished for wasting our time."

Asher swallowed hard against the anger. She needed to stay in control of her emotions. At the moment she could not even find her music due to the roaring in her ears. If she could not find the calm only the wild music would play, and she would be consumed.

She tried to think clearly through the haze. All her instincts were screaming at her to do something. She pushed up her sleeve and reached for the instrument bracelet, but the brute spoke again.

"No funny business from you *Crafter*," he spat the word in disgust. "The Weaver has been declared a traitor. Crafters who support her are to be brought to Ostrin. The choice is yours. Come quietly and nobody else gets hurt."

One cue one of the squad pulled the three huddled figures from the cage. They stumbled to the ground.

"Fleur!" screamed Trinity, running past Levi and Ash, down the steps and onto the gravel. She dodged one of the men who stepped forward to grab her, and dropped onto the ground beside Anetta, Cook and Fleur. Sobbing, she bundled her daughter into her arms.

"Are they hurt?" demanded Asher, fear warring with fury.

"Not yet," grinned the Squad Leader, "but they could be."

He lifted the heavy rope, ready to whip across Trinity's exposed back. "The choice is simple. Give yourself up, they live. You fight, they all die."

One of the men pulled a large knife from the sheaf in his boot and casually twisted it in the sunlight.

Asher looked at the terrified faces of Cook and Anetta, at the damaged bodies of the innocent maids. She thought of her mother and Evie. The dragons of D'rona, the Laneisian and the Undulan Dolphinmen. And she thought of the Weaver. A woman who had dedicated her life to forces beyond human comprehension, to maintaining balance for all magical and non-magical creatures, so that life endured. She could not allow this travesty to be done in her name.

"I am the Weaver's Heir," she whispered to the wind. It caressed her face.

"I can't hear you," growled the Leader. "What did you say?"

"Release them all. I will come with you." Her fingers dropped away from the bracelet and she stepped calmly towards him.

Behind her Kate inhaled sharply. "Asher, no."

Asher did not slow her pace. Steadily, deliberately, she moved towards the carts, her back straight and her head high. The men stepped back, uncertainty clear in their eyes. Even the Leader was unnerved by the serenity of her capitulation.

"Search her," he barked at one of his men.

Reluctantly the man stepped forward.

"Do not touch me," said Asher, her clear grey gaze fixing on him. Quickly he stepped back.

"Oh well," shrugged the Leader, feigning a nonchalance he no longer felt. "It's not as though she has a piano with her. And what good is a Pianist Crafter without a piano."

He forced a laugh.

"Untie the girls and let everyone go free, without further injury," instructed Ash.

But the Leader was not going to take orders from a despised Crafter. His eyes glittered with malice.

"You can have the maids. They are of no further use to me. But I think I'll keep the others. As insurance for your continued good behaviour."

Asher's mind was racing. How could she negotiate freedom for Cook, Anetta and Fleur? And probably Trinity too, now that one of the guards stood over her.

"Let everyone go," said an imperious voice. "I am the Weaver's grandson, and I demand you release our staff and be on your way."

Levi strode to her side, his voice filled with conceit and pride. Asher clamped her mouth shut so it would not drop open in amazement and give the game away.

Levi stared down the guards, his face and manner as regal and disdainful as any spoiled aristocrat might be. He had often said he was descended from the great Indian Maharajas, a claim Asher and Kate had rolled their eyes at more than once. Whatever the truth, his performance was believable enough to convince the thugs.

The Squad Leader considered him carefully. Then a great smirk split his ugly face. "The Weaver's grandson you say? You're worth more to me than those frail old women. How 'bout we make a trade? You for them."

Asher could not believe how easily the Squad Leader had fallen for Levi's plan.

"Oh no!" cried Kate dramatically as she ran down the stairs. "Please don't take my cousin. With my aunt the Weaver gone, he is all the family I have left."

That decided it. The Squad Leader imagined the glory that would be awarded to him for bringing the last of the Weaver's family to the Queen.

"Take them," he commanded the Squad. "Leave the others. The maids spoke of one other. The Glass Crafter. Where is she?"

"I am here," called a soft voice.

"No Fleur, no," cried Trinity, trying desperately to hold onto her daughter.

Fleur gave her a gentle hug and whispered softly, her words for Trinity's ears only.

"Jenah and Evone need you to care for them, to heal them. Your place is here. I am a descendant of the Great Bonnerwen, and a child of the Ap'an. My destiny is not to wait, nor to hide. My place is to fight beside the Weaver's Heir."

Trinity nodded. She squeezed Fleur tightly then released her with a kiss on her forehead.

"Return safely."

Fleur walked over to Ash, Levi and Kate. The four of them stood in silence, heads held high.

"The deal is done," said Asher softly.

The Squad Leader gestured to one of his men. "Put the bracelets on them."

The other man shuffled awkwardly. "We don't have any left."

The Squad Leader grunted. "Then we'll do this the old-fashioned way. A threat is as good as some piece of rock," he laughed maliciously.

He pointed at Asher. "Any Crafting attempt by you will be met by blood, and lots of it."

She nodded to let him know she understood.

"Untie the maids," snapped the Leader. "And get this lot into the cage."

Finally the ropes were cut and the beaten girls slumped to the ground. Cook, Anetta and Trinity rushed forward to a gather them. Slowly, gently, they supported the girls to the house.

As the heavy oak doors closed firmly behind them, Asher released a deep breath and felt some tightness ease in her chest. At least the girls were safe. They would sort out their own captivity soon enough.

"What if they follow them into the house?" worried Kate, peering through the bars of the cage as the heavy lock clanged into place, sealing them in.

Sure enough, the Leader yanked his head in the direction of the manor, indicating to one of the men that they should follow.

"Bastards," raged Levi, pulling fruitlessly at the thick metal bars.

"They cannot enter E-Langren," murmured Fleur. "Only those who wish no ill upon the Weaver may cross the threshold."

They watched with bated breath as the man approached the wide stone steps. He had barely put a foot on the bottom step when he was thrown backwards with great force. He landed awkwardly, painfully, on the gravel.He pulled himself up, approaching the house with dogged determination. Again he was thrown backwards.

Locked in the cart Levi could not help but laugh.

The Squad Leader growled, glaring first at the hapless minion and then at Levi. Then something dark and cruel flared in his eyes. He went to the supply cart and pulled out a large drum of oil.

His thick arms bulged with the weight as he carried the drum as close to the steps as he dared to go, and then poured it out as he walked a line along the front of the house. He tossed as much as he could onto the front façade of the building.

Dread rose in Asher. She stood up, grabbing at the bars.

"Don't you dare!" she yelled.

The Leader turned to her with an evil grin. He threw the barrel towards the steps and sauntered back to the carts.

"Pour the other barrels. Then light it up," he commanded the men.

Asher could not control her outrage, yelling curses and threats, pushing and shaking the unyielding bars. The Squad Leader strode over to her.

"I've had enough of you," he said.

With one swift movement he reached between the bars and thumped her on the head. Asher collapsed to the floor.

Chapter Twelve

Edriene

Asher sat up slowly, acutely aware of the pounding in her head. With a groan she opened her eyes, fighting down nausea from both the injury and the bumping of the cart. She blinked hard to clear the fuzziness.

"Thank goodness!" exclaimed Kate, "we've been freaking out. Are you okay?"

Asher gingerly ran her fingers over the sore spot on her head. Though it was tender, there was no blood and not much of a lump.

"I think so, but that is an experience I never want to have again," she croaked. Kate gave her a hug, being careful not to squeeze her too tight. "How long was I out?"

"Long enough for Levi to completely lose the plot. He caused such a commotion that – well, see for yourself."

Asher turned her gaze to Levi. He was sporting a black eye and his wrists were tied to the bars of the cage.

"Levi," she breathed in shock, "what happened?"

He grinned as though he did not have a care in the world. "Turns out our thug companions did not appreciate my behaviour after they thumped you."

"Oh Levi."

Remorse flooded through Asher. Once again her friends had jumped into her chaos, and this time things were getting serious.

People were getting hurt. She could see the red chaffing of Levi's wrists where he had been straining against the ropes.

"Is there some way we can get those off?" she asked quietly, so the guard driving the cart wouldn't hear.

"I can help with that," murmured Fleur. From the deep pocket of her dress she pulled out a pair of sharp dressmaker's scissors wrapped in soft leather.

"My mother is a seamstress and I often assist her," she said by way of explanation. "I always have some sort of kit with me."

She glanced at the supply cart trailing behind them. It was far enough back that perhaps the driver would not be able to see clearly what they were up to. Fleur sat herself beside Levi while Kate and Asher blocked the view. Carefully Fleur sawed through the ropes.

With relief Levi yanked his hands free and shook out his arms.

"Thank you!" he grinned at Fleur, then impulsively gave her a jubilant hug. Her dusky skin blushed a deep red, but she allowed the hug and smiled warmly.

"I cannot tell you how good that feels." Happily he rubbed his wrists and hands, restoring blood and feeling.

Ash smiled at him, then memory hit with a sudden slap in the face. The last thing she remembered was a flaming torch being thrown at the Manor.

"E-Langren! Did it burn?"

"We don't know for sure, but it looked like the front rooms were alight," said Kate unhappily. "We couldn't see much past the fire as the carts left."

Asher stood up to peer over the back of the cart, trying to see beyond the trees. The cart rocked with the change in balance.

"What's going on back there?" yelled an unfriendly voice. "Sit back down now."

Kate pulled Asher back to the bench. "Don't you dare get bashed on the head again."

"We need to get back," Ash hissed urgently. "We can't have travelled too far. Once we overpower them we can take a cart."

She pushed up her sleeve and reached to unhook the tiny flute from her bracelet.

"Before you do anything, look over there." Fleur's soft voice drew her attention to the other cart, travelling just ahead of them.

In that cage three women were huddled, guarded by the brutish Squad Leader. In his hands he toyed with the large knife. He caught Asher's gaze and mock saluted her with the blade.

"Those are Crafters from the village outside E-Langren. We picked them up after we left the manor. Two are young, one is aged and weak. They possess only middling Crafter ability. He is holding their lives hostage to your good behaviour."

Asher looked at the scared women, and the man who threatened them so casually, almost gleefully. The dark music swirled inside her. He would be sorry. Her face must have given her away, for the Squad Leader's eyes widened. Then something ugly flashed across his own face and he grabbed the woman nearest to him by the hair. It was the Candle Crafter Asher had observed on that first journey to Ostrin.

He pulled her head back and placed the large knife against her neck. She froze in fear. His eyes goaded Ash, daring her to do anything that would give him a reason to spill the woman's blood.

Asher slumped back in defeat, burying her head in her arms. In the other cart the guard released the young woman who flung herself into the old woman's arms. Their terrified sobs carried across the distance to the silent group of friends.

Ash fought to contain her own tears. Her throat and chest burned with the effort. She did not know how the Threads were meant to be woven. Should she have sacrificed the one life to save the others, or would they now all face death at their destination? How did the Weaver know when to intervene and when to let grim situations run their course? It was too much to comprehend, but she did know she could not be the reason an innocent woman was murdered.

She had made her choice. She needed to follow this path and save whoever she could, and E-Langren would burn.

Her heart ached with a pain unlike any she had felt before. The loss of the Weaver's home felt like a symbol that Hesta herself was lost forever. She hoped with all her might that Cook and the others were safe.

Kate put her arms around her friend and held her tight. She said nothing, but the warmth of that steadfast embrace gave Asher comfort. After a few minutes she drew a deep breath, then another.

"This is not over," she muttered to herself, "I will defeat Darven and I will set them all free."

The fierce vow gave her strength of purpose and a sense of calm. It cut through the grief enough for Asher to lift her thumping head.

"We see where this journey takes us," she said quietly to her companions, "and I promise you, I will find a way to get us safely home."

Fleur, Kate and Levi nodded, their faces sombre and their eyes full of trust. Asher reached for their hands and squeezed them, praying and hoping she was worthy of their faith.

It was a tense, uncomfortable journey. Their throats burned with thirst, and their stomachs grumbled mightily for the lunch they had missed. As the air cooled further, Ash was glad of her warm dress and tights.

When they arrived at Varossa the carts stopped in the main square, allowing everyone to see the prisoners. It was designed to intimidate and influence the already fearful residents. And it did.

The Squad Leader stood and cracked his heavy rope on the cobbled stone, demanding the townsfolk turn over their Crafters. After long minutes of silence a small group dragged a frightened woman into the square. Two small children cried and ran after her, before their father swept them up in his arms and hurried them away beyond the buildings.

"She is the last," said one of the group gruffly, pushing her forward.

The Crafter turned to look squarely at the man who fidgeted beneath her gaze, then he looked away.

"It is for the good of everyone," he blustered, refusing to look her in the eye.

"When the flowers die on our parents' graves, and your garden no longer blooms, remember this moment," the Crafter said. Then she turned her back on him and stood silently, awaiting her fate.

The Squad Leader walked to Asher's cart and unlocked the cage.

"Get in," he called to the woman.

She walked proudly across the stones and climbed onto the cart, taking a seat beside Fleur. She said not a word. Behind her the heavy cage door swung shut and was locked with a loud click. It was not until the carts were beyond the edges of the town, taking her away from her family and home, that she turned her face away and cried.

Hesitantly Fleur put her hand over the Crafter's. The woman flinched, and it seemed she would pull her hand away, but then she curled her fingers around Fleur's and accepted this small comfort.

"My name is Fleur," offered the younger girl.

"I am Edriene."

Levi and Kate introduced themselves. Edriene gave Levi a quizzical look but did not ask why a young man was being held captive with Crafters.

Then she turned her face to Asher. They looked at each other appraisingly. Edriene was in her mid-thirties with olive skin and straight black hair. Her eyes were a startling shade of green, the colour of rich, vibrant moss. Wrinkles, from a lifetime of squinting in the sun, furrowed around her eyes, and her hands were rough and calloused. Her energy was strong.

"I am Asher."

Surprise flared in Edriene's eyes, then quickly she shuttered the reaction. "You are the Heir."

Now it was Asher's turn to be surprised.

"How did you know?" she asked.

"Raya told me of your encounter a few days ago. That you promised to save Simeona. You were on your way to Ostrin. How did you end up here?"

"It's a complicated story," said Ash.

"You are very young."

They looked at each other in silence. There was no response to give. Asher thought of her mother on Earth with no way to travel the Void, and Carowen, gone without a word. *I may be young, but I am the only one left.*

Edriene spoke again. "The Queen has declared the Weaver a traitor. Is that true?"

Asher shook her head. "Absolutely not. I was there when the Queen and Darven attacked the Weaver. It was an ambush. She was not the aggressor."

"Then where is she? We need her. Until she shows herself all Crafters are paying the price."

"I don't really know," said Ash honestly. "But I will find her."

Edriene took a moment to consider what she had heard.

"The man who betrayed you in the square. Is he your brother?" asked Fleur quietly.

Edriene's eyes flashed. "Yes."

"And he handed you over to the squad?" Kate's voice was outraged.

"It too is complicated." She fell silent, turning her face to stare at the green countryside. Nobody pushed her. Edriene would share what she wished, in her own time. The cart rattled along the ill-kept road.

"I am a Gardener," she said softly. "I can grow anything, anywhere. Crops, plants, fruit and vegetables. I can coax life from the barren earth, even when the rains are sparse, and the frosts are long. My Crafting has been a blessing to our family and our town. So when the raids first started weeks ago the townsfolk protected me, even as others were taken. It was extremely difficult for all of us."

Her voice hitched, and she coughed to clear her throat.

"As mothers, daughters, sisters and wives were rounded up and taken, the townsfolk began to resent my concealment. Why should my family be spared the grief and loss they were all experiencing? My husband and brother argued for me to be protected, for the good of the entire town. Then a few days ago my niece, only eleven, was taken. She is just a child. So young and trusting."

Her eyes swam with tears.

"My brother was broken by her loss. Yesterday word came that the Weaver had attacked the Queen and we were all guilty by association. He refused to protect me any longer. I could use my Crafting and fight my way out of this cart, but what would be the point? Where would I run to? Where would I go? If I am declared a fugitive my own children will not be spared."

The tears ran freely now. The pain of everything she and her town had experienced could no longer be quietly endured.

Kate's face dripped with silent tears of sympathy. Fleur put her arm around Edriene and offered a calm place, which seemed to help, as Edriene's tears eased and she closed her eyes.

"Your brother loves you beyond price," said Fleur. Her voice was as soft as always, but the conviction was firm. They all heard the ring of truth.

"He agonised over this betrayal, but he gave you up in the hope that you will find his daughter and be her strength and support during this nightmare. He cannot bear to think of her alone and scared. He understands that what he did to you may be beyond forgiveness, but he would do it again and again for the hope you will be there with her."

Edriene raised her face, her eyes blotchy and swollen from crying. "How do you know?"

Fleur shrugged self-consciously. "It was there in his face. To me it was as clear as if he were yelling it across the square."

"Who are you?" asked Edriene in wonder.

"I am simply Fleur," was the solemn response.

"I thank you Fleur, for sharing that with me," Edriene squeezed Fleur's hands. "I pray that I find Metka."

Kate dashed the tears from her cheeks.

"Asher will find her, she will," she blurted impulsively. "She will find the stolen Crafters and she will set them free. And she will find Hestawen and restore the balance."

Edriene's eyes lit up. She turned to Asher. "Will you? Can you?" she said.

In the face of her hope, Asher had no choice but to nod. For the first time Edriene smiled, her face shining with relief.

This new promise settled heavily on top of those Asher already carried, but she shouldered the weight without regret. She knew for sure now that she had made the right decision. Returning to the house would have been the wrong thing to

do; she was needed here. E-Langren had fallen, but the Crafters
would be saved.

Chapter Thirteen

Groush

They travelled on. At Harthe the same call for Crafters was sent through the village. But there was no-one left to take. The villagers cowered in their homes, occasionally peeking through their curtains. Nobody approached the carts.

Through Harthe and onto Mat'drin they continued, still without food or water. The guards meanwhile ate and drank their fill from the supply cart, mocking the captives as they did so.

Finally Levi had had enough. Kate was starting to feel dehydrated and light-headed and while she would not say anything he was more than willing to.

"Ahoy there! You driver!" he called imperiously. "We need to stop and stretch our legs, and answer the call of nature as it were. And we require food and water for everyone."

The guard slowed the pace of the cart, automatically responding to the authority in Levi's voice.

Ahead of them the first cart came to a halt when the Squad Leader realised what was happening. He jumped out of the cage and locked it tight, then strode back to their cart which was now at a standstill. The horses whinnied, tossing their heads and stamping their feet.

"What is happening here?" he growled.

The driver looked uncertain, then nervous. "The lad said they needed to stop."

"Since when do you take orders from a prisoner?" snarled the Leader. "Get moving."

"Listen here man," said Levi, thoroughly embracing his spoiled, stuffy aristocratic character. "We need to stretch and we need food and water."

The Squad Leader laughed roughly. "Good for you," he said, turning to stride away.

"My cousin the Queen will not be pleased when she hears of my maltreatment. I've always been her favourite. I'm sure you've heard her speak of me with affection. Denison this, and Denison that. That's me by the way – I'm Denison."

"You said you were the Weaver's grandson," growled the Leader.

"Yes indeed, and she is the Queen's aunt, as I'm sure you are well aware."

The Leader had not been well aware of this but was certainly not going to admit it. He hesitated, his back to the group. He wanted to spit in Levi's face and let them suffer for the entirety of the journey, but Levi's words made him pause. He did not want to admit that he had never had any sort of conversation with the Queen, and therefore had no idea how she felt about her cousin.

"I know she's cross with old grammy," continued Levi conversationally, "but she won't hold that against *me*."

Asher almost choked when he referred to Hestawen as old grammy. Beside her Kate buried her head in her folded arms, smothering her laughter. Fleur's serious face gave nothing away; Edriene just looked perplexed.

The Squad Leader wrestled with his own thoughts, then with a furious kick of the dirt he growled to the driver.

"Let them out. Get them something to eat and drink. Watch them carefully. And no funny business from you lot, or I'll start slitting throats," he gestured to the women in the other cage.

"We'll take it in turns then," declared Levi, "they can have their break first, then we will have our turn."

And so they did. Everyone relished the release from the uncomfortable, back-aching seats and relentless bouncing of the carts; walking and stretching for the few minutes they were allowed. Asher made sure to stay close and visible the entire time, so the Squad Leader had no excuse to use his knife.

They gulped down fresh water and bread and cheese, their bodies instantly responding to the nourishment. When they were locked back in the cart, the girls grinned at Levi, mouthing 'thank you'.

"Are you really the Queen's cousin?" whispered Edriene.

He grinned and replied in his normal voice.

"Family trees can be complicated, and every now and then a cousin pops up on a precarious branch whom you completely forgot about. So today yes. And maybe for a while longer. We'll see how it works out. And I wasn't completely lying. My mother's name is actually Denise, so I am in reality, Denise-son. It's important to keep the details as truthful as possible."

Edriene seemed dazed but she did not ask any more questions. They settled in for the last part of the journey, wondering what awaited them at Ostrin.

However it soon became apparent they were not going to Ostrin. The carts rolled into Mat'drin but they did not continue on the road to the large gates that led to the castle. Instead, they headed in the other direction, to the very edge of the city, where a collection of rough and ready inns sat dark and cold in the shadow of the mountains.

Asher shivered, and it was not only the intense cold that gave her the chills. The faces of the few people on the streets were harsh and unwelcoming. The buildings were grey and grim. This was the last shred of civilisation before the formidable mountains climb.

She tilted her head back to look at those harsh peaks, most of them obscured by thick cloud. She knew without asking that they were being taken to Groush. Trinity had told Levi that Darven had lived in an extensive cave system there, and it seemed like a place you could hide stolen Crafters indefinitely.

She was both apprehensive of what awaited them in the mountains, and hopeful that they would find the other missing women there. She resolved to be as small and unremarkable as possible, to draw no unnecessary attention to herself. She needed to get up to Groush without incident. She layered her charm.

The carts rattled to a stop. The Squad Leader jumped out of the cart and locked the women inside. He glanced in the direction of Asher and her friends, but he seemed less focused on her than previously. The cloak was working. Then he headed to a nearby inn, banging open its grimy door and striding inside.

A few minutes later he thumped his way outside, grumbling to himself. He went into the inn next door. When he strode out soon after he was clearly angry. Twice more he went in and out of the inns, each time exiting in a fouler and fouler mood.

He returned to the carts bursting with anger.

"Useless, no-good, pathetic scum. I should set the buildings on fire, that would get 'em moving." He laughed meanly.

Asher, Kate and Levi exchanged curious glances but said nothing. They were unwilling to draw his ire in their direction. The Squad Leader's men seemed to know what he was referring to. One of them spoke up, braving the Leader's short temper.

"If none of them will make the climb, does that mean we are heading up the mountains ourselves? The horses need a rest.

We're tired too. The road will be dark and we don't know the way."

"I know that you fool," scowled the Leader. "You'll leave at first light."

The men muttered under their breath, clearly unhappy with the situation. None of them were keen to make the mountain climb without an experienced guide.

"What about them?" The Guard gestured in their direction.

The Leader smiled. "We'll just leave 'em here, see if they survive the frigid night air."

A new thought occurred to him. "Except him." He jerked his head at Levi. "Bring him. I don't want to risk losing the Queen's cousin."

Kate grabbed at Levi's hand in panic, her eyes wide. As dreadful as it was to be locked in this cage for the night, it was more dreadful to be separated.

"I hear you are looking for a driver," came a low voice from the dark.

Asher's ears strained. That voice – it sounded familiar.

"What's it to you?" growled the Squad Leader.

"I know the paths well. I will guide your carts in the morning light. For a reasonable fee of course, paid tonight in advance."

A man stepped out of the shadows and Ash bit her lip to stop a small gasp from escaping. Joseph!

Kate and Levi grabbed her hands, the three of them sharing small smiles. Joseph did not so much as glance in their direction.

The Squad Leader sauntered over to the other man and the haggle began. Asher did not care what terms they settled on, she was just relieved to see a friendly face. Money changed hands.

"And of course the prisoners will have to be moved from the carts overnight," Joseph was saying, his tone neutral and calm. "The horses must be unhitched, brushed, fed and rested. The carts will need to be stored out of the freezing air so the wheels do not warp. The mountain paths are treacherous, we don't want any mistakes. The prisoners can be locked in the empty stables. With your men on guard there will be no issues."

The Leader did not like being told what must happen. He was a man who gave orders, he was not particularly inclined to take them from anyone he considered his inferior. But he understood the sense in what the man was saying. And he was ready to be warm and to rest himself.

He nodded brusquely.

"Do it," he instructed his men. Then he strode away to a nearby inn, intending to drink and carouse late into the night. He would sleep well into the morning, for he would not be making the climb. The companions in the cart watched him stride away, relieved to see the back of him.

The guards muttered and grumbled but they did as Joseph had suggested. Before long Asher and her friends were curled up in fresh warm hay in the stables, along with Edriene and the three exhausted Crafters from the other cart.

A rustle at the adjoining stall drew Asher's attention. Quietly she crawled out of the hay and stepped over to the dividing slats.

"Crafter," said Joseph by way of greeting. He was as solemn as ever.

She smiled broadly at him. "Hello Joseph, goodness I am pleased to see you!"

He lifted a large basket over the wall. The delicious scent of fresh bread and cooked meat wafted around Asher. Her mouth watered and her tummy grumbled.

"Thank you," she said gratefully, staggering slightly as she took the heavy basket from him.

"Are you planning an escape?" Joseph asked so quietly Asher had to strain to hear his voice.

She shook her head. "No, I need to find the others. I suspect there are more Crafters held in the mountains."

"That is so. The mountain guides talk of the prisoners they have escorted. Many have been taken up. None have been brought back down."

He nodded in farewell and disappeared into the gloom. Asher hauled the basket over to the group.

"What is that amazing smell?" asked Levi, propping himself up against the wall.

"Shhh," admonished Ash in a whisper. "We don't want to alert the guards. Everybody, gather around."

Mouths salivating, the eight of them clustered around the basket, pulling out a plate of warm sliced meat, fresh crusty bread, apples, spiced pear cake and flasks of warm tea.

For the tired and hungry captives it was a feast. Mindful not to draw attention to themselves, they ate hastily in silence. When they finished they exchanged smiles and nods of appreciation, and silently settled down to sleep. Asher tucked the empty basket into the back of the stall.

She lay in the clean, slightly prickly hay next to Kate and wrapped her hand around the warm globe. It remained silent, as it had all day, but its very presence gave her comfort.

The day, which had started with such possibility, was ending with sorrow and uncertainty. She wondered how Anetta, Cook and Trinity were. *Where* they were. How the young housemaids were recovering.

She deliberately turned her thoughts away from E-Langren and its lost treasures.

Her full belly rumbled contentedly, filled with the kindness and generosity of Joseph. It reminded her that all was not lost. Amidst the chaos and treachery of Andera and its queen, the Weaver still had friends, *she* still had friends.

***

The night passed quickly, and by first light they were on the move once more, traversing the dangerous mountain paths. Nobody was enjoying the experience.

The wheels of the cart caught on the rough, rocky pass, and the cart shuddered, tipping precariously close to the cliff edge.

Asher and Kate jumped quickly to the other bench, trying to restore the balance with their extra weight.

The cart thumped back onto the ground, jolting them into the air. Their terrified driver swore loudly. They had been travelling for three gruelling hours and everyone was on edge.

"He is not having his best day," commented Levi.

"*He's* not having his best day?" replied Kate incredulously. Her voice was tinged with barely controlled hysteria and she was clinging desperately to the bars.

"He's not the one locked in a cage, watching the wheels send rocks careening down the mountains side. At least he can jump off the damn cart if we tumble off the edge."

She removed her left hand from the bar and covered her eyes, but almost immediately removed it. It was far worse not being able to see what was happening.

Asher nodded at Kate in wordless sympathy. Nausea roiled in her own belly. The jolting of the cart, and the fear of imminent death were an unpleasant combination. She swallowed the urge to vomit. At least they had not eaten this morning. The less food in her system, the better.

"How much longer?" asked Kate in a small voice.

Ash shook her head helplessly. She really had no idea.

Joseph was driving the front cart, with the three village Crafters and Edriene onboard. One of the original Squad drove their cart with fresh horses from Mat'drin, who were used to the mountain roads. Indeed, the animals were the calmest of them all.

The four of them were squashed in with boxes of supplies, that rattled and slid as the cart rumbled along the paths.

The mountains rose around them, uncaring and disinterested in the plight of the tiny humans who toiled upon them. Wild flowers pushed through the rocky ground, turning their faces to the small amount of sun that peeked through the mist. Tufts of grass fought for life among the stones. Great flocks of birds circled above, calling to each other as they surfed the mild currents. The higher they climbed the colder the air became.

It was ruggedly beautiful and inhospitable. They were completely out of their element.

Asher held the flute in her clenched fist, ready to play if they did fall off the cliff, though she was not sure how the logistics of playing a flute while falling through the sky would actually work. Still, the flute had seemed a better option than the piano, or the guitar. Fleur had watched with wide eyes when Asher had unhooked the tiny instrument and commanded the flute to grow.

"Without the Squad Leader threatening the others, there is no reason for you *not* to play. Could you play to help settle the driver and stabilise the cart?" suggested Levi.

It was a good idea, and she raised the flute to her lips, bracing her body against the swaying and jolting.

She remembered Hesta saying that changing another person's state was difficult and tiring. So instead she focused on creating music that settled herself, and hoped it would have the same effect on the others. And it must have. For the next hour Ash played, the light notes swirling around them all, steadying their driver and calming the occupants of the cart.

Even when she ceased playing and moved the flute away from her dry mouth, the memory of the music had a lasting effect. They sat in comfortable quiet together listening to the sound of the wheels crunching and the horses whinnying, the driver no longer yelling and cursing at the hard-working animals.

The morning slid into the afternoon without a break, and without lunch. Nobody mentioned their hungry tummies or their pounding heads, for they were all in the same nightmare and sharing their misery would only compound it.

Levi pulled out his phone and scrolled through the photos they had taken in the library.

"I knew I read something about these mountains!" he exclaimed, holding a picture out to Asher. "Look at this."

Asher ran her eyes over the screen. With growing excitement she read out loud.

"It lies within the caves beneath the village of Groush. These caves form part of a connected river system that runs through the Mat'drinian Mountains from Ostrin to Faerla Grun. If the pieces can be retrieved, they can be re-joined to form the silver globe. When the gold and silver stars combine, it is possible to move beyond the Weave for a moment in time, restoring that which is lost."

She raised shining eyes to Levi. "Do you think that *beyond* means *The* Beyond? That which is lost must be Hesta. But what is 'it'? What lies within the caves?"

"I don't know," he replied, "but it's worth a shot. Maybe there's more information on a another screen-shot."

Asher scrolled through the photos, stopping abruptly when she saw the word D'rona.

"Here's something. *At the heart of the Weave lies Andera, the centre and source of all magic. Everything exists within the Weave, except that which is beyond it. There are four additional universes, connected to Andera by their planet of power. Each of the planets – D'rona, Earth, Elliptica,*" she paused, swiping through the photos. "I can't find the next line."

"Here, let me have a look."

Levi took back his phone and carefully swiped through the photos. After a few minutes he slumped back against the bars of the cage.

"Nope. Missed it. Sorry Ash." His voice was as despondent as the expression on his face.

She shook her head at him. "No way Levi, this is fabulous. This is the best clue we have so far. We just need to find some pieces of a broken globe in the caves beneath Groush. It seems to me that everything is coming up Asher."

She grinned, waggling her eyebrows, hoping to restore his natural good mood. He sighed, wanting to wallow in his melancholy a while longer, but true to form he could not help but laugh.

Fleur cleared her throat. "Excuse me, may I ask what you are talking about?"

Asher nodded. "I think that's fair Fleur. We're all in this together."

Over the next fifteen minutes she told Fleur about her travels to D'rona and the Laneisian. About the Weaving Room and the Guide, and her vision of Hesta and Penn sleeping in the place Beyond. She chose not to mention the Portal Doors, heeding the Guide's comment that they belonged to the Weaver.

"And of course, we are from Earth, so we are quite familiar with that planet." She concluded.

Fleur raised her brows. "That explains so much."

The three Terrans grinned at her.

"I'm going to take that as a compliment," declared Levi.

The were still laughing when the cart slowed to a stop. Deep in their discussion about the caves and the Beyond they had not noticed the cart had moved off the narrow path and into a small, uninspiring collection of buildings that might generously be referred to as a village.

The driver jumped down with a groan. A minute later he hobbled around to the back of the cart and turned a key in the heavy padlock. The door to the cage swung open.

"Get out," he said.

Awkwardly they climbed out, their bodies screaming as they moved limbs and muscles that had been cramped and tormented for hours and hours. The guard limped slowly away in the direction of one of the houses, clearly not concerned with thoughts of their possible escape. It soon became apparent why.

The little village of Groush was nestled high in the shadows of the towering mountains of Mat'drin. The only road in or out was the precarious cliff-edge path they had just traversed. On foot that journey would take a couple of days, and there was nowhere to hide. A hungry and cold escapee would be quickly retrieved. The other option was to climb higher into the mountains themselves. Without adequate knowledge or supplies that meant certain death.

Two men appeared from a nearby hut and hauled the supplies from the carts. They did not look at the new arrivals, nor attempt any sort of contact with them. The crates and boxes were taken to a building at the end of the small village. The men disappeared inside and did not return.

A light rain began to fall. The fog settled in around them. A new level of cold seeped through their clothes and made them shiver.

Ash watched the Crafters from Joseph's cart stumble onto the ground, their eyes filled with despair. For them this bleak place signalled the end of hope. But for Ash it meant something quite different.

She looked around eagerly as she stretched her back and legs. For the first time since Hesta had been poisoned Ash felt she was on the right path to find the Weaver. Somewhere close by were the caves, and within them was surely the path to the Beyond.

Chapter Fourteen

Void Matter

A row of small squat huts was built into the harsh rockface. The door to the nearest one flung open. In the doorway stood two women. One of them called across to the new arrivals.

"Come quickly inside, out of the rain, the fire is warm and the kettle is boiled."

Edriene, Kate and Levi went to help the other captives, supporting them into the small house. Asher wandered over to Joseph's cart, on the pretext of helping with the horses. Though the Squad guard had disappeared into what she presumed was the guardhouse, she did not want to take any chances and reveal Joseph as an ally.

"Excuse me," she said loudly, for the benefit of any listening ears. "Do you need assistance with the horses?"

He eyed her up and down, as though they had never met before.

"You any good with them?" he asked gruffly.

She nodded. "Yes, I am used to horses."

"Let me ask the guard."

Joseph headed to the guardhouse and rapped loudly on the door. The guard opened it with a scowl.

"The girl wants to help with the horses. That okay with you?" He pointed at Ash.

The guard considered, weighing the pros and cons. He was not a bright man, and making decisions was not usually his responsibility.

The head guard had just gone to the supply hut to mark off the new inventory. Before he left he had clearly told the guard to sort out the horses. But the guard had no desire to leave the warmth of the hut and be out in the rain. This had been his first trip up the mountain and hopefully his last. His head pounded and his body was still wobbly from the intense drive. When the Queen's Advisor arrived in two days he hoped there would be a changing of the guards and he could leave this forsaken mountain forever.

He peered at Ash from the doorway. To be honest, he barely remembered the girl. She was not particularly remarkable.

"One less job for me. No funny business mind. If she does anything call for us."

Joseph inclined his head and walked back to Asher.

"Right lass, I'll unhitch these two and you lead them into the stables, over there. I'll go get the other pair. Work fast. This rain is no good for them after that climb."

She did as she was told, talking to them softly as she led the two nickering horses to the stables. Once inside Ash removed the damp coats, then brushed down one horse and then the other. Joseph worked beside her in silence.

"Cold place this," said Asher conversationally.

Joseph nodded. "There are fresh coats for the horses in the tack room. Follow me."

In the tack room they pulled the heavy coats off the hooks, the weight making Asher stumble. Joseph reached out to steady her.

"The only way off these mountains is through them," he murmured. "There are tunnels and caves weaving beneath the surface."

"You alright? The wool is heavy," he said in his normal voice.

Asher heaved the coats in her arms and balanced the weight. She nodded.

"Right then."

They worked in silence for the rest of the time. An unfamiliar guard appeared at the doorway; he watched without interest, his face dull with boredom. Once the horses were dry, warm and settled, the guard ushered her out of the stables.

Ash felt a pang as she was herded to the hut without a backward glance. *Good bye Joseph, and thank you.*

Four anxious faces turned as the door to the small hut was pulled open and she was thrust inside. Fleur, Levi, Kate and Edriene crowded around.

"Where did you go?" demanded Levi, "we had no idea what happened to you."

"I went to help with the horses."

"We assumed they had taken you," said Kate crossly, her blue eyes dark with recriminations.

"Sorry," muttered Ash contritely.

"Come and eat," said Fleur gently.

The mention of food made Asher's stomach growl loudly. Gladly she followed Fleur to a small table laden with surprisingly wonderful cakes and bread. As she ate she looked around at their new accommodation.

They were in a small, drab living room crammed with a few hard chairs and two worn and frayed armchairs clustered around a fire. There was no sofa, which made sense as Asher could not imagine how it would be transported up the mountains. The open fire burned merrily, filling the small space with heat. There were three doors leading off this main room. One was open and she could see into the tiny kitchen. The other two were closed. She presumed they were bedrooms or a bathroom.

The room was dark, lit by small lamps and the crackling flames. The windows let in no light, as they were covered by heavy, faded curtains. It was hard to imagine this grim little cottage might have once been welcoming and bright, perhaps some-one's home.

As well as the four of them, there were another four women crowded in the small house already. Asher looked at them carefully as she sipped her tea. Two were women in their forties. The other two were much younger, only a few years older than her.

They were talking quietly with Edriene and her friends, swapping their stories, paying her no attention.

"Where are the others who travelled with us? The women from our village?" she asked Fleur.

"They are resting in the bedroom," said Fleur, nodding in the direction of the closed doors.

Ash raised her eyebrows. "Eleven of us will share this small space?" Her voice was incredulous.

"Have you been spoiled by the luxurious conditions of the cart?" smiled the other girl.

Ash laughed, appreciating the joke, particularly coming from serious Fleur. She took a final sip of tea. The food was simple and filling and really delicious. Her hunger sated, other needs became more pressing.

"Is there a bathroom?" she asked.

"Just beyond the kitchen," pointed Fleur.

"Thank you."

Asher stepped through the small kitchen and into a tiny washroom, with a toilet, a shower and a sink. Above the sink was a small mirror, the edges tarnished with age and moisture. As Asher washed her hands she peered at her reflection.

Her hair was wild. Tangled and unkempt, it framed her face in a most unflattering way. Beneath that messy halo her face was filthy. Travel dirt stained her pale skin. Her sapphire earrings dangled merrily from dirty ears, their golden beauty undiminished by her overall grottiness.

Carefully she washed her face and neck, then ran her fingers through her hair, which made absolutely no difference at all. If anything her hair looked worse. She was turning to leave when her shoe caught on a small piece of wood, loose on the floor.

A thought popped into her mind. Perhaps she could Craft this piece of wood into a hairbrush. She had never attempted such a thing, and really did not know if it was possible, but she was eager to try. Not simply to brush her hair, but to test her Crafting, to see what could be done.

She pulled the case from her pocket and chose the flute. "Play."

Once the flute was at her lips, she played a soft melody of growth and change. She closed her eyes and poured her energy into the wood, imagining it transforming, blossoming into a hairbrush. After a few minutes she opened her eyes and gasped with delight.

On the sink lay a hairbrush. Simple, still wooden, but with very definite bristles firmly in place.

Asher tucked the flute into her pocket and set about brushing out her wretched hair. She grimaced and clenched her teeth as the bristles caught on every tangle and knot, but with persistence her hair was soft and smooth again.

A few minutes later she made her way back to the living room. Her friends were perched with Edriene, talking with the other Crafters.

Wordlessly she joined them, taking a seat on the floor next to Kate. The strangers barely glanced in her direction. Clearly her charm was working. But what was curious, was the lack of energy emanating from the women.

Edriene pulsed with power, and the life-forces from Levi, Fleur and Kate surrounded their bodies, but from the other

Crafters, nothing. Where there should be life and energy there was blankness. An emptiness, a coldness. It was the complete opposite of energy. It was almost like being in the Void.

Dread crept up Asher's spine and she shivered.

Her companions were sharing a greatly edited version of who they were and the events that had brought them here.

"I am hoping to find my niece here, and anyone else from our town. My niece's name is Metka," added Edriene.

One of the young women nodded enthusiastically. "Yes, she is here. She was moved to one of the other houses yesterday."

Edriene jumped up with joy. "Where? How do I find her?"

"We're not allowed to leave the house," one of the women said with a shake of her head. "The punishments for disobeying the rules are brutal."

Edriene collapsed back on the chair, her face stricken.

"It will be alright Edriene, we will find her," said Asher. "I am sure of it."

Four curious faces turned her way, as though realising for the first time that she was there. A dark-haired woman pointed at each Crafter in turn as she repeated the introductions Asher had missed.

"Isobel, Fruda, Aga, and I am Mara."

"I am Asher. May I ask why Metka was moved?"

"They are sorting the Crafters into ability, as per the orders of the Queen." Mara explained.

More like the orders of the Queen's blackguard Advisor, thought Ash, remembering the dynamic between the helpless Queen and the overpowering Darven.

"We are all Wens, Metka is still young and her Crafting in its infancy. The young, inexperienced Crafters are held together. A few men have accompanied their women folk, for various reasons." She looked at Levi. "They do not last long."

Levi swallowed. "What happens to them?"

"We do not rightly know, but we suspect they are taken to work in the mines of the mountains. They never return." Mara's voice was grave.

Kate reached over and grabbed Levi's hand. They sat there in silence, holding tight to one another.

"That will not happen to Levi," declared Asher, shaking her flute in anger.

Mara's eyes grew wide. "Hush!" she commanded. "If the guards see your instrument they will take it. Not that it matters. I still wear all my jewellery and it is useless!"

Her voice was bitter and despairing.

She did indeed wear beautiful jewellery. Gold and silver chains, encrusted with gems of all colours, circled her neck and wrists. Gleaming ruby earrings dangled from her earlobes. One small diamond stud adorned her nose. Even her unwashed hair was held in place by large silver clips decorated with onyx.

Asher knew they should be radiating Crafting power, filled with energy for Mara the Jeweller to access. But for all their beauty they were silent.

While everyone's attention was drawn to Mara, Asher quietly shrunk her flute and attached it back to her bracelet. Edriene was clearly as perplexed by the lack of energy as Asher.

"What has happened to your Craft?" she asked.

The women lifted their left arms, struggling with the weight of their own limbs, as though something incredibly heavy was holding them down.

Around each wrist was a thin silver chain. Hanging from the chain was a small silver disc. Into each disc a miniscule black dot was embedded. So tiny it was hard to see in the gloomy room.

Edriene reached out her hand to touch the disc, trying to see it more clearly.

"Don't!" cried Mara fearfully, trying to pull her arm away, but unable to move fast due to the weight of the disc.

"What is it?" asked Edriene.

Mara shook her head. "We do not know. Whatever it is negates all Crafter power. Upon being captured we each had one clasped upon our wrist."

"How can it do that?" demanded Edriene. "What has the power to negate energy created from life?"

Awareness prickled at the back of Asher's mind. Dread followed, accompanied by fear. Ash knew exactly what it was.

"It is Void-matter," she said quietly, her throat dry.

Edriene recoiled from Mara as though she had burst into flames. Horror was reflected on all of their faces.

"How is that possible?" said Fruda.

Asher thought of the book she had read in Hesta's library only yesterday. She had almost skipped the section on the Void-matter, keen as she was to find information on the Beyond. But the reference to the portals had caught her attention and she had read on.

'Void-matter is incredibly rare and dangerous to mine, existing only in miniscule amounts. It can leak from tears in the fabric of space, where portals have been opened and not properly sealed.'

"It leaks from portals that are not properly sealed," she said to the others.

She felt sick to her stomach when she considered how she had torn open portals of her own. No wonder the Guide had been so cross. She sincerely hoped that none of her portals had leaked any of the matter.

The book had gone on to say that Void-matter in such miniscule amounts was normally consumed by the energy of the environment around it within days and posed no threat to the inhabitants. It might leave a barren spot on the earth, or a dried river bed, but otherwise there was little consequence.

But when Void-matter could be mined and stored in pure silver it held onto its properties indefinitely, negating all energy within a certain radius, depending on the size of the Void-matter.

"Clearly Darven has found a way to mine and capture just enough Void-matter to negate a Crafter's ability," she said.

"Do you think he deliberately leaked Void-matter when he opened the portal to take Evie?" asked Kate.

Asher nodded emphatically. "Yes, that makes sense. So the mine is in the mountains, wherever the portal was opened. Maybe that's what he's using the men for. Unlike female crafters they would not be susceptible to it."

Ash, Levi and Kate looked at each other, everything clicking into place for them. However the other inhabitants of the room, including Fleur, looked thoroughly confused.

"What are you talking about? What is this news of Darven? How do you know about this Void-matter?" asked Mara, clearly the designated leader of the four women.

The three Earth friends exchanged a long glance, agreeing without words that they should not share anything further. The women were in too much danger already. They thought of the innocent maids, tortured for simply working in the Weaver's house. Knowing about Asher and Evie and Darven and the Weaver put everyone here at risk.

"I'm sorry Mara, I'm just thinking out loud. It's just something I read once, when I was doing Wen training."

A new thought occurred to Ash. "Are you a Wen Edriene?"

The other woman nodded. Which meant Edriene would be kept here with these four. Asher had no idea how she would be categorized. She was not a Wen, yet she was training with the Weaver. She suspected she and her friends would be separated, and Levi sent to the Void-matter mine.

"When do they put the bracelets on?" she asked Mara.

"Mine was put on when they stole me from my home," the Jeweller answered, looking at the others who all nodded.

"Can you take it off?"

The women shuddered, their faces bleak.

"The bracelet burns like ice on the skin. I cannot touch it for more than a second or two. After I tried my fingers were numb and sore for hours," said Mara.

"Well clearly they have forgotten about us. Perhaps we should see what we can Craft before they remember."

Edriene's face was thoughtful. "If I throw some seeds in front of their door, I could grow a vine across the Guard House and trap them inside. I have bags full of seeds hanging inside my skirts. That would give us time to get the others. Then what?"

She looked at Asher. *Yes Ash, then what?* Mocked the voice of doubt. *You made a hairbrush, what can you do with that?*

Questions without answers swirled in her mind. Should they trap the guards and break the Crafters free? Then what? What about the men in the mines? Even if she could collect them all, where would they go? If they survived in the mountains, how far could they run before Darven's squads found them again?

Asher looked at the solemn group gathered in the dim room. She felt paralysed by indecision.

Her priority had to be finding Hesta. That seemed the only way to properly restore order. Without the Weaver Ash feared any attempt at rebellion was doomed.

She shook her head, retreating into her unremarkable aura. She did not want these Crafters to look to her as their Leader.

"What do you think Mara?" she deferred to the experienced Wen.

"I think it is foolhardy and puts everyone at risk. Until we are all released from these cursed bracelets it is far too dangerous. The young ones are the most vulnerable and we cannot be certain we can protect them."

They all nodded, feeling deflated. A harsh bang on the door made them jump. Before they could clamber to their feet the door was pushed open.

Two burly guards stepped into the room. Their large presence overpowered the small space. Their faces were twisted in the semblance of grins, and from their gloved hands dangled seven silver bracelets.

One pointed to Levi, then to the doorway behind them. "You, over there."

Levi glanced at the girls; their eyes were wide with fear. He gave them a tight smile, hoping to reassure them. It did not have the desired effect.

One of the guards grabbed Edriene roughly while the other clipped on the bracelet. Her whole being seemed to shrink into itself. Ash watched in horror as bracelets were clipped on Fleur and Kate; then it was her turn.

As the thin bracelet touched her wrist an overwhelming sense of cold seeped into her skin. Within seconds it had enveloped her body, sinking into her soul, leaving only an emptiness. All her doubts seemed to overwhelm her. She felt hopeless and worthless. It was almost like being in the Void, but not as intense.

The guards made their way into the bedroom, roughly waking the sleeping E-Langren village Crafters and clipping on their bracelets. Then they pushed and shoved those confused women out of the cottage.

Ash reached for the music in her mind, but for the first time in her life there was nothing. The quiet soundtrack that had always accompanied her was not silent, it was simply not there. Panic rose fast. Instinctively she grabbed at the bracelet to yank it off and screamed as pain seared her fingers.

"Enjoy," smirked the guards maliciously.

They grabbed Levi and dragged him from the hut as Kate yelled feebly in protest. She was barely keeping herself upright as the horror of the Void re-established itself in her mind.

Asher sunk into one of the armchairs, her body sapped of strength and her mind struggling in the fog. She could not lift her left arm, and the fingers of her right arm were numb from touching the bracelet. Pain was her companion.

Levi, must save Levi.

Mara's voice was soft and reassuring. "It will pass soon," she said comfortingly, "don't fight it, it will pass."

"Levi," Asher whispered. But he was gone.

Chapter Fifteen

The Secret of the Caves

Fruda, Aga, and Mara bustled around, covering the cold women with blankets. Isobel brewed very sweet tea and encouraged each of them to sip as much as they could, the warmth slowly restoring them from the inside.

As Asher's body and mind were released from the numbness of the Void, worry for Levi became all consuming. Where had they taken him? What would happen to him? Would they be able to find him again?

Kate crawled over and curled up beside her on the floor, the two of them united in their anxiety and sense of loss. It was late. Outside the world was dark and freezing, the stars hidden behind thick fog. They were exhausted and frightened.

The women tucked pillows beneath their heads and stoked the fire. Asher longed to leap up and run in search of Levi, but her body would not respond, and her head ached with pressure.

"Sleep now," said Aga gently, her kind face filled with compassion. "You can do nothing tonight. You need to rest and recover from the battering of the Void bracelet."

Ash was certain that the all-consuming fear for Levi would keep her awake despite the exhaustion of the Void-matter, but within minutes both she and Kate were sound asleep on the floor. Fleur settled into the armchair beside them, curling herself into its faded, battered seat. Edriene slept on the other side of the fire. Mara and the others turned off the lamps and headed to the bedrooms. The tiny hut settled into silence.

Through the night Kate sobbed as the void nightmares tormented her sleep once more.

In the morning the smell of baking bread tickled Asher's nostrils, waking her from sleep. At first she was confused. Why was she lying on the floor? Where was she? Then the events of the last two days came rushing back and she remembered Levi being dragged out of the hut. Abruptly she sat up, immediately regretting the move as her head pounded in protest.

Beside her Kate stirred. Fleur woke, stretching as she sat up in the armchair, her neck and shoulder aching from the awkward night's sleep. The three young women looked quietly at each other.

"Are you two okay?" asked Asher.

Kate stretched her arms above her head, her left arm decidedly heavier than her right.

"I'm okay. Sore and miserable, but the Void feeling has eased. Now my arm just feels heavy."

Ash turned to Fleur. She stood up from the armchair and stretched her back and neck.

"I'm okay," she said quietly.

"Let's eat first," said Asher. "Then we need to work out how we get out of this hut, save Levi, find the caves and discover the door to the Beyond."

The three of them packed up their makeshift beds and stepped across to the table, where the other woman were clustered, eating bread and sipping tea. The bread was fresh, still warm from the oven. Hungrily they slathered their slices with soft butter and sweet strawberry jam.

Fruda was in the tiny kitchen, pulling more loaves from the oven.

"She is a Baker Crafter," explained Mara.

"I didn't know that was a thing," said Asher in surprise.

"Oh yes. A Baker Crafter can bake anything from the simplest of ingredients. A Wen can create food from almost nothing, just from the energy around her. Of course Fruda is unable to Craft with the bracelet on, but she is still an amazing cook."

Asher munched gratefully, torn between fear for Levi and thankfulness that Kate and Fleur were safe.

When they had finished eating the three girls offered to clean up; and soon they were jammed into the tiny kitchen, washing dishes and cleaning trays.

Asher opened a long cupboard beside the bathroom door, expecting it to be a pantry to store the flour, but to her surprise it was empty inside. And far bigger than she was expecting. Hesitantly she reached inside the pantry. Defying all possibility the space inside was huge. On a hunch she climbed into the cupboard and found herself able to walk right through it.

"Ash!" called Kate frantically. "Where are you?"

Asher pushed her way back out of the pantry to find Kate and Fleur staring at her in shock.

"It's huge in here," whispered Asher excitedly, "I think there's a passage back there."

Kate frowned in confusion. "I just opened that cupboard. It had normal shelves and a solid back. I saw it."

"A perception filter," breathed Fleur. "Clever."

"How come I can see through it, but the others have not?" asked Ash. "They've been here for a few days. They would have discovered it by now."

Fleur considered this for a few moments. "All I can think is that you are the Heir. You wear the globe. The rules are different for you."

Kate fiddled with the silver bracelet on her wrist, flicking the small silver disc anxiously. "Are we going in?" she asked in a small voice.

"We sure are," said Ash enthusiastically.

Kate nodded bravely, but her face was pale and her eyes glittered with unshed tears.

"What's wrong Kate?" asked Fleur gently.

"It's just that, I'm not good with dark places, or small spaces," whispered Kate. "The Void…" she shuddered. "It really messed with my head."

Asher felt dreadful. She had been so caught up in where the passage might lead, that she had completely forgotten how badly Kate had been impacted by the crossing.

"Stay here Kate," she said softly. "You don't have to do this."

Kate shook her head. "No, I do. We're a team." But her face was grey and her voice shook.

"You absolutely have to stay here," said Ash firmly. "You need to cover my absence with the others. Tell them I am sleeping in the bedroom."

"Our absence," said Fleur with a small smile.

"Are you sure?" asked Kate, wanting to support her friend, and wanting to avoid the dark passageway in equal measure.

"Go." Asher shooed her away. "Make a diversion."

"Do you have your phone on you?" asked Kate. "The torch function should work. Mark the tunnels as you move through them. If the air is stale, back up. Be safe."

Then she went into the small loungeroom and made a fuss about her leg, drawing everyone's attention to her. Quietly Asher and Fleur stepped through the narrow cupboard doorway and into the dark.

The passageway was wide enough for the two of them to walk carefully next to each other. The torch of Asher's phone shone a welcome beam onto the hard rock, illuminating their steps. The tunnel was clean and clear, no fallen debris or rough edges. It had been well made and maintained. Perhaps most surprisingly the air was fresh.

"There must be exits, or at least vents to the outside," murmured Fleur.

Asher thought she should feel nervous or uncomfortable about where the path may be taking them, but in truth she was bubbling with excitement. She just knew this path was leading them into the caves, and she was confident they would find what they needed there.

After a few more minutes Asher was certain she could see light ahead. She picked up her pace, eager to find what lay ahead. The light turned out to be a lamp on the wall ahead, illuminating two tunnels. Ash peered at the lamp curiously.

"You know, I've been wondering how things are powered here. I haven't seen any cords or power points."

Fleur wrinkled her nose. "Power points? What do you mean?"

"Where is the power coming from? How does the electricity work? Even our phones have not gone flat. Their batteries are staying charged."

Fleur shrugged. "I don't know what you are talking about. All I know is that the energy of Andera is channelled by Crafters into items, and that energy remains."

Asher whacked her forehead with her palm. Of course. Andera was the centre of energy Crafting in the five universes. Naturally everyday items could be powered by such force.

"Talk about green energy," she joked.

The words meant nothing to Fleur, so she chose not to respond. Instead she peered down one tunnel and then another.

"Which one will we choose?" she asked.

Ash pointed at the right one. Fleur dug into her pocket and pulled out a ribbon and a small roll of hemming tape. Carefully she cut the ribbon with her scissors and attached a piece to the wall of the passage they had just walked down.

"Clever," admired Asher.

"It was Kate's suggestion. It is lucky I have some bits and pieces with me."

They headed down the right tunnel. Every few metres another lamp was attached to the wall, creating pools of light. This was clearly designed to be used as a thoroughfare. Asher turned off the phone and tucked it away.

In silence they walked for a while longer; the heavy stillness of the tunnel only perforated by the sound of their footsteps on the stone. Until Ash thought she heard another noise. A very faint *clink*.

She paused to listen. Fleur immediately stopped beside her. *Clink, clink.*

"I think it's coming from further down the tunnel," Asher whispered, "but it's hard to tell. The sound is distorted down here."

Being mindful to tread lightly, they walked on, the *clink clink* becoming louder as they moved further along the path. The tunnel soon ended, opening out to a huge cavern. They stopped in awe, hiding in the opening to their tunnel, to avoid being spotted by the men at work.

Before them was a large underground quarry. Perhaps a dozen exhausted, dirt covered men of all ages laboured with small pick-axes, hacking into the rock. They wore no protective gear, so small cries of pain could be heard as sharp pieces of stone hit them on the face or body. Their clothes were badly worn, suggesting they had been captive for a number of days, if not weeks.

"That stone is polari," explained Fleur in an extremely hushed voice. "It is a very rare precious gem that is used in sorcery potions, or to decorate powerful Crafter items."

"So not the Void-matter?" said Asher disappointedly.

Fleur collected a couple of stray pieces of rock that had previously been flung across the quarry and were laying near her feet. She looked at the stones carefully, then shook her head. "Definitely polari."

Ash scoured the scene before her, looking for Levi, or any clue to where he or the Void-matter might be.

Off to the side two bored guards kept a disinterested eye on the labouring men. Another two tunnels headed out of the quarry. The one on the far left was dark and the other to the right, behind the guards, was well-lit. Ash took a guess that it led back above ground, wherever the men were being held. That in itself was interesting, for perhaps that was where Levi was now.

But the dark tunnel – that one really grabbed her interest. She took a step forward, and would have walked straight into the quarry if Fleur had not grabbed her arm.

"Where are you going?" murmured Fleur.

"I want to see where that tunnel leads," Ash replied quietly, pointing at the dark passage.

"The only way to that tunnel is through the quarry," said Fleur, "and we will definitely be seen. Unless of course we return when the men are finished."

Asher's face lit up. "That's a great idea. We'll come back tonight. In the meantime, let's go see where the other tunnel at the start of this one leads to."

Quietly they turned and retraced their steps back up the passage to the first intersection. This time they chose the path on the left.

Immediately it was apparent that this path was not in regular use. There were no lamps, and small rock-falls littered the passage, making each step treacherous. Without the light from Asher's phone they would have been unable to continue. The air was no longer clean and fresh, and cobwebs caught in their faces and hair. Every now and then one of them would cough as dusty air caught in their throats.

Common sense screamed at Ash that she should give up and turn around, but something was impelling her to continue. Beneath her stained and dirt covered dress the golden globe began to pulse for the first time in days.

Welcome back she muttered in her mind.

Fleur did not complain. She walked carefully behind Ash, as in this tunnel there was no room for them to walk abreast. Without warning, Ash stopped so abruptly that Fleur bumped into her back.

"Sorry," said Ash, "But I think we've come to the end of the path."

The two girls stared at the huge rockfall that blocked the tunnel. There was no way over or through it.

"I was so sure this was something important," sighed Ash disappointedly.

"And I think you are right," replied Fleur excitedly. "Some-one has gone to a lot of trouble to create this rock-wall."

She reached out and touched the cold, dusty stones. "They even feel real."

Asher wrinkled her nose and reached out her own hand. The stones did indeed feel real. As real as they looked.

"Now press harder," said Fleur.

Ash pressed harder and to her surprise her hand continued straight through the rock.

"It's a very very sophisticated perception filter, not just visual, but also tactile. That takes an incredible amount of talent and power. Particularly to leave it here in place indefinitely." Fleur's voice shone with admiration. "I suspect that most people would not even be able to push their way through it, that's how dense and strong it is."

"Then how come we are able to?" asked Ash.

"Probably because you wear the Weaver's globe. How is it responding right now?"

"It's pulsing with energy. Almost like it is encouraging me to keep going," said Ash.

Fleur smiled in the dim light. "Then let's keep going. I might have to hold your hand so the globe's protection extends to me."

Hand in hand the two of them stepped into the rock-wall, and then out the other side. This time they both stopped suddenly, gawking at the incredible sight that greeted them.

Before them was an enormous cavern, even larger than the polari mine. It was bright and well lit by many torches around the walls. There did not appear to be any other entrances to the cavern other than the one they had used, but as theirs was so well disguised as a rockfall it was highly probable that other tunnels were disguised also.

The most incredible feature was the huge lake that glimmered in the heart of the cavern. Its still waters sparkled with a hundred different colours, shimmering and glowing.

A wide path encircled the lake, allowing any visitors to walk around it with ease. The air was sweet and clear, more than normal. Asher and Fleur took deep breaths, filling their tired, sore bodies with energy. The aches and pains they had acquired over the last couple of days seemed to loosen and then melt away.

"What is this place?" whispered Asher, reluctant to break the spell of this magical grotto.

Fleur shook her head, the same wonder on Asher's face reflected on her own.

"I've never heard of anything like this."

"Dare we drink the water?" asked Asher. The desire to drink was strong, the impulse growing by the minute. The globe continued to pulse steadily.

Fleur was clearly torn. She too felt the urge to drink from the shining rainbow lake, but sense was warning her that they were in the presence of great power, and they did not know its purpose or intent.

"I'm not sure," she whispered.

Slowly, filled with anticipation and some nerves, Asher squatted down and reached her hand out to touch the lake. The moment her fingertip touched the cool water fire burned through her body.

She screamed in shock and pain and fell backwards, convulsing.

"Asher!"

Fleur dropped beside her. "Are you okay? What happened? What's wrong?"

The shuddering eased. Asher ran her tongue over her dry lips.

"The power of the Void bracelet," she croaked, "It was annihilated by the lake. It is gone, I can feel my energy, hear my music. It's completely gone. But by the stars that was painful. The Void-matter put up a fight. My body feels crippled though my Crafter energy has been restored. I'm not sure I can stand."

She shivered, her body still throbbing with pain.

"That's incredible," said Fleur wonderingly. "I wonder..." she paused.

"What?"

"I wonder if you touch the lake again if it will heal your pain."

It was worth a try. Her heart beating fast, Asher stretched out her shaking hand, and touched the gleaming water.

This time coolness coursed through her body, eliminating the fire and the pain caused by the Void-matter disintegrating, and nourishing her body and spirit. The globe burst into exuberant song. Ash plunged her hand in, then wiped the drops across her face.

"How do you feel?" asked Fleur, but the question was almost pointless judging by the huge grin on Asher's face.

"I feel amazing. Are you going to stick your hand in and destroy your bracelet?"

Fleur's eyes filled with fear.

"I don't know," she said quietly. "That was incredibly intense. You are the Weaver's Heir. You wear the Golden Globe. Perhaps-" her voice shook, "perhaps I won't survive the battle."

It was a sobering thought.

In silence they sat together by the lake, soothed by its presence and buoyed by the crisp, pure air.

"Let's not risk it," said Asher eventually. "We'll find another way to get these cursed bracelets off you all. It's probably time we headed back. It feels like we've been gone for quite a while. The challenge will be sneaking back in without being discovered."

They stood up, ready to leave.

"Wait," said Ash. "Do you have a container of some sort in your pockets? Something I can collect some water in?"

Fleur dug around, pulling out a small cylinder filled with pins and needles. Carefully she took each one out and wove them through the hem of her dress. Then she handed Asher the little container.

Asher reverently dipped her hand into the lake and filled the cylinder. It was only enough for one mouthful, if a person were to drink it. But Asher had no intention of drinking it. She screwed the lid on tightly and zipped it safely away in her pocket. She felt sure this was the most precious liquid in this world, possibly this universe.

"Thank you," she whispered to the lake. "I will guard it with my life."

Minds full, the two girls wordlessly stepped through the rock-wall and made their way back up the passage. At the intersection they chose the tunnel Fleur had already marked, and she was careful to remove her ribbon and tape. There was no need to notify anyone that uninvited visitors had been exploring the caves.

"I feel like we have more questions than answers," said Ash pensively, as they ascended the final tunnel back to the house.

"Where is Levi? Where is the Void-matter being mined, and how? What is that lake? Who is hiding it so cleverly? How did it destroy the Void-matter?"

Ash did not expect Fleur to reply, and she did not.

At the top of the tunnel Ash pushed very very slightly on the cupboard door. She peeked through a tiny crack, trying to determine if anyone was in the kitchen. The coast looked clear. As quietly as possible she and Fleur climbed out of the cupboard.

They could hear the women talking in the living room. Ash looked at Fleur's dirty face and hair and imagined hers must look quite similar.

"I think we should at least try and clean some of the dirt off," she suggested, closing the cupboard door and turning to the bathroom.

She leapt in surprise and swallowed a small scream.

Marawen was standing in the doorway to the washroom, her eyes full of speculation. She raised her brows, eyeing their dusty clothes and the cobwebs in their hair.

"And what exactly have you two been up to?" she asked.

Chapter Sixteen

Allies and plans

"Well... the thing is..." Ash stopped talking. Her mind was racing and she really had no idea how she was going to explain their sudden appearance from the cupboard. As her mouth tried to form a believable story she could feel the tell-tale flush warm her neck. She had always been a dreadful liar.

Marawen stood patiently, her brows still raised. She could see their discomfort but she was not going to make it easy on them and let them off the hook.

After a minute of squirming, Asher decided the best option was to tell the truth. Well, part of the truth. She would not share the details of the lake or its effect on the Void-matter. If Mara did not ask directly about a lake of power in the heart of the caves then she would not be forced to lie. Ash felt quite comfortable with this reasoning.

"We were putting away the breakfast items, and we stumbled across a doorway to the caves. So we went exploring."

Mara's brows settled back into their normal position above her eyes. "Did you find anything of interest?"

"Yes, we found a mine where the men are working. They are mining polari."

Fleur dug into her pocket and pulled out a small piece of rock.

Mara exhaled in surprise, reaching out for the precious stone.

"This is incredible," she breathed, "polari is so rare and such a powerful gem. I could Craft something wonderful with this."

"Then it is yours," said Fleur.

Mara smiled and tucked the stone inside her own pocket. "When this damned bracelet is removed I will Craft a pendant."

The bracelets! Asher fought the urge to fiddle with hers, knowing if she did Mara would wonder how she could touch it without pain.

"We were hoping to find my friend Levi, but he was not in the mine with the others." As she said the words worry for Levi gnawed at her stomach. Where had they taken him?

"I have just boiled the kettle," said Mara, correctly reading the anxiety on Asher's face. Her voice was warm with compassion, but she offered no hollow words of comfort which Asher appreciated.

"Would you like a cup of tea?"

They both nodded eagerly.

"Then wash up and come join the group. We expect that you will be sorted soon enough," Mara said.

Mara's tone was calm and neutral but the words impacted Ash badly. Levi was already taken from them. Would she and Kate and Fleur be separated?

Troubling over what might happen, Asher washed her face and hands and brushed away the cobwebs and dust from her hair with her brush. She longed to clean her teeth but could not risk Crafting a toothbrush when the rest of the household believed she was still Void-matter impacted. She wondered when she should tell them, and how she would explain it. She rinsed her mouth, swiped away the worst of the mess from her dress, and returned to the gathered women.

Kate was sitting cross-legged on the floor, playing with the small disc on her bracelet anxiously. She looked up when Asher entered, relief clear in her eyes.

'Levi?' she mouthed.

Asher gave a slight shake of her head. Kate's face fell and she dropped her gaze back to the silver chain.

A memory tickled at the back of Asher's mind. In the kitchen this morning Kate had been touching the bracelet without any ill-effect, as she was now. That was incredibly curious. Ash made a mental note to ask her about it. Then, with the unexpected violence of a cymbal falling to the floor with a discordant clang, an idea burst into Asher's head.

If Kate could touch her bracelet perhaps she would be able to touch the others' bracelets. If so, she might be able to remove them. It was so brilliant that Ash found herself grinning like a fool. She plonked onto the floor beside Kate. Fleur joined them a few seconds later.

"Kate," said Ash in a low voice, her words meant for Kate and Fleur only, "when you touch your bracelet, what does it feel like?"

"I didn't realise I was touching it," said Kate in surprise. Tentatively she lay her right thumb against the disc.

"Nothing!" she exclaimed softly. "It feels like nothing. Well, not nothing, just a normal cold silver disc. But there is no pain at all. In fact, my whole arm feels normal." She lifted her hand up and down enthusiastically.

Mara appeared beside them with a wooden tray and plain mugs filled with steaming tea. The unadorned mugs reminded Asher of the beauty and Crafting that had been lost when E-Langren had burned. Resolutely she turned her thoughts away from that grief, to focus on the present.

"You must have travelled across the Void," said Mara.

The three girls looked up in surprise. They had not realised she had heard Kate's remarks. Kate nodded.

"And I am guessing you are not a Crafter."

Kate nodded again. Mara stared at her thoughtfully for a moment before turning her gaze to Asher.

"What about you Asher? Can you touch your bracelet?" There was an edge to her tone that warned Ash not to lie.

Slowly Asher nodded her head. "But not for the same reason that Kate can. Mine is disabled."

"How have you done that?"

Ash dropped her eyes to the floor. "I cannot tell you." She knew she was risking Marawen's trust but she felt strongly that she could not reveal the lake.

"I think it is time we had the truth from you girls. About who you are, and what you are doing here." Mara's voice was hard, suspicion flaring in her eyes.

The rest of the room had fallen silent, their attention drawn to the tense interaction now taking place. Asher looked to Edriene, seeking guidance. She was unsure if she was putting everyone at risk by revealing her relationship to the Weaver. Mara followed her gaze and scowled at the Gardener.

"Are you in on this too Edriene'wen?" she asked fiercely. "Are you keeping secrets?"

Edriene did not flinch. "It is not my tale to tell. Asher will share what she chooses to. But know this. I vouch for her. I put my trust in her. When the time comes, I will stand beside her."

The softly spoken words hung heavily in the air.

Asher felt the honesty and faith in Edriene's words nestle deep in her core. She realised she needed to offer that same honesty and faith to the women whose lives were being held to ransom for a fight they had not chosen.

"My name is Asher el Ginarwen," she said slowly, softly.

Some deep emotion raced across Marawen's face, but she stilled it quickly. Across the room Aga sucked in her breath. "That cannot be. Ginarwen died in the Void long ago. She was my friend, I knew her well."

"Then perhaps you will see her in me, though Hesta tells me I look like my great-grandfather. I was born on Earth, sixteen years ago, raised without knowing of Andera, or the Weaver, or the great Threads of Existence. One week ago I travelled across the Void with my Earth friends, Levi and Kate. We find ourselves caught in the tangled Threads."

"And who are you Fleur?" asked Mara.

"She is my cousin, somewhat removed," replied Asher. "She is the granddaughter of Myrtawen, Hesta's cousin, but she is not a Crafter."

She fell silent, allowing time for everyone to process her revelations.

"And you Asher? Are you a Crafter?" asked Fruda in a quiet voice.

Rather than answer, Asher stood and went into the kitchen. There she unhooked the small violin charm. She ran the bow over the strings to check the tuning, noting without surprise that it was ready to play.

She returned to the living room, enjoying the surprise on everyone's faces when they saw the bow and violin in her hands.

"Yes I am a Crafter," she replied, and lifted the bow to play.

It had been so long since she had held a violin in her hands. Asher relished the sharp sound of each chirpy note. As she played she Crafted, sending her energy around the room. In her mind's eye she could see the streams of colourful notes as they flowed from the bow. For many minutes her music swirled around the space, lightening the heavy atmosphere and teasing their spirits. When the Crafting was done Asher removed the violin from beneath her chin and lowered the bow.

The women looked at each other, initially with bemusement and then with joy, as they realised what she had done.

They were all clean. Their dresses were no longer dirty and stained; they were restored to their original state. The old, faded

armchairs were renewed; their fabric as fresh and colourful as
the day they had been made; their cushions soft and plump once
more. The carpet beneath their feet had reclaimed its deep pile,
glowing golden in the lamplight.

Everywhere they looked everything was beautiful. The paint
on the walls was refreshed, making the room brighter than before. The once dingy curtains were lively and colourful, adding
vibrancy to the previously gloomy space. As the women exclaimed in pleasure and shock, Asher stepped into the kitchen
and returned the instrument to the bracelet. She would offer no
explanation for its appearance and disappearance.

She returned to the living room and every face turned her
way.

"I am Asher el Ginarwen, granddaughter of the Weaver. I am
an Earth human and I am a Crafter."

"You are the missing Heir," said Mara in wonder.

Asher nodded.

Mixed emotions ran across the faces of the women looking
at her. Fruda was beaming and Edriene smiling proudly. Mara
seemed relieved, but there was also uncertainty. Aga and Isobel
shifted uneasily, their faces clouded. Finally Aga burst out.

"The Weaver has abandoned us! She attacked the Queen and
tarred us all with her traitorous act. You pose a great risk to us.
All of us. We should turn you over to the guards in exchange for
our release."

Kate leapt up, her eyes blazing.

"None of that is true! None of it. How dare you speak
to Asher that way. It is not the Weaver and Heir against the
Crafters. We are suffering too. Levi is taken. Ash found a way
to dismantle the Void-matter, which means she could bust out
of here and leave any time she wanted, but instead she is risking
everything to find the Weaver and save Andera. This is not our
war! Don't you see what Darven and the Queen are doing? They

are tearing you all apart! Maybe we should just go back to Earth and close the damn portals. Leave you all here to rot!"

Her fury spent, she burst into tears and turned away from the shocked group. Fleur immediately went to her and wrapped her in a hug. Uneasy silence followed Kate's outburst. The distress in Aga and Kate's voices and the pain on their faces was a stark reminder that emotions were high and people were at their limit.

A moment later, Mara spoke up.

"Kate is absolutely right. We cannot turn on each other. Do you honestly think the guards will release you Aga? You will be just as imprisoned as you are now, but without the power the Heir offers."

Aga's face flushed.

"Asher is a secret we must all swear to keep, to protect," continued Marawen. "Without the Weaver she is the beacon of light for the Crafters of Andera. She is our hope."

The Jeweller turned to Asher, her blue eyes gleaming as brightly as her jewels.

"When I had nothing, Hestawen offered me everything. I swore allegiance to the Weaver and her Heirs, and I will honour my oath," she said softly, her voice true. "Whatever comes Asher el Ginarwen, I will stand beside you."

Fruda came forward and reached for Asher's hands, giving them a squeeze. She offered the same promise, with great gusto. As did Isobel, far more shyly. A thick knot of gratitude and overwhelm settled in Asher's chest and she swallowed thickly, humbled and terrified by their faith in her.

Aga hung back, her eyes clouded with inner conflict. After a minute she shook her head.

"I cannot make such a vow," she whispered, her voice husky with pain. "I have lost too much already, and the Weaver has not protected me or mine. Why should I offer such loyalty to her?"

Asher nodded in understanding, but had no words to offer in reply.

Kate turned her blotchy red face back to the group. "I'm really sorry for my outburst," she said hoarsely. "I just feel so helpless and out of my depth, and now Levi is gone."

Her eyes swam with tears and she took a shuddering breath. "But please believe me. The Weaver is not the villain in any of this. Your Queen and Darven are weaving a complicated plot, and we are all victims of it."

Mara nodded. "I think it's time we heard the whole story. Asher, please tell us what has been going on."

So Asher gave them a brief summary of who she was and how she had come to Andera. She told them about her mother the Painter, raising her on Earth away from the Weaver and her Threads. Of Evie, her non-Crafter sister, kidnapped by mistake and the decision for Asher to cross the Void and rescue her. And finally of the attack on Hesta and her disappearance.

By the time she had finished the gathered Wens looked grim.

"This is extremely concerning," said Fruda, her brow furrowed.

"Why would the Queen and Darven want to eliminate the Weaver?" asked Edriene. "I cannot make sense of it."

"Neither can we," said Asher. "She had no intention to interfere in his kingly ambitions. She told me herself."

Mara stood up and paced around the small room, then disappeared into the kitchen. Her body brimmed with agitation. She clearly wanted a moment alone.

"On a completely other topic. I think we should try and remove your bracelets," said Asher.

"What?" exclaimed Fruda.

"How?" asked Isobel.

"I think Kate will be able to unclip them," explained Asher. "It's worth a try."

Eagerly Edriene thrust out her arm. "Absolutely worth a try!"

With a small amount of trepidation, Kate put her fingers on Edriene's bracelet, bracing herself for the shock and pain. But nothing came. More confidently she unclipped the silver clasp.

Edriene gasped in relief as the small chain fell from her wrist and was left dangling in Kate's fingers.

Edriene shook her hand and raised her arm up and down. On impulse she reached into her pocket and drew out a small handful of seeds. She threw them into the air and blew on them as they fell. Instantly they transformed into small white flowers, that drifted through the small room, carried by her breath.

Everyone laughed with pleasure.

"ME!" shouted Fruda, holding out her arm.

Kate grinned as she unclipped the young woman's bracelet.

"Woohoo!" celebrated the Baker, dancing a small jig as she waved her arms around. The others had to duck away from her flailing limbs, but they did not mind. Everyone pulsed with excitement.

Isobel and Aga followed, both laughing as the dreaded Void-matter was removed and their Crafter energy returned.

Mara returned from the kitchen, keen so see what all the frivolity was about. Soon enough both her and Fleur's bracelets were removed. Mara closed her eyes and lifted her hands above her head, relishing the feeling of her arms moving without pain.

"The first thing I am going to do is lay a perception filter on the room," said Mara. "We cannot risk the guards barging in here and discovering our refurbished prison. All will be revealed then."

Edriene offered her help, and the two Wens moved around the room, layering their energy. Asher watched them carefully but could not see any changes in the room, it looked to her just as she had made it.

After the celebrations had died down the women settled back into the living room with far more optimism and hope than they had felt for a while.

"So what do we do now? Attack the guards? Sneak off? Try and release the others?" asked Fruda.

Mara shook her head.

"Trying to leave Groush on the mountains pass is virtually impossible. I do not know how we could do that without being pursued, and we would have to leave the women and girls in the other huts behind. I am sure none of us want to do that. I shudder to think what punishment they would receive for our escape. I think…" she paused, as she sorted through her thoughts. "I think we need to find a way to end this, once and for all."

Asher and Kate nodded, but the others were dumbstruck. They glanced at each other.

"Us?" squeaked Fruda. "What can we do? Darven has defeated the Weaver. She is more powerful than all of us combined. If she can fall, then how are we to succeed?"

"More importantly, *why* should we?" said Aga, her face flat. "My family are dead. My town has turned its back on me. There is nothing for me here. I am happy to leave and cross the Void. Settle far away."

Mara's eyes were sad. "I do not think you can outrun this Aga. If the Weaver is not found and the Threads tangle and tear beyond repair, then every life-form in the five universes will feel the impact. Across the galaxies new stars will cease to be born. Supernovas and black holes will form where they were never intended to form. Storms will roil across the cosmos. For the planets of power it will be catastrophic."

Asher's ears pricked up.

"What are the planets of power?" she asked.

The Crafters looked at each other.

"The structure of the five universes is not common knowl-edge," replied Edriene. "It is part of advanced Crafter studies. Clearly you have not reached that point in your Wen training."

Asher shook her head. "No. My training was interrupted," she said drily.

"Then we will try and resume it," smiled Mara. "We need our Heir trained for the battle ahead."

Her tone was light, but the words sent shivers down Asher's spine. War and prophecy, prophecy and war... was there a way to escape it? All she could think was to find Hesta. The Weaver would know what to do. Asher needed to get back into the caves. She needed to find the doors to the planets and the Beyond.

"I think..." she stopped, embarrassed when all eyes turned her way. She cleared her throat. "I think as a first step we need to explore the caves further, see if there is a way through the mountains that we can use to escape. We might even find the Void-matter mine and be able to shut it down."

Isobel and Fruda, the youngest of the Wens, looked uncertain. Mara and Edriene nodded in agreement.

"It is a good place to start," said Mara. "Asher, you and I will investigate. Edriene, you keep an eye on the activity of the guards. If it appears they will discover our absence then do what you need to do. If we can find a way to get through the mountains we might be able to seek safety with the people of the great plains."

Asher swallowed a protest. She had been hoping she and Fleur would have the opportunity to search for the Beyond. But she had no way to disagree with Mara without disclosing her greater plan.

"There is one thing I would like to do before night falls," said Edriene. "I would like to find my niece. If we are planning an escape and a fight then I want her by my side, where I can protect her."

"And I want to find Levi," added Kate.

"How to you propose to do that?" asked Aga. "Do you think you can just wander out there into the square and go from house to house? Knock on the doors, call out their names? Hmmmm?"

An idea bubbled into Asher's head and she grinned.

"What if we don't even need to leave the cottage?" she said excitedly, her smile wide. "It's a terraced row of huts. We could simply Craft our way through the walls."

Chapter Seventeen

The Day Before

Asher's suggestion generated much discussion among the group. Some comments were supportive while others were more sceptical. Concerns about how they could actually break through the walls without alerting the guards or injuring some-one on the other side were top of the list.

Ash had to swallow her impatience a number of times as the pros and cons of her suggestion were debated. Eventually she left the experienced Crafters to decide on how it could be done and went into one of the bedrooms for some space and quiet.

The bedroom was small, which was to be expected considering the size of the house. Three single beds were crammed into the room, with a very small space between each bed. Her Crafting had not encompassed this room, so it remained drab and uninspiring, the furnishings worn and dull.

She chose the flute this time and blew an upbeat melody of rejuvenation and new life. She was really pleased at the level of control she was managing to maintain. When she was finished and the room was gleaming and bright, Asher lay on one of the beautiful quilt covers and stared at the ceiling. Now that she was lying down, weariness settled like a cloud around her and the temptation to close her eyes and rest was too hard to resist. It felt like a lifetime since she had experienced a good, restorative sleep, with a calm mind and a comfortable body. And though her mind was far from calm, the newly plumped pillow and soft mattress offered the comfort her body sorely craved, and soon Asher was asleep.

Aggressive thumping on the door to the hut woke her with a start. She sat up too quickly and her head spun as she struggled to wake up. Gruff voices in the other room were met by the quiet tones of Mara, and then the door banged shut.

Within a few seconds the bedroom door swung open. Mara and Edriene stood in the small doorway.

"It looks like our plans will have to move faster than we might like," said Marawen. "The guards have advised that Darven arrives tomorrow. They took great pleasure in letting us know that he takes Crafters and they never return. It appears this is merely a sorting pen." Her voice was bitter.

Darven. Just the thought of him being in Groush made Asher's stomach roil with nausea and fear. She swung her feet over the side of the bed and stood up, taking a few deep breaths to wake up.

"I suggest you have something to eat Asher and then you and Mara get moving into the caves. See what you can discover," said Edriene. "Aga, Isobel, Fruda and I will work out how to create doorways into the other cottages. Even if we cannot escape through the caves at least we can get everyone together, remove their bracelets and make a stand."

The words were simply said, but the meaning was clear. Tomorrow the Crafters would bring the fight to Darven. Asher shivered.

In the kitchen Fruda had baked up a storm. With her Crafting restored she was able to create beautiful pastries, breads, fruit-loaves and pies from incredibly simple ingredients. From the soil of a droopy pot-plant Edriene had Crafted fresh carrots and cucumbers, and shiny red apples.

Asher ate her fill, thanking both Crafters for the abundance of good food. Fruda smiled at her appreciation and set to work baking yet more loaves and pies.

"What is all that for?" asked Kate curiously.

"For the others, when we reach them. I'm sure they have not been well-fed," was Fruda's reply. It was a glum thought. "And also, for our escape through the caves. Always best to have supplies."

Marawen entered the small kitchen, which meant Kate and Fruda had to shuffle out to the living room.

"Alright Asher, show me this doorway to the caves. We must make haste."

She blew a low whistle of appreciation when Asher showed her the cupboard.

"That is certainly a powerful perception filter," Mara said, angling her head back and forth to admire the depth of the charm. "Even very experienced Crafters would be fooled by that. We certainly were while wearing the Void-matter."

She smiled at Asher. "Lead on."

Kate and Fruda watched from the doorway as Ash and Mara climbed into the cupboard and disappeared.

"Kate would you please monitor the pies, remove them from the oven when they are golden and brown," said Fruda, wiping her floury hands on her dress. "It's time to break through some walls."

***

Down through the tunnels Asher led Mara, to the first intersection. She pointed to the left passage.

"That way is crumbling and blocked. It seems abandoned. That one, to the right, led us to the polari mine. In the cavern of the mine there were other passages. One of them might lead us to the Void-matter."

Mara nodded, and the two of them continued down to the mine. They paused warily at the opening of the tunnel, but it was quickly apparent that the quarry was empty, the men having finished for the day. Still, they did not want to be foolish, so slowly and silently they emerged from the passage and walked into the large cavern.

Mara's attention was drawn to the heavy rock wall that had been hacked into small pieces. She fossicked among the pieces on the ground, picking up and discarding fragments. Many of the stones were nothing more than rock, but every now and then the Jeweller called out with excitement. Soon she had four pieces of stone in her hands. To Ash they looked pretty much the same as the pieces she had discarded, but from the joy on Mara's face she supposed they contained polari.

"There is not much left here to mine," Mara said. "Which is both a shame and a good thing. We do not want too much of this gem in Darven's hands. I dread to think how much he has already collected. But I am happy with my little find." She smiled and tucked her treasure into her deep pockets.

Asher eyed the tunnels leading out of the quarry. She was torn. The well-lit tunnel might lead to Levi. The dark tunnel might lead to further caves and tunnels, and possibly the Weaver, or escape.

Down here in the caves time was hard to measure. If they were not careful they could be exploring for hours, and risk the guards discovering their absence.

Mara seemed to sense her uncertainty. "You want to find your friend," she said.

Asher nodded, her throat thick.

"Then let us try that first. Too many of our friends are lost, we must save the ones we can."

Ash nodded again, unable to speak past the emotion in her throat. She was grateful for Mara's understanding and support.

They headed up the brightly lit tunnel, treading as lightly as they possibly could, all their senses heightened. As they neared the top the passageway grew lighter, indicating that daylight was not too far ahead. They slowed their steps, even more cautious. And their caution was rewarded. The sound of voices outside the tunnel entrance stopped them in their tracks.

Asher indicated to Mara that she would creep ahead and see what she could see. Mara nodded in agreement, mouthing 'be careful'.

Moving slowly, and barely breathing, Asher rounded the bend at the top of the passage and reached the opening. It was not a big entrance; many of the guards would not be able to squeeze through the narrow break in the rock. Carefully she edged as close as she dared.

She was looking at the open square of Groush. On the far side was the row of huts where the Crafters were being held. To the right were the stables and a collection of houses. Still small and plain, but in better repair than the prison huts. Asher supposed that was where the guards lived.

Two of those guards were seated nearby at a faded and badly maintained wooden table. They were not monitoring the entrance of the cave, instead they were playing some type of card game and drinking from two foul smelling flagons. They argued over the play and the scoring, each gulp from the flagon adding fire to their tempers and language.

There was no sign of Levi, or any of the other men. The disappointment cut deep.

She crept back to Mara and shared what she had seen. The Wen thought silently then she smiled.

"I think we should seal in the entrance," she said, "so they cannot access the caves. That will give us more time when we bring the women down here to escape."

"What if there are other entrances?" asked Ash.

"We can only deal with what we know," said Mara.

This was entirely reasonable and it was a good plan. But part of her felt despondent that she had not found and rescued Levi. She feared that closing this entrance meant she might not find another way to him.

"How should we create the rockfall?" she asked. "Playing any of my instruments will draw too much attention."

The Jeweller smiled. "Leave that to me. I suggest you move back."

Asher watched in fascination as Mara closed her eyes and took a deep breath. When she opened her eyes she was glowing with energy. The rings on her fingers gleamed, radiating power. The Wen raised her arm and pointed a finger at the passage ahead of them. She whispered under her breath, commanding the rocks to crumble and fall.

An ominous cracking filled the air. Ash took a few hasty steps back. The walls around them began to shudder.

"And now we run," said Mara, picking up her long skirt and heading back down the passage.

Asher did not need to be told twice. She followed the small woman quickly, slipping and sliding on the stone floor which had been well-polished by thousands of boot clad footfalls. They skidded to a halt back in the cavern, the last of the rock-fall still echoing among the dust it had created.

"That was incredible," said Ash, still breathing heavily from the run and the adrenaline rush.

Mara gave a small bow.

"Are all Wens that powerful?"

"Mostly, depending on the Craft," said Mara. "And you will be too, probably even more so. What you achieved with your violin was extraordinary. Imagine what you will be able to do when you can Craft without your instruments."

Asher blinked in surprise.

"Craft *without* my instruments? How?"

Mara smiled at her and raised an eyebrow. "That is the secret of Wen training. Once we are free of this place we must begin in earnest. If you are a true Wen, it will be possible. If not, then you will still be a powerful Musician. Right now, let us see what the other passage offers."

Asher followed the Jeweller as she moved across the quarry and into the mouth of the other tunnel. Her mind was buzzing. It had never occurred to her that she could learn to Craft without an instrument in her hand.

This tunnel was not lit and certainly not regularly used, but it was accessible. Ash remembered she still had her phone in her pocket and pulled that out, turning on the torch.

Mara's eyebrows shut up.

"It's an Earth gadget," said Asher.

With the tunnel no longer encased in darkness they could see that it ran for miles ahead of them. They continued on for another fifteen minutes, but it became apparent that they could walk indefinitely without encountering a cross-road or another cavern.

"What do you think?" asked Ash.

"I hope this is probably part of an extensive tunnel system that may take us through the mountains. But I cannot say for sure. I do not know if there is value in us continuing this path today. We could stray too far from the village."

Reluctantly Asher agreed. She was feeling hot and bothered in the stale air of the tunnel and frustration was gnawing at her. They had not found Levi. They had not established a sure escape route through the mountains, and she was no closer to finding the door to the Beyond and Hesta than she had been a day ago.

She scowled as she and Mara retraced their steps, kicking stones and stomping in annoyance. The older woman said nothing and Asher was glad of it. She wanted to wallow in her anger and frustration.

Ash did not know how much time had passed when she and Mara climbed back through the cupboard, but at least her temper had settled. Kate and Fleur were waiting with Isobel in the living room, but the others were not there.

"Where is everyone?" asked Ash.

The girls grinned. "They have almost broken through the first wall. They are in the bedroom. We are on look-out duty."

Marawen hurried into the bedroom, keen to see what had happened in their absence. Ash slumped into one of the armchairs and stared into the low flames of the fire.

"I cannot find Levi," she said in resignation. "I think he is in one of the huts near the stables, but short of walking across the square I don't know how to reach him."

"We'll work it out," said Kate, trying to be encouraging, but there was fear in her voice.

There was no time to wallow, as a cry of joy flowed from the bedroom. The girls jumped up and crowded around the little doorway.

Edriene was hugging a young girl so tightly it seemed she might snap her spine. Both of them were crying, and laughing, and talking a million words a minute. Then they fell silent and just held each other. The little girl's tears of happiness were soon consumed by huge sobs of released fear and anxiety.

Edriene held her niece close, absorbing all that emotion. "All is well now Metka. You are safe. I will keep you safe."

The girl nodded in her arms, trusting the word of her aunt. Her sobs eased. Above Metka's head Edriene's fearful gaze met Asher's, piercing her deep in the heart. Edriene was making a promise that she did not know how she could keep, and Asher understood that all too well. But at least there was hope. Edriene had found Metka.

One by one the women and girls in the hut were embraced by the Wens. Fruda passed around cakes and pies which were eagerly consumed. Kate handed out apples and cucumbers, which were snatched out of her hands. After days of small amounts of poor quality food the captives were ravenous.

Mara, Fruda and Edriene took charge of the seven women in the second hut. After they were fed, the Wens sat with them in the little living room and explained what was happening. They did not tell them who Asher was, or about the escape plan through the caves. They just spoke of uniting them all together.

Asher noticed they did not offer to remove their Void-bracelets, and it had not yet occurred to the less powerful Crafters to ask how the Wens had crafted through the wall.

When Mara returned through the hole to their side she asked her directly.

"Would you like Kate to remove their bracelets?"

Marawen shook her head. "No," she said quietly, "They are exhausted and frightened and very susceptible to the bullying and threats of the guards. If they are too scared I fear they will reveal all our secrets. Tonight everyone needs to eat well and rest well. First thing in the morning we will begin the evacuation. If there is trouble, we five Wens will handle the guards and Darven. Your job will be to lead the women through the caves."

Asher's hackles immediately rose. She did not want to skulk away, leaving Mara, Edriene, Fruda, Aga and Isobel to face the danger.

"But-"

Mara held up a hand to cut her off. "I do not want Darven to know of your existence."

Asher swallowed the words of argument that were tumbling around her mouth. There was no point in arguing about it now.

For the next few hours the Wens worked quietly and carefully at the thick stone wall between hut number two and hut number three. With Mara now here to help, Fruda was able to return to the kitchen and continue baking, in anticipation of feeding the hungry women on the other side of that wall.

Small stone piece by small stone piece they opened the hole, creating another huge pile of rubble. Ash wondered where any of them would sleep that night, as the bedrooms were covered in dust and stone.

She sat in the filthy bedroom of their little house, a room that only hours ago she had restored to beauty. Everyone was occupied elsewhere; she was alone and unobserved. She would make the space lovely for the exhausted women. She pulled out the flute and closed her eyes.

This time she deliberately set the intention before she started to play. She wanted to reduce each large block to one tiny glass bead and clean up the dust and mess.

With the image clear in her head Asher raised the flute and blew gently, finding the right music. She played and she played, fighting against the heavy energy of the rocks, wrestling them into submission, forcing them to release their very forms and shrink into something made of glass and reduced to the size of a pebble. She was careful not to sink into the energy of the stones, instead she fought to master it with her own. She pulled deeper and deeper from her own energy, as the tussle continued. Finally, exhausted, light-headed and gasping for breath, Asher pulled the flute away from her mouth and opened her eyes to see what she had Crafted.

The room was clean and fresh once more. A small pile of glass beads gathered neatly on the floor. But she had pushed too far. Her body swayed; black spots danced before her eyes. With a small 'humph' Ash collapsed onto the nearest bed.

A cold cloth on her face brought her back to consciousness. Mara helped her sit back up and Asher held the cold cloth to her forehead, hoping to ease the pounding. It did not seem to help, and soon enough her stomach joined the affray, roiling dangerously.

"Here, drink this." Edriene passed her a mug full of fresh apple juice. The sugar in the cold drink soon did its job, sending a rush of energy through her system. The headache eased, leaving only a dull aching. That would not bother her. An aching head had become a regular companion since she had arrived on Andera.

Her stomach settled enough that she was no longer in danger of vomiting all over the Jeweller.

"What were you thinking?" scolded Mara fiercely. "That was incredibly dangerous. You are very lucky you did not consume your life-force."

Asher was surprised by Mara's intensity.

"I don't know what you mean," she said. "I was only removing the rocks and cleaning the room."

Mara shook her head. "No you weren't *removing* the rocks. You were *changing* the rocks. Altering their cellular level, forcing them to be something other than what they are. That is extremely difficult and ill-advised. It's like you were *trying* to destroy yourself," she said crossly, her face red and her eyes blazing.

Edriene laid a steadying hand on Mara's arm.

"But she did not," she said calmly. "And indeed, she did alter the composition of the rocks. An incredible feat, though foolhardy."

Asher looked from one Wen to the other, her confusion clear on her face.

"But I've seen you both alter things. Edriene you grew vegetables in a matter of seconds. Mara you created a rockfall from a wall of solid rock."

"That is completely different," said Edriene. "We took an existing object and found the energy within it and coerced it into a new shape of the same cellular structure. For example, my seeds already have the imprint of the vegetables within them, that possibility already exists. I am merely crafting that possibility into being. Manipulating what exists into another version of itself. It is easy to *grow* one thing into another version of itself. Mara creating a rockfall is simply asking the rock to no longer be over here, but to now be over there. There is no change to the entity itself, merely its location. What you did was to force a very old piece of energy into a completely different shape and structure, reducing it, *diminishing* it, changing it. It would have been easier to turn them to dust. Do you understand what I mean?"

Asher was not sure if she understood or not. There was sense in what Edriene was saying, but she still had so many questions that she could not articulate. Her mind was too dulled to make sense of them. Gingerly Asher stretched her back and rolled her shoulders, wincing as her body ached with weariness. Her energy levels were so low she was struggling to sit upright. The idea of standing seemed overwhelming.

Edriene seemed to understand. "We will discuss this more later. There is much you need training on, but this is not the time nor place."

She stood up. "We are through to the final cottage. There are only five women in there, including the three from the Weaver's village. Apparently there were another five but they were removed two days ago."

Edriene's kind face was filled with sadness. "Most of these are simple women. Crafters of low-level ability, using their Crafting purely in the context of village life, to sew a neater line, to fix a broken pot, to soothe a crying baby. They pose no threat to anyone, and particularly not a sorcerer and a Queen."

The three of them looked at each other, the same thoughts swirling around each of their heads. This had gone on too long. The weak had been stolen and abused, caught up in Darven's twisted schemes. But no longer. They could not wait for the Weaver to return, they needed to act now; to face Darven's power with their strength.

They were going to create a new possibility in the Threads. From tomorrow a new weave would be woven.

Chapter Eighteen

The Escape

The afternoon was spent meeting and feeding the women and girls from the other cottages, as well as cleaning up the rock debris by pushing under the beds, rather than Crafting it into marbles. Mara and Edriene spent considerable time layering perception filters on each of the openings. They did not want to risk discovery by the guards this close to freedom.

There was much animated chatter and sharing of stories. Who they were, where they were from, how long they had been in Groush. It turned out that no-one had been there for more than a few days. It was simply a 'holding pen' as Mara had rather caustically described it.

The incredibly thick stone walls which had taken such effort to breach provided exceptional soundproofing, which was important considering the amount of chatter and laughing taking place inside the cottages, despite Edriene's regular requests to 'hush'.

They now numbered twenty in total, a rather unwieldy group when considering their escape plans. If Marawen was concerned she hid it well, maintaining an air of calm and confidence.

Kate and Fleur helped where they could, but Asher's energy levels were low. She felt unusually exhausted, and eventually retreated to the second bedroom for some quiet and rest. Kate and Fleur joined her soon after.

The bedroom was even smaller than the other one, with two beds crammed against each other. Asher had no energy left to transform the room, so they sat on the faded, grimy bedspreads and avoiding staring at the peeling paint and mucky walls. A particularly vile gloopy stain on the ragged curtains made Kate heave. She screwed up her face and turned her back to the offending material.

"So what's the plan?" asked Kate softly, unintentionally mimicking Levi. She realised it immediately, and her eyes filled with tears, which she roughly swiped away.

Asher squeezed her hand. "Mara wants everyone to sleep well tonight, and then before the dawn tomorrow we will leave through the caves."

Kate's face blanched. "The possibility of me sleeping well tonight just evaporated."

"Did you find the way through?" asked Fleur.

Ash glanced at Kate and hesitated. If she told the truth, that they were *hoping* they could find a way, then Kate would never willingly descend into the tunnels. But if she lied, would Kate trust her again? It was a risk she had to take. Kate being angry with her was better than Kate left behind.

"Yes," she said.

The other girls grinned with relief.

"And Levi?" said Kate.

Asher looked at the closed door, reassuring herself that even Mara could not hear through walls.

"Once everyone is settled tonight, I'm going to find him," she whispered.

"I think you mean *we're* going to find him," replied Kate sternly.

Asher did not mean that at all, so she chose to change the subject instead.

"I can't believe how tired I am," she said. On cue a huge yawn split her face and she curled up on the lumpy mattress.

"I'll just close my eyes for a moment," she murmured as her friends crept out of the room. Within a few breaths Asher was fast asleep.

She was woken the next morning by Mara, before the dawn.

Asher pulled back the grimy curtain an inch and peered into the silent square, feeling frustrated and annoyed. Damnation! She had slept through the night and lost her opportunity to find Levi.

Fog lay heavily on the village of Groush, giving it an atmosphere of otherworldly gloom. Ash shivered. She hoped it was not indicative of how the day would end.

"We must get everyone into the caves," whispered Mara, "I'll rouse the other cottages."

Stuck against the far wall, Ash considered Kate and Fleur who were asleep on the bed between her and the door. Either she would have to climb over them, or they had to wake up and move. She gave Kate a light shake. Kate stretched and grumbled. Without opening her eyes she rolled over and settled back into sleep.

Asher gave her a sharp pinch on the soft skin of her underarm.

"Ouch!" Kate's eyes flew open.

"Oh good, you're awake. We need to get up and moving."

Kate glared at her, and opened her mouth to protest, but her words were swallowed by a giant yawn. Beside her Fleur sat up and scooted off the bed. Yawning and stretching the three of them stumbled into the living room.

Mugs of coffee and fresh pastries were waiting on the dining table. The Wens were already clustered there, sipping and murmuring quietly to each other, Metka glued to Edriene's side.

Asher's stomach roiled at the thought of eating and drinking this early in the morning, but she forced a few bites. The day ahead was uncertain; they may not eat again for a while. She chose a mug of water instead of the bitter smelling coffee.

Around them the room started to fill with sleepy and confused Crafters. When all twenty women and girls were crammed into the rooms of the cottage Mara cleared her throat.

"Good morning to you all," she said quietly. "Today will be a strange day, as have been the days that preceded it. Today we are leaving this place, we are escaping."

A murmur of excitement and fear rose and fell like a wave through the group.

"All will be explained once we are safely far away. For now I ask that you trust us to lead you from here."

The women looked at each other and slowly nodded. There was nothing left to lose by trusting Marawen. Staying here meant certain torture or even death. They had all heard the stories.

"Are we climbing the paths over the mountains?" asked one woman nervously. The mountain paths were known to be treacherous even for those who were well prepared and in good weather.

"We will be travelling through the caves." Mara replied.

The caves! The murmur increased in volume. Most of them had not been aware that caves even existed, and for many of them the idea of being in them was daunting.

"Where will we go?" asked another woman timidly. "Nowhere is safe."

"We will travel through the mountains to the Great Plains and seek refuge there."

The murmurs exploded into a muddle of words and exclamations. The Great Plains...

"Shhhh...." hissed Marawen. "The walls are thick but we must still take care. This is Asher. She will lead you through the caves."

All eyes turned to Ash. The familiar glaze of 'Oh, I didn't see you there' was reflected on many of the faces. They lost interest in her soon enough and returned their attention to Mara.

"When do we leave?" asked another voice.

"As soon as we are able," replied Mara.

"*Quietly,*" she added as the chatter rose once again. "Make use of the bathrooms, gather what belongings you have. Collect some food from Fruda."

Quiet chaos followed this announcement as the Crafters bumped and knocked against each other, trying to navigate the small spaces in a rush.

Marawen murmured quietly to Asher. "After you lead the group into the caves, Aga, Edriene and I will seal all the windows and doors. Then we will follow you in. All going well we should be long gone before Darven arrives. By the time they break into the cottages it will be as if we vanished into thin air." She smiled reassuringly.

Asher returned the smile, but she could not shake the gnawing fear that it would not be that easy. And once the women were safe she still needed to find Levi.

Thirty minutes later the group was finally ready, clustered together silently in the living room once more. Fleur was on watch at the window in the small bedroom, peering through a tiny crack in the curtain. The soft dawn had finally penetrated the fog, which was slowly drifting away. All was still and calm.

"It's time," said Mara softly.

She stood at the cupboard doorway and pointed a bejewelled finger. Her rings flared. The cupboard shook a little, then settled, just as it was. Mara frowned.

"The charm is stronger than I expected. And old. The energy has deepened and strengthened over the years. I may not be able to open it without major destruction."

Aga shuffled her way between the milling bodies to stand beside Mara. They raised their hands together. The cupboard rattled and the door flew open, but still the perception filter remained and the narrow structure held. Breathing deeply, Mara and Aga conceded defeat. They could not risk blowing it open and perhaps damaging the cottage.

"You will have to climb in and squeeze through," Mara told the group.

Uneasy murmurs greeted this directive. No-one was keen on climbing into a dark cupboard. Kate stepped forward.

"Asher will go first," she said, "then you." She pointed at the woman nearest to her. "Followed by you and you." More finger pointing. "Then me, then you, you and you. Everyone else follow behind. Fleur will bring up the rear. Got it?"

Everyone nodded. Ash grinned. Kate waggled a finger at her. "Let's go."

Trying to be as quiet as possible, the women and girls followed Kate's instructions. One by one they climbed through the cupboard and into the tunnel. Metka lingered behind, holding tight to her aunt, reluctant to be parted from her. Edriene kissed the top of her forehead and gave her a slight push.

"Go. I will join you soon."

Ash led the group down to the first junction, where they paused for a headcount. Fifteen, including her. Only Mara, Edriene, Aga and Fruda were to stay behind. Some-one else was missing.

"Fleur," Kate said suddenly, "Fleur is not here."

It was the excuse Asher needed to return to the surface and find Levi. She pointed at the right hand tunnel.

"Walk down there. You will come to a large cavern, a quarry. Wait for us there. I'll go back and check what is happening. Kate, when you get to the quarry remove their bracelets. Kate and Isobel are in charge."

Kate and Isobel nodded solemnly, herding the others down the tunnel. Asher turned and sprinted back the way they had come.

***

The remaining three women were waiting to climb into the cupboard when Fleur heard the horses trot into the square. The last of the mist lifted as Darven and two Squad Leaders rode in. One of whom looked awfully familiar.

The ride up the Mountain path must have been terrifying in the fog, as the Squad Leaders looked decidedly grey. Darven looked as confident and handsome as he had at Ostrin when he had defeated the Weaver.

Fleur's heart sank. She crawled over the beds to the doorway.

"Marawen," she hissed. "Darven is here."

The colour leeched from Mara's face. "Make haste," she called softly to the Wens who were sealing the doors and windows in the other huts.

She climbed over to the window Fleur had been spying through and sealed the window shut. If she felt an increase in the energy around her, it never occurred to Mara that Fleur was the source.

The living room window was sealed next. Then the two of them cracked open the front door less than an inch, to watch and listen.

The soft aura of energy behind them drew Mara's attention. She frowned in disapproval when she saw Asher, but with the door open she dared not say a word. She scowled fiercely instead, shaking her head. Ash crept up beside them, deliberately avoiding eye contact with the Jeweller.

Across the square the door to the Guard House flew open.

Six men stumbled through the door, pushing each other in the haste. Some were pulling on their coats, others their boots. They assembled themselves into a raggedy line. One was still holding his mug. When he realised, his eyes flared in horror and he flung it away in panic, flinching as it smashed against the rock.

From atop his horse Darven eyed the line silently, his face impassive.

After a long, tense perusal, Darven twisted gracefully and leapt off his horse. The two Squad Leaders followed suit, far more awkwardly. One of the guards hurried forward and grasped the reins, leading the three horses towards the stables.

Asher could almost feel his relief at having an excuse to be far from their illustrious, terrifying leader.

"What news?" asked that same dread leader. "The Polari Mine."

A guard stepped forward, his body shaking.

"We have mined one hundred grams," he squeaked nervously.

"Bring it to me."

The man hurried back into the Guard House, returning a minute later with a small pouch. He placed it in Darven's outstretched hand. The sorcerer held it carefully, judging its weight. Then he opened the sack and poured a few pieces into his open palm.

"I am pleased," he said. "You have done well."

He returned the pieces to the pouch and tucked it into his large black coat. From another pocket he pulled out a handful of gold coins. He threw them at the guard, who scrambled to catch them. The guard's eyes gleamed as he clutched the gold.

"Thank you Your Great Exellencyness," he said.

"Next report," demanded Darven. "Tell me what Wens you hold captive."

Two guards stepped forward, eager to give their update in anticipation of being well rewarded.

"We captured the Lady Marawen. She has evaded other Squads as you know, but we weren't going to be beaten by the likes of her. She put up a fight, so we used the dust you gave us, and it paralysed her long enough to clap the bracelet on her wrist."

They beamed proudly.

"And her jewellery?" asked Darven, "Did you bring that?"

"Yes sir. She is wearing it, but unable to use any of it." They laughed viciously.

Darven nodded approvingly and smiled. An unpleasant twisting of his mouth that sent shivers down the spines of the hidden watchers.

"Excellent," he cooed. "I have plans for the lovely Lady Marawen. And her jewels."

He threw another handful of gold at the two puffed-up guards who shoved and pushed at each other in their greed. Mara was practically shaking with fury.

"We should leave now," whispered Edriene.

Reluctantly Mara nodded. She was itching to fling a bolt of energy at Darven's cold face, but she knew escape was the right decision for now.

The guard who had brought Asher and her friends to Groush stepped forward, desperate to be rewarded for his own ill-deeds.

"I have the Weaver's grandson," he blurted.

Asher froze.

Darven stared him up and down. "Who are you?"

"He's one of mine Lord," said the brutish Squad Leader quickly as he swaggered forward, keen to be included in any praise and gold.

"I see. And you have the Weaver's *grandson* you say," said Darven carefully.

"Yes sir," they replied in unison, puffing out their chests.

"Well bring him out then," said Darven, his face still and his voice cool.

The guard rushed off to another building beside the stables. Asher was paralysed. Her companions were hissing at her to close the door and step back. They wanted to seal it and be gone. But she was barely aware of their presence. Her entire focus was on the young man stumbling behind the guard.

Levi did not appear hurt or mistreated, just filthy and tired and struggling to move properly with his wrists tied and his legs shackled by a short chain.

Relief coursed through Asher.

"Thank you," she whispered gratefully.

"You must come now," murmured Edriene.

"You go. But I will not leave without him," replied Ash. "He would never abandon me." Her tone left no room for negotiation or argument.

The Wens looked at each other with uncertainty. Mara made a fast decision.

"Fruda, Aga, Edriene – go. You too Fleur. Wait in the tunnel. If we do not follow in ten minutes, destroy the entrance, seal yourselves in."

Fruda and Edriene hurried to the kitchen, but Aga and Fleur refused to move.

"There is great evil here," said Aga quietly, "greater than what I had realised. The picture in my head..." she shuddered. "I cannot run."

"And you Fleur?" asked Mara.

"My place is beside Asher."

Mara nodded. There was no time to argue.

"Be ready," said the Jeweller, "we will only have one chance and maybe not even that."

Across the square Darven ran his eyes over the gangly lad before him.

"So this is Hestawen's grandson, hmmm?" he asked.

The guard nodded, so eager to be rewarded that he did not see the anger in the eyes of the sorcerer.

"Do you think I'm a fool?" roared Darven.

The gathered men jumped back in fear. Darven's face contorted with rage. "The Weaver has no grandson. You are trying to con me."

The sorcerer turned blazing eyes on the now shaking guard. "No... my Lord... he said he was," stuttered the terrified man.

"Oh *he* said, did he?" Darven's voice was suddenly soft and calm. His face and body seemed to have relaxed. The speed at which his temper swung from one extreme to another made Asher's head spin. His strange calm was almost more horrifying than his fury.

Darven stared consideringly at the shell-shocked guard, then he pointed a finger at the man. Tiny sparks crackled from its tip. The Squad Leader stepped quickly away from his underling, distancing himself from the man and his fate.

"He was at E-Langren, with the Glass Crafter. We brought them both," screamed the guard in a last attempt to save his life.

"Is that so?" said Darven reflectively. He returned his gaze to Levi, dropping his finger, and the guard slumped with relief.

"So you live at E-Langren?" he asked Levi pleasantly.

Levi nodded.

"And you know it well? Including the Weaver's study?" Darven's eyes were shining brightly.

Levi nodded again.

"Tell me, what books line the walls?"

Levi frowned at the unexpected question. "There were hundreds of books about the universe, the star systems, the planets and the Threads."

Darven's gaze intensified. "I am most interested in one specific book. With a purple cover. Do you know the one I mean?"

Levi nodded once more. "Yes, I think so. It was in a section I could not access."

"Of course not," said Darven dismissively, "It is well beyond your understanding." He laughed crazily. "Soon they will all be mine. The secrets of E-Langren. The secrets of everything."

"No they won't," said Levi boldly. "They are all gone."

Abruptly Darven stopped laughing. "What did you say?"

"The books are gone. Everything is gone." Levi pointed at the Squad Leader and his underling. "Those two burned E-Langren to the ground."

Mara and Aga sucked in horrified breaths.

"It cannot be," whispered Aga.

Darven seemed frozen in place as tiny tremors wracked his body. His handsome face turned a shade of purplish red that Asher had never seen before. For a moment she thought he might actually explode. And then the moment passed, and the Lord Adviser seemed calm and in control, as though he had never been aggravated at all.

When Darven next spoke to the guard, he sounded almost pleasant. The hairs on the back of Asher's neck stood up in trepidation.

"Did I hear that right? Did you burn the Weaver's home?" he asked in a friendly manner.

Duped by the Sorcerer's dulcet tones the brainless guard and the Squad Leader nodded eagerly. Maybe this was their redemption. Unfortunately for them, it was not.

On the square Darven began to convulse, consumed with rage.

"You imbeciles!" he screamed.

The two men were paralysed in fear. The guard opened his mouth, but no words came out. Darven did not care. He was not interested in an answer. He raised a shaking hand in the direction of the Squad Leader and guard. Sparks flew from every finger. Eyes wide, the condemned men scrambled to run away from the Lord Advisor's deadly fury.

They had not taken more than three steps when great bursts of fire enveloped them both, burning them to cinders. Darven howled like a banshee as the flames roared around him.

"Now," hissed Mara, as the occupants of the square scrambled in fear and confusion.

The four women flung open the door and ran towards the remaining guards, who were in a state of panic and disbelief.

Mara raised her hands. "Who would like a taste of my jewellery now?"

Energy streamed from her fingers, encircling the hapless men and pulling them together like a shimmering, glowing lasso. Futilely the five of them struggled briefly before collapsing in a heap on the ground.

Asher and Fleur ran for Levi. Behind them Aga was frantically scribbling in the dirt with a large stick.

Through the red haze of his temper, Darven finally realised what was happening. He whipped around, pointing a blazing finger at Mara.

"Oh no you don't," called Aga, swirling her hands above her stick drawing, lifting the picture off the dirt and crafting it into reality.

A giant metal box appeared above Darven's head. With a mighty thump it landed on the ground, capturing him within. From inside the box they could hear him banging and cursing.

Aga flinched as she held the box firm against his attacks. Mara rushed to her side.

"As soon as you release the box he will leap free."

Aga nodded. Sweat beads were forming on her brow. "Hurry," she said through gritted teeth.

Mara sped off to help Ash and Fleur who were struggling to untie Levi's ropes and chains.

"Drag him if we must, but we need to leave *now*. Aga cannot hold Darven for much longer. He is far more powerful than I feared, and he is in possession of a large amount of polari. We cannot fight him. We must retreat."

Fleur ran to Aga and stood beside her, weaving her energy in with the Artist. Aga felt the additional energy surge through her, strengthening and supporting her. She smiled gratefully at Fleur. Inside the box Darven threw charms at the walls, causing both Aga and Fleur to gasp.

Asher and Mara helped Levi to his feet and Mara broke the chains with a bolt of lightning. Asher's heart was pounding so hard she was surprised her body was still able to move.

"This way," she called to Levi, pointing to the hut.

They had stumbled halfway across the square when a figure leapt from the overhanging rock 200 metres above, landing nimbly on the ground in front of them.

"Give him to me and I will let you pass safely through my caves," he said.

Brawn.

His hair and beard were more matted and filthier than the last time they had met, if such a thing were possible. The pelt of a mountain lion hung over his shoulders, protecting him from the cold air. His face and body were lined with dirt and scars. He was the very image of a mad man, except his grey eyes were clear.

Mara recoiled in shock and disgust.

"Hello young Crafter," he greeted Asher amiably.

"Hello Brawn."

"You know this wild man?" asked Mara in surprise.

Behind them the metal box shook, pounding the ground like thunder.

"Levi is coming with us," said Ash hurriedly.

"Then you and your little band of escapees will never make it out of my caves alive." He chuckled, displaying a mouth half-full of brown teeth. "Those caves run for miles in all directions, twisting, turning. It took Darven years to learn to navigate them. You won't last two days."

He dangled a large torch in front of them. "To find the true path, you will need this."

Asher stamped her feet, frustration and anger building inside her. "Why are you doing this?" she yelled.

"Choose little Musician. The boy or the torch, and safe passage for all."

The box rattled ominously.

"If you wait too long it will be a moot point," added Brawn cheerfully. "Darven will get you all anyway."

"I thought you were on our side," said Asher accusingly.

Brawn grinned. "How many sides does an avalanche have?"

"Brawn!" hissed Ash angrily. "We don't have time for your riddles."

The Mountain Man shrugged, as though he had not a care in the world.

"Hurry!" pleaded Aga, her brow dripping in sweat and her body shaking.

"Go," said Levi firmly. "I will go with Brawn. Get everyone to safety and find Hesta. Stop this madness. I believe in you Asher."

Tears welled in her eyes; angrily she swabbed them away. She hugged Levi tightly.

"I can't just let you go," she said. "When we were four years old, and nobody else wanted to be friends with the odd little girl who played piano in the dirt, you took me under your wing. You've never made me feel weird or different. You always believe in me. I can't do this without you Levi."

Levi squeezed her in return and then stepped away from her, towards Brawn.

"We don't know if you are safe with him." Asher threw a reproachful glance at Brawn who was not the least bit concerned. "We have no idea what side he's on, what game he's playing."

Levi grinned reassuringly. "I'll be fine. We have a lot in common, Brawn and me. We both like riddles, and I've recently realised a new appreciation for speaking in rhyme. Most importantly, we both like sausages."

Asher did not smile in response. She was desperately close to bawling.

"Of course you can do this without me." Levi continued. "And you *are* weird and different. That's what I like best about you. You are special Ash."

Asher immediately started shaking her head.

"Special," he repeated insistently. "Even before all this began you were special. And now you are a real witch Ash, with incredible power, on a huge adventure."

Asher shook her head again, her eyes full of misery and fear. "I don't think I can do this. I'm not strong enough. I get exhausted and I pass out. That's useless against Darven. I can't seem to control it when I need to."

Levi smiled at her affectionately. "Then learn. Now go save the world. And tell Kate -" he stopped, his eyes clouding a little.

Kate and Levi had never shared their feelings for each other, but Asher had long suspected what neither of them had said. A split second passed then Levi grinned again, his normal bonhomie determinedly in place.

"Tell Kate I'll see her soon."

He stepped beside Brawn and nodded at the wild man.

In response Brawn handed Asher the torch. Then he wrapped a scrawny arm around Levi's waist and leapt into the air. He carried Levi easily, as though he weighed no more than a bag of stolen sandwiches. Asher stood staring into the space where they had disappeared, her heart aching and her throat tight.

"Fleur, Aga, come on," called Mara.

After one last glance at the empty space, Asher turned and followed the others. They ran towards the hut, rushing through the open door.

"If we don't hurry Edriene will trap them in, and us out." Mara pushed the door closed with a bang. "Wait, where's Aga?"

She turned her head frantically, scanning the room. Ash and Fleur stared back at her in panic.

Mara pulled open the door and screamed into the square. "Aga! Run now!"

"*Go,*" came Aga's voice in their minds. It was weak and strained. "*I can hold him for another minute only.*"

"*No Aga, you run. I will cover your retreat.*"

"*He is too strong for us Mara. We cannot risk your defeat and Asher's capture. I will slow him down. Leave now. Save our Heir, stop this evil, restore the Threads.*"

Then her voice was gone.

The words pierced deeply into Asher's already sore heart. *Save our Heir.* Aga was sacrificing her life for her. Levi was sacrificing his freedom for her. She struggled to make sense of what was happening. They had lost Aga and alerted Darven to their plans all because she had been determined to save Levi. And she had failed at that.

Beside her Mara dashed away hot tears. "You heard her," she said grimly.

And they sealed the door, leaving Aga to her fate.

The trio climbed through the cupboard with heavy hearts, weary and sad to the depths of their beings. Edriene and Fruda grabbed at them joyfully, then quickly realised something was wrong.

"Where's Aga?" asked Edriene, looking from one to the other.

They shook their heads, their throats too thick to speak the words. The ground above shook with a fearsome force.

"Destroy the tunnel," said Mara. "It's time to go."

Chapter Nineteen

The Legend of the Great Plains

There were hugs and tears when they joined the group in the cavern. Isobel cried out when she heard of Aga's sacrifice, refusing to be comforted. Aga had been her friend and mentor, her last link with home and a life before this madness. Edriene and Fruda hovered close by, to offer any support when she was ready.

Telling Kate that Levi was gone was one of the most difficult things Asher had ever done. Her friend's face flushed red, then blanched white as her body processed the shock. She swayed unsteadily.

Fleur and Asher grabbed at her and tried to ease her into a sitting position, but Kate vehemently shook her head.

"No, no! I don't need to sit down like a wilting flower. Aga and Levi deserve better than that."

Kate glared at them both as though they had contradicted her. "Tell me this Asher Blake, and don't sweet talk me. Is Levi lost for good? Or can we still save him?"

Asher would not have dared to sweet talk this fierce version of Kate, so she gave the question the consideration it deserved. Was there still hope to rescue Levi?

"Yes, I believe we can find him. And I truly, truly believe he is safer with Brawn than with Darven."

Kate nodded. "Okay then. So let's get out of these caves and find a way to defeat Darven once and for all."

She brushed roughly at her dress, a useless gesture considering how dusty they all were, and took a deep breath. Then she strode away.

Ash watched Kate curiously as she moved among the Crafters, removing their bracelets to their enormous relief. Mara came and stood beside her, following her gaze.

"Is something amiss?"

"I'm not sure really, it's just that there is something different about Kate. She is normally quite claustrophobic, and since the first Void crossing she has been struggling with dark and heavy places. Two days ago she wouldn't even step through the cupboard, now she seems completely at ease here in the caves."

In contemplative silence they watched Kate for a moment longer.

"Perhaps ask her about it, when she is not so distressed," suggested Marawen.

Ash nodded and made a mental note to do so.

Conscious of Darven searching for them above, Mara hustled the group to get moving along the passage she and Asher had taken yesterday. Once everyone had passed into the tunnel, she and Fruda and Edriene set a seal over the entrance. They hoped the complicated layers of Crafting would be challenging and time consuming to unravel.

Asher led the group along the tunnel; nervous anxiety creating a blanket of silence as they trod over the uneven stone. For weeks their lives and those of every Crafter in Andera had been under a cloud, but it was only in the last few days that they had been dragged into politics well beyond their understanding. And today's terrifying events had shaken each of them to the core.

They did not know where they were heading, or why, but the Crafters considered themselves lucky to have escaped.

Asher walked a few steps ahead, scouring the tunnel for any sign of problems or exits. Brawn's torch created a wide beam of light, making it easy to see all around.

Just when Asher was beginning to wonder if this tunnel would continue forever, it came to an abrupt end, branching out into three new options. Each one of the tunnels looked exactly the same as the others.

Ash shone Brawn's torch down each tunnel. For the first two the torch dimmed. Ash frowned and gave it a shake, wondering if its energy source was fading. But when she pointed it at the third tunnel it flared brightly, sending a strong white beam into the darkness.

"This way," she called to the group, hoping she sounded encouraging and upbeat.

"How can you be sure?" called a hesitant voice from towards the back.

It was a good question. Ash could only trust that Brawn had not played them false.

"The torch lights the way. It will lead us safely," she said confidently. "We'll stop for a rest and refreshments at the end of this passage."

The women murmured in assent and followed her lead. Again the three Wens blocked the passage entrance, but this time they blocked all three, hoping to cause confusion.

This tunnel twisted and turned until it opened into a large grotto, complete with underground spring. It was well-lit by lamps positioned high on the walls, their light reflecting off the slow-moving water onto the stone walls. There was plenty of space for everyone to spread out and sit down, which they did gratefully.

The cavern had a high ceiling which eliminated any sense of claustrophobia. The water itself danced and shimmered, creating a peaceful atmosphere. One of the group cupped her hands into the water and tentatively raised it to her lips. Her eyes widened in pleasure.

"It's fresh and delicious," she said the others, before scooping more water and slurping it eagerly.

While the Crafters drank from the spring and ate from the supplies they carried, Ash wandered the grotto, shining Brawn's torch into the many tunnels that exited the space. For most of them the torch light shone weakly, and for one it went completely dark. Puzzled, Asher stepped closer to the mouth of that passage and immediately a chill of dread ran down her neck. Goosebumps rose on her arms. Hastily she backed away.

The next tunnel was clearly the right path, for the torch shone brightly. Out of curiosity Asher shone the torch down the final tunnel, assuming it would also be dim. However this time the torch pulsed, sending staccato shocks of light into the passage.

Fleur came to stand beside her and the two of them considered the flickering light.

"Do you think we should investigate?" asked Fleur.

Asher wrinkled her nose. She was unsure how much time they had before Darven started breaking through the passages they had sealed behind them, but her intuition was telling her to follow the torch.

"Let's be quick," she replied, before heading swiftly up the passage, her cousin close behind.

The pulsing torch led them only a short distance along the stone passage before they found a heavy wooden door barring their way. Behind the door terrified hushed voices could be heard.

"Hello?"

There was no answer to Asher's greeting.

"Are you Crafters?" she called again. "I am a friend."

"Hello?" the soft voice was tentative and filled with fear.

With her flute in hand Asher drew on her energy to weaken the bolts of the door, to slide the strong iron out of the hinges, and to pull the lock free. She pushed against it, but the door did not budge. Even without its fastenings, it had warped shut.

Asher raised her brows at Fleur and indicated the door with a twist of her head. "Would you mind?" she asked. Fleur nodded.

"Stand back," yelled Fleur. With a leap she was off the ground and spinning her body to kick the door in.

It crashed to the floor of the cave with an almighty thump, wood splintering. The noise must have carried back to the main chamber, for Mara and Edriene came running up the short passage.

"Asher!" yelled Marawen, "What is happening? Are you okay?"

"More than okay," called Asher, her face split into a giant smile. "We've found the stolen Crafters."

Twenty more women and girls were huddled in the large room behind the broken door. Their bodies were battered and malnourished; the evidence of Darven's blood leeching clear from the scars they bore and the sickly pallor of their skin.

Two small lanterns were their only light, and makeshift bedding their only comfort.

Asher and Fleur helped the confused and frightened captives to their feet, and the four of them took it in turns to support the women on the walk back down the tunnel as their wobbly legs took the first steps to freedom.

As they entered the large cavern, the newly rescued Crafters squinting in the light, the other members of their original groups clustered around, offering support, food and water.

"They will need some time to rest," said Mara, coming to stand beside Asher who was watching the women eat and drink. "They are not strong enough to move quickly. I suspect they have been bled of all use to Darven and they were left here to die."

"Do you think there are more?" asked Asher.

"Most certainly," replied Mara grimly.

"Then we must search the caves, check every tunnel."

Mara's blue eyes were sad. "We cannot Asher. We do not have the time. We must keep moving before Darven breaks through our defences."

"But we can't leave them here! Mara, please. We must find as many as we can." Asher could hear the desperation in her voice and feel the tears burning behind her eyes.

The Jeweller shook her head, her own eyes glimmering with tears. "We must save the women we have found. If we do not get moving soon, everyone will die."

She was right and Asher knew it, but the decision weighed heavily on her.

"I will return and find them all," she whispered fiercely, "I will find them all."

Asher turned her attention back to the newly rescued group. Some of them were known to the escapees from Groush, and there was a great deal of excitement as old friends hugged and laughed.

Asher noticed Edriene was in the midst, holding tight to three other women. The Gardener looked up and smiled at Ash.

"Asher, come meet my friends from Varossa."

Ash forced a smile onto her face and walked forward to be introduced.

"This is Alana, and Johava, and this is Simeona."

Asher gasped.

"Simeona, Raya's sister," repeated Edriene, her face glowing with joy. "You found her Asher. Just as you promised."

***

Once the group were rested they resumed their journey. Hour after hour they traversed the caves, following the path chosen by Brawn's torch. They could not move fast, but thankfully everyone kept moving. Each slow step was a step closer to freedom.

Finally, after stumbling up a particularly steep passage, Asher saw daylight ahead.

"Daylight! I think we're at the end!" she called excitedly.

Her words spurred on the weary walkers; even the most exhausted amongst them finding a burst of energy. At the mouth of the cave she stepped onto a huge ledge, reminding Asher of the dragon caves of Dor'atar.

One by one the Crafters emerged from the dark passage, blinking in the late afternoon sun. When their eyes adjusted to the daylight there was more than one gasp of shock.

They were part-way up the mountain, looking down on the vast plains below.

A crumbling path led the way down from the ledge to the plains, but not onto the green fertile lands they could see spreading to the horizon. Running along the base of the mountains lay only barren sandy soil, creating a kilometre wide barrier between the mountains and the thick woodlands of the plains.

"What is that?" asked Kate, shielding her eyes against the sun, and trying to peer as far as she could.

"Sinking sand," replied Mara, her voice subdued. "I had heard the legends, but I did not know what to expect. I rather hoped they were exaggerated."

The quicksand was effectively a moat, separating the mountains from the plains themselves, except there was no bridge to cross. Travellers descending from the mountains would have to brave the scorching sinking sands to reach the haven and protection of the trees beyond. It seemed unlikely anyone would survive the crossing.

A wave of fatigue and disappointment washed over the group, and many of them sunk onto the ledge, their faces stark with hopelessness. Mara too seemed deflated.

"What is its purpose? Surely all that quicksand just keeps people away?" asked Asher, her eyes roaming the sand.

Mara nodded. "Yes, that's exactly the point. It's all part of the rather sordid history of the Ostrin Royal Family. You see, what we now call the King or Queen of Andera is actually only the ruler of Ostrin and its surrounds. All the land from that side of the mountains to the ocean. This side of the mountains is known as Faerla Grun, the prosperous lands. The story goes that almost one hundred years ago Ostrin was beset by drought and famine. The people were hungry and poor, overcome by taxes and landgrabs. The King of Ostrin, the current queen's great-grandfather and the man responsible for his people's dire state, sent emissaries to Faerla Grun, requesting aid and assistance. The emissaries returned with the welcome news that the King of Faerla Grun would provide food and water as required. In fact, a caravan of carts was a day or two behind them, travelling over the dangerous mountain paths, the Crown Prince himself leading the way. The King was filled with relief, but as the returned group shared stories of the fertile lands and the great riverbeds sparkling with gold, the Ostrin King became greedy. He hatched a plan to invade Faerla Grun and seize their lands for himself, declaring himself King of all Andera."

"Oh this is not going to end well," murmured Kate.

"Indeed it does not," said Mara. "After accepting aid from his neighbours, the Ostrin King took the Faerla Grun prince hostage, demanding the people of the prosperous lands surrender to his rule. The Faerla Grun King was furious and sent soldiers to retrieve his son. The Ostrin King executed the young prince in the square and invaded Faerla Grun. A vicious war ensued. Though he was victorious, the people of Faerla Grun never accepted him as their king. They swore he would never have what he wanted from their lands."

"What happened next?" asked Asher, slightly breathless from the intensity of the story.

"After a torturous year of occupancy and rebellion, the wondrous royal city was destroyed, and the people of Faerla Grun fled onto their vast plains. The story goes that the nomads found a great power which gave them the means to protect the plains. They ousted the Ostrin invaders who retreated back across the mountains, to the fury of their King who demanded they return and rebuild the city. He refused to believe he could not have it. Even without the city, he wanted the bounty of the fields and rivers. But when the Ostrin soldiers crossed the mountains once more they were greeted by a river of quicksand, cutting them off from the prosperous lands forever. It is said that many attempted to cross the sinking sands and none survived." Her voice trailed away.

They all stood silently, staring at the sea of sand and the trees and plains beyond, the weight of its violent history hanging heavily in the air.

"So what do we do?" asked Edriene. "Return the way we came? Try and find a way to defeat Darven now?"

An enormous explosion echoed from somewhere deep in the caves behind them. Asher exchanged an uneasy glance with Kate and Fleur.

"Our pursuers are not as hampered by our obstacles as I hoped they would be," said Mara, her brow crinkled with concern. "His power is greater than I could have imagined. I don't think we can make a stand against him yet. Our Crafters are weak from their captivity and the Void-matter, and our Heir is not ready."

Asher's stomach tightened. Mara spoke the truth. Her Crafting was strong, but the exertion of that energy usually resulted in her passing out. She had to find a way to control it, so it did not control her.

"We need to get off this mountain and onto the safety of the Plains beyond the quicksand," said Mara. "We need to find a way."

"Why will we be safer on the plains? Won't Darven just follow us?" asked Kate, her eyes anxious.

Mara returned her gaze to the vast lands below.

"The people of Faerla Grun were farmers and scholars. Their city was famed for its beauty and culture, for its music and art. But they were strong warriors too. The King of Ostrin could never have defeated them with his army alone. The records show that he used dark sorcery to win the war. And when the Ostrin soldiers returned to reclaim Faerla Grun they discovered the sinking sand barrier was not the only change. Sorcery no longer worked. The Great Plains are protected."

Another crash, closer now, startled Mara from her story telling. She looked anxiously back down the tunnel and then anxiously at the deadly sands. Indecision was clear on her face.

As the women murmured around her, Asher closed her eyes and tuned in to the music that was dancing on the light breeze. It was telling her a story of a besieged city and a grieving queen, pregnant and alone. Of a river and a lake, where the water washed over something powerful and strange. Of a city crumbled to the earth and a royal family in hiding. Of a century of songs, silenced.

The music had been formless for so long. It was eager to be played. It buffeted against Asher, teasing her, urging her, begging her. *Play...*

Asher opened her eyes.

"Come," she said firmly, her voice carrying to every set of ears. "We must descend. Walk carefully but quickly. There is not much time. Stop at the bottom and do not step onto the sands until I say so."

Encouraged by the conviction in her voice, the group began the awkward descent. The path had lain untrodden for many years and was overgrown with tangled shrubs. The fallen stones and weather worn rocks made it slippery underfoot. Fleur and Kate offered their arms to the older women, sharing their strength and steadiness.

Asher and Fruda led from the front, clearing brambles and the worst of the loose rocks while Isobel walked with those at the rear, murmuring encouragement and support. Edriene hung back with Mara, the two of them moving carefully down the path while keeping an eye on the mouth of the cave above.

Step by cautious step they all moved further from the danger above to the danger below. Until they were standing on the last broken steps.

Asher reached for the instrument bracelet at her wrist, the music of the Plains pulling at her ears impatiently. With the flute in her hand the notes would no longer be denied. She raised the instrument to her lips and blew.

The melody tickled the top layer of the sands, sending small plumes into the air. It raced over the wide moat, leaping among the trees that grew densely on the vibrant, lush plains. It swirled around the group of Crafters, filling their ears and their souls with its story. Asher played until she felt light-headed, until the urgency of the music had eased.

She pulled the flute from her mouth and used it to point at the sands, which were now undulated and pulsing to her music.

"This way," she said. "Kate, lead the way."

She raised the flute again and blew each note with care. As she played great rocks rose from deep within the sands, providing a firm bridge of sorts for them to walk across.

Beside her the women gasped in wonder, but Asher paid them no mind. She needed to play to keep the bridge intact. She knew as soon as she stopped the stones would disappear below the sands, along with anyone still standing on them.

Kate stepped over the stones as quickly as she dared, followed by Fleur, the two of them supporting the exhausted old Crafters. The others fell into line, moving carefully but with haste. Finally everyone was on the bridge. Asher brought up the rear, playing and walking. In the past she had played for many hours longer than this, but never before while walking and Crafting after hours of physical exertion. She willed her shuddering body to not pass out.

Finally, finally they stepped off the last of the boulders and stumbled onto the lush, soft grass.

"Over here," urged Fleur, "just a little further, under these trees."

The women limped painfully; the blisters on their feet rubbing against the dirt and dust in their shoes. All of them sank gladly onto the ground, taking deep breaths of the clean air and relishing the fresh grass and the wide blue sky above.

Asher dropped her arms, her body throbbing with the effort of her Crafting. Behind her the great stones sank back into the sand, the moat once more impenetrable. The flute shrunk to its tiny form and Ash clipped it onto the bracelet with a silent prayer of thanks.

"That was extraordinary," smiled Edriene, coming over to her. "Well done Asher."

"How did you know?" asked Fruda.

"The music wanted me to cross over," said Asher. "It wants me here. I don't know why." She shook her head, forestalling any more questions.

Around them the Crafters sat or lay on the soft grass, but Mara remained standing, her watchful eyes never taking their gaze from the cave entrance far across the sands.

"Are we sure Darven can't use his powers?" asked Fruda nervously.

"Sure is a rather definitive word," replied Mara. "But one thing is certain..." she raised her hands and pushed forward slowly. The grass before her flattened to her will. "We sure can."

As the weary group regained their breath, Fruda passed around the last of the food, knowing that tomorrow they would need to find water.

"We should settle here for the night and see if we can find the people of the plains tomorrow. We need a safe place to train you." said Mara.

"Can *you* lead the Crafters?" asked Asher. "You are powerful, they trust you. It makes more sense."

Mara kept her eyes trained on the cave ledge. Asher wondered what she could see from such a distance. For a long moment it seemed the other woman would not answer her question. Then Mara sighed. She opened her mouth to speak but gasped instead.

"Look," she said quietly to Asher, trying not to alert the others.

Ash followed her gaze. On the ledge they had only recently vacated, Darven now stood, flanked by the remaining members of his squad. The distance was too great to see the expression on the Lord Advisor's face, but his body radiated fury as he pointed to them on the plains. A fire-ball flared from his fingertips and sputtered out long before it could cross the sands. The tiny figure of the sorcerer jumped up and down in anger. Beside him the guards shuffled uneasily.

Darven must have found a way to magnify his voice, for his words carried easily across the large space between them.

"Run and hide little mice, but have no doubt, I will find you." The words, full of menace, made Asher shiver.

"And as for you Lady Marawen, I look forward to our re-union. Until then, my love, know that you have already given me what I need to become the most powerful being in this universe, and beyond. For that I thank you."

Maniacal laughter filled the air and then abruptly stopped. Darven disappeared back into the cave, leaving the unhappy guards on the ledge.

All eyes turned to Mara, who continued to stare at the empty cave mouth.

"Mara?" Fruda broke the silence. Her voice was gentle.

The Jeweller sighed deeply, her body slumping.

"Let us settle for the night and I will share my story. I assure you of this – Darven does not have my loyalty, or my heart." Her voice was bitter. "I swore my allegiance to the Weaver a long time ago and I mean it. I will stand with Asher, whatever comes."

It was clear she would say no more for the moment. Burning with curiosity Ash helped Kate start a fire, while Edriene and Fruda combined their Crafting to create a light supper.

Everyone was exhausted and a little cold, but spirits were high. For the first time in many days they were free.

Light laughter caught Asher's attention and she turned her head to find its source. The Varossa Crafters were sitting a small distance away on the soft green grass, breathing deeply and laughing with the pleasure of being free and outdoors. They were eating slowly, savouring each bite of Fruda's delicious bread and cake.

Raya's sister Simeona sat among them, her long, dark hair hanging in a tangled and dirty plait down her back. She was painfully thin, her face and clothes filthy and bedraggled. Her hands were torn and marked with dry blood, as though she had spent days, or weeks, pulling at the earth and stones that held her captive.

But despite the pain of her body, and the terrors of captivity, her eyes shone with joy, and her face was filled with hope. Simeona turned her head and caught Asher's gaze. She nodded her head in acknowledgement and a smile of thanks creased her dirt smeared face.

Edriene came to stand beside Ash and waved at her friend. Simeona waved in response and returned her attention to the group she was with.

"It won't be long before their spirits and Crafting are restored," said Edrience, her voice filled with emotion. "They will get stronger every day. As will you."

Asher nodded without speaking. Edriene was right. She could feel the Crafting growing within her. It exhilarated and terrified her, for she still did not know how to control it fully. But she had found Simeona, and made good on her pinky swear to Raya, and that filled her with hope.

"Come," said the Gardener, "rest for a moment. You have done much today, and you too need to be restored."

Gladly Asher capitulated to Edriene's suggestion, finding a quiet place to sink onto the grass. The final setting of the sun sent glorious streaks of orange and pink across the cloudless horizon. Asher closed her eyes and breathed deeply, filling her lungs with the tart evening air. The smell of grass and trees was a welcome change after days in the small hut and the dusty caves.

Birds cawed to each other as they farewelled the day. When she opened her eyes, the sun was gone and the sky was turning dark.

On the far away ledge the guards were slumped onto the hard rock. They were clearly staying put for the night, maybe hoping to solve the puzzle of how the women had crossed the quicksand.

Asher pulled her aching body from the ground and went to join Kate and Fleur who were seated in a small circle with Mara and the other Wens. As they waited patiently for Mara to share her tale, Asher realised something peculiar. Now that she was just sitting and staring at the Jeweller she was aware that Mara's bright blue eyes, the shape of her chin, the line of her nose… they were all so familiar.

Before her tired brain could puzzle together the answer, the Jeweller began her tale.

"I have been Mara or Marawen the Jeweller for almost twenty five years. It has been so long that my life before seems almost a dream, or a story I once heard. I was born in Ostrin Castle, the youngest child of the King, and sister to the Crown Princess Magda. My name was Deltamara."

Mara took a deep breath, her eyes glazed with memory.

"I always knew I was different to the rest of my family, and I also knew that Crafting and Sorcery in royal children were forbidden, so I hid my growing talent. Revealing my ability meant renouncing my place in the line of succession, and there were reasons why that was undesirable. I hoped the Crafting would simply shrivel and fade without use. But by the time I was thirteen it was becoming more and more difficult to ignore. By fifteen I knew I had to leave the castle. My uncle Horace and Hesta had been regular visitors to Ostrin throughout my childhood and they had always known who I really was. I knew I would be welcome at E-Langren, so that is where I went. I spent five years there, becoming Marawen."

Asher glanced at the rapt faces of the silent listeners, each of them as surprised and intrigued as she was.

"Of course I renounced my royal title, and any claim to the throne, but for the first time in my life I was truly me. My father granted me lands by the sea and a new honorific, styling me Lady Mara. Then one summer, twenty-one years ago, I met a young man and fell madly in love. We planned a life together, but he was killed when his boat was caught in a wild storm and sunk. I thought I would die from the grief, and indeed I hoped I would, such is the intensity of youth. Then I discovered I was with child."

Kate gasped softly, but nobody said a word. The pieces of a complicated jigsaw started to click into place for Asher.

"I was alone, heartbroken, pregnant. I could not bear to stay in my house by the sea, staring at the very waters that had taken my love. I decided I should return to Ostrin and raise my child there, supported by my family. Magda was now Queen and herself pregnant. I imagined our children could grow together. But my sister refused me. Her mind, impacted from a childhood illness, was weakening as she aged. Pregnancy seemed to make it worse. She denied she had ever had a sister. She would not let me see our mother. She declared me an imposter and had me thrown out of Ostrin. That is when I met Darven."

Mara's tone was bleak.

"I encountered him on the road home from Ostrin. I poured my whole sorry story into his sympathetic ear. I was so vulnerable and he was so comforting. Making me feel cherished and cared for. Assuring me that he would help me with the babe, that he loved me. I was desperate to believe him. For months he stayed at my side and I grew fond of him."

She laughed lightly at the horror on Kate's face.

"It's hard to believe now, but he was a charming, kind and attentive companion. Clever and witty, and so very handsome.

He was very interested in the baby, counting down the days until her arrival. He was captivated by my Crafting, keen to learn everything he could about it. For a woman who had grown up in an environment where she had been frightened of ostracization, it was very seductive to be so adored. All seemed idyllic, until the day I entered his study uninvited and unannounced."

Marawen took a deep breath. "Darven had been called away unexpectedly. I was in the last weeks of pregnancy and choosing to stay close to home. I wanted a book from the study and wandered in without his prior permission. Usually the door was locked, but he had left in such a hurry he had forgotten to turn the key. On previous occasions, everything had been locked away, but this day his journals and papers were spread across the desk. He must have thought them sealed behind the locked door, safe from discovery. The words 'royal babe of Crafter born' caught my eye and I started to read. It was a prophecy that told of a baby of royal blood, born of a Crafter, whose blood could grant powers beyond imagining, if the child was sacrificed on a night of five red moons. Darven had star charts and notes calculating when that night would be. Sometimes they are decades apart, but the next one was only a few months away. I was beyond horrified. Sickened and terrified I longed to flee the house, but sense told me I would not get far before Darven hunted me down. So I needed a plan. By the time he returned I had forced myself to act as normally as possible with him. I told him I had received word from Ostrin and needed to return immediately. He had business to attend to, so I put on a show of reluctance to be separated from him. In truth I was desperate to be gone. Willingly he organised the coach and driver, saying he would follow in a few days. There was still a week or so before the baby was due. It was an extremely uncomfortable two days travel. By the time I arrived at Ostrin my labour had commenced. Luckily my mother was there to welcome me, and I was housed in luxury in my old room, with midwives to attend the birth of my daughter."

Asher was holding her breath. Her racing mind was slotting together the pieces of the story as quickly as Mara was sharing them. Those eyes and that nose...

"The Threads weave a complicated pattern. That fateful night both women of the royal house laboured at Ostrin, both bearing daughters of their own. Only one child survived to see the morning light. The Princess Evelyn, the daughter of the Queen."

Mara stopped speaking.

"But she was not the daughter of Queen Magda," said Asher, everything finally making sense. "She was your daughter. The child of royal blood and Crafter mother. You swapped her with the dead Princess. To keep her safe."

Mara nodded, her face grey with grief. "I grieved the death of my baby while watching her flourish as my sister's child. Unable to love her and care for her as a mother, having to find contentment that she was safe and would one day sit on the Ostrin throne. For Magda's birthing was so traumatic that the midwives were certain she would never carry a child to term again. And she never has."

Mara shook her head, as if to clear the old memories. "And then one day my greatest fear was realised. That Darven would realise what I had done, and my baby would no longer be safe."

Asher nodded. "So you asked your cousin Ginarwen, with whom you had lived at E-Langren, to protect her. But something went terribly wrong. The baby disappeared, presumed dead, and Ginarwen was injured before she vanished into the Void."

Mara's eyes were stricken, shining with unshed tears. "This time the grief was all-consuming, for both Magda and me. It tipped her further into instability. It was meant to be such a simple plan. Ginarwen was going to take Evelyn and hide her at E-Langren, far from Darven's reach. But on that dreadful night everything went wrong. Ginarwen and Darven battled ferociously. She was much more powerful than him and should have prevailed, but somehow Darven escaped, and Evelyn was lost. The search for the baby continued for weeks, but she was never found. As for Ginar, we heard later that she had died in the Void, though how Darven managed that, I do not know. With both my child and my cousin lost, I did not have the heart or the will to follow Darven into the Mountains and finish him. I was broken in mind and spirit. I returned to my home by the sea to nurse my grief over Evelyn and my guilt over Ginarwen and put him far from my mind. I thought it was all over."

"Except it was only just beginning," said Asher quietly. "Darven nursed his grudges as he was learning his sorcery, and Evelyn was being raised far from Andera, setting in train events that have brought us to this moment now."

Mara's head whipped up.

"What did you say?"

Asher's grey eyes were filled with sadness. Evie's deep sense of loss, of not belonging, had started at birth, when she had been taken from one mother and given to another. Then mere months later it had happened again. Deep within her infant mind, uncertainty about who she was and where she belonged had taken root.

"Evelyn was not lost, and she did not die. Ginarwen took her across the Void. We were raised as sisters."

Mara opened her mouth and then closed it again. Her eyes were glazed with shock. "So she is safe on Earth?" she croaked.

Asher shook her head.

"No. Almost two weeks ago Darven sent a squad across the Void. She is the sister they stole from our home, and brought here to Ostrin. She is the sister I travelled to Andera to rescue.

I wanted to take her home to Earth, but she was determined to stay. She is at the castle now."

Horror leeched the last of the colour from Mara's cheeks.

"By the stars, that is what Darven meant. I have given him what he needs. He has found Evelyn and knows that she is my daughter. When he spills her blood on the night of the five red moons he will become the most powerful being in the universes." Her voice cracked. "Dark sorcery and blood charms and the polari gems mean his power has grown beyond anything a normal Crafter and even a Wen can match. If he manages to use Evelyn's blood..." Mara shuddered.

"We need the Weaver," said Fruda.

"We don't have the Weaver," replied Edriene, "but we have Asher."

"But I am useless," cried Asher in despair. "Crafting exhausts me and the music in my head can be overwhelming. What use is an Heir that passes out from the pressure of the energy?"

The little group looked at her solemnly. Then Fleur reached over and squeezed her hand.

"This is your destiny Asher. You will learn to control it. You must."

After the revelations of the Lady Marawen, it had taken a long time before the small group of Wens and Fleur and Kate had finally settled into slumber. Mara had sat with Ash for some time, asking a hundred questions about Evelyn. Asher had willingly shared the stories of their childhood, and Evie's bright, bold nature. Mara had laughed and shed tears. Celebrating and mourning the lost years.

Now Asher sat alone.

The fire burned low, its soft glow illuminating the weary travellers as they lay on the ground. Above them the stars of the universes twinkled, reminding Asher that this fight had repercussions far beyond this group or even this planet.

She looked at the women and girls in various stages of sleep, drawing comfort from the companionship they shared. All of them scared, all of them brave, and all of them trusting her to save them. They believed in her, they had followed her from captivity, through the depths of the mountains, across the sinking sands and onto the Great Plains. From one uncertain situation to another.

Her thoughts turned to Hesta and Penn, then Evie, and lastly to Levi. Her chest was tight, and her throat was sore, but her eyes were dry. Tears would not serve her now. She had saved Simeona, she would save the others.

Asher pulled back her sleeve and peered at the small instrument charms hanging from her bracelet. Edriene had once said that she was very young, and perhaps she was. But a weariness and a knowing beyond her years had settled in her soul. She had aged years in this last week. She was no longer quiet, weird, invisible Asher Blake, hiding from the world, dreaming her life away, lost in the music in her mind. And she could not be the Crafter whose energy overwhelmed her, who collapsed with the effort. She needed to learn to control and shape her music.

Carefully she unclipped the bracelet and held it between her fingers. She touched each cool charm in turn. The piano, the flute, the violin, the guitar. Instruments of power. *Her* instruments of power.

Tomorrow everything would change. Tomorrow she would shake off the cloaking that had hidden her all her life. It was time Andera met the Musician.

Chapter Twenty

Arvana

Before dawn the next morning the group woke to begin the trek further into the woods, in search of water and shelter. Their bodies were stiff from lying on the cold hard ground, and their feet protested each step, but they walked without complaint. Isobel had discovered an overgrown track leading through the trees. Slowly they walked or limped along the neglected path, moving away from the towering mountains and their captivity.

On the cave ledge Darven's guards slumbered on, unaware that their prey was moving further and further out of sight. By the time they woke an hour later, the women and girls were long gone.

Asher had slept extremely poorly, her racing mind making it hard to relax. But when she had finally woken, a sense of peace and purpose had settled deep in her soul.

Edriene fell into step on her left, then Mara on her right.

"Let us begin," said the Jeweller.

Ash blinked in surprise. "Now?" she asked.

"Do you have something else to do, perhaps somewhere else to be?" asked Mara, a smile tickling at her mouth.

Ash could not help but smile in response.

"So tell us, when the energy rises within you, what does it feel like?" asked Edriene.

Asher told them how the music would swell within her, capturing her mind and senses. She told them about the terror in Hesta's study when the anger and rage had almost consumed her, and she shared with them the story of the fire-dragon's birth and the crystals of the Laneisian.

The two older Crafters listened carefully, nodding, asking questions to clarify.

"Such power!" said Edriene wonderingly. "The things you speak of, the fire-dragon, the crystals, even what you did with the bridge over the sinking sands. These are enormous feats of strength Asher. Clearly you are gifted, as we would expect the Weaver's granddaughter to be. Generations of powerful Crafters run through your blood. So what I don't yet understand is why you are passing out afterwards. You might feel tired, but it should not render you unconscious. When you reduced the great stones at Groush to small pebbles, where did you draw the energy source from?"

Ash wrinkled her nose. "I'm not sure I understand Edriene. I just used my own energy. I always do."

Mara and Edriene stopped walking, their mouths dropping open in shock.

"What do you mean, you use your own energy?" said Mara.

"I use my own energy to play the music, to Craft. I feel the music in my body and I channel that," Ash said self-consciously, feeling stupid. It was clear from the look on their faces that she had been doing something wrong.

"No wonder you feel weak and light-headed!" exclaimed Edriene. "I'm surprised you haven't imploded."

Asher flushed a hot red. "I didn't get much training time with Hesta," she said quietly.

"Then we will make up for that lost time now," said Edriene. She stood still, raising her arms out to her side. "Can you feel that?"

Asher closed her eyes.

"All around you is the life of the forest, the energy of every living thing on the planet. Reach out and feel the energy of the trees, the grass, the soil and the insects. When I Craft I feel the energy within the plants themselves. For Mara, she feels the energy of the gemstone. That is what we draw upon."

"It's just a buzzing mass," Asher said, trying not to feel frustrated.

"Settle your mind. Relax. Feel for the space between the physical world and the buzzing sensation. Feel." Mara's warm voice washed over her.

Asher was reminded of that day in the music room with Hesta, it seemed so long ago, when she had felt the old energy in the instruments around her. Now, when she opened her mind and spirit, the immensity of the world around her was awe-inspiring.

Then unexpectedly she remembered the pressure of the stones of Mat'drin, and for a brief moment she felt the struggle of being held in the energy of the ancient stones. Her eyes flew open in panic.

"Asher?" asked Mara, "are you okay?"

Asher took a few steadying breaths before nodding. Haltingly she shared the experience of Mat'drin with Mara and Edriene.

Mara nodded knowingly. "Yes, I understand the experience. I too have sunk my energy too far into stones. They are enormously dense and as old as Andera itself. You will learn to only skim along their surface. You are extremely fortunate that you were not lost within them."

"So how do I use the energy around me? Edriene, you said you feel the energy in the plants and use that to Craft them. How do I do that with music?"

Edriene smiled warmly, without ridicule.

"You've already answered that question yourself. The music you heard when you created the bridge, that is the energy around you. You talk of feeling music within you, your whole life. Reach out. Feel the music of the world."

So Asher did. Eyes closed, body still. She quietened her mind and opened her senses to the melody that played within the life-force of everything around her. It was glorious and humbling. All her life she had thought she was creating music, but really she was receiving it. The great symphony of life.

She stood like that for a long time, lost in the ebb and flow of the music of existence. At first it was a jumbled cacophony of sound, but as she deepened her connection she was able to distinguish individual songs - the soft notes of the dying grasses; the brash notes of a new born chick squawking for food, the deep chords of the old trees.

"Now what?" Ash asked softly, her eyes still closed.

"Now feel the energy, borrow some of it, not too much – you don't want to destroy that life-force. Take a little from many." Mara's voice was low and hushed, so as not to disturb Asher's concentration. "Practise gathering that energy and then releasing it. That will be your lesson today. To gather a little of the music around you, hold it and then return it."

For the next two hours they hiked through the trees. The women chattered to each other but Ash did not join in. She focused on tuning in to the musical energy around her, and gently taking small amounts, adding them to her own energy. The sensation was amazing. She could feel her energy increasing, blossoming. Her whole being itched to pull out an instrument and channel that power. Instead she did as Mara suggested, releasing the energy back into the environment.

Further into the woods they stopped. Some of the women needed to rest, their feet still sore from the long walk of the previous day.

"We need to find water soon," worried Fruda. "There is plenty of edible plants in the woods that I can use for food, but water is our most pressing need."

A small woman with a leathered and lined face stepped forward. Her skin was worn from a lifetime of exposure to the elements and her small frame was slightly stooped as though she spent a great deal of time hunched over. She was clothed in sturdy leather pants and a woollen tunic, both of which were marked with old grease and oil stains.

"There is water nearby," she said shyly. "I am a Boat Builder. The river calls to me."

"That is wonderful!" exclaimed Fruda. "Thank you Maeve. But wait, we will need something to carry water in. Ivenia, you mentioned you are a Potter."

"Yes I am a Potter," replied a voice from the group, "but my talent is only middling," she added apologetically. "Perhaps I can use the damp earth of the woods to fashion a bowl."

"Thank you Ivenia," said Fruda with a smile. "Let's get to work."

Asher marvelled at Fruda's ability to remember each of the Crafter's names and felt slightly guilty that she had not really introduced herself to them individually. The thought of doing so made her feel awkward and uncomfortable.

"We could wander these woods for days without having a sense of where we are going," said Isobel, staring at the thick canopy around them. She shuddered slightly. "It is overwhelming."

The decision was made that Ivenia would make a vessel to carry water in, assisted by the other Crafters. When that was done they would continue to the river, then on to the fields, and hopefully encounter people. As the plans were discussed Asher found herself struggling to concentrate and participate.

The lively music of Faerla Grun played loudly in her head. It urged her up on her feet and along the path towards the river.

"Asher?" called Kate, "Where are you going?"

"I'll return soon," she replied vaguely, "Wait for me here."

Asher meandered her way through the trees, surrounded by the soft rustle of unseen creatures and the wind in the branches. Here, far below the canopy, it was cool and dark and smelled like moss and damp earth. Only the most persistent of sun rays manoeuvred their way between the large branches and thick foliage. It was soothing and invigorating at the same time. She opened her senses to the life of the forest and immediately music flooded in.

She walked on until she met the river. At the small bridge Asher paused. *What now?* The music danced around her, directing her off the path and into the woods, along the river's edge. To her right the water burbled and gurgled, tripping over rocks and branches. She closed her eyes and breathed in the melody that swirled around and within her. There was no-one to see her wide smile of delight, or her spontaneous twirl with her arms flung out wide. If there had been, Asher would not have cared. She felt fully at peace.

In time she opened her eyes and resumed walking alongside the stream. The globe, which had been silent for a while, hummed against her chest. It too seemed restored now it was far from the Mountains, captivity and the Void-matter.

If the path had once been well-maintained it certainly was no longer. Brambly shrubs snagged her dress, and moss and fallen branches and overgrown vines made each step hazardous.

But Asher truly did not mind. The stream burbled beside her, its clear fresh water gleaming in the sunlight. She was walking against the current, heading upstream to the water's source it seemed. Gradually the trees and shrubs thinned out slightly, before coming to an abrupt end.

Asher stopped a few feet before the forest's edge. She hesitated to walk beyond the cover of the trees and into the grove that lay beyond. The muffled sound of crashing water served as a backdrop to the picturesque scene that lay before her.

The music pushed at her impatiently, but Asher held firm.

She scanned the large clearing and the village it contained. A collection of various sized houses clustered along the edge of an enormous lake. More were built along a modest road that led out of the village to the right, over the river and away into the fields.

Though it was nearing the end of Autumn, and the coming winter was making its presence felt everywhere else across Andera, here in the grove it seemed to be eternally Spring. Bountiful vegetable and flower gardens bursting with life were woven between the houses. Flowerboxes hanging from the houses spilled over with colourful blossoms. Trees that should have already shed their leaves still proudly wore their green cloaks.

The air was warm and filled with the scent of fresh grass and fragrant plants.

Far beyond the houses and the lake she could just see a large waterfall that tumbled from the mountains. The pool below was hidden from her view. This was clearly the source of both the lake and the river that ran from it.

The sun drenched everything in a soft, warm light.

People bustled in the gardens and in and out of the houses. They laughed and talked with ease, seemingly without a care in the world. Asher had just decided to step out of the woods and seek their aid, when a hushed, curious voice whispered beside her.

"What are we staring at?"

Asher leapt three feet into the air, before falling backwards with a yelp and landing on her bottom.

"Sheesh!" she exclaimed, clutching her chest to stop her wildly beating heart from escaping. "You scared the daylights out of me."

The grinning young man who had crept up so silently beside her, reached out a tanned, calloused hand to help Ash to her feet.

"What are you doing?" he asked once she was standing once more.

Ash thought she should take a moment to decide if he was friend or foe, but the enthusiastic swirling of the Plains music decided for her. It pushed and prodded her.

"Wow, you're certainly popular," she said.

The new arrival raised dark eyebrows in query.

Ash shook her head. "Never mind. My name is Asher. I'm a Crafter from beyond the Mountains. Our people are being persecuted by the Queen's Advisor. We have come seeking shelter while we work out what to do."

He pursed his lips thoughtfully as he digested her small speech. Asher used the time to consider him in turn. His tall, athletic body was tanned a deep honey, a sign of the many hours he spent outdoors. A shock of neglected golden brown curls sat atop a warm, open face. The faintest of laugh lines were just beginning to etch themselves around his eyes and mouth even at his young age. Combined with the bright humour in his grey eyes they gave the impression of a good nature and an easy temper. He wore the soft leathers of a hunter. The bow slung over his back and the knives strapped to his calves seemed to confirm this.

Now that they were standing, Asher was aware of how proudly he stood and the sense of authority he exuded.

"What is your name?" she found herself blurting.

"A question without an answer," he answered lightly, though his eyes were serious.

The music swirled with delight. Its obvious pleasure in the young man made Asher feel self-conscious, as if some-how she was flirting with him. To her mortification she realised she was blushing. Embarrassed, she scowled fiercely.

"Alright wise guy. What are you called?"

"Niem. He is Niem." A voice behind her answered.

This time Asher did not jump quite as wildly, nor did she land on her bottom, but the shock of the new arrival still set her heart into palpitations.

"Jeepers Creepers, you people are as silent as cats!"

The small girl grinned at her briefly before launching herself into Niem's wide embrace.

"Finally! You are home," she said happily, "did you find what you were seeking?"

He shook his head.

"Never mind," she said, wrapping her small arms around him and burying her face against his chest. He held her tight. A few seconds later she pulled back, her face wrinkled in disgust.

"You smell foul!" she exclaimed.

Her nose twitched in Asher's direction. "As so do you," she said bluntly.

Ash could not help herself. She laughed. The indignation on the child's face was simply too adorable. And to be fair, she was certain she must smell rather fragrant. She could almost hear Levi saying that when you could no longer smell yourself that's when you knew the pong was next level bad.

Niem laughed with her, and the girl scowled crossly, stamping silently on the mossy undergrowth.

"Well you do. You'll need to bathe before you come into the house or the Lady will toss you straight back out."

She spun back to Asher. "I'm Treen. Where did you come from?"

Asher hesitated for only a brief moment. She was seeking sanctuary and their help. She owed them her honesty. As much as was sensible.

"My companions and I have come from Ostrin, through the mountains."

"Over the sands?" Niem's voice was deceptively casual. "That's interesting."

Asher squirmed. She knew without a doubt that his next question was going to be 'how?', and she suspected her newly formed resolution to be honest was going to be tested.

She was saved by Treen, who was decidedly uninterested in how Asher had crossed the sands.

"What's your name?" she said.

"I'm Asher."

Treen nodded in acknowledgement. "Hurry up then. The Lady is desperate to see you Niem."

She spun around and headed off towards the houses, calling out as she ran, letting the village know that Niem was home.

The hunter lifted his pack off the ground and swung it onto his broad shoulders against the bow. He set off in the same direction as the girl at a far more subdued pace, but paused after a few steps when he realised Asher was not walking with him. He turned back towards her.

"You coming?"

Asher hesitated. She wanted to ask about sanctuary for her companions.

A small flash from the woods to her left, over Niem's shoulder, caught at the edge of her vision. She blinked to clear the gleam, but a millisecond later it was there again. Instinct knew it for what it was, even without the clarity of sight. Every atom of energy in and around her focused on that flash, that out of place shard of light.

A blade.

Ash felt the energy of the dagger as it cut through the air, aimed straight and true for Niem's chest. She felt the malevolence of the unseen assailant who had thrown it from the shadows of the trees. She felt her own heart beating. All noise disappeared. Time slowed.

With a giant leap she closed the small distance between her and Niem, throwing her body against his and sending them both crashing to the ground. As soon as she hit the earth, sound and feeling returned. Beyond their heads the twelve-inch dagger thudded harmlessly into a tree.

Ash lay on the hard damp ground breathing rapidly as her senses stabilised. Her head spun from the adrenaline that still coursed through her body, and from the brutal thump on the ground.

Niem was not so affected. He leapt to his feet in one fluid motion. He ran in the direction of where his would-be assassin had been hiding, pulling a short sword from its strap on his outer calf as he ran. The ease with which he handled the sword suggested he was not just a hunter. He disappeared into the woods. Three men from the village were close behind.

Asher sat up gingerly, grimacing as she adjusted her weight. A flurry of movement brought two women to her side, offering their support as she stood up.

"Are you alright lass?" asked the shorter woman, looping an arm around Asher's waist to steady her.

"Yes I think so." Asher shook out her body and stepped shyly away from their concerned clucking.

"What was that all about?" she asked, pointing at the wicked looking dagger still wedged in the tree.

The women exchanged dark glances.

"Somebody wants Niem dead before tomorrow. Whoever it is best be fleet of foot, or they'll find themselves dragged before the Council."

It seemed the perpetrator was indeed fast enough, for Niem and the village men were re-entering the grove, empty handed.

"Come. The Lady will want to meet you." The small woman gestured towards the houses. "After you bathe."

***

Asher sank beneath the warm scented water and massaged the soapy lather out of her hair. She let the heat ease her battered body.

She was lying in a large tub in one of many bathing rooms contained in a large purpose built hut by the lake. Fresh water was pumped from the lake and heated for the individual bathing rooms. There had been the option of a shower, but the lure of soaking in the tub had been irresistible.

She had initially protested, wanting to speak with Niem or the Lady about her friends. Saffen, the small woman, had assured her that she would speak with the Lady and they would organise for the group to be brought here to the village.

Asher lay in the water and let herself rest in the energy of the lake, listening to the distant falls and the birds that congregated on the water's edge. When she finally pulled herself out of the tub and dried off, it was not only her body that felt restored. She felt a strong sense of calm and connectedness to the energy around her.

In the change-room adjoining the bathroom she discovered her torn and soiled dress had been taken away and replaced with a selection of dresses and a pile of trousers, a long-sleeved top, a warm woollen blue tunic, and clean underwear and socks. Gladly she chose the trousers and tunic.

Asher had never been so excited to put on clean clothes in her life. She silently vowed that she would never take such luxury for granted again.

Lying beside the clothes was a small, brown leather bag with a long strap.

Once she was dressed she retrieved all her precious knick-knacks from beside the tub and tucked them into the soft leather bag, then slung the bag across her body.

The excited chatter of familiar voices attracted her attention, and Ash hurried outside to greet her friends and companions. Kate and Fleur ran straight over when they saw her.

"Gosh, you look so clean! I hadn't quite realised how filthy you were until now you're not," said Kate.

"You should see yourself then," replied Ash drily. "The bath was amazing."

"I can't wait to be clean," sighed Kate. "This village is lovely. Incredible find Asher. Quite a few of the women were getting nervous that it would be another cold, damp night on the ground."

Saffen walked towards them, along the lake path.

"Well you certainly look and smell far more palatable," she said with a pleased smile. "The Lady is currently with her nephew, but she will want to meet with you soon. Asher, you come with me. As for you two..." she wrinkled her nose, "head straight to that hut. There are a number of bathing rooms prepared for you. The girls will organise fresh clothes."

Kate and Fleur thanked her sincerely before running off eagerly to the hut.

"Who is the Lady?" asked Ash as she fell into step beside the swiftly moving Saffen.

"Quinn, Lady of the Falls. You will meet her soon enough."

As they walked through the village Ash realised it was bigger than she had first thought. Forty or so houses lined the shores of the lake and the road that led out of the grove and into the open farmland.

The villagers smiled at her and Saffen as they passed. They seemed genuinely happy to see her. There was none of the animosity or fear that had surrounded them in the towns and cities on the Ostrin side of the Mountains.

"The people here are very friendly and welcoming," said Asher.

Saffen laughed merrily. "Why wouldn't they be?"

Ash shrugged self-consciously. "A group of strangers, exiled Crafters, from the lands of Ostrin. You might think we bring trouble."

"Do you?" Saffen stopped walking. She tilted her chin to look Asher square in the eye.

"Maybe," answered Ash softly.

Saffen resumed her brisk pace. "And maybe not. But no matter what, you saved Niem's life. There is a debt that is owed."

They walked for a few minutes more, until Saffen stopped outside a large cream and red painted wood house. She pushed open its merry yellow door and waved Asher inside.

"Here we are. Make yourself comfortable. Your friends will join you here, and I will return to collect you when the Lady is ready."

"Thank you," said Ash to Saffen's departing back.

Alone, she took a moment to absorb her new surroundings. She was standing in a small hall. A peek into the room on her left revealed a large bright kitchen and eat in dining room. Further along the hallway a set of narrow stairs led up to a second floor and presumably bedrooms.

The door to her right opened into a spacious sitting room, richly painted in blues and yellow. A cheery fire crackled merrily in the fireplace, warming the room. Cushions and rugs adorned the many sofas and chairs, inviting a weary traveller such as herself to snuggle and relax.

Asher could not refuse such an invitation.

She choose the large sofa beneath the window, kicked off her boots and curled up in the comfort of the cushions. She sighed happily and closed her eyes.

Sometime later she was startled awake by the sound of chatter, as the newly washed and changed Mara and Edriene entered the room, followed by Fleur and Kate. Her friends were dressed in similar outfits to her. The older Wens were wearing thick jumpers and warm woollen skirts. Their skin glowed and their spirits were high.

"Were you asleep?" asked Kate.

"I don't think so," said Asher, then immediately yawned. "Well possibly."

"This is like a wonderful dream after days of nightmares," sighed Kate, sinking into a soft armchair.

Fruda stuck her freshly washed head through the doorway, her face glowing.

"Oh the kitchen! It's fully stocked. We'll eat well soon enough. If you need me, you know where to find me," and she disappeared back across the hall, humming happily.

"Where is Metka?" asked Ash, surprised not to see Edriene's niece shadowing her.

Edriene smiled. "I sent her upstairs to rest. She is exhausted. The rest for mind and body will do her good."

Fleur, Mara and Edriene gratefully relaxed into their chosen seats.

"Everybody is very relieved you found safety and shelter Asher," said Mara. "Their spirits are much restored. Perhaps we can take a breath and plan the next move, rather than just running."

A cursory knock on the open front door was shortly followed by Saffen striding into the room.

"The Lady wants to see you now Asher." She ran a speculative gaze over the rest of the group. "Would anyone else care to come along?"

All four immediately stood up. Saffen laughed.

"I rather thought so. Alright then. Follow me."

The Lady of the Falls lived in a large house beside the lake, on the far edge of the village. Enormous windows allowed a magnificent view of the water from every room, and particularly the falls in the far distance. A large porch wrapped around the lakeside of the house, and Asher imagined the occupants would often sit out there and be close to the water.

Before she followed Saffen and the others into the house, Ash paused and closed her eyes. She relaxed into the energy that hummed from the lake and its myriad of life-forms, practising her new method of skimming energy and releasing it.

It was becoming easier and easier to tap into the great melody. To feel the music of each living being and connect with her own energy.

She opened her eyes and looked around for something to practise on. By the water's edge a scattered collection of stones caught her attention. Perfect. Tentatively she reached for the energy within them, and the air and the earth they lay upon. When she felt the energy meld with her own, Ash pulled the flute from her bracelet and started to play.

The stones responded easily to her command, dancing lightly into the air before settling on top of each other to form a tower of rocks. Ash held them there for a minute as she played, until a final discordant blow sent them tumbling to the ground.

For the first time, she had not expended a single atom of her own energy, she had simply manipulated what already existed. It was exhilarating.

She laughed jubilantly. Her whole being tingled. It was a completely different sensation to the exhaustion and depletion she usually felt after Crafting. Moving the rocks was only a small achievement, but it felt great.

Mara's soft query interrupted her happy dance.

"What have you learned?" she asked.

Ash grinned, her grey eyes bright. "We are all the energy, every one of us."

Mara nodded with a smile. "And how does it feel to be immersed in that energy?"

Ash took a moment to consider, to find the right way to describe what she was feeling.

"Limitless," she said softly. The globe hummed against her chest.

A thrill ran down Mara's spine and her eyes widened in surprise. She quelled the urge to shiver.

"That is a very powerful word."

Asher nodded slowly, feeling the energy pulse through her body. She smiled. "Yes."

For the first time since this nightmare had begun the Lady Marawen felt true hope flicker into life deep inside her. The tall girl standing before her was more than the daughter of Ginarwen the Lost, or even the Granddaughter of Hestawen the Weaver. This girl, glowing with energy, was Asher the Musician.

With every breath Asher was becoming stronger, more powerful. One day soon she would shake off the limitations of her instruments and become a Wen like no other. She would be their salvation. Then Darven should tremble.

Mara smiled with satisfaction and followed Asher into the Lady's house.

Chapter Twenty-One

The Lady of the Falls

Quinn d'Arvana stood at the wide window of her library and considered the girl making her way up the steps into her house. She had wondered about her since Niem had told her what had transpired in the woods, including the rather startling fact that she and her troop of weary wanderers had somehow crossed the Sinking Sands.

Behind Quinn the accumulated wisdom of those who had stood here before her was captured in the pages of hundreds of books. She had studied them for decades, never expecting they would come to life in the form of the girl now entering her home.

Without warning her human eyes lost all vision, and the glistening waters of the lake and the flame haired Crafter disappeared, replaced by a swirling mass of multi-coloured energy.

She felt no fear. It had been many years since her first immersion into the energy of the lake's waters, and while she was never quite prepared for when it might happen, it did not terrify her as it had done as a child. Indeed she welcomed it.

Quinn breathed deeply and centred her focus on the sensation of sinking below calm waters. Here she always found the source of her truth and illumination. But something was different today. The water spirits were agitated and overly excited. They pulled at Quinn, desperate for her to understand.

She sunk deeper into the tumultuous depths and opened her being.

In the wide doorway of the room the small group of Crafters halted. They saw a tall woman with long silvery blue hair flowing down her back. She was clad in a dress the colour of translucent aquamarines, that clung tightly to her willowy frame and swirled around her calves. Her skin shimmered like fish scales in the light of the many lamps that lit the large room.

Asher sucked in her breath in surprise, for she could see the silvery aqua aura of the Lady shimmering and swirling around her. Pure energy. She had never seen the like.

The Lady turned towards the silent observers, aware of their presence but not seeing them with ordinary vision. Her wide, sightless eyes swirled with clouds of blue and green and grey, as she observed the very souls of her guests. The Lady Quinn's gaze moved slowly from one to the other.

On the far left bloomed a garden, lush and alive. Filled with life, its deep roots were pure and strong. It pulsed with the urge to protect and nurture all living creatures.

Beside the garden shone a dazzling crown, covered in hundreds of precious gems. Its brilliance and its power were blinding to behold. Its heart was fierce and loyal.

The space beside the crown was puzzling in its dense emptiness. Quinn could sense a soul cocooned inside layers that hid it from her gaze. It was like nothing she had ever seen before and she wondered what this meant.

She did not wonder too long though, as she could no longer keep her attention from the pulsing music that was swirling around the last of the figures in the doorway. She knew without seeing that this was the Musician who had saved Niem, who had crossed the sinking sands, whose presence so agitated the Water Spirits.

Without the shackles of sight Quinn could see her clearly, all that she was and could be. And the Lady of the Falls was troubled.

She had seen what the Spirits had wanted her to, and Quinn expected the vision to clear and her human sight to return. But it did not. So she waited patiently, knowing there must be more to see.

A shift in the energy at the doorway caught her attention. A large beam of golden light joined the group, providing sunshine to the garden and power to the gems on the crown. When that golden beam merged with the darkness Quinn could finally see the form of the figure there. Courage and sacrifice. A bird aflame.

But it was when the beam blended with the energy of the music that Quinn felt the full force of its power. The music roared, the melody and multiple harmonies combined in a symphony that almost overwhelmed Quinn. She shook with the force of that combined energy as she was hurtled out of the trance, and into the bright, familiar surrounds of her library.

Shocked by the intensity of the Water Spirits departure, Quinn stumbled to the nearest chair and collapsed there, breathing deeply as her human senses were restored.

The women and girls in the doorway shifted uneasily, exchanging questioning glances. Should they leave? Should they stay? The decision was made moments later when the Lady turned her face towards them, this time with clear, almost mortal eyes.

She smiled at them.

"Welcome to Arvana, the Sacred Falls. I am the Lady. You may call me Quinn." Her low voice washed over them like gentle water on smooth rocks. She smiled warmly as she greeted each in turn.

"Gardener, please come in. Sit here beside me."

Edriene started with surprise and took the seat she had been allocated.

"My name is Edriene," she offered, bobbing her head in respect.

The Lady nodded in acknowledgement, then turned her attention to Mara.

"Princess of Ostrin, please – join me here."

Mara inclined her head regally. "Princess no longer, simply Marawen the Jeweller."

A small smile played at Quinn's mouth. "As you wish."

Then it was Kate's turn.

"Girl with the soul of a firebird and the courage of a lion. Welcome. You intrigue me child. I have never seen your like."

Kate's eyes were wide. "Me?" she squeaked. "I'm just ordinary Kate Reynolds."

Quinn smiled kindly at her. "There is nothing ordinary about you Kate Reynolds."

Kate blushed fiercely under that warm regard and hurried to her seat.

Quinn turned her attention to the two young women who remained motionless in the doorway. With her ordinary eyes they were not particularly remarkable, with slightly damp hair and dressed in the trousers and tunics of the villagers.

But her mind could not forget the vision of the music and the light. She was both thrilled and troubled by it.

She caught the grey, clear gaze of the tall redhead. She was barely more than a child, hovering on the precipice to adulthood. And yet there was such gravitas about her, so much knowing. Quinn guessed she already knew the heavy responsibility that would one day be hers.

"Do you know who you are?"

The musician inclined her head.

"Do they?"

Asher nodded again, mesmerized by that bottomless gaze and that deep voice.

"Then welcome to Arvana, Asherwen the Weaver's Heir. Your presence honours me and terrifies me. Once you would not have been welcome in my home, but the animosity of the past must be put aside."

Asher jerked with shock at the unexpected words. "I wish you no ill Lady Quinn."

The Lady nodded. "I know. However your presence here means great evil is to follow. Perhaps we could have avoided it, protected here on the Great Plains. Perhaps not. No matter. Today you performed a great deed for the people of Faerla Grun, for me personally. When the time comes, I will stand beside you Asher."

"I thank you Lady," replied Asher gravely.

Then Quinn turned her attention to Fleur.

"What is your name child?" she asked softly.

"I am Fleur el Jesper e Trinity," was the proud response.

"And do you know *what* you are?"

The Lady's voice was kind and gentle. Uncertainty flickered across Fleur's face. She was not sure she understood the question.

"I am Ap'an, and I am of the Bonner line," she replied.

"Ah, so you are kin to the Weaver."

"Yes."

Though the warmth of her voice did not change, Quinn's swirling gaze bored into the girl with unblinking intensity. "Have you heard of the Gaela, Fleur?"

Fleur shook her head. "I don't know what that means," she said in a small voice. Her eyes were wide as her hands restlessly twisted the edge of her tunic, unconsciously mimicking her mother.

Quinn's gleaming face was solemn and calm.

"There is an old story, not well-known or often told, of two sisters bound by the Threads. One was the Weaver, and the other was Guilana, known as the Gaela. Guilana had no Crafting ability of her own, but wherever she focused her energy that power was enhanced and Crafting was enriched. Do you know of what I speak?"

Fleur nodded, her eyes bright. Against her chest, Asher felt the Weaver's globe begin to burn.

"The Endless Weave had created the Gaela to deepen moments of importance in the Threads. To ensure that things that were meant to happen, did happen. The Gaela would be incarnated into human form when the need was greatest. But Guilana was a gentle, guileless girl, easily manipulated. She believed all who came seeking her aid had only good intentions. One day she gave her energy to a Crafter who sought power at all costs. A fierce battle between the Weaver and the Crafter ensued, depleting the Gaela until she was weak. The Crafter fled, but she did not escape the Weaver."

Fleur was completely mesmerised by the story, by the lulling rise and fall of the Lady's voice.

"What happened to Guilana?" she asked.

Quinn's face was soft. "The Weaver knew Guilana was not strong enough. Her gentle mind had been ravaged by the battle. The Threads had not chosen the vessel wisely. She had to be protected from further manipulation and treachery. So the Weaver unwove the power of the Gaela from her sister and captured the energy into an unbreakable pendant. A disc of solid silver. The disc was hidden, lost to legend. Guilana lived out her years as an ordinary woman."

Fleur's hand flew to her chest. The Weaver's Globe hummed erratically. The Lady of the Falls did not take her eyes off the young Ap'an girl breathing rapidly before her.

"Do you wear the pendant Fleur?"

Asher's heart was beating so loudly she was sure the others must be able to hear it. Fleur's eyes glimmered with unshed tears.

"Yes," she breathed.

The occupants of the room collectively exhaled. Quinn nodded, unsurprised.

"In one of her moments of lucidity, my great aunt gave to it me as a small child. She said she could feel my energy when she was Crafting. She said the pendant was my birthright, but I had to keep it hidden, even from my mother. I never had the chance to ask her what it meant, as she was often in a state of madness."

Carefully, reluctantly, Fleur pulled the silver pendant from beneath her tunic. She had kept her secret for so long, it was both a relief and a terror to share it. The disc spun in the light, and Asher could feel its pleasure radiating around the room. Her globe hummed happily in response.

"Have I done something wrong?" asked Fleur in a small voice.

The Lady shook her head, setting off a cascade of white blue waves down her back, like foam atop a crashing wave.

"No Fleur. You are the Gaela. The pendant has claimed you. It is yours. But you are a secret that must be kept. There are many who would do nearly anything to have control over you."

Fleur tucked the disc back beneath her clothes, and Asher's globe finally eased its burning and humming.

"Let us eat," said the Lady in a far less solemn voice, smiling at her guests once more. "And you will tell me what brings you to the Great Plains and to my humble village."

She reached for the small bell on the table beside her, giving it a firm tinkle, summoning a maid.

"Lady Quinn," said Fleur, her soft voice now firm and steady once more. "You said Guilana was of gentle mind and disposition. That she was easily beguiled."

The Lady nodded. Fleur drew herself up. Her dark skin glowed and her eyes shone.

"I am no gentle girl to be manipulated and ill-used. I am Ap'an. I am a warrior. And my place is beside the Weaver. No matter the pain, no matter the cost. For now I will remain a secret. Not because I should be protected, but because I should be feared. I am a weapon for the Weaver. I am not a pawn."

Her voice rang around the room. Quinn D'Arvana, the Lady of the Sacred Falls, felt the words weave into the Threads. The elements were coming together. She quelled the urge to shiver.

"Who or what is it you run from?" Lady Quinn asked.

"Darven, Lord Advisor of the Ostrin Queen," said Asher in a clear voice. "He is persecuting Crafters, stealing their energy, using their blood for dark sorcery. We believe he plans to sacrifice the Ostrin princess on the night of the five red moons, and grant himself some kind of ultimate power. We don't know how he will do this, or what it truly means. But his power is growing and his ambition is out of control. He has already defeated the Weaver. The Threads are in chaos. He needs to be stopped."

Quinn's soft scales flushed red with outrage. "Defeated the Weaver? How is such a thing possible? I have felt the chaos in the Threads, but I did not understand their meaning. My own Water Sprites are disturbed. Balance, there must be balance."

Two young maids entered the room, easing some of the intensity that had been building since Asher and her companions had arrived. The girls carried trays of sandwiches and cakes and all kinds of fruits.

"Please eat," invited Quinn.

Her guests did not need to be told twice. They filled their plates with food and chatted quietly as they munched.

Quinn did not join them. She made her way to the bookcase and climbed the ladder to claim a small, rarely touched book from the top shelf. The mere touch of the purple leather beneath her fingers sent an unpleasant shock through her skin, momentarily lighting up her scales. She frowned fiercely at the book.

"I do not intend to use you as a guide," she muttered sternly, "but to learn your contents only."

The book was not appeased, but Quinn would not be deterred. She held firmly to the seething book and climbed back down to re-join the group.

"Asher, you mentioned Darven has plans to sacrifice the princess. How do you know of this?"

Asher turned to Mara. The Jeweller cleared her throat and took a long sip of water before sharing her story with the Lady. Quinn listened carefully, asking questions to clarify and be sure she understood.

"What you speak of is not unknown to me." She brandished the small book.

"There are only two of these in known existence. Once there were three. It is the prophecy of the K'ratig." The word was harsh and guttural. "It means, the Ultimate Power. These books are considered incredibly dangerous, and it was often argued among people of power, both magical and not, that they should be destroyed. The counter-argument was that it is better to know than to be ignorant. The decision was made that they would be held in protected places. One of these books is kept in the Weaver's study. The other was destroyed when the Palace of the Pallegorian was invaded many centuries ago. My copy came from our Illuminated City, rescued when it was also destroyed, by the grandfather of the Ostrin Queen."

Her voice and face remained calm and even, but Asher wondered if bitterness remained.

"Then that is the last copy," she said softly, "for E-Langren is gone."

Quinn furrowed her brow in confusion. "What do you mean? Gone where?"

"Burned to the ground by Darven's men." She said the words as steadily as she could, but they sat heavily on Asher's heart, and the feelings of loss and grief that she had pushed deep inside roiled in her stomach and chest.

"Not possible," said Quinn calmly. "E-Langren is the heart of the Weave. If E-Langren had burned the universes would have collided."

"But we saw the flames engulf the house," said Kate.

"Whatever you saw, I am certain E-Langren stands. I would have felt it fall." She smiled at the Fleur and Asher, whose faces were brimming with hesitant hopefulness.

"But Darven was so angry when he heard," said Asher. "He truly believed it had burned. He was in a rage about a book-" she stopped talking as realisation hit her hard between the eyes.

"That book," she breathed, "he wanted *that* book."

"I'm sure he did," said Quinn grimly. "For this book tells him exactly how to claim the Ultimate Power. Let us hope he remains ignorant of E-Langren's survival, and unable to access her secrets. Now please, sit."

They sat, Asher and Fleur and Kate grinning madly at each other. The relief in the air was palpable, and their spirits were high. E-Langren had not fallen. Cook and Anetta and Trinity were safe.

"The night of the five red moons is only seven days away. Ironically, if he had killed the baby all those years ago he would never have acquired the Power he craves. He needs more than the princess, which he clearly did not know at the time. He also needs the sacred dagger, the eternal gem, and this book. All of which are so well hidden I do not know where they are. We can hope that he cannot locate them in time, and that you can find them first."

Quinn had barely finished speaking when a huge explosion rent the air outside, making the house shake. A roar filled the sky, followed by a large flash of light. Screams filled the air.

Quinn leapt out of her seat and ran through the door. Asher was close behind. All she could think was that Darven had found them.

The sight outside brought everyone to a shocked standstill.

Above the lake two huge dragons hovered in the sky, roaring with fury as Niem and his men showered them with arrows. Their great wings churned the air around them. They sent large plumes of flames towards the men, but it seemed to Asher they were defensive and not intended to actually harm. She knew first-hand how accurate the dragons could be with their fire, and these two were deliberately missing the men and burning the arrows.

The villagers were screaming and running for cover. Niem was yelling instructions at his men. The Lady was raising her arms, churning the waters of the lake, intending to overwhelm the dragons with the water.

Amid the chaos Asher focused her attention and held up her hand to shield her eyes, trying to get a better look at the dragons backlit in the afternoon sun. When a cloud covered the bright sun, Asher could see them clearly. A jet-black adult dragon, and a somewhat blue, somewhat golden adolescent.

Frantically she yanked the flute from her bracelet and blew a long, loud note into the fray, drawing on the energy of every living being around her. The music pulsed, momentarily knocking everyone backwards, including the dragons, who flapped fiercely against it.

"STOP!" she yelled, projecting her voice across the lake, across the grove. "Cease fire immediately! These are friends."

Shocked into submission, Niem and the others lowered their bows.

"Finally!" growled the Black, his words only clear to Asher. Everyone else covered their ears against his roar.

With a thump Dor'tiem and Hr'tom landed on the ground beside the house. The earth shook and a few people screamed. Niem raised his cocked bow in warning.

Asher put up her hand, beseeching him to hold his arrow.

"Please," she called to the men. "I know these dragons. They are friendly."

The dragons roared again "fact!", momentarily deafening the human ears.

"Stop it!' said Asher crossly. "Unless you have a dragon's tooth for everyone, you are going to blow their eardrums, then Niem will really finish you off."

"I would like to see him try," muttered Hr'tom, but he took care to keep his roar muted to a low grumble.

It's time to change young dragon.

Asher heard the thought as clearly as if Dor'tiem had spoken the words. She frowned in confusion. Change? Change what?

The air around the dragons undulated and thickened. The gathered humans gasped and stepped further back as a thick grey fog engulfed the giant creatures until they were no longer visible. Then after a few long minutes the fog cleared, fading back into nothingness. Lying on the ground were two men, one dressed entirely in black leather, the other in blue.

The shapeshifting Dragons of D'rona had arrived.

Asher rushed over to them, followed closely by Quinn and then Niem. Everyone else hung back.

"Dor'tiem! Hr'tom! Are you okay?"

Slowly they sat up, rubbing their heads.

"Is this better small Crafter? Can you all hear without pain?"

Asher grinned at Dor'tiem and resisted the urge to throw her arms around him. He was as familiar to her in human form as he had been in dragon form. She looked to the Lady.

"Can you hear him speak Lady Quinn?"

The Lady of the Falls nodded, her eyes wide. Asher had the impression not many things normally surprised the Lady Quinn, and today she had experienced quite a few.

"Oh damn it!" muttered Hr'tom in despair, twisting his arms back and forth. "Blue. I am blue."

Asher crouched beside him and smiled. "Your clothes are blue, but your hair and skin are golden. As golden as golden can be."

"Really?" his deep blue eyes were hopeful. She nodded.

She felt ridiculously happy to see the dragons. Her face still wide with a grin she introduced them to Niem and Quinn. The Lady was fast regaining her composure.

"Welcome to Arvana," she said calmly. "It is quite a trip you have undertaken. It is a dangerous Void crossing from D'rona to Andera."

"Not in dragon form," replied Dor'tiem, his human voice as warm and mellow as his dragon voice. "We are well protected. I know of a small Crafter who made the crossing more than once, in her weak human form. Now that is something to be admired."

Asher wriggled her nose at his praise.

"But still, we do not cross the Void lightly. Dragons belong on D'rona. Fact."

"So what brings you to Andera now?"

Dor'tiem climbed to his feet, pulling Hr'tom up beside him. The Head of the Dragon Council stood as tall as Niem, a middle-aged man in his prime. Hr'tom was shorter than Asher, a gangly, not yet fully grown boy of perhaps twelve or thirteen. He scowled when he realised she was taller than him. Asher was tempted to ruffle his golden hair but thought better of it.

"We come in search of the Weaver. We scried for the Weaver's globe, and it led us to you. We must speak with Hestawen. It is a matter of great importance."

The Lady looked at Asher with a raised brow, offering her the opportunity to explain.

"I'm sorry Dor'tiem. Hestawen is missing. There is only me. Her heir."

Deep in her heart she knew now was the time to declare herself, to be known. Without hesitation she pulled the globe from beneath her clothes, letting the shining pendant on its gleaming gold chain fall onto her chest.

Dor'tiem inclined his dark head.

"Then small Crafter, we bring you grave news. We have failed in our duty. D'rona is breached. The Eternal Gem has been stolen."

Chapter Twenty-Two

Nobody's Song

"Let us speak of this inside the house," said Quinn, her eyes wary. "Niem, send everyone home. We will organise a reception this evening for the villagers to meet Asher, the Crafters and the Dragons. They will want to send you off in style for tomorrow too."

"Quite an eventful day in our little lakeside village," said Niem with a grin for Asher. She smiled absently in return, her mind churning over the news the dragons had brought. Surely there was only one explanation for the stolen gem.

"Indeed," replied the Lady. "The world has changed much in the last few hours."

Niem excused himself from the group and strode back around the lake, organising the curious, lingering villagers.

Quinn and the others headed to the house. Asher stayed close to the transformed dragons, who were wincing as they struggled to walk steadily on their unfamiliar legs. She offered tips to help them shift their weight, but she knew better than to offer her arm for them to hold. Dor'tiem was just as intimidating in his new form, and Hr'tom would rather crawl than admit he needed help from a 'small human Crafter'.

Step by step they found their balance, their confidence growing as their movements became more fluid.

"It has been many moons since I have walked in human form," said Dor'tiem. "It never ceases to amaze me just how ridiculous it is. No tail, no wings, no counterbalance points. The lungs and heart are small, so endurance is diminished. The depth and periphery of vision is incredibly limited, while the hearing seems to only work for a few metres at best. And the skin! So soft and unprotected. It is a marvel that humans have survived as long as they have."

The sky above them was darkening as heavy clouds rolled down from the mountains. The wind that had previously been gently whipping through the trees and across the water was gathering in momentum and volume. The uppermost branches of the canopy were swaying wildly. A storm was not far away.

Asher sent up a small prayer of gratitude that they were not sleeping rough in the woods tonight.

She and the dragons had just reached the steps to the veranda when the first heavy drops of rain plopped onto their heads. Hr'tom squealed in surprise, almost losing his already precarious balance.

"Our soft skin is also rather susceptible to the elements," said Asher seriously, her eyes dancing. "We get cold easily and overheat all too fast. It's best not to get caught in a heavy storm."

Dor'tiem snorted. Hr'tom did not respond, just gritted his teeth as he hauled one leg after the other up the stairs, hanging on to the banister for dear life.

A few long minutes later and the dragons shuffled into the house behind Asher, moving slowly but growing in confidence and strength. Still, it was with relief that they manoeuvred their new bodies into the human chairs.

They had not been seated for more than a few seconds when Niem strode into the room, water dripping from his hair and clothes. He seemed completely unconcerned about the moisture. With a grin for Asher, he took the seat beside Quinn.

The Lady of the Falls turned her expectant gaze upon Dor'tiem.

"I was not aware the Dragons had stewardship of the Eternal Gem. Its theft is worrisome indeed, and unfortunately I suspect we know who the culprit is and that raises some very concerning questions. But let us start at the beginning. Please Dor'tiem, tell us the story of the Dragons and the Gem."

Dor'tiem cleared his throat. His deep, smooth voice rolled over them as he told his tale.

"Many moons ago, perhaps one hundred human years, a creature wearing the form of a human arrived on D'rona. He appeared to travel without need of the portals, suddenly appearing at Dor'atar one morning and requested an audience with the King. He seemed surprised when I informed him, as Head of the Council, that the Kings of D'rona had ceased to exist many thousands of moons before. He said he brought an object of great power from the Weaver and asked for a private discussion. He refused my suggestion to gather the Council, insisting that his news was for my ears alone."

He paused, sensing a question from the Lady.

"You said 'wearing the form of a human'. What did you mean by that?"

"To a human eye he looked like a human. But to a dragon eye he was clearly Ralshok." He snorted. "I am uncertain if he thought we would be fooled by such a disguise, but as he had chosen to present himself in such a ridiculous manner I never asked him about it."

Mara and Edriene sucked in surprised breaths.

"This cannot be," whispered Edriene to Mara. "The Ralshok were lost to legend centuries ago, if they ever existed at all."

Her whisper did not escape Dor'tiem's sharp hearing. He turned unblinking black eyes upon her.

"Ralshok he was. Fact."

Edriene coloured under that intense gaze.

"It is rare that a dragon is curious," continued Dor'tiem. "Very little of what happens in the human worlds matters to us, and since the clan wars we have rarely left D'rona. But this was curious to me, so I granted him a private discussion. He spun an odd tale of a human war here on Andera, and the destruction of a city and a culture. All interesting I am sure to the people of Andera, but of no interest at all to me. Until he drew a large, glowing blue orb from beneath his cloak. I knew immediately what it was. The Eternal Gem."

"How did you know?" asked Asher, totally caught up in the story.

Hr'tom snorted, eager to contribute. "It is a fact that all gems of power are created on D'rona. Of course Dor'tiem would recognise it."

Asher grinned at him, as filled with affection for this scrappy teen as she would have been for a younger brother. He scowled at her in return and deliberately turned his face away. The sulky gesture only increased her amusement.

Dor'tiem continued, ignoring both Asher and Hr'tom.

"The Ralshok asked me to keep the gem. He said there would be great danger on Andera, and the gem must be hidden. He was most insistent that if the gem should ever be taken by some-one other than him, that I find the Weaver and inform her. He said the fate of the universes depended on it. Then he disappeared and I have not seen him since. I knew the importance of keeping this particular gem hidden, its unlocked power could be world shattering. I placed the gem deep within my own cave system, expecting it would be safe there for all time. One hundred human years has passed in the blink of a dragon's eye and I have grown accustomed to its presence, its energy greeting me each morning. Until this morning, when there was no energy, and no gem."

Silence greeted the conclusion of his story. The Lady of the Falls was deep in thought, her brow furrowed.

"Is it possible some other dragon found the gem and has taken it?" she asked slowly.

Dor'tolen raised his head as though to roar in outrage, then realised his puny human form would not respond in such a way. He settled for harumphing.

"Never!" he declared. "Dragons do not steal. Besides, nobody knew of the gem except for me and the Ralshok named Marten."

Asher and Fleur's heads whipped up in unison.

"Marten?" they said simultaneously.

The dragon man inclined his head.

"What does this name mean to you?" asked Quinn sharply.

The girls exchanged a glance.

"He works for Hesta, at E-Langren," replied Asher. "He is the one who rescued the Weaver from Darven at Ostrin."

"How? How did he rescue her?" Her voice and gaze were intense.

"It was like the air rent open and the outline of a figure reached through and pulled both Hesta and Penn into the opening. Then just as quickly as it ripped open, the air sealed shut and they were gone" said Kate.

"Have you ever seen this Marten, in the flesh?" asked Quinn.

The three girls shook their heads.

"Is this possible?" asked Mara, "can Ralshok be here on Andera, working with the Weaver?"

Quinn looked at the assembled group sitting in her library. An Ostrin Princess, Crafter Wens, Shape-shifting dragons, the Gaela, an invisible Firebird and the lost Heir. Only twelve hours before she would never have imagined such a gathering. She smiled.

"If I have learned anything this day, it is that anything is possible."

"What is this Ralshok?" asked Niem, speaking for the first time since he had entered the house.

Quinn turned her gaze to him. "They are creatures of the Beyond. They exist beyond the Weave, beyond the Void, beyond the five universes, beyond all known matter. Very little is known about them. Except that they appear to be immortal, living longer even than myself."

Asher's ears pricked up. The Beyond. If Marten was Ralshok, then that was how he had taken Hesta and Penn to the Beyond.

"Could this Marten have returned and taken the Eternal Gem without your knowledge?" asked Niem.

Dor'tiem gave the question a moment's consideration, blinking slowly as he gazed at Niem.

"Considering he can travel beyond the portals, this is possible," he conceded. "It is the most likely explanation."

A general feeling of relief permeated the room, but Asher could sense that both Quinn and Mara were not so easily appeased.

"But why would he take the gem? And where would he take the gem? And without informing Dor'tiem?" asked Mara, shaking her head. "It is too much of a co-incidence that Darven needs the gem and now it is missing."

An uneasy silence followed this announcement. Outside the rain and wind lashed against the house, rattling the windows. A heavy fog had descended on the grove, obscuring the view of the lake and village. It felt as if they were cut off from the outside world, trapped by the raging elements. In the library the small fire crackled comfortingly, a contrast to the wild, uncontained elements outside.

"If it is Darven, then all he needs now is one of these books, and the dagger," said Quinn.

"And where is that?" asked Asher, her stomach churning.

Quinn shook her head. "I do not know."

Mara jumped to her feet, her eyes blazing. "We cannot wait until Darven finds the dagger. We need to mount an attack on him now! Stop him before he can grow even stronger. It is terrifying to consider the amount of power he required to cross the Void to D'rona, unnoticed by the Dragons themselves. We need to rescue those Crafters that are held captive and remove that power source. Please Lady Quinn, we need to speak with the Faerla Grun High King. We will need his support, his armies, his conjurers."

Her body was quivering with energy and passion. With her new connection to the energy around her, Asher could see what the Lady of the Falls had seen clearly from the start. A princess, a leader, a gleaming, glowing crown.

Quinn and Niem exchanged a look, then the Lady sighed quietly.

"The King is dead," she said softly.

Mara's brow furrowed. "Then who is his heir? There must be an appointed King."

"Nobody," was the Lady's solemn response.

"That is not possible," insisted Mara.

"The new King is not yet chosen."

Mara raised her brows in disbelief. "What are you not saying Lady Quinn?"

The Lady of the Falls stood abruptly and went to stand at the large window, staring out at the storm. They were waiting for her to speak but it was Niem's quiet voice that broke the silence.

"I am the king's son. By birth I am his heir. But I cannot inherit, for I am nobody. If the king dies without an heir the next in the line of succession would normally inherit, or the Council would appoint a king, but as I am still living it has caused confusion and delay."

Asher wrinkled her nose, trying to make sense of what he had said. She was not an expert on kings and lines of succession, but if Niem was the king's son, and the king's son was meant to inherit, then surely that was pretty straightforward.

Mara sat down with a large exhale of breath.

"Niem..." she breathed. "It means Nobody in the old language."

He nodded, his eyes grave.

When it seemed no further explanation would be offered, Asher cleared her throat. "Can you please explain what you mean?" she asked, "for the Earthlings among us."

"And the Dragons," rumbled Dor'tiem, an unexpected gleam of humour glinting in his eye.

Quinn spun back from the window. Her scales undulated restlessly.

"In the lands of Faerla Grun, every child is born with a song of their own, a song that is created within the mother as the child grows within her. At the time of their birth the song is released, surrounding the child and sung by the women who attend the birth, naming the child, anchoring them into our lore."

The music that had guided Asher across the sinking sands and through the woods started to swirl around her once more.

"Every song is individual, created from the energy of new life, and from the plains themselves. The song links the child with their history and their future. It will play for them their entire life, and when it plays for the last time, death is nigh. Without it they are nameless, nobody."

A huge blast of wind rattled the windows of the library and Kate gasped.

Hr'tom shifted his strange new body uncomfortably in the unfamiliar chair. He was ill at ease in the house, the chair, with the humans. He longed to lie on the ground, but his pride resisted the urge. If Dor'tiem could manage, then he would manage. He swallowed his fear of the rising storm.

"Niem's mother was my niece, the daughter of my sister. She married the King when she was very young but did not conceive until her fortieth year. She poured all her energy into conceiving and safely growing her child. By the time the birthing came she was all but spent."

Quinn's misty blue grey eyes swirled with memory. She turned again to the storm outside.

"It was a night much like this one, exactly twenty years ago." Her voice was low, but Asher did not need to strain to hear the words.

"The King brought her to my home for the birthing, to be supported by her mother and myself. It was a difficult labour and a difficult birth. In the early hours of the next morning he was born. The baby survived, the Queen did not."

The wind howled and water smashed against the stone moorings of the lake. Asher glanced at Niem. He was staring at the wildness outside, seemingly oblivious to the story being told, but the white knuckles of his clenched hands told other-wise.

"And in the intensity, and fear, and sorrow, his song was never sung. Hers was ending as his should have begun. By the time we attended to the baby, the grief-stricken King and of course, the body of the Queen, the sun was rising and the song was gone."

Quinn turned to smile at her great-nephew, her ageless face shining with love, though her eyes were full of tears.

"Your father and your grandmother and I loved you very much. You were a blessing to us all. It was our greatest sorrow that we could not sing your song for you. Your father was de-termined that you would wear the crown of Faerla Grun after him and he raised you to be the next King. He tried everything to find your song."

"As have I," said Niem, his voice tired. "The Council allowed me twelve months after his death to find it, and I have travelled from one end of Andera to the other, to no avail. Perhaps it is as we feared - that my song entangled with my mother's, and she took them both to her grave. Tomorrow is my twentieth birthday. Tomorrow I stand at the ruins of the Illuminated City and cannot stake my claim to my ancestors' throne."

"What happens then?" asked Mara.

"The other contenders will present their case and the Council will elect the next king."

Mara asked another question, but Asher could not hear her. Her ears were filling with the roaring of the storm, and her heart was beating as wildly as the wind.

She scrambled to her feet and lurched towards the door, unaware of the startled exclamations and questions that followed her. Out onto the covered front porch she stumbled, pulled by the energy of the storm. She stood there with her eyes closed and her arms thrown out wide, feeling the wind whip around her body. She was surrounded by chaos and yet even that chaos had a distinct melody running through it, filling her head.

She breathed deeply, immersing herself in the music. She felt that if she stepped off the porch and into that wildness she could be consumed by the energy and become one with it, no longer trapped in her human body. It was so very tempting.

And then she heard it. Something new. Within the symphony of the storm there existed another tune, a smaller song caught in the much more powerful energy, trapped within the chaos. It called to her, reached for her. It had been travelling with the wind for a long time, and it wanted release.

Asher reached for the instruments dangling at her wrist and chose the piano. This music was a ballad, it needed keys.

"Play," she whispered as she threw the charm into the air.

The gathered group watched with amazement as the tiny silver piano expanded to full size and settled on the wooden boards, complete with a small stool.

Asher settled herself on the stool and ran her fingers along the keys. Perfectly tuned, as she expected. She closed her eyes and let the small melody come to her on the wind. Then she started to play. Her fingers moved lightly, and the notes were quiet at first, but second by second the music grew louder, more insistent.

Niem stepped forward, compelled by each note. Soon he was standing beside the piano. His eyes glowed with rapture as the music seeped into his soul. A moment later he was joined by Quinn, then Mara, Edriene and Fleur.

Asher raised her face to his and smiled. She could feel the music enveloping him as she played, she could see the wonder of it in his eyes. After twenty years trapped in the wind, the song had found its home.

The man without a name opened his mouth and started to sing.

At once the wind hushed and the rain ceased. The people of Arvana stepped out of their houses and raised their eyes in wonder at the vibrant rainbow that illuminated the sky above them, and the music that danced within each of its colours. Hearts full of joy, they felt the song swirl into each of their beings.

And so it was that the Prince of Faerla Grun sang his own name into existence, at the base of the Sacred Falls, accompanied by Asher the Musician.

Around them the Lady and the Crafters, the villagers and the Gaela, raised their voices in harmony, and wove him into the Threads.

The Lady's Weave

Asher woke at dawn the next morning well rested and clear of mind. Today she planned to travel with the prince to the ruins of the Illuminated City to see him crowned King. Then she hoped he would mobilise his men and help her and the Wens storm Ostrin and free the stolen Crafters who were being bled to power Darven. If they could stop him finding the dagger, and even steal Evie away before the night of the red moons, then they might actually have a chance at overthrowing him and restoring order.

The thought of Darven with the book, the gem and Evie filled her with dread. If they failed to stop him and he retrieved the dagger in time then all would be lost.

Her desire to find Hesta was now secondary to her desire to save her sister and Andera from Darven's madness. Once Darven was contained she could focus on finding Hesta and restoring the Threads.

Fleur and Kate were fast asleep in the other beds, Kate still fully dressed and snoring lightly. Asher had no idea what time the celebrations had ended, or when her friends had finally tumbled into bed, but she guessed it was quite late. She herself had not attended the night of joyous dancing and feasting. After separating the song from the storm, a great mental and physical weariness had consumed her, and she had headed to bed soon after the prince's name was claimed.

Ash pulled on the thick robe that was hanging on the end of her bed and grabbed her clothes. Down the hall was a small washroom with a shower. It was not as luxurious as the bathing hut, but the water was warm and refreshing.

Outside, birds were joining the dawn chorus, celebrating the calm new day. Plenty of tasty morsels had been displaced in the woods during the wild storm of the previous evening, adding to the birds' morning joy.

Dressed once more in her borrowed tunic and trousers, Asher headed downstairs quietly, not wanting to wake the others. Despite the early hour Fruda was already in the kitchen, humming happily as she baked many small loaves of bread. A full tray was cooling on the counter. Ash's mouth watered as the smell danced around her nostrils, and her stomach gurgled in anticipation.

Fruda straightened from her inspection of the hot oven and saw the Musician hovering in the doorway. Her rosy face creased in a welcoming smile.

"Come on in Asher, help yourself."

Asher did not need to be invited twice. She ducked into the kitchen and scooped up three little loaves, slathering them in butter and fresh sweet raspberry jam.

"You are riding to the Illuminated City with the Prince, I assume," said the Baker.

Asher nodded. "How did you know?" she mumbled inelegantly through a mouthful of bread. She winced guiltily at the crumbs that sprayed when she spoke.

"There was much talk of it last night. The whole village is in an uproar at their prince claiming his name and the throne. Many wanted to accompany him today, but the Lady was adamant that only a small contingent should go. Herself, Marawen, you, Fleur and two of the prince's soldiers. The young girl Treen was mightily put out. Carried on so much she was sent off to bed."

Asher munched silently as she considered this information.

"Tea?" asked Fruda.

Ash swallowed the last of her breakfast.

"Yes please."

"While the kettle is boiling you can help me pack the bread and cakes for today. From what I understand the Illuminated City is a pile of ruins, not actually a city as such, merely a figurehead of power. You'll need to carry all your supplies, there won't be anything there."

"So where does the King live? And his soldiers?" asked Asher as she helped Fruda lift trays of food out of the cupboards, realising she had no idea if Faerla Grun even had an army to support her cause.

"The previous King lived in the new city a number of miles beyond the ruins, built after the old city was destroyed. That's where the current court remained after his death. I suppose the Prince will live there once he is acknowledged as King."

Asher drank her tea and helped the Baker pack supplies, then excused herself and headed out to the lake. She felt the need to see the water, feel its energy and timelessness. The thought that it had endured for centuries, seeing kings and conquerors rise and fall filled her with a sense of hope. That soon enough this madness would pass and become part of history too.

Most of the village was still and quiet as she made her way along the cobbled paths, with the exception of the clucking chickens and occasional dog bark. The houses were shuttered and silent as the inhabitants slept off their celebrations. Ahead of her the lake shone like molten silver in the pre-dawn, and the sound of the distant falls echoed softly across the water.

A movement much further along the lake caught her attention. Lady Quinn was disappearing off the path and into the trees. Without thinking Asher automatically followed her.

She found Quinn sitting quietly on a wooden bench beside a row of stone markers that rose from the ground. Even protected in this clearing under the canopy of trees, the stones were worn by the elements in varying degrees. On some of the stones the writing was still clear, but on others it was worn and much harder to read.

Asher paused, realising too late that she had blundered uninvited into a private graveyard. She hesitated, then turned to leave, hoping Quinn was unaware of her intrusion.

"Musician." The Lady's voice stopped her. "Come and join me."

It was a request Asher could not refuse. Reluctantly she walked towards the bench, hovering awkwardly beside it until Quinn indicated with a wave of her hand that Ash should sit.

Quinn pointed to the stones on her right.

"My mother, my sister and my niece, the Queen." Her voice was soft and calm, but Asher could feel the sadness and the grief radiating around her.

"And here lie my children, buried beside their father." She pointed to the tallest stone on the left. "Torim, who loved me well. When we promised our lives to one another we knew this would be our fate, but still, it was hard to watch him wither with age as my own body remained strong and young." The Lady's eyes glistened.

"Beside him lies our eldest son Aron who died as a child, almost eighty years ago now. Then Sylvie who died in her prime, fifty years ago. Strange to think she has now been gone longer than the years she lived. And Lula." Quinn's voice hitched, and she cleared her throat. "Lula who died in my arms a few months ago, at the age of eighty-two, surrounded by her children and grandchildren, and Treen, her great-granddaughter. A life well lived."

"I am sorry," whispered Asher.

"Our gifts, they are a blessing Asher. But to outlive your children, and their children, and theirs..." Quinn stared off into the distance.

Asher sat silently, unsure what she should say, if anything at all.

"The Weaver is blessed. Her Heir is found. I must wait a little longer."

Unexpectedly she twisted to face Asher, her water-coloured eyes luminous in the shadows of the trees.

"I met your great-grandmother, you know. She was the Weaver when Ostrin invaded Faerla Grun. She came to the Illuminated City a year before the invasion. I have often wondered if she knew what was to pass. I was only a child at the time, perhaps eleven or twelve. She had been the Weaver for two decades already, without a daughter to name as Heir. It was another thirty years before your grandmother was born."

Asher puzzled through what was saying. "That doesn't really make sense. How could she be so old before she had a child?"

Quinn smiled softly. "Age is an illusion Asher. Such as we are not bound by it."

Ash tucked this away to consider later. "Have you met Hesta?" she asked.

Quinn shook her head. "Indeed I have not. She has made overtures during the years and I have always rebuffed her, unwilling to make friends with the woman who refused to offer assistance when Faerla Grun desperately needed it. Who could have ended the war with a weave of her Threads and chose not to."

Asher frowned. "But didn't you say that it was Hesta's mother who was the Weaver when the war happened? Hesta wasn't even born."

"The Weaver is the Weaver. Her actions are those of her forebears and her descendants. That is the continuity of the Threads."

Asher thought of her grandmother, dedicated to the Weave, and her mother who had long ago forsaken any responsibility in her pre-destined role. And she thought of herself, fumbling her way through this new world. She shook her head.

"No," she said quietly, surprising herself.

Quinn's pale eyebrows shot up.

"No," repeated Asher slowly, trying to articulate her jumbled thoughts clearly. "I don't believe that is true. Nobody is defined by those that came before, or those that come after. We get to choose who we are, how we behave, and what we stand for. That is the power of the Weave. It is never still. The Loom clacks even now, spinning threads that are constantly changing. No-one's threads are pre-woven. And no two weaves are the same. That includes Hesta's and Ginarwen's and mine."

"And my Weave? How are the Threads spun for me?"

Within a heartbeat, Asher was no longer seeing the grove, or the gravestones, or the Lady herself. Before her she could see the giant loom, and the glowing strands that told the story of Quinn, Lady of the Falls. It unfolded clearly before her.

"As a small child you made a vow that you would never abandon Faerla Grun as you felt the Weaver had. You dedicated yourself to protecting this place and began to believe that only you could do so. Your living vow has woven you so tightly into the Threads that you are not able to leave. Your Heir will come, Lady of the Falls, when you are ready to forgive and let go. When you have the courage to trust that another will care for this place, for this land, as fiercely and as devotedly as you have. When you make space for her."

Quinn stared at the Weaver sitting beside her in the shape of a girl.

"So there is an Heir to follow me?"

Asher nodded, her eyes fixated on what the Threads had woven.

"Can you see who?" Quinn asked hesitantly. "Is it Treen?"

Asher shook her head. "I cannot interpret the unwoven Threads yet. I'm kind of surprised I could actually see your past. This is the first time I've done anything like this."

She grinned sheepishly, and in an instant the Weaver fell away, leaving only Ash once more. "Well that was incredibly strange! I have no idea how I did that, or if I could even do it again."

Quinn found herself smiling in response.

"I thank you. Now I offer you a truth in return young Musician. The Crafting within you is strong and every day it grows. You are learning to control it and that is imperative. You will be a powerful Weaver. But there is anger and resentment that burns deep within your being, and you must release this before you can truly be whole. You have spent too many years denying yourself. If you cannot master your anger, the Crafting will destroy you."

Asher's eyes widened in surprise, but before she could say anything the Lady of the Falls continued lightly.

"Take it from me, it's no fun harbouring resentments and anger."

Asher nodded slowly. Before the arrival of the Weaver in her life, she would never have considered herself in such a way, preferring to believe her veneer of calm collectedness. Of contentment with her small, quiet, mousy life. But now she was learning that her music had been a shield and a distraction. A way to protect herself and to avoid the anger and resentment that were indeed seething inside her. Anger at her mother for being so fragile. Anger at her father for constantly shushing her. Anger at her sister for not sharing the load. And resentment that she must be always perfect, quiet, and malleable.

They sat together in companionable silence for a while longer, as the sun rose above the village and the bleary-eyed people began the rituals of their day.

"Come now, it is time to go back. We must get the prince to the Illuminated City before noon. And the Spirits are very keen for you to accompany him, if you so desire."

Asher nodded as the two of them stood up. She would not miss it for the world.

Chapter Twenty-Four

The Illuminated City

They gathered at the Lady's house, the small contingent who would accompany he who was no longer Niem to the Illuminated City. Asher, Fleur and Mara watched quietly as the prince and his men organised the horses they would ride upon.

Fruda and Saffen had carefully loaded packs with food and water to last them for two days, and these were now being slung across the saddles. Inside the house the Lady was busy with Treen who was furious and rebellious at being left behind.

Asher's thoughts kept returning to the moment with Quinn in the grove, when the great Loom had appeared before her, as real as if she was standing in the Weaving Room. She knew if she had reached out her hands she could have actually touched those luminous threads. Instead she had asked the Weave to show her the Lady's life, and somehow she had known exactly how to read the colourful pattern. Then just as unexpectedly as it had appeared, the Loom was gone.

"Righto," said the prince beside them, startling Ash back to the present moment. "Can you three ride?"

Mara and Fleur nodded confidently, Ash a little less so. Her riding experience was limited to a few hours here and there at Kate's family property.

One of the soldiers brought over a small wooden block and another led over a chestnut mare for Fleur. The younger girl stepped onto the block, grabbed hold of the saddle and smoothly pulled herself onto the horse, gently stroking the animal's neck and murmuring soft words of comfort as she did so. A moment later she picked up the reins and pressed her knees into the horse's flanks, giving the command to walk on.

Mara stepped on the block next, her usual long dress discarded in favour of a pair of heavy brown cotton trousers and a cream knit jumper. Her thick dark hair had been washed and styled into a large, loose bun on the top of her head which was pinned in place with gleaming gems. Asher wondered whether the Jeweller was aware how much the flashing diamonds and rubies and sapphires resembled a tiara. Her wrists and fingers were encircled with gold and precious stones. Asher could feel the power radiating from her.

The men brought over a large black stallion for Marawen, and effortlessly she swung her leg over the saddle and sat atop the huge horse. He whinnied with pride and threw his head from side to side.

"Stop that," commanded the Crafter sternly, and the horse ceased his thrashing. "Better," she said approvingly and he tossed his head slightly.

"That's going to be an interesting battle of wills," murmured the prince from beside Asher as they watched horse and rider prance away, "my money's on Gallead. The horse," he clarified. "He's a fantastic ride, but incredibly spirited."

Asher laughed. "Some-how I think Marawen will have that horse bowed to her will before we leave the village."

"You could be right. Now what about you?"

Asher wrinkled her nose and said nothing. Her stomach was churning with nerves but she did not want the prince to think she could not keep up and decide that she could not come at all.

Knees weak, she stepped onto the block.

The soldier brought forward a mid-size honey coloured mare whose blonde mane had been plaited together neatly. Asher froze, her mind blank. Though she had just seen both Fleur and Mara climb onto their horses, she could not seem to remember where she should put her feet and hands.

"Put your right foot in the stirrup and swing your left leg over the saddle," murmured the prince softly beside her. "Hold onto that part there."

Asher threw him a small grateful smile, then turned her attention to scrambling onto the patient horse. After a few awkward minutes she was finally seated somewhat confidently.

"What's her name?" she asked, stroking the horse's neck and silently thanking her for being so calm.

"Honey."

Ash grinned. "Of course it is. Who named her? Treen?"

The prince huffed, his face affronted. "I did, thank you very much."

"That took imagination," she said cheekily as she nudged the horse with her knees and shook the reins. "Come on Honey, let's go join the others."

The sun was rising above the mountains as they trotted out of the grove and onto the main highway. The prince and Quinn led the small group. Asher, Mara and Fleur made up the middle posse, and two of the prince's men brought up the rear.

Once beyond the woods Asher could see why the lands of Faerla Grun were referred to as the Great Plains.

All around them endless green and yellow fields ran to the horizon, dotted with the occasional farmhouse or collection of buildings. Far off in the distance to their left she could just make out the outline of a large town, but the wide road they were on seemed to be taking them to nowhere. As hard as she could squint she was unable to see anything ahead of them except more grasslands and farmers' fields.

With every passing minute, the woods and the Mountains fell further behind them. Uncertainty and excitement about what lay ahead bubbled in Asher's stomach.

The sun climbed higher as they rode, but the late Autumn day was not warm. The cool air was a welcome relief on Asher's sweaty face. She was so focused on not embarrassing herself and falling off that her jaw was starting to hurt from how tightly she was tensing her face, and her wrists felt stiff from their firm grip on the reins.

Fortunately Honey was a beautifully mannered mare, and seemed willing to accommodate her rider's inexperience, for which Ash was incredibly grateful. She knew if she did fall it would not be Honey's fault. More than once she thanked the stars that she was not riding the black stallion. He tossed his head and pulled at the bit as he cantered along, testing the aptitude and strength of his rider. Mara was undeterred by his antics, pulling sharply when required and applying a firm grip with her knees to keep him in line. In fact, she almost seemed to be relishing the small battle between them.

Unsurprisingly Fleur was a confident, competent rider. Ash envied her the ease with which she sat atop her horse, curiously surveying the wide lands around them.

They rode without speaking, everyone focused on their own musings, including the prince.

Ash stared at his straight back and wondered what he was thinking as they drew ever closer to his destiny. To the ruins of the royal city, the place his ancestors had built and then been forced to abandon as the enemy had razed it to the ground. Marawen's ancestor. As though he felt her gaze, the prince glanced over his shoulder at her and quirked his brows.

Asher immediately straightened her spine and endeavoured to look like she was born to the saddle. The prince grinned, not fooled for a moment. Asher grinned back, feeling completely at ease, until Honey mis-stepped and Asher bounced awkwardly. She stared off into the distance, avoiding the knowing grey eyes of the prince, who was now chuckling to himself.

Minutes passed into hours and the stiffness of her legs and back melded with the numbness of her bottom. Teeth gritted she retreated to the music in her mind. Instantly her body responded, relaxing overly tensed muscles and softening her clenched face.

She spent the rest of the ride that way, playing music in her mind, filling her brain and body with the energy of each note. She paid very little attention to her surroundings, or to the passage of time, so it was with surprise that Ash realised they were no longer surrounded by fields, but by the vast stone debris of crumbling, abandoned buildings.

In silence they clip clopped along the wide roads, awed and humbled by the enormity of the Illuminated City and all that had been lost.

The music of Faerla Grun swirled within Asher and filled her senses. Seconds later a great light filled her vision, momentarily blinding her. She blinked hard. When she opened her eyes Ash was no longer seeing the ruined city in the present, but instead was seeing it as it had been for centuries, filled with life and music and colour and people and energy.

Around her residents of the city laughed and talked with each other, hung out their washing on lines strung high above the streets, pushed carts full of produce, walked in groups dressed in richly made colourful garments.

The whitewashed stone buildings gleamed in the sun. Crushed opal had been mixed in with the whitewash, giving the buildings a shimmering, otherworldly feel. The streets were lined with large pavers, which gleamed with veins of gold. Illuminated indeed. The whole city radiated energy and prosperity.

As their small group rode along the bustling, vibrant streets, the residents called out and waved to them, but only Ash waved in reply.

"This city is full of its ghosts," murmured Mara quietly to Fleur. "Do you feel them?"

Fleur nodded, her face solemn, her eyes flicking around the empty ruins. They could feel them, but they could not see them.

But to Asher the city and its residents were as real as the Jeweller and her cousin riding beside her. They were certainly not ghosts. She was not seeing an image or a memory from the past, she was in the past, while simultaneously existing in the present.

They rode through the many streets of the city, heading toward its centre and the glorious palace which housed the Kings and Queens of Faerla Grun.

As they turned the last corner Asher gasped in shock.

"Oh my stars," she breathed, "it's incredible."

Mara turned a quizzical eye toward her. "What is?"

Ash pointed at the gleaming golden palace rising out of the enormous square, its large windows sparkling in the sun, each one embossed with shimmering diamond dust. Burbling fountains and large stone pots overflowing with lush plants and flowers surrounded the building, providing an atmosphere of peace and tranquillity.

This was no fortress, protected by gates and soldiers. Instead it was the heart of the city, a place all were welcome. Many inhabitants sat on brightly painted wooden benches in the lush green park to the left of the palace, under the shade of large trees.

Ceremonial guards adorned the wide palace steps, more of a decoration than a security detail.

"This place, it's so vibrant I almost want to close my eyes."

Mara frowned, unable to see whatever it was that so enthralled the young Musician, but Asher was oblivious to the Jeweller. Her eyes were darting right and left, trying to take everything in.

The huge doors to the palace were flung open as they approached and a woman dressed in a voluminous red and gold dress hurried down the steps, followed by a retinue of servants and courtiers.

"Weaver Merriwen!" she called to Ash, her face shining and her voice rich with pleasure. "Welcome to the Illuminated City! His Majesty and I are thrilled to have you here at last."

Asher opened her mouth to respond, but her words were drowned out by Mara.

"Asher. Asher! Did you hear what I said. What are you staring at so intently?"

The music evaporated, as did the glorious city and its residents, as she was pulled firmly back to the present. Asher blinked rapidly to clear her vision, trying to reclaim what was lost. But the palace was gone, and in its place was only a massive pile of worn and discoloured stone.

They had come to a standstill in the ruins of the large square. The road ended here, there was nowhere else to go.

The manicured park was no more, instead wild grasses grew haphazardly among the fallen rock, and tenacious ivy curled around the piles of rubble. In some places nature had completely reclaimed whole sections of the city, burying the old buildings beneath dirt and grass.

Asher whipped her head around, desperately seeking any evidence of what she had once existed, but all around her the great city lay in ruins, illuminated no more.

"No..." she whispered, "no."

"Are you okay?" asked Mara gently, her voice more than a little worried.

"The city..." Asher shook her head. She could not say anything more or the thick tears that were welling in her throat would pour forth and she would not be able to hold them back.

The enormity of what had been and what was lost almost overwhelmed her. A thousand years of history, of culture, gone. Destroyed by greed and ignorance. A gentle, scholarly civilisation scattered to the winds.

The grief she was feeling was so very real, so very personal, far greater than that she would feel from a vision of the past. Ash tried to focus through the pain, to make sense of what she was feeling. As her mind and racing heart settled, only one explanation remained.

'Quinn,' she called out with her mind. *'I can feel your grief. It overwhelms me.'*

The Lady of the Falls turned in her saddle to face Asher. Her face was pale and her eyes were full of tears.

'Every time it is like this for me. I cannot bear to be here, yet with every coronation I must return to bear witness. This is the third time I have stood among the ruins to crown a monarch. I pray this is my last. You saw the city. You know what was lost.'

Asher nodded.

'Then tell me Musician, explain to me why the Threads were spun that way. Why the Weaver could not, would not, intervene.'

Tears Asher could no longer contain rolled down her cheeks.

'I don't know,' she whispered into Quinn's mind. *'I simply don't know.'*

"Welcome," a solemn voice greeted them across the ruins, pulling Asher out of Quinn's mind and grief.

As she dashed away the wetness on her face and adjusted to the present, Asher realised they were surrounded by perhaps twenty-five other people, clustered in four groups. They stood together in the remains of the great square but in separate groups. By accident or design three of the groups had formed in the far corners of the square. She glanced from group to group.

The three groups in the corners were assembled much like theirs. A young man who appeared to be a contender for the throne, and his family or supporters. The fourth group were mingling around the middle of the square and had the puffed up importance of officials, wearing heavy robes and great golden chains. They were there to oversee the proceedings and most likely make the final decision on who would be king. On a large stone a thick red velvet cushion had been placed. Atop it sat the gleaming, gem encrusted golden crown of Faerla Grun.

The general air was serious and tense. No light banter filled the air. People spoke quietly to each other, their words muted and hard to discern. This was an unusual coronation. For the first time in many generations there was no pre-appointed heir. Today the future of Faerla Grun and its noble families would be decided. Anything was possible.

The great ruins of the Illuminated City lay silently, an observer to this ritual.

The Lady of the Falls swung her left leg over her horse and leapt lightly to the ground. The clustered men and women inclined their heads in respect, greeting her solemnly. She acknowledged each person in turn, greeting them by name with a smile, and clasping their hands as she walked among them.

Her presence seemed to lift the mood of the attendees, who offered their own small smiles in response.

Around Asher, the members of her own group were dismounting and leading their horses to an area of the square where water and hay had been prepared. With growing trepidation she watched as first Mara, then Fleur, echoed Quinn's casually controlled leap off their horses. She had never had to dismount in such a manner before. At Kate's farm she had simply ridden back to the mounting block and some-one had always held the horse still for her. Honey seemed to sense her uncertainty, or maybe she was simply eager for a rest after the long ride, for she shifted restlessly and nickered softly.

With each passing second Asher knew she risked becoming conspicuous by remaining on the horse. Soon enough she would draw the attention of the other people, and she really did not want that. She had been hoping to be an unobtrusive observer to this whole situation.

Just when she was starting to think she would need to either ask for help or attempt the leg swing while some-how holding onto the saddle and keeping Honey still, the prince appeared at her side with a smile.

"Need some help Musician?" he asked softly, his face full of humour and his eyes alight with suppressed laughter.

His mirth somehow made the situation worse. Asher was tempted to scowl at him and tell him that she was perfectly fine on her own. She fleetingly wondered if it was worth the risk of breaking a leg just to save her pride.

"Or not," he offered with a grin, reading the expression on her face correctly. He turned slightly, as though he would walk away.

"Oh fine," she hissed as Honey shifted again, and Ash slid awkwardly in the saddle, "yes please."

Keeping his voice low, he offered advice on how she should shift her weight as she brought her leg across the saddle, then gently placed his hands around her waist and supported her as she slid to the ground.

"Thank you," murmured Ash, refusing to look into his laughing grey eyes. Her face was burning with embarrassment.

"You're welcome," he replied lightly, then he turned and strode into the middle of the square, where the three other young men had gathered with the Council members.

The soldier named Simon quietly led Honey away, and Ash walked over to where Mara and Fleur were standing with Quinn.

"What happens now?" she asked softly.

Before Quinn could answer, a long single note blew across the square, piercing the tension between the humans and the layered atmosphere of the ancient stones. Immediately Asher felt her own music rise in response, and the Golden Globe sprung to life.

Hush she commanded them.

"It begins," murmured Quinn, her voice sending shivers up and down Asher's spine. "We cannot leave now, until a king is named, by consensus or by blood."

Chapter Twenty-Five

The King of Faerla Grun

The trumpet continued to play for a few minutes more, the rich notes dancing around the four young men standing proudly in the centre of the square. And then the music was gone, the final note lingering for three or four seconds before fading away into the dust.

The oldest and most senior of the Council stepped into the centre of the square. He was resplendent in golden robes that swirled around him as he moved. His eyes and brows were dark, a startling contrast to the bushy white hair that fell to his shoulders.

"Welcome to the Illuminated City, Council Members, Dignitaries, Lady Quinn of the Sacred Falls, families and friends. We meet here in the place that was the heart of our people, the home of our Kings and Queens for a thousand years. The place where every King and Queen has been crowned."

For just a moment Asher's vision blurred and she thought she could see hundreds of men and women superimposed on the scene in front of her, each kneeling as the gleaming golden crown was laid upon their heads. Music pounded like a drum around the square. She blinked hard and the blurred figures and the harsh drumming were gone.

"Before us stand the noble sons of Faerla Grun, those who claim the crown through kinship to the late King Rudorph, a wise and just king. May his song be ever sung."

"May his song be ever sung." Murmured the crowd reverently.

"In ages past, any dispute would be settled by combat, the victor taking his or her place as king or queen, and the contenders sentenced to exile, or even death. Today, we seek a more peaceful way. Each claimant will have a chance to sing his song for us, and then to share why he should be elected the next King. If the song cannot be sung for any reason," the old man's eyes flicked briefly to Niem and then back to the crowd, "that claimant, and any sons or daughters of his line, is eliminated from the line of succession. They can make no future claim."

"That seems harsh," whispered Asher to Mara.

The former princess shrugged. "It is the way of things. It eliminates messy allegiances and claims as the generations pass by. The last thing anyone wants is confusion over who is the rightful ruler and heir."

"Like babies swapped at birth?" Asher threw her an arch look but the Jeweller resolutely ignored her.

"Lord Maken, step forward."

A tall, gangly young man with long dark hair and a nervous manner stepped into the circle the Lord Chamberlain had drawn on the ground. He gulped a shuddering breath and then began to sing his song.

The listening crowd tried hard to conceal their winces. Whether it was the nerves, or just a general ineptitude with tone and pitch, it was a difficult listen.

When he finished the crowd clapped enthusiastically, pleased for both him and themselves that is was over. Asher could not recall a single word that had been sung.

"I am Maken, son of Plymer. My father was first cousin to King Rudorph. Their grandmother, my great grandmother, was the queen prior to King Rudorph. I claim my right to the throne through him." Maken's voice shook as he delivered his prepared speech, and it was with audible relief that he stepped out of the circle.

He resumed his place with the others, and smiled happily at his young wife, standing with his support group. Her face was twisted with annoyance, and she was mouthing an admonishment at him. It took him a minute to work out what she was saying, and then Maken's face coloured in dismay when he realised he had not presented his reasons as to why he should be king.

He opened and closed his mouth repeatedly, unsure whether he should speak up now, but it did not matter, his opportunity had passed.

"Lord Stober," called the Lord Chamberlain.

Stober sang his song with gusto, rattled off his lineage with pride, and then spoke passionately about his love for Faerla Grun and his deep desire to serve as a good king.

The five members of the Council and the Lord Chamberlain nodded encouragingly. Asher found herself liking him and his kind, earnest spirit.

"Lord Lyel."

A man a few years older than Niem stepped into the circle. His face was similar to the young prince, suggesting a close blood relationship, but instead of Niem's warmth and compassion, Lyel's face was cold and haughty. He swaggered with the arrogance of a man who believed himself entitled to the world and everything in it.

"I am Lord Lyel, and I claim the throne through my mother, the Princess Gladriol. She is the sister of the late king Rudorph.

I am his nephew and the closest relative with a legitimate claim to the throne. No offense to my nameless cousin."

He smirked at the prince, his eyes gleaming with meanness.

"I was born in the royal palace in Sedendria, not some backwater village beside a lake, and the king himself was in attendance to hear my song sung for the first time. I have spent the last year since the king's death immersing myself in the court, not gallivanting around the world, unlike others. I know what it takes to be king. I know how to command. I have the lineage, the strength of mind and body, and the fortitude. Not to mention, my song."

Asher hated him. She just knew he would have a dreadful song, full of harsh notes and a discordant melody, a perfect fit for his loathsome personality. So she was extremely disappointed when Lyel sang a beautiful song in a rich baritone.

She glared at his retreating back as he stepped out of the circle. He resumed his place beside a small, richly dressed older woman who smiled lovingly at him, her eyes bright with maternal pride. He ignored her. Instead he muttered to the man who stood to his right, and the two of them sneered nastily at the group from Arvana.

The Lord Chamberlain cleared his throat, sliding his glance to the final member of the claimants.

"And finally, our prince."

It was known to all that the prince had no name, but Asher was glad that the Lord Chamberlain had not referred to him as niem – nobody.

He stepped into the circle, tall and proud and radiating calmness. Asher realised he was actually the youngest of the group, but his maturity and sense of self made up for his years.

"You all know my story," he said, his warm voice swirling around them. "I was blessed to be born without my song, without my name. Blessed because I had the opportunity to decide the person I wanted to be, supported and loved by my father and my aunt and my grandmother."

Quinn's eyes shone with pride and tears.

"My father always expected me to be king after him. And after my birth in Arvana, the village of the sacred falls, I was raised in Sedendria, as you all well know. Each of you is familiar to me as are your families. We have shared meals, and stories, and griefs and joys together."

Around the square people were smiling and nodding. Lyel's face was dark with displeasure.

"When my father died a great hole opened up in my heart, in my soul. I longed to be the king you deserve, but without my name we all knew this was not possible. The Council in its wisdom and compassion gave me a year to find my name, to find my song. I thank them for this opportunity."

He clasped his hand together and bowed to the old men who accepted his thanks with genuine smiles.

"It is with great pleasure and no small amount of relief that I sing for you now, the song of Rhion."

And Rhion son of Rudorph raised his voice to the skies above the Illuminated City and sang.

Prince Rhion. The murmur spread through crowd. As the last notes echoed around the stones, Lord Stober thumped his left hand over his chest and bowed his head.

"King Rhion, I swear allegiance."

His declaration spurred the gathered crowd who started clapping and cheering.

"Thank you everyone, thank you, please calm down," called the Lord Chamberlain. "Let us not get ahead of ourselves. The Council needs to –"

"He is cheating!" interrupted a furious voice. "He has no song, he is nobody, NOBODY!"

"Lyel, hush," whispered Princess Gladriol frantically, reaching for his arm. Her enraged son swatted her away.

"There is only one way he can have a song. He has stolen it."

A collective gasp of outrage and horror burst from the crowd. Rhion's and Quinn's faces blanched with shock.

"Lord Lyel!" breathed the Head of the Council, "that is a serious and dangerous claim to make. Should we attribute this to a moment of disappointment? Do you wish to retract this accusation?"

Lyel hesitated for a moment, his eyes darting from person to person, his face flushed with his anger and ambition.

"Please Lyel..." whimpered his devastated mother, "do not pursue this vile claim against our new king."

She laid a gentle hand on his stiff shoulder.

That desperate plea seemed to incite him. He turned scornful eyes on the fragile woman. "You disgust me," he hissed to her, "you always have. The throne is mine, father knew it. He would never have allowed this travesty."

Violently he shook away her touch, elbowing her so hard she stumbled and would have fallen if Mara had not rushed to her side.

"What is happening?" whispered Asher to Simon.

The soldier's face burned with anger. Though he answered her, he did not look at her. His attention was completely rivetted on the scene before them, his body thrumming with readiness, his hand resting on the handle of his sword.

"Lyel the Grotesque accuses King Rhion of stealing a song. The only way to do that is to murder a newborn child as the mother sings the song and then steal that song for yourself by murdering the mother. It has only been done twice before in our known history, by desperate, evil men. A stolen song requires despicable acts, but it also twists the stealer's soul, turning them into something depraved. It is the worst accusation you can make to a son or daughter of Faerla Grun."

"None of this is true," said the Lady of the Falls calmly, her deep voice washing over all of them. "I was there as witness when Rhion received his song. It had been waiting for him in the wind since the night of his birth. It was his, freely given and received."

Everyone sighed with relief, and the Head of the Council almost sagged with released tension.

"Then that is resolved. Lord Lyel retracts his accusation, and the Lady Quinn stands as witness to the origins of our King's song. Council, I ask you now - all in favour of appointing Rhion el Rudorph as the King and Custodian of the lands of Faerla Grun, raise your hand."

Five hands reached high.

"NO!" screamed Lyel. "You take her word for it? His own kin? She most likely orchestrated the plot."

Outrage swelled within the crowd. Furious words burst from everyone.

"Lord Lyel! You go too far. The Lady is above reproach. Her integrity is beyond question." The Lord Chamberlain's voice was stern, his face hard. "You will apologise. Now."

Lyel shook his head.

"Never will I apologise to that pretender or that witch."

The sound of steel dragging against steel cut through the air.

Asher's eyes flew to Rhion, who had drawn his sword. The stain on his own name was something he would have shrugged off, but this horrendous accusation against his aunt would not be allowed to go unpunished. His grey eyes, normally so gentle and full of humour, were dark with anger. His lively face was set and still.

The devastated princess Gladriol sobbed in Mara's arms, completely ignored by her son.

When Rhion spoke, his voice was hard and low. It carried across the square, echoing against the stones of the ruined palace.

"Lyel, I challenge you. For the honour of our Lady of the Falls, and the integrity of the Crown. Bring forth your weapon."

For the first time uncertainty flashed across Lyel's face. He seemed to finally realise that he had gone too far. He glanced from one stony face to another, and then at the new King holding his sword with such fierce intent, and a tendril of fear curled within his eyes.

Rhion, ever kind, saw that fear and was moved by it. He lowered his sword.

"Lyel, cousin, it has been a difficult time for all. All my life you believed it likely you would be the next king. I understand how strange and unsettling today's events must be. Retract your accusation against the Lady and all is forgiven and forgotten."

He stuck the point of his sword in the dirt.

Murmurs of respect and appreciation buzzed around the watching crowd. Asher could feel their relief. Nobody wanted bloodshed on this auspicious day, nobody wanted to see cousin fight cousin. People were already starting to smile and relax, seeing the danger as passed. The moment of madness eased.

Asher's body was thrumming and her hearing and eyesight seemed amplified. Around her the ruined city was humming with Rhion's song, celebrating the crowning of a new king. Her own energy churned in response. Beside her the soldier Simon had relaxed his grip on his sword. Opposite her the members of the Council were nodding proudly at each other. A tentative sense of relief and even celebration was returning. People were no longer paying any attention to the vile Lord Lyel. She wondered why she alone was so on edge.

The music of Faerla Grun buzzed urgently in her ears. It would not let her relax. And then the flash of light caught the edge of her eye. The scrape of a dagger being drawn from its concealment inside a long sleeve whispered at the edge of her hearing. The slight whoosh of steel cutting through air.

And just like in the woods Asher reacted without thinking.

She ran faster than she had ever thought possible, speeding past the whirring blade and leaping in front of the new king. She was unaware of the gasps and screams of the people watching. Every ounce of her being was focused on the dagger spinning relentlessly towards her.

Asher did not know if the Weaver would interfere in this assassination, or if she would let events run their course. She did not understand how an entire city had been allowed to fall, or why. She did not know how it was determined who would live and who would die. She only knew that Rhion's threads would not end here, not if she could help it. This city would not lose another king, and she would not lose another friend.

"No," she whispered to the blade, reaching for the music of the Illuminated City, still murmuring after all these years. The old stones poured forth their dormant energy, eager to help her stop this killing. Too many had shed their blood in this ancient place.

There was no time to choose an instrument, she simply raised her hand.

"No," she said again, the word echoing like thunder across the square as she channelled her energy towards the spinning blade.

The dagger exploded into a thousand shards of light. It burned furiously for a millisecond before crumbling into cinders which floated harmlessly to the ground.

For a heartbeat everyone stood frozen in shock, then Rhion's soldiers leapt at Lyel, drawing their swords and surrounding him with their blades. His face contorted with fury and fear, but his body shook with defiance.

Rhion grabbed Asher's shoulders and gave her a small squeeze.

"Don't ever do that again," he said. "I felt my heart stop. Quite literally stop."

Asher wrinkled her nose as she peered at him. His face was certainly pale. She pulled his hands away from her shoulders and held them in her own for a moment, offering comfort and reassurance.

"If you stop having knives thrown at you, then I won't have to keep rescuing you."

Her little joke seemed to help. Rhion took a deep breath and smiled.

The silence in the square was absolute. Even the shocked members of the Council said nothing. Everyone was darting their gazes between Asher and Rhion and Lyel, their eyes wide, their mouths agape.

Asher turned to look at Lyel. Cousin to the king. Traitor and would be murderer. She took two steps towards him. He immediately stepped backwards, and into the tip of Simon's blade.

Asher eyed him up and down, her dislike clear. Anger seethed within her, and music thundered in response. She could feel it rising in her mind, tingling in her hands. She swallowed it down.

"That is the second dagger you have thrown at your cousin, the king. The second time in as many days that you have tried to murder him and claim his throne." Her tone was light, almost conversational, but her eyes were unforgiving.

"You have brought dishonour on your family and yourself."

She took another step, slowly closing the gap between them. Music pounding with retribution egged her on. Lyel's eyes flashed, as his mother whimpered his name. He shot the princess a look of pure loathing, before returning his gaze to Asher.

"What are you going to do to me?" he hissed.

Asher took a long moment to stare him down. She let him see the full force of the energy swirling in her eyes, and then she shook her head and let the energy ease. Quinn was right, she needed to let go of her anger, before it consumed her.

"Nothing," she said softly. "It is not my place to sentence you. I leave your fate in the hands of your King, and his Council."

She turned away and walked back to Fleur. The incredible energy was dissipating, as was the anger, and it felt like she was shrinking, returning to normal. Her head was pounding a little and her throat was rather dry. She was desperate for a glass of water.

The Lord Chamberlain finally found his voice. "Guards, tie Lord Lyel to the horses' trough. We will deal with him soon enough. Young lady," he called to Ash.

Asher turned around and raised her face to the old Councillor.

"Who are you?"

She looked at Mara, who was smiling at her like a proud mother. She looked at the Lady Quinn, who inclined her head in respect. All eyes were upon her, truly seeing her, for perhaps the first time in her life.

Who am I? A daughter, a sister, a musician, a friend. A simple, ordinary girl from a planet far away. And something more. The last vestiges of the concealment charm shattered and fell away.

Deliberately, slowly, she pulled the humming globe from beneath her tunic and held it high for all to see. Then she closed her fist around it, allowing its energy to burn into her palm. Asher raised her voice to swirl around the square, to fill every listening ear.

"I am Asher the Musician. I am the Weaver's Heir."

A beam of sunlight illuminated the ruins of the palace, sliding across the stones and the humans gathered there, until finally coming to rest on her.

Asher lifted her face to the sky. The warmth on her face was soothing and invigorating. Far away, lying forgotten on a side table in the Weaver's library, a small brown book glowed, and spidery words began to fill the pages. Along the spine golden letters appeared, spelling a single word. *Asherwen.*

"The Weaver's Heir?" repeated the Lord Chamberlain in surprise. "What are you doing here?"

"I seek your assistance. Andera is at war. The Lord Adviser to the Ostrin Queen has banished the Weaver and disrupted the Threads. Crafters are being pursued and persecuted. I require your army, your support."

"What does any of that have to do with us? We are not interested in the affairs of Ostrin," said the Lord Chamberlain fiercely.

"This is greater than Ostrin sir," said Asher respectfully, "greater than Andera. The universes are in peril."

Indecision flashed across his face, and he turned to mutter with the other members of the Council.

"Please," implored Asher, "In the name of the Weaver I request your support."

It was the wrong thing to say. The faces of the old men hardened, their eyes went flat.

"The Weaver?" said the Lord Chamberlain. "What loyalty do we owe the Weaver? In our time of greatest need, when our lands and people were being decimated, our people turned to the Weaver for assistance, and were denied. Her war is nothing to us."

His words hit Asher hard in the chest and she felt the air whoosh out of her body. With every ounce of strength she kept her face calm and her body upright.

The old man shook his head in dismissal. "We appreciate what you have done today for our new king. But we want nothing to do with Ostrin or the Weaver. You may leave now."

Shocked and feeling helpless Asher turned desperate eyes to Quinn. The Lady of the Falls stepped forward.

"My Lord," she interjected, her warm, liquid voice filling the spaces between them all. "I too have carried my grudges and my scars. But this threat is far bigger, far greater than a century old dispute with a woman long dead."

Almost on cue a great rumble of thunder roared across the plains, and a hole ripped open in the sky. From deep within the chasm they could all see a huge cosmic storm twisting and churning, hurtling towards them from the far reaches of space.

"What, by all the songs, is that?" gasped the Lord Chamberlain.

Quinn's eyes were wide with horror and her voice was strained when she replied.

"*That*, Frances, is the bigger threat. Welcome to a world without the Weaver."

Chapter Twenty-Six

The Storm arrives

Asher gaped at the tempest raging above them. Could this be the Laneisian storm? Had it somehow broken free of its own planet and was racing across the universe? If it had, then surely that meant the Laneisian were lost.

Agonising pain tore through Asher, and she stumbled to the ground, gasping for breath.

Fleur dropped immediately beside her. "What is it?"

Asher closed her eyes, breathing deeply to ease the pain. In her mind's eye the great Loom hitched and shuddered.

"The Weave..." she whispered, every word an effort, "I can feel it inside me. Something is very, very wrong."

And then the Threads tore, and the Weave twisted erratically. Asher screamed. A planet had been devoured by the storm. Thousands upon thousands of magical and non-magical beings did not even have time to plead for mercy as their world was destroyed. Asher felt their loss deep within her being. Every fibre of her soul was burning in pain.

She cried out as her body shook ferociously. She was caught in the storm and would be torn apart. She could not fight it, could not survive it. The lost souls pulled at her; their agony was hers.

Then Mara and Fleur were at her side. Her friends linked their arms into hers, keeping her upright, anchoring her to the hard earth beneath her feet. Giving her a solid place despite the cacophony of music and mayhem that swirled within her.

They stood like that until the shuddering stopped. Slowly, slowly Asher felt her mind settle and her spirit ease. But as she returned to her own mind and body, Ash felt the pain of the lost planet lodge itself within her soul. She would never forget how that felt.

"What is happening?" demanded the Lord Chamberlain. "Is this some kind of ruse? What has made that storm?"

"The Threads," Asher rasped, "they are tearing. We need to stop Darven and find Hesta."

"We will," Fleur assured her. "We will."

Asher smiled gratefully at her friend; the cousin she had not known existed only a few weeks ago.

"But I think we should do something about that storm in the sky first," continued Fleur, her dark eyes wide with fear.

Around them the nobles of Faerla Grun muttered to each other in small, scared voices. The horses tied at the far end of the square began to whinny and pull at their ropes.

"Any ideas?" asked Fleur.

Asher stared at the storm pulsing at the edge of Andera's atmosphere, threatening to unleash chaos on everything it touched. She had no idea how long it would be before it broke through.

Then Quinn let out a large moan and grabbed at her heart as though it was going to explode.

"The Sacred Falls," she whimpered, "I am under attack."

With a great gasp she staggered forward, into Rhion's steadying embrace.

"What is happening Aunt? What type of attack?" he said gently.

"The storm tears at the protections that encase the grove," she whispered in agony. "If it penetrates the barrier the lake will be polluted and Faerla Grun will fall. I must return. Without me they are too vulnerable."

She pulled away from Rhion and took a few steps in the direction of the horses before collapsing to the ground. Immediately the king was at her side, helping her to her feet once more.

"I will come with you."

Quinn nodded in thanks, but then her already pale face leeched of all remaining colour.

"Too late," she whimpered, "too late. I will not make it in time. I must go within. Rhion, protect me."

He seemed to understand what she was about to do, for he nodded. "I swear you will be safe," he vowed grimly.

Carefully he supported Quinn as she sank to the ground, crossed her legs and closed her eyes. Within the space of an exhale the Lady of the Falls sent her consciousness deep within. A large shimmering bubble enveloped her, and the Lady was soon completely encased in a glowing, watery orb.

"Mirren, stand guard." Rhion directed his man. "Lady Quinn is no longer with us, her consciousness and spirit have returned to the lake. She will return for her body when all is safe once more. Your job is to guard her physical being. Keep it safe for her return."

The soldier nodded and stepped forward immediately with his sword drawn. His fierce eyes dared anyone to come close.

Asher and Fleur exchanged terrified glances. The one thought bounced between them. *Kate.*

"I have to go find Kate," Asher murmured desperately to Fleur. "I can't let anything happen to her."

Fleur looked up at the raging storm. "What about that?" she asked in a small voice.

"I don't know." Ash shook her head frantically. "I need to save Kate. I need to."

Fear was threatening to overwhelm her. She had already lost Levi, and Penn and Hesta. She could not cope with the thought of losing Kate as well. Mara stepped forward.

"Asher, we need to deal with the storm," she said firmly.

"But Kate-" began Ash desperately, her gaze leaping from left to right, frantically searching for someone, something, anything that would help her leave and get to Kate.

"Asherwen." Mara's voice was firm.

Power and authority thrummed in that one word. It drew Asher's attention reluctantly to the Jeweller.

"Asherwen," Mara repeated, and Ash felt the overwhelm begin to subside. She took a few deep breaths.

"You must control that storm and seal the sky. That is the surest way to save Arvana and your friend."

Asher gaped at her. "Me? I can't do that."

Mara reached out and grabbed Asher's chin, forcing Asher to focus her eyes on the Jeweller. Within those piercing blue eyes, so like Evelyn's, Asher saw kindness and compassion and a will of steel.

"Yes you can. And you will. And Fleur and I will help you."

Asher pulled away from the smaller woman and shook her head. She opened her mouth to argue, to protest. She was not trained, not strong enough. She had failed at saving everyone who relied on her. Levi, her sister, the Laneisian, *Aga*...

"Asher, you can do this," repeated Mara sternly, "you must do this. If you do not, more people and beings will die, not just now, but over the coming days and weeks. Do you understand?"

Asher did understand. The lost souls cut deep into her own being, and she knew she would always carry the scar. She was responsible for the lives and safety of one hundred million magical creatures among one billion beings. She could not allow Darven to inflict more death and destruction.

"This is what it means to be the Weaver," she whispered to nobody in particular. Fleur and Mara nodded in sympathy.

Asher took one slow inhale and held it for as long as she could. She closed her eyes and felt her heart beating, pumping her life-force around her body. She thought of Levi, and his favourite quote from a movie made long before his birth. *We're not in Kansas anymore...*

Carefully she exhaled the breath and opened her eyes.

"It is a lonely, difficult road she walks," said Asher quietly, feeling more affinity with her grandmother than she ever had before. And more compassion for her mother, who had been too scared to walk it.

"Difficult yes, but lonely?" Mara reached out her left hand to Asher and her right hand to Fleur. Both girls grasped the offered hands tightly. "It doesn't have to be lonely. And it doesn't have to be alone."

With a flash of insight Asher realised that Hesta had it wrong. She had made herself an island, with nobody to help her when she was flagging, to strengthen her when she was weak, to guide her when she was lost. Hesta thought that the Weaver was a solitary role, that the Weaver stood alone and apart.

She was reminded of Penn's wise words, said to her a lifetime ago.

'You are surrounded by friends Asher el Ginarwen. Keep them close. There is no requirement that you do this alone'

With a smile of gratitude and relief Asher squeezed Mara's hand. She raised her face to the storm and sent her voice with the wind.

"I am Asherwen the Musician. I am the Weaver's Heir. And I am not alone."

Perhaps it was her imagination, but it seemed that the furious advance of the storm seemed to pull back, if only a little.

"So what do we do?' asked Fleur.

Ash bit her bottom lip as she scanned the faces of the watching, frightened crowd. She needed some direction, or a plan.

She threw a fleeting glance at Quinn still encased in the bubble. She hoped the Lady was prevailing in her protection of the grove. The quicker she sorted this storm, the quicker she could get back to help Kate and the others in the village. She pulled the bracelet off her wrist, touching each of the small instruments in turn.

"Which instrument do you think I should use?" she asked Mara fretfully, "I don't know which one has the right power to combat the storm."

Mara shook her head. "You don't need an instrument Asherwen. You only need to feel the energy within you and channel it through you, just as you did when you destroyed Lyel's dagger."

Asher looked at the Jeweller, her grey eyes clouded with uncertainty. "Are you sure? Because I don't really know how I did that before."

"Sink into the energy Asher, let it fill you. Then release it. That is all. Everything you need is within you."

"Okay." Asher nodded, steeling her nerves.

She took a few deep breaths and reached out her awareness to the great energy of the Illuminated City, its fallen stones, its wild nature, the creatures that now called it home. This time she also tapped into the life-force of every being whose blood had soaked into the stones. Heeding Hesta's warning, she was careful not to take any energy from the living people around her. She felt herself filling with power and strength beyond anything she had ever experienced before.

"Fleur, can you feel that?"

The younger girl nodded, her eyes wide with awe.

"Can you use it?"

Fleur nodded again, and Ash felt her cousin's energy merge with her. The surge was so huge Asher was almost knocked off her feet. She staggered slightly, then steadied herself.

"I feel like I could burst!" she exclaimed. Energy pulsating from her entire being. She shone so brightly the gathered crowd had to shield their eyes.

"Now I want to pull the storm towards me, but we need to control it, contain it somehow. If it gets loose on Andera, if I am not strong enough…" she shook her head to clear the dread that thought created.

"We will be strong enough," said Fleur with a tight smile. "You and me."

"And me," said Mara grimly, "And I have just the thing to contain this beast."

She pulled a pendant from beneath her clothes, a heavy silver amulet with a piece of polari embedded within it. She handed it to Asher. Then the Jeweller whispered to the rings on her fingers and they shimmered with power. Perusing them carefully she chose a large ruby ring and pulled it off her hand. She held it up to the sky.

"Use this Asher. Focus your crafting through the stone and we will use it like a conductor to capture the storm and send it into the polari pendant. Ready?"

Through gritted teeth Asher and Fleur nodded.

Asher called to the music within her. It leapt eagerly to her summons. Slowly and carefully she created a glowing net from the energy of her music, and strengthened it with the energy of the ancient place and the lost people of the Illuminated city. Using both her mind and her hands she threw that net over the twisting, churning fury of the storm, encasing it within. The storm pushed and pulsed against Asher's net, challenging her hold.

Asher jerked and almost lost grip of the net, but she held firm. Then, when she knew she had contained it, she tried to condense it down, to reduce its size and fury. Ash felt like a tiny fish swimming in a thrashing, fierce ocean, trying to control that which was never meant to be controlled. Her body jerked and twisted with the strain.

Just when she thought she would lose control, the red, vibrant energy of the Jeweller bolstered her, strengthened her.

Asher remembered the agony of the lost planet and gritted her teeth. She wrestled with the storm, tightening the net, forcing it to shrink, smaller and smaller until at last she could pull what was left of it through the atmosphere of Andera.

Chaos erupted. The noise of the diminishing storm thundered across the sky, and wild winds made it hard for Asher and her steadfast allies to keep upright. Standing back to back they leant into each other, the three of them focused on the churning mass they were pulling ever closer to themselves.

If the people and animals around her cried out in fright, Ash was unaware. Her senses were filled with the almighty roaring of the furiously pulsating winds.

With a final gasp and surge of energy from Fleur, Asher pushed the storm into a small writhing frothy ball and hurtled it towards the ring dangling from Mara's outstretched hand. The moment the storm touched the glowing ruby it was sucked through the stone and then streamed back out as a single beam of red light.

Mara shook with the huge charge that poured in and out of her ring, but she tightened her jaw and held firm. Asher leapt forward and captured the red beam within the polari pendant.

But they were not done yet. Inch by inch Asher and Mara pushed the ring across the sky, and sealed the hole shut.

Finally, when the last millimetre was sealed and the sky had returned to normal, the Crafters and Fleur released their focus and sank to the ground, exhausted. Huddled together they breathed heavily, too spent to even celebrate their victory, the polari pendant dangling from Asher's limp hand.

Rhion ran to their sides, carrying a flask of water and some of Fruda's bread rolls.

"What was that?" asked one of the Council, his voice shaking.

"That," replied Ash without raising her head, her own voice hoarse and barely able to be heard, "that is what happens when Lord Darven is allowed to bleed Crafters and tear apart the universe. That is what we are fighting."

"Eat," Rhion urged. "You must all be exhausted. What just happened is beyond mere mortal comprehension. You are right Asher. I fear this is only the beginning. This is a war, and Faerla Grun must stand beside you. Whatever you need Asher. I promise you."

Asher smiled weakly, gulping down some water. She was physically and mentally wrecked, but she had not passed out. That was a good sign.

Mara lifted her bleary eyes to stare at the now calm sky.

"We have saved ourselves for now," she said quietly, "but the damage it has caused will ripple across space and time. One planet is already destroyed. Who knows what other consequences this will have. I find it hard to believe that the storm found its way here by accident or chance."

Asher considered this. "Do you think a part of the Laneisian storm had been ripped apart deliberately and sent here? How could that be?"

"It would take incredible power, a universe rattling, terrifying amount of power."

Asher felt sick to her stomach. The Jeweller continued.

"Whatever it was, we have dealt with it for now. We are even more aware of what is at stake, and what he is capable of."

Asher nodded. Yes, now everyone knew. As frightening and exhausting as the battle against the storm had been, it had given her allies where before there had been only hostility. Asher thought of the thousands of beings annihilated by Darven's ambition, of the many more at risk. The worlds within the five universes needed protecting. They were all relying on her, though none of them would ever know it.

When she felt ready she turned and faced the silent crowd. Their faces were pale with shock and horror and fear, and no small amount of awe. Many eyes darted to the glowing pendant dangling from Asher's fingers, then quickly away.

The Lord Chamberlain did not speak. His old face was grey and drawn with worry. The events of the day were unlike anything he had ever experienced in his seventy years of life.

Rhion reached out a hand and helped Asher to her feet. His calloused hand was warm and strong. Her fingers tingled as the wild music within her melded with the ancient songs of Faerla Grun within him, and for the briefest of moments they were bound by the music. Weaver and King. A knot in the Threads.

"Asherwen," he said seriously, inclining his head. "Thank you."

She squeezed his hand in acknowledgement of his friendship and support, and offered a tentative smile to the watching crowd.

"Asherwen," said Lord Stober slowly, bowing his head and thumping his fist across his heart. "Asherwen," repeated his family, bowing their heads.

Around the small assembly the word rang out. One by one the Council and nobles of Faerla Grun bowed their heads in respect.

Asher's eyes filled with tears. She was tired, and she was more than a little scared by what had happened and what was to come, but the acceptance and the respect of those around her was humbling. For so long she had been so frightened to be seen, and now there was nowhere to hide.

"Thank you," she said quietly, hoping her voice was not shaking as hard as her heart was thumping.

Feeling self-conscious she looked away from the gathered nobles, her eyes moving around the square until they rested on Quinn. She had not yet emerged from her bubble. Immediately Ash thought of Kate, and the Crafters she had left there.

"I think we need to head back to the village, if even a small amount of the storm broke through, they could be in chaos," she murmured to Fleur and Mara.

Mara frowned thoughtfully as she glanced at the low hanging sun and the gathering clouds. The gems in her dark hair glistened in the late afternoon light.

"I'm not disagreeing, I'm sure we are needed. But it was a ride of many hours, and the horses may not be up to it, particularly after the spooking they just experienced. The sun already moves across the sky, soon enough we will lose the light. Our choices are either to camp for the night, or ride to Sedendria, which I believe is less than two hours away. However it is in the opposite direction to Arvana."

Indecision roiled within Ash. She was anxious to see what was happening with the village and her friends, but she was exhausted and unsure if she could actually stay mounted for a five-hour ride. Plus the horses needed a rest, and what would happen to the Lady Quinn? They could not leave her alone and unprotected here in the Illuminated City.

As if on cue, the bubble encasing Quinn began to pulsate, faster and faster, before bursting open spilling water everywhere. The Lady herself fell to the ground with a great gasp, sucking in air as her body heaved.

Rhion and the Lord Chamberlain moved swiftly to her side, holding her steady as she stood.

She was soaked from head to toe, her beautiful hair hanging in tangled, dripping strands down her back, and her movements were slow. Her body slumped wearily, as though she had been swimming for hours in a strong current and her legs were yet to recover their land strength.

"Are you alright my Lady?" murmured Rhion.

She nodded, though when she spoke her voice was laboured. "The village is safe. The lake remains unpolluted. The water sprites fought hard and we have prevailed. The dark threat has retreated, gone with the storm." She took a deep, restorative breath. "Thank you, I am fine now."

The two men dropped their arms and immediately Quinn wobbled precariously. Quickly they steadied her once more.

"It appears that my body is not yet responding fully," she added ruefully. "I may need some time to recover."

Nobody said anything though Asher suspected they were all thinking similar thoughts. There was nowhere to recover here in the ruins. Where once a luxurious bedroom in a great palace would have been ready for the Lady of the Falls, now there was only dust and rock and the rambling vines.

They needed a place for Quinn to rest. For all of them to rest really. The energy users were exhausted, and the non-magical humans were also tired, on edge, and overwhelmed from the terrifying events of the afternoon.

Though she was desperate to return to Arvana and check for herself that her friends were safe, Ash knew the most sensible thing was to ride to Sedendria. The notion of camping here in the abandoned city sent chills down her spine.

She cleared her throat, drawing Rhion and Quinn's attention.

"I think we should head to Sedendria, if there is a place we can stay."

Rhion grinned, the quirk of his lips lighting up his face. For a moment he looked like the travelworn hunter she had encountered in the woods only yesterday, and not the regal king he now was.

"Of course Asherwen. There is the Royal Citadel which is at your disposal. A rather grand palace to be sure, but to be honest it's not particularly warm and welcoming." He looked across at the Lord Chamberlain almost guiltily, hoping he had not been overheard.

"To be fair, there has not been a king in residence in a number of years, so it's more of an office than a home. If you are happy with humbler surroundings, there is my home which has plenty of room for you all."

Ash turned to discuss their options with Mara and Fleur, who both agreed that a ride to Sedendria was preferable to a night on the hard ground. Simon offered to re-saddle and prepare their horses.

Around them everyone was making the same preparations in readiness to leave. Horses and carriages clacked across the stone, and many voices were raised in farewells. Everyone was keen to leave this place.

A loud commotion interrupted the activities as Simon came running back into the main square calling for the king.

"My Lord! Lyel is gone."

Rhion's face was impassive. "Did he slip the bindings?" he asked.

"No sire. The ropes were cut. Somebody assisted him, most likely when we were all distracted by the storm. His horse is missing also."

Murmuring and general unease met this announcement. Somebody in the group had assisted an enemy of the crown, a man who had tried to kill the king, his own cousin. People glanced warily at each other until one by one all eyes turned to the Princess Gladriol. As one, the crowd drew away from her until she was standing alone. Somebody whispered the word 'traitor' and it carried on the wind, swirling around the small woman.

The princess was perhaps only five years older than Marawen, but her frailness and nerviness gave the impression of a woman much older than her years. Her tear swollen, blood-shot blue eyes flared with fear, and her hands twisted and pulled at each other anxiously as she glanced from one uncertain face to another.

"No, no," she muttered, her voice catching. "I swear... Rhion..." she pleaded, "I mean, my Lord..."

Rhion smiled at her gently. "It is alright Aunt. Nobody suspects you of anything untoward. Nobody."

The last word had a hard edge, a warning to the gathered crowd not to frighten the terrified woman any further.

"Though we could understand a devoted mother wanting to help her insistent, rather manipulative son, we are also fully aware that your gentle hands would be unable to hold a blade long enough or tightly enough to saw through bindings that strong."

His words directed their collective gaze to her swollen knuckles and bent fingers.

"The seamstress' curse," murmured Fleur, "I have known others with such deformity, brought on by years of plying needle and thread."

Ash nodded. "We call it arthritis. Musicians are also afflicted."

"Which means," continued Rhion, his voice as warm as steel scraping against stone, "somebody else assisted Lord Lyel. Would anyone care to step forward?"

The crowd murmured and shuffled as they looked one to the other, but nobody came forth with a confession. Rhion did not seem surprised.

"No matter, there is nothing more to be done now, but be assured that I will discover the truth of what has happened with Lyel. If you wish to speak with me before then, I strongly recommend you do. Right now everyone is tired. Let us return to our homes before we find ourselves travelling at night and at the mercy of the elements."

The crowd murmured their assent.

"Let us ride then," said Rhion. "We have perhaps an hour until darkness, and another thirty minutes of travel after that."

Mara stepped closer to the young king and spoke quietly, her words for his ears alone.

"Are you sure you do not want to interview the attendees and discover who is Lyel's accomplice or assistant in this matter while you have the might of the Council beside you? While people's memories are fresh. If the person remains at large you might be at risk."

Rhion nodded thoughtfully, considering her words.

"You might be right Lady Marawen, but I fear that most people are too shocked and scared by what they just experienced to be of much help. Keeping them here any longer while we hold an investigation and a mock court will do more harm than good. I do believe that with some time the culprit will become relaxed and complacent, making it easier to identify them. I will speak with each person once we return to Sedendria, in an informal setting. These people have been known to me my whole life, they are my family and friends. I don't wish to cause ruptures on my first day in the job."

He grinned at her, and she smiled back. "In the meantime I will be careful."

Mara nodded in acceptance of his decision and stepped away to attend to her own horse. Rhion turned to Quinn who was sitting on a large rock drinking hot tea from a flask. Her hair and dress were completely dry and restored to their previous immaculate state. Her skin was no longer translucent and scaly, but its normal soft, watery sheen.

"Are you recovered enough to travel my Lady?"

She nodded and stood up lightly.

"Indeed."

"You can travel with me if you wish Quinn," offered the Princess in a small voice. "There is plenty of room in my carriage."

Quinn shook her head.

"That is a very kind offer Gladriol. Thank you. However I am feeling hale and whole, and I do love to ride."

The princess' eyes filled with tears of shame.

"Of course," she said in a wobbly voice, "I understand."

And in that moment Quinn also understood. She understood that the fragile princess was feeling lost and broken now that her beloved son had treated her so badly and attempted to murder his cousin.

For many years Gladriol had believed she would be mother of the next King, and now she was nothing more than the mother of a traitor, and a woman her extended family and friends had been willing to believe was also a traitor. In one afternoon her whole world had been upended and she was lost and alone.

Quinn feigned a small stumble.

"On second thoughts Gladriol, it appears I am still quite weary. Perhaps we can tie my horse behind the carriage, and I can ride with you for a while. Until I am strong again. It would be a pleasure to spend some time with you. And I am certain I have some sweet strawberries in my pack, which I believe are your favourites."

"Strawberries!" exclaimed the princess, "but it is almost winter."

"Indeed it is," said Quinn, her eyes dancing, "but in my garden it is always summer."

The thought of travelling in a seat, in a carriage, instead of a hard saddle atop a galloping horse, sounded divine to Asher. There might even be a cushion.

"Would you mind," she asked hesitantly, unsure of the protocol of asking a princess if she could travel with her, "would it be okay if I travelled with you? If there is room that is. I'm rather exhausted," she added apologetically.

Gladriol's eyes grew so round they almost consumed her face.

"Of course Asherwen," she breathed reverently, "I would be honoured."

In front of the assembled nobles of Faerla Grun, her head held high and her face shining with pride, the Princess Gladriol led Quinn and Asher to her gleaming red carriage, her honour restored.

Chapter Twenty-Seven

Sedendria

There were indeed cushions in Gladriol's carriage. And warm, woollen blankets, and hot, sweet tea and biscuits. All of which Ash greatly appreciated and enjoyed. And while she really tried to keep her eyes open and her mind focused on the conversation taking place between the princess and Quinn, the gentle bouncing of the well-appointed carriage was incredibly lulling, and soon enough she was fast asleep.

She was woken too soon by Quinn gently shaking her shoulder.

"Asherwen, we are almost there. You don't want to miss our arrival into Sedendria, it is something to behold."

Asher sat up slowly, her head still groggy from the deep, dreamless sleep. She had been warm beneath the thick blankets, and her head had been well cushioned, but her left hip and shoulder were sore from lying on the carriage bench, which had been obstinately hard despite the gaily coloured cushions. She stretched her back and rolled her shoulders, hoping that the stiffness would ease once she was out of the carriage. But no matter how sore she was she would absolutely not complain. She was incredibly thankful she had not had to ride this far.

Her tummy rumbled slightly and she noticed with regret that at some point the small, silent lady's maid had packed away the tea and biscuits into a basket beneath her seat. She considered asking if they were easily accessible, and if so, could she please have some, but one look at the wide-eyed maid changed her mind.

The young woman was clearly horrified and awed that she was riding with both Quinn and Asherwen, and her eyes darted fearfully between them. She had shrunk herself as small as she possibly could, which was impressively small, and she had inched as far away from Asher as the carriage confines would allow.

Everything about her body language screamed 'don't notice me!' and Asher empathised. She had been there too many times herself. She would not make the woman any more uncomfortable by forcing conversation upon her.

Instead Ash turned her attention to the large glass window closest to her and peered curiously outside. She was riding backwards in the carriage, so her view was of the road they had already travelled.

The sun was in its final descent over the horizon, staining the thick clouds vibrant shades of red and orange, like a trail of volcanic lava across the sky. The lands around them were enveloped in shadow, so it was hard to determine the structure of the landscape, but from the flatness Ash guessed it was more farmland. Great Plains indeed. She squinted her eyes, wondering if she could see the ruins of the Illuminated City far behind them, but visibility was low in the fading light.

"Look over there, to the left," directed Quinn.

Ash twisted around to look where the Lady was pointing, and her mouth dropped open.

"Incredible, isn't it?" said Quinn proudly.

Ahead of them, rising out of the plains, was an enormous rock. The top of the rock was flat, and built upon it was a sprawling city, gleaming in the last rays of the sunset. At the very heart of the city was a large citadel. Standing proudly above the buildings, it served as a guardian surveying the land, warning off intruders.

The only way up to the city was the winding road that had been carved into the rock. There was simply no way you could make that climb without the inhabitants knowing you were coming, and allowing you to do so.

Sedendria had learned the lessons of the Illuminated City. It was glorious and awe-inspiring in its own way, but it was not welcoming and would not be easily invaded. Sedendria was a fortress.

Ash silently nodded in answer to Quinn's question. There were no words to describe how she was feeling as she stared at the monolith before them.

The music within her was rich and deep, a march of conquerors, or perhaps a final stand. The colours of the music were rich purples and dense crimsons. She wanted to close her eyes and just feel it, but she was rivetted by the immenseness and unable to look away.

The occupants of the carriage had fallen silent. Even the princess and her maid, natives of this city, were subdued beneath its shadow. As the final rays of sun disappeared behind the rock city of Sedendria, enveloping it in a deep mulberry hue, the thunder of wheels against the hard road beat in time with the galloping hooves of thirty horses. It was a sombre and eerie sound in the twilight.

Asher shivered slightly.

Within minutes they reached the bottom of the rock mountain and began the sloping climb. Ash held her breath, the memory of the terrifying journey through the Mat'drin Mountains still fresh. However this was a vastly different experience. The road to the city above was wide and well cared for, with plenty of room for the carriage to travel without fear of the edge, and for four or five horses to ride abreast if required.

Embedded into the rock were large lanterns, spilling a bright and welcoming light over the road.

Asher frowned in puzzlement.

It seemed counterintuitive to build a fortress city at the top of a wide rock, and then make the road to access it so welcoming and comfortable. Perhaps she had misunderstood its purpose.

Then, just as Ash was feeling relaxed, she noticed that the road a few hundred metres ahead of them simply disappeared.

With a gasp Ash grabbed at the side of the carriage, certain they were about to plunge from the rock face to their deaths. Across from her Quinn chuckled.

"Wait for it..." the Lady said eagerly, mischief sparkling in her voice.

Asher took a deep breath and swallowed her heart back into her chest. If the Lady was not panicking, then surely everything was going to be just fine. She took another deep breath and slowly released it, 2..3..4.

The cliff edge drew ever nearer. Ash resisted the urge to cry out in warning.

Don't panic, don't panic, don't panic, don't panic.

The words looped through her brain, but it seemed her body refused to receive the message, for her stomach was churning and her hands were simultaneously cold and sweating. She wasn't sure she still had legs.

"Move to the other window," instructed Quinn.

Ash did not want to move. She felt compelled to watch the road ahead, even if it meant watching them canter off into thin air, but Quinn raised her brows and nodded at the window on the left hand side of the carriage. Reluctantly Ash moved across the seat and peered through the glass.

And there it was – salvation. A huge opening in the rock, like the portcullis of a castle, its enormous steel doors flung open for the carriages and horses to safely enter inside.

One by one they trotted in, into the heart of the rock itself.

It took a second for Asher's eyes to adjust to the dim light, and when they did they widened in amazement. The path they were riding on was far narrower than the mountain road had been. They could only travel in single file. The light was poor, and the stones beneath the horses' hooves were uneven which meant the going was slow. It was not long before Ash realised why the road was so poorly laid. On either side small windows had been carved into the rock and the tip of a cannon peeked through each one. She guessed that all manner of weapons were hidden behind them. Bows and arrows, oil and fire... If an unwelcome intruder somehow made it through the steel gates, then they would be dealt with here.

It had been one hundred years since the last war, and it seemed the people of Faerla Grun had never stopped preparing for the next one.

Asher felt a little breathless at the depth of the anger that had created this place. She had not appreciated how wide the division was between the people of Faerla Grun and the people of Ostrin.

It was truly a wonder that Quinn had welcomed her and Mara into the village at all - the Weaver's Heir and a daughter of the Ostrin royal house - descendants of those she despised. Lyel had done Ash a great service by trying to kill Rhion, she thought ruefully. Her saving his life the first time had opened Quinn's heart.

They travelled on through the grim and silent battlements, ascending all the while, until finally they passed through another immense steel door and into the fresh evening air.

After the last of their party had passed safely through, the door was pushed shut behind them, and giant bolts clanged into place, effectively trapping any unfortunate souls inside. Ash shuddered with horror. What a terrible fate that would be.

She felt slightly ill from the oppressive journey through the rock, and tension pounded in her head. Sedendria must be a foreboding place, filled with stifled anger and churning resentment. Those long-lost inhabitants of the Illuminated City would have wept.

It was as if Quinn read her mind, or more likely, her face. Which was quite pale and stark.

"Look around you Asherwen," she said eagerly, "The beauty and culture of Faerla Grun is alive here."

Obligingly Ash peered through the glass at the brightly lit city, glad to turn her thoughts away from the grisly fate of being trapped in the rock.

They were travelling on a wide road which meandered between tightly packed buildings of every colour imaginable. A small moss-green house butted against a towering pearly pink building, which in turn sat next to a sprawling blue complex of buildings which seemed to be a school. Though the colours were festive and seemingly uncoordinated, there was nothing ramshackle about the buildings. Everything was solid and sound, each one built with intent and care. The road was well-maintained, and the city planning appeared structured and ordered.

This was not a city that had grown organically over centuries.

On the streets people in vibrant clothing engaged in lively conversation with their neighbours, and children ran around with their friends, laughing and arguing over games of marbles and tip. Intricately detailed flags flew proudly above many of the buildings, and great murals decorated the wide straight lanes that ran off the main road.

In the early evening Sedendria thrummed with life and vibrancy.

Everyone turned towards the returning riders and carriages with excitement and expectation. A new king had been named in the Illuminated City, and they were eager to learn who it was.

In groups or one by one, the people of Sedendria joined the slow-moving procession of carriages and horses, winding through the streets towards the Citadel. Energetic children ran alongside, calling out to the riders.

Ash could not help but smile when two young boys ran up to the window of their carriage and peered inside, falling back in surprise when they saw the gleaming, scaly face of the Lady Quinn grinning at them.

A few moments later the boys were back, this time with friends, staring in awe and pointing at the Lady of the Falls as they jogged alongside the clattering carriage. It had been many years since the Lady had visited Sedendria, and for most of these young children she existed only in stories.

Quinn waved regally, then gave them a wink. The children hooted with pleasure.

"A rock star welcome," laughed Asher.

Three sets of puzzled eyes turned to her.

"This rock is not a star Asherwen, merely a formation of the earth," said Quinn seriously.

"Yes I know, I mean, that's not what I meant. It's a saying. It means you are as popular as a rock star. A famous person."

Three blank faces.

"A famous person," continued Ash doggedly, "A person who is well known."

"Well, yes, I am well known. But what does that have to do with rocks?" asked Quinn.

Ash bit her bottom lip and shook her head with a small smile. "Nothing. Never mind."

It was not much longer before they rolled into the main square in front of the Citadel. Even above the noise of the carriages and horses and cheering people Ash could hear music playing. The rich, joyous music of a brass band. It filled her senses, muting all other sounds. Her hands and feet tapped along to the merry music, as the gloom of the ascent through the rock lifted from her soul.

It was the first time since she had arrived on Andera that she had heard music played by some-one else. It was wonderful. Her fingers itched to play along, but as she was travelling in the carriage she would have to content herself with simply feeling the music.

The princess's carriage pulled to a halt at the steps of the Citadel and the silent lady's maid pushed open the door and carefully climbed down, signally for assistance for the princess. A footman stepped forward and offered his hand to aid first Gladriol, then Quinn. The women stepped gracefully onto the paved ground, their skirts swirling around them.

Asher did not wait for the footman; she was not a fine lady who needed help, and she was very keen to be out of the carriage and on firm ground once more.

Enthusiastically she scooted across the seat and bounded through the open door, landing with a thump on the ground. The cool night air stung her face and chilled her hands, which was rather invigorating, and she breathed deeply of both air and music as the brass band welcomed the weary travellers.

As she stepped away from the carriage, her legs wobbled a little, and for a moment Ash thought she might actually trip over her own feet, but then her balance settled and she straightened, stretching her back and shoulders as she eagerly looked around.

They were standing in a huge stone square, surrounded on three sides by large, grey buildings with flat rooves and square columns that appeared to be a courthouse and townhall and parliamentary chambers. In front of her the white citadel rose four stories high into the night sky, topped by three magnificent domes. Four forbidding towers with tiny archer's windows anchored the corners of the citadel, and atop each tower enormous fires leapt into the sky, illuminating the gleaming gold of the domes.

The square itself was brightly lit by large fiery sconces that lined the perimeter and pathways, and by glowing orbs that hung from each of the buildings.

Around her grooms helped the nobles dismount, before leading the tired horses away for feeding and rest. The growing crowd chatted and laughed excitedly, calling out to friends and family, yelling their support for their favourite heir. The band played with gusto. And nobody spared more than a fleeting, disinterested glance for the unimportant, red-haired girl in travel-stained tunic and trousers.

As Quinn and the Princess Gladriol were led to a VIP area off to the right, the rowdy crowd jostled and elbowed Asher out of their way, vying for prime position by the steps.

She shuffled and shimmied out of the crush, scanning the growing crowd, looking for Mara and Fleur.

A huge roar went up, drawing Ash's attention back to the giant stone steps of the citadel, which were now further away than they had been only minutes before.

The Lord Chamberlain and the other members of the Council were standing at the top of the steps, between the towering columns that held up the enormous portico. They were dwarfed by the proportions of the citadel, but their vibrant red and purple robes ensured they stood out against the stark grey and white building.

The excited crowd pushed closer together, knocking against Ash, who hastily stepped out of the way.

The Lord Chamberlain raised his hands, and the music ceased. Calls to 'shush' and 'be quiet' rang out around the square for a few minutes, until finally everyone fell silent.

"Welcome," called the Lord Chamberlain, his voice carrying easily across the square. Some-how it was being magnified, but Ash could not see a microphone or speakers.

"Today is the day we name our King."

The crowd roared in anticipation, and Ash found herself pushed further and further back as the wave of people surged forward.

"I ask the contenders for the Throne of Faerla Grun to join the Council."

One by one Rhion, Lord Maken, and Lord Stober climbed the steps to stand with the aged men, affectionate catcalling and cheering accompanying them. It was not long before the crowd realised that where four men had been bound for the Illuminated City, only three had returned.

Perplexed murmurs rippled through the crowd.

"Lord Lyel is not there..."

"Has anyone seen Lord Lyel?"

One man raised his voice, calling to the noblemen standing silently above them.

"Lord Merth, where is Lord Lyel?"

The Lord Chamberlain hesitated, clearly unsure whether to acknowledge the question, and if so, how best to answer it. The crowd murmured uneasily.

"Why do you not tell us?" called the same bold man. "What are you hiding?"

The Lord Chamberlain puffed out his chest and drew himself up proudly.

"I have nothing to hide. Lyel the traitor accused our new king of stealing a song, then attempted to assassinate him, before fleeing to avoid a trial and fair sentencing. He has exiled himself from Sedendria."

Outrage and confusion rose and swelled among the gathering.

"What!"

"No!"

"That cannot be true..."

As people shifted anxiously around her, Asher found it simplest and safest to step back as far as she could from the crowd. She was feeling tired and hungry and longed to rest. Away from the mass, she again scanned the assembly, looking for Mara or Fleur or Quinn. Any familiar face really. She would even be pleased to see the Princess Gladriol, or the sour-faced maid for that matter. But now that she was at the back of the crush she was only really looking at the back of people's heads, and there was simply too many to easily distinguish one she knew.

"Let us continue," said the Lord Chamberlain firmly, his voice silencing the crowd once more. "No more shall we dwell on Lyel. There is much to celebrate this night. For today, in the city of our ancestors, we crowned a true and noble king."

He gestured to the band who struck up a majestic tune.

As they played, a footman solemnly climbed the steps, his outstretched hands clutching the red velvet cushion, atop which sat the gleaming, gem encrusted crown of Faerla Grun.

The people of Sedendria shuffled and shifted in anticipation.

The footman stopped before the Lord Chamberlain and dropped to one knee, raising the cushion and crown above his bowed head. Lord Merth placed a hand on each side of the heavy crown and lifted it up high. The footman ducked away, taking the empty cushion with him.

Warm, golden firelight danced over the crown, caressing the dazzling red and blue and green sparks that radiated from the glorious hand cut gems. The Lord Chamberlain raised the crown to the crowd who cheered.

"People of Sedendria, of Faerla Grun. I present to you, our king."

The three contenders stepped forward. Kind Lord Stober. Eager Lord Maken. The Nameless Prince.

The crowd held a collective breath.

"All hail King Rhion, son of Rudorph. May his song be ever sung!" And he turned and placed the crown on Rhion's head.

The crowd erupted in cheering and chanting and clapping and stomping. The brass band joined the melee, and people danced and sang. High above the citadel fireworks exploded into the night sky, sending multicoloured sparks across the square. Children and adults alike squealed with wonder.

Rhion grinned and waved to the joyous gathering, his face shining with pleasure.

Alone at the back of the crowd Asher smiled too, pleased for her new friend. There had been so much trouble and fear today, it was marvellous to end the day with a celebration.

Then she sighed, a great weary sound that whooshed out of her body, taking the last of her energy with it. She was certain these celebrations would go on late into the night, and she really was ready for bed.

Rhion had said they could stay at his home, but the problem was she had no idea where that was. Or where any of her friends were, for that matter. A small tendril of anxiety swirled around her stomach and thickened her throat.

Then from the corner of her eye she caught the movement of some-one waving at her from the back of the square. She spun around and realised with relief that it was Simon, Rhion's soldier.

He was standing alone at the far end of the square, near one of the wide streets that ran from the square into the city.

"Gosh I'm pleased to see you Simon," she called as she hurried over to join him. "Are you able to take me to Rhion's house? And do you know where Marawen and Fleur are?"

The soldier laughed at her eager questions and nodded.

"Yes and yes. They are already there. Come, follow me."

With relief, Asher followed the soldier out of the bright, festive square and into the dimly lit streets of Sedendria, all the while chatting happily about the evening's events. Within minutes the noise and gaiety was behind them, and they were deep in the quiet, empty city.

Far across the square, at the foot of the giant steps to the Citadel, Marawen and Fleur craned their necks, trying to locate Asher in the exuberant crowd.

"Can you see her?" Mara asked anxiously for the fifth time.

Fleur shook her head, her dark eyes filled with worry.

"She must be here somewhere," said Quinn reassuringly, "she cannot have gone anywhere. We will find her soon enough."

She turned to the man who had been with them throughout the evening. The loyal soldier was practically bursting with pride at seeing his friend and leader be crowned king, and while he would have loved to join the festivities, he would not abandon his duty to the Lady.

"Don't you agree Simon?"

***

Asher had long since stopped talking as she stumbled after Simon down the empty streets of the city. She was exhausted and struggling to keep up with her guide's brisk pace.

"Is it much further?" she asked, hoping she did not sound too whiny.

The man ahead of her shook his head. "No Asherwen, in fact we are here."

He stopped in front of a dark doorway, his face obscured by shadow. "Before we enter, you will need this."

From his pocket he withdrew a box of matches and proceeded to light a wall sconce that was mounted beside the door. It flickered into life. Then he turned the heavy iron handle on the door and pushed it open. Beyond lay a dark, musty smelling room.

Asher frowned in confusion. This was nothing like she was expecting.

"Are you sure this is the place?" she asked.

"Just take the torch and go inside," answered Simon impatiently. "This is the outer room for dirty boots and coats. The luxurious rooms are beyond. Quickly now, I don't have all night."

Ash hurried forward, feeling guilty that she had kept the soldier from the celebrations. He was one of Rhion's best friends, he must be keen to re-join the party.

She grabbed the torch from its iron bracket on the wall and immediately felt a familiar, dreaded heaviness seep up her arm and overtake her body. In shock and pain she stumbled forward, into the horrible room. She tried to drop the Void-matter coated torch, but her fingers could not release it. It felt melded to her hand.

"Simon..." she mumbled breathlessly, "please... help me. Take the torch. Void-matter... can't let go."

The soldier, Rhion's friend, *her friend* she had thought, sneered at her, extinguished the flame of her torch, then pushed her roughly to the ground. He did not take the torch from her frozen, burning hand.

"Help you?" Simon laughed bitterly. "Oh I don't think so. This is where you die Asherwen. Alone, in the dark. Who knows if anyone will ever find your body?"

He unsheathed the dagger that was strapped to his thigh.

Asher's head was pounding with the force of the Void. Empty, her mind was empty. The music was gone, gone. Panic and fear threatened to overwhelm her. She tried to move, to roll away from the wicked dagger, but her body was heavy and unresponsive under the weight of the Void-matter.

"Why?" she whispered hoarsely, "Are you in league with Darven?"

"Darven?" the man in the doorway laughed. "I don't know anyone with that name. No Asherwen, this is for my Lord Lyel."

And he threw the dagger at her heart.

***

In the place Beyond, Penn was dreaming. He was dreaming of a girl with tangled red hair and serious grey eyes, who had travelled across the universe to rescue her sister and had returned to save them all.

In his dream she was trapped and in danger. There was no-one to save her, no way that she could save herself. She was going to die here, alone in his dream.

He twisted restlessly in his sleep.

The Ralshok known as Marten leaned forward, his brow furrowed. There was no dreaming in the Beyond. There were no dreams. This should not be.

In the small, dark room the blade was drawn. The girl, *Asher*, that was her name, lay frozen beneath its threat. Penn thrashed fiercely against his enforced slumber.

Marten's mind was racing, trying to make sense of what was happening. There were no dreams in the Beyond. There was no time, no matter, no connection to the physical world. And yet, now there was. Something had changed.

Marten reached over and placed both hands on Penn's head. With a lurch Penn sat up, wide awake, his eyes glazed with panic.

"I made a promise to protect her," he said. "An oath, sworn with my blood. It binds me until my death. Am I dead?"

Marten shook his head.

"Then I must go."

Marten nodded. "So you must."

***

The blade whirred soundlessly through the air. It was only a short distance from Simon's hand to her heart, and Asher knew that within a heartbeat she would be dead.

With everything she had left, Ash willed herself to roll, for her mind and body to be greater than the pain and the paralysis of the Void-matter.

And in the fraction of a second between the dagger being released and it burying into her heart, the globe burst into frantic song, infusing Asher with just enough energy to yank her body slightly to the right. Not enough to save her from injury, but enough to save her from certain, immediate death.

She cried out in agony as the blade tore through skin and muscles and tendons, embedding itself into her left shoulder.

Simon, who had already turned towards the door, spun back in surprise. His eyes narrowed and his mouth twisted when he realised he had missed. Then he laughed meanly.

"You've just made this worse for yourself I'm afraid. I'm going to lock this door and leave you here in the dark to bleed out. Enjoy your slow death."

Before he could make good on his threat, a huge flash of light engulfed the room, blinding them both. A roar thundered around the small space as a tall, muscular figure leapt out of the light and into the room.

As Simon turned to flee, Penn thumped him across the back of the head, knocking him unconscious to the ground. Then he dropped to his knees beside Asher, carefully inspecting the dagger embedded in her shoulder. He was careful not to touch the weapon, but he pulled the hated Void-matter torch from her inert hand and threw it against the wall.

"You will be alright Asher, I swear." His dark eyes were fierce.

Asher tried to smile, but her face was not working particularly well. Even with the Void-matter gone, its poison had badly affected her entire system. Her head was spinning and her body felt numb. She did not know if she even had a body anymore. It was an effort to keep her eyes open.

"Penn," she whispered with the last of her strength. "Thank you."

He reached out and touched her face, as her damaged shoulder finally exploded in pain, consuming her mind and body. The last thing she heard before she lost consciousness was the deep bellow of a hunting horn.

* This is the the End of The Weaver's Heir: Book Two – Musician. Thank you for reading, I hope you are enjoying The Weaver's Heir series. *

About the author

TS McCarthy is an Australian Writer, Coach and Possiblist, who lives and works in the beautiful Blue Mountains.

When not working in her corporate career, parenting, or staying connected with family and friends 'IRL', she spends her time on never-ending DIY projects, walking in the fresh mountain air, and imagining and scribbling about people, places and magical things.

She is immensely grateful to the teachers who pretended they did not know she had a book propped on her lap under her desk, and the librarians who let her borrow more than her allotted limit. Those wonderful women nurtured a love for reading that has been a life-long joy and passion.

Home is filled with her family, two black bunnies and an ever-growing collection of books, photographs, mugs, throw-rugs, vases, cushions and lamps. Minimalist she is not.

Writing The Weaver's Heir has been a true passion project, and she is excited to share the series with you.